COURT OF THE T

BOOK THE

CH00687451

# HEROD'S STEWARD

KATRINA D. HAMEL

Published by Long Walk Publishing
Alberta, Canada

Map Illustration by Cay Danielson

Herod's Steward : Court of the Tetrarch Book Three / By Katrina D. Hamel — 1st ed.

1. Christian Historical Fiction 2. Biblical Fiction

ISBN: 978-1-9990338-9-7

*For my husband, Chase*

# HEROD'S FAMILY, AS MENTIONED IN HEROD'S STEWARD

King Herod married ten wives and had fourteen children, three of whom he executed for suspected treason.

By his wife Mariamne I (descendant of Hasmonean royalty), Herod fathered five children including Aristobulus. He was executed by Herod and had four or five children with Salome's daughter Bernice, including Herod, Agrippa, and Herodias.

By his wife Malthace (a Samaritan), Herod fathered Archelaus, who was named ethnarch before being exiled by Caesar. He also fathered Antipas, who became tetrarch and is featured in this novel. His daughter Olympias married her cousin and had one daughter, Mariamne, who married Herodias' brother, Herod.

By his wife Cleopatra, Herod fathered Philip, who became tetrarch and married Herodias' daughter Salome.

By his wife Mariamne II, Herod fathered Herod, who married his niece Herodias, the daughter of Aristobulus. Herod and Herodias were the parents of one daughter, Salome.

Herod had other wives and children, but as I do not name them in this book, I have not included them here. You can find a more complete family tree, including the many marriages within the family, on my website, katrinadhamel.com.

# Timeline of Historic Events

40 BC Herod named King of the Jews by the Roman Senate

37 BC Herod achieves military control of his territory

29 BC Herod executes his beloved wife Mariamne on suspicion of adultery

27 BC Caesar Augustus named Emperor

20 BC Herod starts massive renovations of the Jewish temple

9 BC Aretas IV made king of Nabatea

7 BC Herod executes his sons Aristobulus and Alexander

4 BC Herod executes his son Antipater

4 BC Herod dies

4 BC Archelaus becomes ethnarch, Antipas and Philip become tetrarchs

6 AD Archelaus exiled and Roman prefects rule his territory of Iudaea, which includes Judea, Idumea (Edom), and Samaria

14 AD Augustus dies

14 AD Tiberius becomes Emperor of Rome

23 AD Tiberius' son and heir, Drusus, dies suddenly

26 AD Pilate becomes the fifth prefect/governor of Iudaea

27 AD (approx) Antipas divorces his wife and marries Herodias

28* AD John the Baptist arrested

28* AD Jesus begins ministry

31* AD Jesus is crucified and rises from the dead, and the Holy Spirit descends on Pentecost

31 AD This story begins


*Biblical scholars debate these dates, some of which argue for an earlier date of 26 AD, and others place Jesus' ministry at various dates within 30-36 AD.

# HISTORICAL NOTES

*Dates*
The dates in the chapter headings are Roman, rather than Jewish. In about 45 BC, January 1st was designated as the new year by Julius Caesar. For this series, the year changes during winter.

*Herod's Name*
In the Bible, there are four individuals using the name Herod. For clarity, I call the second Herod by his name, Antipas.

*King or Tetrarch*
Biblical authors sometimes give Antipas the title of 'king', such as Mark 6:14, though he was not a king like his father Herod, but a tetrarch, as mentioned in Matthew 14:1 and throughout Luke's gospel. A tetrarch ruled a quarter of a territory or was a subordinate prince, and he was under the authority of the Roman government.

*Israel*
The name 'Israel' for the land may be anachronistic for this time period, but I felt that in some places, it added clarity for modern, western readers. Within the New Testament, the land is often mentioned by its various territories, such as Galilee. Judea was the name of a specific territory, but also of a larger area ruled by the Roman governors. Often clarified by using the Latin name 'Idumaea', this territory encompassed Judea, Samaria, and Idumea (Edom).

*Historical Accuracy*
I did my best to represent the practices and traditions of the time, and to present them in a way that will appeal to a modern reader. I acknowledge that my research may be in error, or disputed now or in the future. Please keep in mind that this is a work of historical fiction, and is not intended for academic purposes.

Map Illustration by Cay Danielson

*Blessed are those who have been
persecuted for the sake of righteousness,
for theirs is the kingdom of heaven.*
Matthew 5:10

# PROLOGUE

23 AD

"My lord, you don't understand." Perseus wrung his hands. "They won't fulfill the order until your account is paid."

Agrippa gestured to the desk where stacks of receipts lay in disarray. "Then pay them."

Perseus' face gleamed with an unhealthy sheen. "My lord, I can't. There's no money."

Agrippa's gaze narrowed. "What do you mean, no money?"

Perseus opened and closed his mouth soundlessly.

"Speak man!"

Perseus flinched. "You gave the last of it away."

"You mean that gift to Septimus? It was only a hundred thousand sesterces."

"It was all that remained from your inheritance. I had hoped we could invest it, but—"

Agrippa stared at him, trying to make sense of this madness. He had money. Lots of it. His mother had always harped on him to keep careful accounts, but that was why he employed Perseus.

Agrippa stepped around the desk and stood toe-to-toe with his steward, staring down at the smaller man. "You must be mistaken."

Sweat dripped from under Perseus' hair and followed the creases in his face. He looked like the ugliest water fountain Agrippa had ever seen.

Perseus gulped. "My lord, I tried to tell you. You were spending too quickly. Your mother hoped you'd heed her lessons on prudence and economy—"

Agrippa silenced his steward with a slice of his hand. His mother had been a wise woman, but she didn't understand what it took to regain a kingdom. "I can't practice economy and have friends in the imperial palace."

Perseus fidgeted, but whatever nonsense he intended to sputter didn't make it past his thick lips.

Agrippa shook his head. "There must be more money. Check again."

Perseus' face crumpled, but Agrippa had his fill of prophecies of doom. He stormed from the office and drew a cleansing breath as he surveyed the sunny courtyard. Carved marble columns surrounded a lush space filled with greenery and comfortable seating. He had hosted a hundred parties here, feasting men and women from the best circles. Of course, those evenings had been expensive, but they were an investment in his future. A proper steward would understand that.

The pad of bare feet on the polished stone floor made him turn. Cypros strode toward him. Her deep blue peplos glowed in the sunlight, and her silver belt emphasized her small waist. Freckles spread like sparks over her creamy skin, but her brow was puckered over her honey-brown eyes.

"My love," she said, "I just had the strangest conversation with my shoemaker. He insists the bill is overdue. You must speak to Perseus about it."

Agrippa's jaw clenched, but he dragged the corners of his mouth into a smile. "Of course, my dear."

Cypros tilted her head and peered into his face. "Agrippa, what's wrong?"

"Nothing."

His wife saw straight through him. She slid her hand down his arm to knit their fingers together. "Tell me."

He scoffed to cover the uneasiness in his gut. "Perseus says the coffers are empty."

Cypros' complexion paled to the color of thin milk. "Is he right?"

Perhaps it was possible. But his inheritance had seemed limitless, an unending pool pouring a steady stream of coins. His grandfather left him enough to live comfortably for the rest of his life—but apparently not enough to fund his ambition.

He set his palms on Cypros' shoulders. "My friends will loan me whatever we need." Her expression was still troubled, and Agrippa leaned closer. "Everything will be fine. I promise."

As his lips pressed against her forehead, a servant hurried into the courtyard.

"My lord, Antonia is here."

Shame spiraled up Agrippa's spine and into his cheeks. Antonia had been his mother's closest friend. He whispered into Cypros' ear. "Let's keep our money troubles between us, hmm?"

Cypros nodded, her eyes wide.

But as Antonia swept into the room, Agrippa forgot his financial concerns. She rushed toward him, her hands outstretched and her eyes red and puffy.

Agrippa gripped her icy fingers. "Good God!" he cried out, searching her face. "What happened?"

Her face crumpled. "Drusus is dead!"

Agrippa blinked. "Your husband?" But he had died more than ten years ago.

"No," she gasped out the word. "My nephew."

His head reared in confusion. She couldn't mean his friend, Caesar's son and heir. "That's impossible. We just attended the theater together last week."

Antonia's chin trembled as she cupped his cheek. "I know it's hard

3

to believe, but it's true. He's gone."

Agrippa's mind drifted like a rudderless ship. He and Drusus had grown up together. Agrippa had attended his wedding and the naming of his son. One day Drusus would be the emperor, and he had promised to make Agrippa a king.

"How?" Agrippa whispered.

"We aren't sure. He was ill for a few days, but we didn't suspect —" Antonia's hand fluttered to cover her mouth.

Agrippa cleared his throat. "We should go to Tiberius. Comfort him."

Antonia shook her head. "He is overwhelmed by his grief and refuses to see any of his son's friends."

Cypros came to Agrippa's side, and her face was pale with anxiety.

Antonia's tight eyes belied her comforting smile. "I'm sure Tiberius will send for you soon."

Agrippa took Cypros' hand. With Drusus' death, he not only lost a good friend, he lost an entire future. He glanced around at his spacious home, the servant, and his wife's expensive clothes. Though his insides shriveled with grief for his friend, his entire future was at risk. He had to find his way back into Tiberius' inner circle. But that would take money. A lot of it.

# ONE

31 AD
AUTUMN

They were back. Chuza gripped the wooden railing as the port slid into view. Sailors hollered to one another, and the merchant ship shuddered in protest as it was turned toward shore. The ship's prow cut through the white-tipped waves while gulls keened overhead.

"This is your port?" Sadiki asked in his accented voice.

Chuza glanced over. The Egyptian sailor, wiry like the ropes that controlled the sail, waited for an answer.

"It is."

"Then you must make ready. The captain does not wish to linger here."

Chuza peered across the deck of the ship. Joanna and Leah were untying the leather tarp that protected them from the wind and sea spray. He took a half step toward his wife and daughter, but then stopped.

"You are not happy to be home?" Sadiki asked, his brow furrowed.

Chuza hesitated. He was happy at the prospect of leaving this cramped vessel. He was eager to see how their friends fared in Jerusalem. But returning to Israel meant returning to his responsibilities.

"It's complicated," he said. "I must find a way to serve my master and yet allow my wife to serve the Lord."

Sadiki glanced at Joanna, who was wrangling the tarp into a tidy roll. "She is a priestess for your people?"

Chuza's lips twitched. "Something like that."

"Then why is she packing your tent while you stand here and gape at the shore?"

Chuza chuckled and patted Sadiki's shoulder.

Joanna finished binding the tarp as Chuza approached. She straightened, and sunlight played across her wide cheekbones and the line of her arrow-straight nose. Her pregnant figure was half-hidden by the folds of her palla, but the swell beneath her belt was another reminder of the responsibility Chuza carried. So many people depended on him that it felt impossible to please them all.

He reached for their satchels and the heavy tarp. "Thanks for packing up."

Her gaze roved over his face. "You're worried." It wasn't a question.

He forced a smile. "Why should I be worried?"

She chuckled and touched his arm. "Everything will work out. You'll see. We just need to trust that God has a plan."

Chuza's smile turned wry. "If only he'd share it with me."

Leah hitched the strap of her bag over her head. "And spoil the surprise? If you'd asked me four years ago where I'd be today, this would have seemed impossible."

Joanna's expression softened as she looked at Leah. "You've come a long way since then." She glanced at Chuza. "We all have."

Joanna took Leah's arm and strode to the ship's railing. Chuza watched his wife and adopted daughter walk arm-in-arm. Joanna was a decade older than the fifteen-year-old girl, and a full head taller. Over the past few years, Leah had gone from Joanna's slave, to her ward, to her daughter.

As the wind tussled Chuza's hair, he fingered his golden earring. So much had changed, but some things were exactly the same.

He joined the women at the railing as the ship drifted into the harbor. The scent of the city wafted toward them—cook fires and spices, the salty tang of the day's catch, as well as sharp urine from tanneries and belching smoke from potters and glassmakers.

The ship bumped against the pier, and the gangplank was lowered so they could disembark. As his feet hit solid ground, Chuza glanced over his shoulder. The little Egyptian sailor waved his thin arm, and Chuza smiled and returned the gesture.

But his smile faded as he turned away from the ship and led the women through the bustling city streets. It was one thing to lead his family on a journey, and another thing entirely to guide them safely into their new life.

Joanna glanced at the sky. "It's early yet. Why don't we buy something to eat and start for Jerusalem?"

They aimed for the market street. The rumble of carts on cobblestone battled with the cries of merchants and the hum of the crowds.

She bumped his shoulder with hers. "Do you suppose we could buy Balaam back?"

"The donkey?" Chuza said. "I'm sure he's been sold to someone else by now."

Joanna's expression fell.

Leah shook her head. "See, that's why you shouldn't have named him. You grew too attached."

Joanna smiled sheepishly. "I couldn't help it. He was a good donkey."

Chuza readjusted the heavy tarp under his arm. Balaam had carried their supplies from Jerusalem, and it was a long walk back. "We'll take a look," he said, and then amended his agreement. "A quick look."

Joanna picked up her pace.

Booths with colorful awnings sheltered everything from knives to pomegranates. Shoppers perused and haggled while the sun rose higher, the autumn day warm despite the breeze blowing off the sea. While Chuza overheard Greek and Latin, the dominant language was Aramaic, and the lilting tones of his homeland soothed his ears after their time away.

They purchased bread and dates, and Joanna asked for a sample at the wine-seller's table.

She pursed her lips and leaned toward Chuza. "Well, it's wet," she whispered.

The merchant overheard and crossed his arms with a deep scowl.

"She has her own vineyard," Chuza said, and threw the red-faced man an apologetic smile. Joanna stiffened. "Had," Chuza quickly corrected. "She had her own vineyard."

The man's expression didn't change, so Chuza paid his coin, gathered the sloshing wineskin, and hustled the women away.

"There's the man who bought Balaam." Joanna gestured to a paddock at the end of the street. She picked up her hem so she could hurry forward, hopping over a steaming mound of manure.

"Slow down," Chuza called, but she kept going, leaving him to catch up. When he reached the fence, she was leaning against it, searching through a small herd of sheep, donkeys, and goats.

"There he is!" she cried out, and pointed to a soft gray beast with dark markings on his tail and legs. His ears flicked at her voice, and Joanna beamed. "He recognizes me!"

Chuza was dubious about the beast's memory, but he was sure the merchant did not remember them. The man strode forward, his shrewd gaze calculating the worth of their robes and sandals.

"My lord!" The merchant swept out his hands. "Your wife has a good eye for livestock. That is one of my best animals."

"Balaam?" Leah scoffed. "He is terribly lazy."

Joanna shot her a reproachful look. "He had to carry all the supplies. You'd be tired too."

The merchant blinked with realization. "Ah, you are the family who sold me this fine beast. And now you want him back again. Of course you do!" He inclined his head toward Joanna as if imparting a great favor. "For you, I will let him go for a mere one hundred denarii."

"One hundred!" Chuza's voice shot upward with his eyebrows. "I sold him to you for sixty."

"Ah, but he arrived footsore and thin from his journey." The merchant shook his head. "It took much time and expense to bring him to this fine state."

Chuza crossed his arms. Balaam looked exactly as they left him. "I can pay seventy denarii, as you did feed and shelter him."

"Seventy!" The merchant threw up his hands. "You are trying to rob me! I can't let this fine animal go for less than ninety denarii."

"Absolutely not," Chuza said. "We will buy elsewhere."

The merchant's gaze slid to where Joanna gripped the top rail of the fence.

"Oh, Chuza," Joanna said, her shoulders sagging. "I'm sure we could do... eighty?"

The merchant rubbed his chin with an exaggerated, thoughtful expression. "Eighty would be acceptable," he said. "At least I could afford a little bread for my children."

Chuza rolled his eyes at the man's theatrics, but he fished the coins out of his bag.

The merchant opened the gate and handed Joanna the lead. Chuza hid his smile as Joanna crooned over Balaam like a pet. If the donkey made her happy, he was worth every coin.

As Joanna and Leah stroked Balaam, Chuza strapped their belongings onto the donkey's back. He took the lead and gave a tug. Balaam's ears flicked, but he didn't move. Chuza sighed as memories of their last journey returned with painful clarity.

He heaved harder, but Balaam refused to walk until Leah smacked his rump.

Joanna glowed. "See? He's as well trained as Celer."

Chuza opened his mouth to protest at her comparison between this squat beast and his tall, fine-legged gelding, but then he caught the mischievous glint in her eyes. He sighed loudly and shook his head.

9

As evening draped the brown hills in shadow, they rented a room at a roadside inn. The innkeeper's wife provided them with a hot meal and an armful of hay for Balaam. They rose at dawn, prayed the *Shema*, and continued their journey.

They walked in silence for a time, the morning chill waning as the sun rose, gravel crunching beneath their feet. As they drew near to Jerusalem, they passed a vast flock of sheep destined for the temple altar.

"Everything's different now, isn't it?" Joanna said. Chuza looked at her in question, and she flicked her chin at the sheep. "How can God accept sacrifices from those who killed his son?"

He pressed his lips together. They weren't the first to question the righteousness of the priests, but the High Priest was appointed by the Roman governor. And as long as Caiaphas promoted peace in Judea, Pilate had no reason to replace him.

"But what do we do?" Leah said. Her large hazel eyes flickered with worry. "We refuse to take part?"

Chuza cleared his throat. "I'm sure the others have been discussing this. The twelve will decide what to do."

"This is why Jesus sent the Spirit to be our helper," Joanna said, nodding at Leah with confidence. "We're not figuring this out alone." Joanna turned to Chuza and grinned. "I can't wait to see everyone and hear what's been going on."

"Do you think Titus is back?" Leah asked. "It's been nearly five months."

Joanna shot Chuza a weighted glance, one that made Leah blush.

Leah crossed her arms. "I'm just concerned for him as a friend, so you can stop looking at each other like that. I'm not pining after him." Her cheeks darkened even more, and she stammered, "I mean —I had hoped—but things are different now. I just want him to know

10

that Jesus' life didn't end at the cross."

Titus had disappeared the day Jesus died. He had missed the resurrection and then the second miracle on Pentecost.

"I still don't know why he left without saying good bye," Chuza muttered. The Greek soldier had been his friend—his only true friend in the palace.

Chuza scanned the horizon, and his stomach swooped. "We're here."

Jerusalem rose from the countryside. The ancient city engulfed the slope that made up its base. Against his will, Chuza's focus turned to the western side, where the three towers of Herod's Palace pushed their way into the sky. Too many painful scenes had taken place within their shadows.

The Mount of Olives spread to the east, the thick trees adding a bulk of silvery green to complement the white and yellow city.

Joanna took his arm. "Things will be easier now. No more sneaking around Antipas and Herodias."

At least there was that. Antipas didn't care what Chuza believed, as long as he remained loyal.

Loyal to the man who helped send Jesus to the cross.

# TWO

The road curved around the city wall toward the southern gate, passing through hundreds of tents. Jews had traveled long distances for the Day of Atonement and Festival of Booths, but the city couldn't house so many pilgrims. Conversations hummed and children squealed amid the scent of cookfires.

As they strode through the temporary camp, Chuza smoothed his robe self-consciously. They might look like pilgrims, coated with dust and leading their donkey, but he did not feel like one of them.

People turned, searching for familiar faces. Strangers' hands rose in greeting. "Shalom!"

"Shalom!" Joanna returned. *Peace be with you.* They all needed peace these days, though it was a rare commodity as powerful men wrestled over the promised land.

He realized he was tugging on his golden earring and dropped his hand. He beckoned Leah to walk closer as they approached a city gate.

Large as a house, the gateway ushered them through thick walls and into the thoroughfare. The cobbled road that crossed the city north to south was glutted with pilgrims heading to purchase supplies, see what remained of King David's ancient city, or wash in the *mikveh* before visiting the temple.

"It's good to be back!" Joanna said, unconcerned as they bumped shoulders with strangers. Leah, however, followed Joanna so closely she collided with her tall back anytime Joanna paused.

Chuza wondered how many of these pilgrims knew what had transpired in this city mere months ago. Jesus had taught and healed in the temple, faced Pontius Pilate in the Antonia, and carried his cross down the city streets to his death. Women gathered water at the Pool of Siloam where thousands had been baptized in unprecedented numbers.

"This way." Joanna pointed to a narrow side street.

Glancing back at Balaam, Chuza plunged into the Lower City. Yellowish houses of clay bricks were separated by a warren of narrow streets and even narrower alleys, dim and sour with pungent aromas.

Noise spilled through open windows as families worked their trades with clinking, banging, and thumps. Laundry hung on roof tops, attempting to catch the breeze. It was all so close, everyone on top of one another, that Chuza had to force himself to draw a full breath.

They turned down another street and Joanna's pace quickened as a familiar two-story house rose ahead of them. People came and went through the courtyard gate as if it was a bustling synagogue.

Joanna burst into the courtyard.

"Maryam!" she said, rushing forward.

A woman with streaks of silver in her dark hair turned, her crescent-shaped dimples deepening as she squealed in delight.

"You're back!" Maryam met Joanna halfway as they collided in an embrace.

Other women crowded forward, and Leah slipped from Chuza's side to join the tumult. But Chuza hung back. He scratched Balaam behind the ears as he scanned the courtyard for Manaen. The older man was nowhere in sight, but a dozen men, women, and children sat at Matthew's feet. Chuza was struck by the strangeness. A tax collector shouldn't be teaching like a rabbi, yet here Matthew was.

On the other side of the courtyard, a trio of men scooped grain from tall storage jars. Women waited in line, some with small children. Men poured portions into the women's jars as barley dust puffed into the air.

Chuza calculated the cost of the grain, yet no coins were passing hands. A surge of pleased understanding rose in his throat. The disciples were taking Jesus' words to care for widows and orphans to heart. But where had they found the money?

Maryam's son Joses looked over. The young man had traveled with Jesus, and his brother James was one of the twelve. His face broke into a grin, and he raised his hand. "Chuza!"

Joses passed off his scoop and hurried forward, dusting off his hands before he clasped Chuza's wrist.

"How was your journey?" Joses asked. "Did you find…" He glanced at Leah, and concern flickered over his features. He lowered his voice. "You didn't find her family?"

"We did," Chuza said. "But she decided to return with us. Joanna and I have adopted her as our own."

Joses folded his arms and tucked his palms against his chest. "Joanna must be pleased. And you, of course," he added. He looked at his mother, who had her arm around Leah's shoulders as the women talked. "We're all glad to have you back."

Chuza's chest expanded with gratitude. He may not have a large family of his own to offer Leah, but there was no shortage of women here to support and teach his daughter. He scanned the courtyard. They were a new kind of family now, joined through faith in Jesus Christ.

But there was one still missing. Chuza stepped closer to Joses. "Have you seen my friend Jovian Titus? He escorted Joanna a few times when she was going to see Jesus."

Joses shook his head. "No, I'm sorry. We are all Jews here."

"Of course," Chuza said. He should walk up to the palace and ask Titus' former captain if he'd heard from him. But first, he needed to get his family settled.

The disciple's large house was surely cramped. Joanna was accustomed to close quarters, but Chuza wasn't raised that way. It seemed unlikely he could change now.

"Are all the followers staying here?" he asked.

"We've spread out a bit." Joses smiled ruefully. "As much as we enjoy being together, a hundred bodies under one roof brings certain difficulties." He leaned closer and lowered his voice. "Lines at the latrine, for example."

As Chuza chuckled, Joses continued. "Some of us are staying with believers in other houses around the city."

Chuza tried to hide his relief. If everyone had been staying here, Joanna would want to as well. He glanced around at the bustling courtyard and hoped no one would judge him for wanting a quieter place to call home.

He turned back to Joses. "Do you know where Manaen is?"

"At the temple." Joses gestured in its direction. "Peter, John, Andrew, and a few others went up for the hour of prayer."

"Is that wise?" Chuza blurted, and then flushed. "I mean, after what the priests did to Jesus?"

Joses clapped a hand on Chuza's shoulder. "I know how you feel. But we can't hide the wondrous news that the Messiah has come."

Chuza knew it in his head, but his heart feared the risks.

A man hovered nearby, and Joses beckoned him forward with a grin. "This is Stephen. One of our Hellenized brethren, who was with us at Pentecost."

"When my life changed forever," Stephen added, nodding his head. "My wife and I were baptized with the crowds." He beamed around the courtyard. "We are learning about Jesus, one parable, one miracle, at a time."

"I could talk for years and still not say everything," Joses said. "But this one is an apt pupil." Stephen lowered his eyes humbly.

A hurried footstep pulled both Chuza and Joses' attention to the gate. Andrew burst into the courtyard, his face pale. Chuza's tensed. Andrew was one of the twelve.

Everyone in the courtyard stilled, the disciples attuned to the dismay in one of their own.

Matthew rose to his feet as his students swiveled to see what was happening. He spoke into the silence. "What's wrong?"

Andrew worked his mouth for a second, and at last, he dragged the words to his tongue. "It's Peter and John. They were arrested."

# THREE

Joanna stiffened as Andrew's words blew through the courtyard like wind snuffing a lamp.

Joses strode over to Andrew. "By who?"

Andrew dragged both hands through his hair. "The priests."

Fear rippled down Joanna's spine. The same men who sentenced Jesus to death.

Matthew stepped around his students. "What happened?"

Despite his fear, awe shone in Andrew's eyes. "It was incredible. Peter healed a crippled beggar."

A shiver ran over Joanna's arms. Peter *healed*. Just like Jesus. She glanced at Maryam before slipping across the courtyard to stand beside Chuza.

Andrew's voice filled the silent courtyard. "As you can imagine, it drew a lot of attention. Peter took the chance to share the good news of Jesus, but the crowds weren't the only ones listening." His brow furrowed. "The temple guards hauled Peter and John away."

Chuza took a half step forward. "Is Manaen alright?"

"He's waiting with the women," Andrew said, and winced. "Peter's wife is there, along with Mary Magdalene and John's mother." His voice grew quieter. "They're hoping for news."

Joanna slipped her hand into Chuza's, her chest too tight.

"I'm going back." Andrew took a step toward the gate. "But I'll return if anything changes." He left as rapidly as he arrived.

A heavy silence hung in the courtyard. Matthew dismissed his students and they slipped from the courtyard with hunched shoulders. Joses jerked out of his reverie and returned to where the widows waited for grain, their eyes wide and fearful.

"What should we do?" Chuza asked Joanna. His cheeks reddened as faces turned his way. "There must be some way to help."

"There is." Matthew said. "We can pray."

The others murmured in agreement, but Chuza pressed his lips together. Joanna twined her fingers in his. Her husband was a problem solver, but some problems could not be solved by mortal men.

Matthew beckoned everyone closer, and Joanna drew strength from their familiar faces. They'd been through so much already, and they would get through this together.

Matthew lifted his hands to heaven and closed his eyes. "Lord, we ask that you give Peter and John the words to say. Give our brothers wisdom and courage to speak boldly."

Joanna clasped her hands together under her chin. Perhaps she had been naive to hope God would shelter the believers as they waited for Jesus' return. The forces that had arrayed themselves against Jesus still held power over Jerusalem. But as Matthew prayed, she was reminded of one very important fact—the disciples had God on their side.

"Amens" floated in the air.

Joanna rolled her neck as she ran a palm over her round middle. The ache in her soles was spreading up her calves and thighs, sapping what little energy she had left.

Chuza studied her face. "We need a place to stay. I was thinking we would go to your sister's house."

Joanna hesitated. She and Dalia had made peace, helped in part by Chuza's role in freeing their brother Amichai from prison. But Dalia and her family did not believe in Jesus. Neither did Joanna's mother, Miriam.

Leah came up and scanned Joanna's face with concern. Joanna twisted her lips to the side. How bad did she look?

"Dalia's house sounds good to me," Leah said.

"It makes sense," Joanna admitted. "And I would like to see my mother." She turned to pet the donkey, who pushed his nose into her hand. "There will be room for Balaam too."

"We're not keeping him though," Chuza said. His gaze flickered uncertainly. "Are we?"

"I thought we might."

"He could grind grain," Leah said.

Joanna's eyebrows rose. That was a good idea.

Chuza gave Leah a mock scowl. "I thought you were on my side."

Leah shrugged. "There's a mill at the palace we can use. Balaam could save the disciples hours of work."

Joanna shot Chuza a smug glance. "That's a wonderful plan. We should suggest it to the others," she said. "But not until Peter and John are free."

The trio glanced around themselves. The women worked in the outdoor kitchen, and Joses had picked up a broom. Some men were arranging tables for the evening meal. But the cheerful chatter was gone. It was as if everyone sensed the peace they enjoyed these past months had swung over a precipice.

Joanna glanced over at Chuza and saw the problem turning itself over in the depths of his dark brown eyes. Perhaps he would find a solution, but right now she needed to get off her feet.

They left the courtyard and rejoined the busy street.

"Where is all that grain coming from?" Chuza asked. "Can the disciples multiply food like Jesus did with the bread and fish?"

Joanna tucked her arm in his and leaned on him. "I asked Maryam.

Everyone is sharing what they have, giving to any who need it."

"Just like that?" he asked in amazement.

Chuza had always struggled with believing the best in people. But, she reminded herself, he had been raised in Herod's court.

They passed through a gateway in the stone wall that divided the Lower City from the Upper City. The houses stood in tidy rows with pale stone walls, inner courtyards, tiled roofs, and brightly painted shutters and doors.

After a few turns, they arrived at a large house. They approached the side, where an addition was built onto an older home. Joanna drew herself up to her full height, but nervousness poured into her like icy water. Though she and Dalia had parted friends, it was hard to forget years of suspicion and animosity.

"They'll be happy to see you," Chuza said.

"Well, most of them," Leah amended, her eye glinting with mischief.

Chuza shot Leah a pointed glance, but she was right. Alexander's family was distrustful of a woman who would leave her husband behind to follow Jesus.

Joanna squared her shoulders. After everything she'd been through, she could handle a little animosity.

She rapped on the red door, and the three of them stood silently. The door swung open to reveal a familiar face.

"Joanna!" Miriam exclaimed.

Joanna hugged her mother, closing her eyes as unexpected relief burst in her chest. She had so many questions about her pregnancy, ones only her mother could answer.

Miriam released Joanna and wrapped her arms around Leah. "And you brought Leah," she said, sounding pleased. "Did you find your family? You must tell me everything." Without waiting for an answer, Miriam turned to Chuza and pulled him into a hug.

Joanna smothered an amused smile as Chuza flushed and awkwardly patted Miriam's back.

"Come in, come in!" Miriam said, and ushered them forward.

22

Chuza jerked his thumb to the side. "I'll just take Balaam around to the stable."

Joanna watched him walk away. Though this had been his idea, he seemed nervous. He was determined to keep her free of the palace and far from Herodias, for which she was grateful, but she hoped he knew what he was getting into.

"Dalia!" Miriam called. "Look who's here!"

Sunlight spilled through the doorway that led them into the central courtyard. The comfortable space was filled with potted plants, soft seating, a low table, and stairs that led up to the second-story roof. Doorways opened into the original side of the house where Alexander's family lived, as well as the storeroom and the stable.

Dalia rose from her loom. She smiled, and some of Joanna's tension melted away.

"We've been praying for your safety," Dalia said. She gestured to Joanna's middle. "How's the baby?"

"I've felt him—or her—move," Joanna said, spreading both of her palms over her middle. The proof of life within her was both reassuring and terrifying. "Little nudges, but they're getting stronger."

Miriam clasped her hands in front of her chest, her eyes glowing. "You must be famished. Let me get you something to eat." She hurried to the storeroom.

Little Mary came skipping out of her grandparent's side of the house. She stumbled to a halt and stared between Joanna and Leah.

Leah crouched and playfully chastised the four-year-old. "You haven't forgotten me already, have you?"

A wide grin spread on Mary's face, and she leaped into Leah's arms, nearly knocking her over. Leah steadied herself just in time for Samuel to barrel out of the house, hollering and joining his younger sister.

"Gentle!" Dalia scolded as Leah tipped over, but Leah squealed with laughter. Dalia glanced at Joanna in surprise.

Satisfaction spread through Joanna's weary limbs. Between the wonder of Jesus' resurrection and the peace she found through reconciling with her family, Leah was like a different person—full of joy, instead of pain.

Chuza came through the stable door. He watched in amusement as Leah picked herself up off the floor and ruffled Mary's hair.

Miriam emerged from the store room with an overflowing tray of food, and Joanna's belly rumbled. She hastened to help her mother lay out the bread, fruit, cheese, and olives.

They all gathered around the low table, and Miriam looked at Chuza expectantly. Chuza reddened and cleared his throat. He recited the usual blessing, took a loaf, and ripped it in half to give to Joanna. As Joanna took the bread, she held his gaze and gave him a reassuring nod.

The others began helping themselves.

"Where's Alexander?" Chuza asked Dalia.

Dalia glanced up at the dusky sky, gauging the time. "He was at the booth today with his father. They planned to stop at the temple after work."

Chuza stiffened, and Joanna shot him a look.

"What?" Dalia said, catching the unspoken conversation.

Joanna drew a deep breath. She might as well get it over with. "The priests arrested two of our friends for teaching about Jesus at the temple."

Dalia frowned. "But why would they teach in the courts after —" She cut herself off and looked at her mother.

Miriam's eyes narrowed. "You shouldn't be involved with men the priests have deemed troublesome." Joanna's lips parted, but Miriam made a slicing movement with her hand. "You have a family now, and they must come first."

Joanna set a hand on her stomach. "I don't see it as choosing one or the other. We are born Jews first, God's covenant people, before we are called to be mothers."

Miriam shook her head. "If you continue to flout tradition, you will bring shame on your family."

Chuza frowned, but Joanna set a hand on his arm. He didn't need to be dragged into her family squabbles. "God has revealed our Messiah. Did God allow me to witness that moment just to keep it to myself?"

Dalia's eyes narrowed with old resentment. "So God chose you for a special purpose, is that right?"

Joanna tensed at the familiar rebuke. She had dreamed of being used by God since she was a child. Now that God had given her the desire of her heart, she would not turn aside.

"I don't want to argue," Joanna said, "and I have no intention of putting my family at risk." She glanced at Chuza. She knew he worried about how they would hold all the parts of their lives together. But there had to be a way.

Miriam fiddled with her cup. "Well, it is your husband's unlucky duty to oversee you now." She gave Chuza an exaggerated look of sympathy before looking back at her younger daughter. "But you must live with us instead of those disciples. You belong with family. Your real family."

Joanna stiffened. The disciples were her family, too. But Chuza shot her a quelling look, and she smiled tightly at her mother. "Of course, we will stay with you. If Dalia doesn't mind."

"You are family," Dalia said.

It wasn't an overwhelming welcome, but it would do.

Popping an olive in his mouth, Chuza rose. "I'm going to the temple."

Joanna knew he would not be at peace until he had tried to help. "Be careful," she said.

"I will," he promised. He kissed the top of her head, and she tilted her chin back so he could kiss her lips too.

He squeezed Leah's shoulder, nodded at Dalia and Miriam, and strode from the courtyard.

# FOUR

Chuza hurried down the aqueduct road that rose over the Lower City and brought much-needed water to the temple. The massive stones that supported the complex's western side glowed in the setting sun. Chuza climbed the steps to an arched gateway, and he emerged under a colonnade with carved wooden panels and soaring pillars. It surrounded a huge, opulent courtyard.

The Temple was partially hidden by an inner courtyard, but it gleamed with white marble and gold. Chuza paused to let the sight sink into his soul. The priests might be corrupt, but surely their callous hearts could not outweigh decades of incense, sacrifices, and prayer.

The outer courtyard was nearly empty. The rabbis had left with their students, and the worshipers had gone home. A group of Levites chatted as they crossed the courtyard toward their quarters, holding their instruments. Chuza walked past temple merchants covering the cages of cooing doves. Shepherds were cleaning the pens for sacrificial lambs. The swish of brooms from temple workers softened the chink of coins as the money changers secured their trade. A priest closed the heavy door to a massive storeroom and locked it securely.

Across the courtyard, near the Sanhedrin's chambers, Chuza spotted a group of Jesus' disciples. He strode in their direction, his sandals scuffing the colorful, intricately tiled floor, but he was drawn up short by a familiar face amid a knot of well-dressed men.

Relief flooded Chuza's veins. "Manaen!"

Manaen's face lit up, and he clasped Chuza's arm. "It's good to see you, my friend."

Chuza nodded at the others. They were Herodians, supporters of King Herod's heirs.

"Peace be with you," Chuza said.

Omri, the leader of their party, inclined his head in welcome. "Shalom, Steward. What brings you to the temple courts at this hour?" He scanned Chuza's dusty clothes. "And straight from the road, it seems."

Chuza's neck warmed at his unkempt appearance. "I heard there have been two arrests."

Omri folded his hands. "Three. They've detained the beggar."

"The beggar?" Chuza looked at Manaen.

Manaen's eyes promised to tell him more later. "They believe him complicit in some trick."

Omri snorted. "That would be quite the deception. Everyone has seen him at the gates since he was a child. He must be what, forty now?"

Chuza had probably passed the man multiple times himself. "Will they hold a trial tonight?"

"Tomorrow morning," Omri said.

Manaen ran a hand down his beard. "Presumably because it's too late in the day, but—"

"More likely they're trying to rattle them," Omri finished for him.

"Do we need to do anything? Bring witnesses?" Chuza lowered his voice. "Offer a financial settlement?" He smiled crookedly, though he was half serious.

"There is nothing we can do but wait," Manaen said. He bowed his head to Omri, took Chuza's arm, and led him toward the other disciples.

Manaen spoke near Chuza's ear. "I don't know if we can trust them."

Chuza darted a sideways glance at his old mentor. "What do you mean?"

"They supported Jesus' crucifixion, in thought if not in deed." Manaen kept his voice low. "They worked with the Pharisees, trying to trap Jesus into speaking against Roman taxation."

Chuza fought the urge to look over his shoulder. "But we need allies if we hope to free Peter and John."

Manaen shook his head, revealing new strands of silver in his hair. "You're thinking like the royal steward, not as a man of faith." He gestured toward the temple. "Sometimes, my friend, the only ally we have is God."

Chuza squirmed inwardly. He knew God was all-powerful, but he was uncomfortable doing nothing. "Surely there is something we can do."

A priest strode toward the cluster of disciples, his expression sour.

Manaen quickened his pace. "We will do the most powerful thing of all, my friend."

"And what is that?"

"We pray."

Chuza and Manaen reached the others just as the priest approached. He flapped his hands at the disciples. "You must go. It's time to lock the gates."

Peter's wife wrung her hands. "Please, just let me see my husband."

"Absolutely not," he said. "Come back tomorrow."

She opened her mouth to protest, but the other women drew her away. The priest followed them, and shut the gate so quickly that he almost caught Chuza's heel.

Andrew led the women toward the Lower City, and Manaen gripped Chuza's shoulder. "Join us tomorrow."

29

Chuza walked back to Dalia's house as darkness fell, his insides writhing at the unfamiliar feeling of helplessness. He was the steward. Fixing problems was his job. But as he reached the red door, his mind was empty.

He shook back his shoulders and went inside.

Lamps cast patterns on the stone walls and the remnants of a meal. Chuza nodded at Alexander, who sat near his parents. Alexander's expression was open, but his gray-haired father returned Chuza's nod with cold politeness. Alexander's unmarried sister sat with her mother. Both women seemed uncomfortable with their new house guests.

Leah was distracted by Little Mary, but Joanna rose from the table and hurried to him.

He took her hand. "Nothing has changed."

Joanna pressed her lips together and squeezed his fingers. "I saved you some stew."

The bread and olives from earlier were only a memory in his stomach. He washed his hands and joined the others at the table, sitting beside Joanna.

Joanna leaned toward him and kept her voice under the hum of conversation. "I made up a bed for us in the stable loft. I thought you might enjoy some quiet." Thankfulness for his wife warmed him more than fire on a cold night. "Leah will sleep upstairs with my mother." Her smile turned wry. "My mother is upset because we won't be with the rest of the family, but I reminded her that you were not raised in a communal sleeping room."

"True. I just had a snoring master to contend with." Chuza twisted his smile to the side. His first bed was on the floor near his master's couch. He nudged Joanna's shoulder and lifted an eyebrow. "But the good thing is, it prepared me for my snoring wife."

Joanna pretended to smack his arm, and Chuza took a large mouthful of stew, grinning at her with full cheeks.

Chuza, Joanna, and Leah left the house as the sun rose over the city, painting the tops of buildings gold while the rest lay in shadow. The rich tones of a shofar echoed from the tallest temple tower and reverberated over the city. Joanna and Chuza shared a glance. The priests were offering the morning sacrifice.

The courtyard gate of the disciple's house was unlocked, and they let themselves in. They followed the hum of voices to the upper room, Joanna leading the way to a place that had contained both despair and unbounded joy.

Glancing back at him, Joanna pushed the door open. As they slipped into the dim room, they were bathed in the words of prayer. A few lamps had been lit, augmenting the soft light from the window. The upper room was full, but Maryam and her sons shifted closer together and beckoned them to join.

The prayers wove into one another like a tapestry and the sense of unity and holiness was enough to take Chuza's breath away. Across the city, the most powerful men in Judea conspired against Peter and John, but in this room, common women and men interceded on their behalf.

Peter's wife prayed with a wavering voice that made Chuza's eyes burn. She had to be terrified.

Joanna took a turn praying, full of confidence in the goodness of God. He wished he had her unwavering faith. Words of lament pressed at Chuza's throat, begging to be released, but he couldn't reveal his inner turmoil to the others.

Hasty footsteps scraped on the stairs outside. His breath caught in his throat. They were gathered like a flock of quail, easy prey before a hungry fox. He grasped Joanna's arm as the door swung open.

A familiar figure burst into the room.

"Peter!" Andrew cried out.

The room erupted in startled gasps, and Andrew charged forward. He hugged his brother so exuberantly that he lifted Peter off his feet.

The clamor increased as John entered the room, ducking under the questions flying at him. As men and women pressed forward, all speaking at once, John's eyes searched the room. His expression eased as he saw his mother, and the others parted like the Red Sea to let her through.

Peter's wife slipped through the crowd, tears falling silently. She threw herself into Peter's arms, and he leaned to murmur in her ear. She stepped back, wiping her cheeks, and John's brother James clapped his hands on both Peter's and John's shoulders. Even across the room, Chuza could feel their bond. The little group from Capernaum had fished together in Galilee before they left their homes and trade to follow Jesus.

"What happened?" Andrew asked Peter.

Peter moved deeper into the room so everyone could hear him better. "We were brought before the Sanhedrin on charges of blasphemy."

John nodded. "They demanded to know where we got the power to heal." He grinned at Peter. "I think they expected a bumbling recitation from this unschooled fisherman, but the Holy Spirit had other ideas. Peter's wise arguments caught them off guard."

Peter shook his head good-naturedly and faced the group. "They commanded us to not speak about Jesus again. They wanted to punish us, but the crowds had seen the miracle. How could they keep us imprisoned or beat us without upsetting the people?"

"So they lashed us with their tongues instead and sent us away," John said. "If you think about it, our arrest granted us the opportunity to preach to them."

Several laughed at that, their anxiety turning to joy. But Chuza noticed Peter and John's shadowed eyes, a reminder of their rough night and how the trial could have ended. Peter gripped John's shoulder, his lips pressed together for a moment. He turned to face the others.

"Let us pray together, my brothers and sisters," Peter said, his bright eyes shining around at them all. Silence fell.

"Sovereign Lord," Peter's voice filled the room, "you made the heavens, earth, and sea, and everything in them. You spoke by the Holy Spirit through the mouth of your servant, our father David: Why do the nations rage, and the people plot in vain? The kings of the earth rise up and the rulers band together against the Lord and against his anointed one."

The disciples whispered words of agreement, and a sense of unity pervaded the space. They were not a gathering of individuals, but a family bound by blood.

Peter spoke louder. "Herod Antipas and Pontius Pilate met together in this city with the Gentiles and the people of Israel to conspire against your holy servant Jesus, who you anointed. They did what your power and will decided beforehand should happen." His voice grew thick with passion. "Now, Lord, consider their threats and enable your servants to speak your word with great boldness. Stretch out your hand to heal and perform signs and wonders through the name of your holy servant Jesus."

A tremor shook the house, and shock lanced through Chuza's chest. Another sign from heaven.

Joanna gripped his arm as others cried out with joy, not fear. Her eyes were pools of shimmering tears. "See? We don't need to be afraid. God is with us."

# FIVE

Chuza's new sandals scuffed on the wide stone steps. He ran a hand over his freshly trimmed beard and down the front of his robe. Armed guards flanked the entrance, and behind them soared a sky of cloudless blue. He arranged his face to hide his taut emotions. After two months away, he was back at Herod's Palace.

A familiar guard noticed his approach. "Welcome, Steward."

Chuza inclined his head. "Have you heard word from Jovian Titus?"

The guard's brows twitched in surprise. "No, my lord. The captain dismissed him months ago."

Chuza's hope shriveled. "Yes, of course."

He stepped into the courtyard, skirting the verdant garden with its palms, fountains, and streams filled with exotic fish, and strode for his office in the northern wing. No guards were posted at the identical southern wing, meaning Pontius Pilate was not in residence. Chuza sighed with relief. He had enough to handle today.

A parade of servants rushed by with their arms full of linen, following the harried housekeeper. Antipas would soon arrive with his retinue of servants, friends, and family. Everything had to be perfect.

Chuza swallowed his nerves and pushed open his office door.

His office was much like his rooms in Antipas' other palaces. A window illuminated a wall of small cubicles that stored his documents and scrolls. But the sideboard was empty of its usual wine and refreshments, and his couch was draped with a cloth to keep off the dust.

His desk was piled with messages. Still standing, Chuza sifted through them, breaking the wax seals and unfurling the rolls of papyrus. Bills, requests, complaints, but nothing from Titus. He sat heavily in his chair and leaned his forehead onto his palms.

If only he could write to the former guard. But, despite their years together, Chuza had never asked what part of Antioch Titus was from. And even if he knew where to send a message, he had no one to carry it.

Chuza swallowed a pang of loss. When Antipas left Jerusalem, Chuza would go with him for a few weeks, serving a master he could not trust. Titus' companionship would have eased Chuza's burden. Memories of the hours they had spent in the kitchen rose to his mind—Leah working nearby while Titus and Chuza played board games.

Jerking his chin upright, he laid out his writing materials—wax tablets for notes, rolls of papyrus and a sharp knife to cut it into sheets, and his pen and pot of ink. He flicked his wrists to shake his sleeves out of the way and set to work.

A royal household had a dizzying array of expenses. He worked through the stack of receipts that had piled up in his absence, recording the amounts in his ledger, and ensuring the heads of staff were within their budgets.

It was late afternoon when the noise in the courtyard changed. Servants rushed to unload luggage, obeying self-important voices demanding baths and food. Chuza rose, his legs stiff from hours of sitting, and smoothed his robe. His real work was just beginning.

Chuza opened his office door and watched the bustle disperse from the courtyard. Antipas was heading for his usual apartment, Herodias on his arm.

Chuza straightened his spine and strode toward them.

Sensing his approach, Antipas turned. Close-cropped hair was curled over his forehead, and the dark strands were frosted with silver. His once athletic frame had thickened considerably since his second marriage.

"Chuza!" Antipas said, and the pleasure in his tone was unmistakable. "How was Alexandria?"

The tightness in Chuza's chest loosened a fraction. "We had good weather, and I'm pleased to say that Leah is now my daughter."

Antipas burst into laughter and smacked Chuza's back. "Now you will know the struggle of marrying off a daughter." He beamed at Herodias, but his exuberance seemed overdone. "Am I right, my love?"

Herodias smiled sweetly. "You are right, as always." She turned her dark eyes on Chuza. "I pray your daughter will make a prosperous match."

Chuza inclined his head, thinking of Herodias' daughter Salome, who lived in Caesarea Philippi with her much-older husband.

Antipas turned away. "We have business to discuss, now that you're back. But first, I need a bath. Join me in an hour."

"Of course," Chuza said and bowed.

At the appointed time, Chuza stepped into Antipas' opulent room and was greeted by soft music. Plush couches were placed among delicately carved tables, with statues, tapestries, and golden bowls of fruit. It was all layered over a mosaic floor and a mural depicting an idyllic garden scene.

Chuza blinked in surprise to see his master sitting at a desk instead of relaxing on a couch. Antipas was studying a sheet of papyrus, his expression unusually eager.

Herodias sat gracefully on an elegant chair as she plucked on a lyre. Her dark hair was piled on her head and bound with a ribbon, and her robes were arranged to show every curve of her figure. Chuza stepped forward, and her sharp eyes regarded him coldly.

"Ah, Chuza, there you are," Antipas said, and beckoned him forward. As Chuza approached, Antipas held out the papyrus. "I have already placed orders for armor and weapons, but I need you to ensure they are being filled—and on budget."

Chuza scanned the list and his eyebrows rose. The tetrarch wasn't permitted an army, yet he had ordered enough to outfit a thousand soldiers.

"Have tensions worsened with Nabatea, my lord?" Chuza asked.

"A few border testings." Antipas waved his hand. "No bloodshed, but it's only a matter of time. I must be ready to show my strength."

Chuza avoided looking at Herodias. Had she pressed for this?

"What about a nonviolent resolution?" Chuza asked. "War with Nabatea will be costly, my lord, and I'm sure Emperor Tiberius would prefer if you could maintain the peace."

The music paused.

"We are not the instigators," Herodias said testily. Antipas cast her a conciliatory smile, and she resumed her music.

Antipas lowered his voice and leaned toward Chuza. "I suspect King Aretas still nurses a grudge about..." he trailed off, his eyes darting to his wife. Antipas' first wife, Phasaelis, was King Aretas' daughter. Phasaelis had been forced to flee when Antipas decided to divorce her, and Joanna's part in the escape had made her a suspicious figure in Herodias' eyes ever since.

Chuza returned the list and folded his hands behind his back. Before he left for Alexandria, he had vowed to speak up when he believed Antipas was making a poor decision. That vow was simpler in the abstract.

"Allow me to write a letter to King Aretas. Open talks," Chuza said. As Antipas opened his mouth to protest, Chuza pushed on. "Prepare for battle, but in the meantime, we can try for peace."

Antipas tapped his fingers on his desk. "Of course, peace is preferable," he muttered. "Fine. Draw up your letter and bring it to me for approval. I must not appear weak, you understand."

"Of course." Chuza inclined his head. "I only want what is best for you and your kingdom."

Antipas' eyes roved over Chuza's face as if testing the veracity of his claim. Lately, Antipas had done little to garner Chuza's loyalty, but Chuza meant every word. Thirty years together forged a tie not easily broken. Antipas had lost his way, but Chuza would steer him onto the proper path—if it was at all possible.

Antipas' lips parted as if he wanted to say more, but his gaze flicked to his wife. He nodded at Chuza. "You may go."

Chuza bowed and turned for the door, but Antipas called after him. "When we return to Tiberias, we must go for a ride, you and I."

Chuza glanced back. An earnestness shone in his master's eye. It was the closest to an apology Chuza could expect. He smiled. "I look forward to it."

"Why do you let him talk to you like that?"

Antipas' fingers tightened on the papyrus, but he feigned confusion. "Who?"

Herodias rose with a rustle of expensive cloth and set aside her lyre. Her hips swayed delightfully as she approached, coming to stand behind him with her palms resting on his shoulders. She leaned forward so her lips were right beside his ear, and her perfume filled his nose.

"Your steward. You should not allow a slave to question you." She kissed his cheek and began massaging his shoulders with her strong fingers.

Antipas' head drooped as his muscles relaxed. "He may be my slave, but he would make a poor steward if he didn't share his concerns."

"His concerns should be limited to budgets, productivity, and staff," Herodias said. "He can never understand your responsibilities or the weight of power you bear."

"Perhaps not," Antipas admitted, "but he's been with me most of my life. He is one of the few men I trust completely."

He winced as her thumb dug too deep.

"A trusted slave is a worthy possession, but he cannot be a true friend."

Antipas frowned, glad that she could not see his face. True, he and Chuza were not equals, but they were friends all the same.

Herodias' hands stilled. "I'm just saying, don't let him hold you back with needless worries. You may think he's your friend, but he's been pulling away from you, little by little, ever since he married that woman." She shifted so she was leaning against his desk, facing him. "While he's letting his wife fill his head with religious nonsense, you've been ruling your territories with a sure and just hand."

Antipas was flattered by her jealousy. He pulled Herodias into his lap, and she came with a giggle. He nuzzled her neck. "You, my dear, are my greatest strength. Don't worry about Chuza's doubts or questions. We know what we're doing."

She wrapped both her arms around him and smiled coyly. "Of course we do."

Chuza set a large ornate box on the empty table. Stars spread across the night sky, bright in the crisp air.

A footstep made him turn. Joanna walked toward him, her bare feet padding on the cold courtyard floor. Her belly pressed against the thin cloth of her linen tunic and tendrils had slipped from her braid. She drew her shawl closer around her shoulders.

"How was work?" Joanna asked.

"It was awkward," he admitted, "but not as bad as I expected. I don't need to go tomorrow, but I must return after the fast."

"You'll be able to celebrate Sukkot with us, right?" Joanna wrapped her arms around him, her shawl pleasantly warm. He burrowed his face into her neck and pulled her closer.

"In the evenings," he said.

She stepped back and gestured to the box. "What's this?"

He opened the lid, revealing his entire collection of ancient texts. "I want to give them to the disciples. A synagogue needs scriptures."

Her fingertips brushed over the scrolls. She had read many of them herself. Years ago, before they were friends, he lent her the scrolls of Isaiah. He smiled, remembering the day she teased him about reading Song of Solomon. After their marriage, she had asked him to buy the prophecies of Daniel.

He jerked, feeling like an idiot. "I'm so sorry. These are yours as much as mine. I should have discussed it with you first."

She smiled coyly and closed the box. "Perhaps you should have, but I think you're doing the right thing. The disciples will be grateful."

He sighed, relieved she understood. "It's one of the few things I can give."

Joanna cupped his face with her warm hands. "You have much to give."

He swallowed hard, and her gaze held his. She kissed him, and the swell of her belly pressed against him. He wrapped his arms around her and the stress of the day melted away.

"What would I do without you?" he asked.

She laughed and led him toward the stable loft.

So much was changing, but his wife's steadfast trust in Jesus was a rock he could cling to as his faith was broken down and rebuilt.

But Joanna wouldn't be with him when he traveled with Antipas after the festival. Neither would Leah or Titus. An ache widened in Chuza's chest. What if more trouble befell the disciples while he was away? He reached up to tug on his earring. Such a small piece of jewelry, yet it bound him tighter than the heaviest manacles.

# SIX

Jovian Titus raised his sword just in time, parrying a slice aimed at his throat. He hefted his heavy shield back into its proper place. Fool! He must stay focused.

He blinked away the grisly image of a man upon a cross and countered the next blow before offering a few of his own. His arm reverberated with the force of his strikes. They caught his opponent's shield, nothing more. Sweat trickled down his forehead, and sand slid beneath his sandals. His tunic clung to his skin beneath his leather armor. Shifting his stance, he pushed forward to knock his opponent off balance, and he was rewarded when the man stumbled.

Eager for victory, he lunged to strike, but his overconfidence cost him. His opponent seemed to evaporate, spinning beside Jovian and slamming his weapon into his back.

Jovian cried out at the sting across his shoulders and collapsed. Sand ground into his cheek, and his arm was trapped between his shield and his chest. His back was exposed. He rolled over, but a grin pinned him beneath the point of a blade.

"Galen is the victor!" a voice shouted.

Shaking his unruly curls out of his eyes, Galen tossed his practice sword to a ludus slave. He extended his hand to Jovian.

Galen was never one to gloat, but he also wasn't the one lying on his back in the sand. Jovian's pride stung, but as his blood cooled, he grinned and accepted Galen's help, rising to clap his childhood friend on the shoulder.

"Well fought." Galen inclined his head. "But what made you lose focus?"

Jovian handed off his weapon and shield as the ludus captain arranged the next bout. "Does it matter? It would have cost my life on a battlefield." He unstrapped his leather armor, ready for a bath and a massage. He rolled his shoulders and winced. More bruises for his mother to complain about.

Galen studied his face. "Is something troubling you?"

Jovian grimaced and rubbed his tired eyes. Nightmares plagued his sleep, and the images chased him into the waking hours. But it wasn't something he wished to discuss.

"It's nothing," he lied.

Galen did not look convinced, but he joined Jovian as they stored the faded practice armor and drank from a krater of wine and water.

Jovian gathered up his cloak and slung it over his shoulder. Galen wasn't the only one who had questions. Jovian had arrived back home with nothing to show for his five years away, and his parents were pressing him for answers. But that didn't mean he wanted to talk about it.

He eyed Galen. "Why don't you come for supper?"

Galen seemed pleased. "I'd be happy to. If your mother won't mind."

"Mind? My mother would adopt you if she could." Jovian laughed. "She likes to remind me how well you're doing in your family's business."

"The merchant's life isn't so bad, you know," Galen said. "Would you rather scrounge for odd jobs, like when you were a boy?"

Jovian made a face. Back then, he had longed for Galen's easy life, with a private home and a servant to do the chores. Now he didn't know what he wanted.

The friends let themselves out of the ludus and stepped into the wide, paved street. A group of young women giggled as they passed, but their fluttering lashes were aimed at Galen. Jovian did not begrudge his friend their admiration. A broken nose had marred Jovian's chance at good looks, but he refused to have it broken and reset in exchange for a little admiration.

The sun was sinking by the time they left the bathhouse, their hair gleaming with scented oil instead of sweat. Galen steered Jovian to a booth and selected a cluster of plump grapes, so purple they were almost black. Joanna grew similar fruit on her vineyard. But Galilee was a world away from Antioch.

Admirers called Antioch the Golden City. It was resplendent with impressive architecture, some gilded with actual gold. The city sprawled over a river, spanned by dozens of bridges, and walls divided the city into four quarters. A large island housed the palace and an enormous circus. As they strolled past lush gardens, wide market streets, and insulae reaching ten stories tall, Jovian pushed all thoughts of humble Galilee out of his head. It was not part of his life anymore.

They turned down a wide street lined with private dwellings built of light-colored stone and topped with sloped, red-tiled roofs. Pots of herbs flanked Jovian's front gate. He knocked. The slave, Tomas, unbolted it and let them in.

"Good afternoon, my lord." Tomas grinned. He was younger than Jovian, with wide shoulders topping his skinny frame. "Your parents are gathering for supper."

Jovian winked at Galen. "Just in time."

The men walked through the courtyard and into the atrium. The airy space was open to the sky with a large tiled pool in the center. Jovian followed voices deeper into the house.

Couches bordered the triclinium, forming three sides of a square with a table in the middle. Their maidservant set down a tray with dill soup and fresh bread. The scent made Jovian's mouth water.

"Galen!" Jovian's mother beamed and rose with practiced grace. Golden brown hair, lightly touched with silver, was braided around her head. Her eyebrows were thin and her lips full, contrasting the sharp planes of her cheekbones. She was not strictly beautiful, but her expressions were captivating.

Thea kissed Galen's cheek. "I'm so happy Jovian invited you. Sergio and Cassandra are dining with friends tonight, and our conversation could use a little variety."

Galen bowed with a flourish and offered his grapes.

Thea accepted them with delight. She turned to her son, and her easy smile was replaced with consternation. "Another afternoon at the ludus?"

Jovian kissed her cheek and sat on one of the couches. "I needed the exercise. I'm afraid pouring over ledgers isn't the physical exertion I'm used to."

Galen sat beside him and lifted his brows. "Perhaps your father can put you to work unloading ships."

Jovian chuckled, but Belen's sharp eyes assessed his youngest son like a new shipment of goods.

"I didn't work my way up from a dockworker so my son could become a common laborer," he said. Galen cast his eyes down.

But Jovian shrugged. "We are only jesting, Father."

Belen's frown deepened. "Every day you are at the ludus. Training for what?"

Jovian didn't have a ready answer. He had given up the idea of enlisting in the army, but he was drawn to the ludus like a horse to a bucket of grain.

Belen shook his finger at the sky. "We are Greeks! The people who brought art, literature, and science to the Romans. It is time you sought greater rewards than the spoils of battle." He looked at Thea affectionately.

"We cannot all be so fortunate," Jovian said.

Galen slapped his shoulder. "We have time yet, my friend."

"Not that much time." Thea raised her brows. She began handing around the bread, serving her husband first.

"A young man needs exertion," Belen conceded as he dipped his bread in the soup. "But when a man needs as much exercise as you, he's trying to outrun something in his head."

Jovian's cheeks warmed. His parents surely imagined all sorts of reasons why he fled Judea. They would be shocked if they knew the truth.

Thea noticed his discomfort and relented. "No matter why you returned, we're glad you're here."

"You can train in the early mornings," Belen said. "But you will spend the rest of your day working with your brother and me. It is time for you to settle down, my son. You will forget whatever business chased you home from Judea."

Jovian's throat tightened at the jab, and he inclined his head with difficulty.

The maidservant returned to the triclinium with a platter of steaming fish, and Jovian rubbed his palms together, as ready to fill his rumbling belly as he was to turn the conversation to other topics.

Shadows claimed the hallway to Jovian's bedchamber, but a flickering light around the corner drew him toward the family altar. In a niche in the wall, Thea's lamp bathed the bronze goddess in a golden glow. Bread and salt were placed in the little serving dishes, and Thea poured a few drops of glistening oil over the goddess' head.

Thea knelt with clasped hands. Every day she prayed for her family's health and safety. She insisted her prayers had lifted them from poor laborers to a comfortable middle class, and maybe she was right. All her prayers had been answered.

Jovian crossed his arms and leaned against the wall. The Jews insisted there was only one God who heard prayers. They called him the one true God, the God who sees, the God of Abraham, Isaac, and Jacob. They would not even speak his name, calling him *Hashem*— The Name—or *Adonai*, which meant Master, or Lord.

Who was right—his mother, or an oppressed but proud people?

Jovian slipped away. Moonlight shone through the high window of his bedchamber. The narrow room was barely large enough for a bed, chest, and a basin, but it was the one place where he could give way to the painful memories that pursued him from Jerusalem. Not that Judea had been all bad. Most of it had been wonderful.

Five years ago, he'd left home, determined to enlist in the Roman army and get as far as possible from Antioch. A chance encounter led him to the temple in Jerusalem, and he experienced God amid the songs of the priests and the scent of burned offerings and incense. Wanting to stay close to this mysterious deity, he joined Antipas' private guards.

But learning about the Jewish God was difficult. Jovian was an outsider, an uncircumcised Greek, regarded with distrust or outright animosity. The best he could achieve was the tenuous status of a righteous Gentile—a God-fearer, as they called it. A God-fearer was not held to Jewish purity standards, but he was taught to govern his life by seven laws.

If not for Chuza, Jovian wouldn't have gotten any further in his quest to understand this unseen God. The steward invited Jovian not only into friendship, but into the Jewish faith. And then there was Joanna, Chuza's wife. Passionate and driven, her dedication to a prophet gave Jovian the opportunity to witness the miracle-working Jesus of Nazareth for himself.

He squeezed his eyes shut, shoving back the image of Jesus on the cross—beaten, bloodied, and dying. He tried to paint over the image with better memories of Jesus in a field near Bethsaida, his hair blown by the wind. Strong. Powerful. An enigmatic figure Jovian struggled to understand.

Jovian could comprehend God as described in the scriptures, a powerful being who conquered nations and raised up heroes like Gideon, David, and Joshua. But Jesus was like the mysterious prophets with their mingled message of doom and hope. Jesus spoke impossible riddles and lessons, like the poor being blessed, or telling his followers to love their enemies. It was the opposite message Jovian expected a prophet to give to a subjugated people. And yet, Jovian admired Jesus, and even wished to be more like him.

Jovian's lips quirked to the side. Perhaps it was good Jesus had focused his ministry in a quiet place like Galilee. If a man with his gifts had appeared in Antioch, the priests would name him a god, place him on a throne, and start a system whereby supplicants could exchange money for miracles.

But not the Jews. Jovian's smile melted away. They refused to believe Jesus was a man of God, despite how many cripples he healed, or how many lessons of love and mercy he taught. God had given his people an incredible gift, but they nailed him to a cross.

Jovian rubbed his forehead with his fingers and thumb. Everything he learned about God from Chuza collided with that cross and fell lifeless to the ground. What kind of god allowed his prophet to be tortured and killed?

Jovian threw himself back on his bed. Maybe there was nothing to be found in faith, only futility. A chasing after the wind.

After a moment, he heaved himself upright, pulled his wool robe over his head, and hung it on its hook. He crawled into bed wearing only his thin linen tunic. Pillowing his head with his arm, he peered out the window. The moon shone in a sea of deepest blue, cold and distant.

Thoughts of Leah pushed their way forward, and his throat contracted with shame. He should never have let himself become so familiar with the young Jewish woman. She had fascinated him with her sharp edges and sarcasm, yet she had been vulnerable too. Inquisitive. Clever.

Pretty.

Groaning, he rolled over. There was no future for a Jew and a Gentile. He knew that, and yet he let his feelings run away with him. He had assumed the admiration was all one-sided, but then she turned into his arms for comfort.

He made a fist, tapping his forehead with disgust. Flippant with his own feelings, he engaged hers, and now she must hate him for leaving without even saying goodbye. He sighed. She was better off without him.

He would make a new life in Antioch, far from the God who let Jesus die. Whatever was happening in Judea had nothing to do with him anymore.

# SEVEN

The royal retinue jostled toward the city perched on the south-western shore of the Sea of Galilee. From atop his restless stallion, Antipas surveyed Tiberias with pride. Beneath the palace, an impressive theater overlooked the sea, and below that, the city was arranged in rows of tidy houses and cobbled streets, with a colonnaded market and government buildings. A new public bathhouse was an easy walk away, utilizing natural hot springs with healing properties. None of this had existed before him. He may not have an heir, but this city would be his legacy.

He grinned at Chuza. The steward sat astride his bay gelding and peered uncertainty at the palace. Antipas' smile faded. Chuza had spent months with his wife. Surely he could live without her for a few weeks.

Antipas cleared his throat loudly. "It's good to be home!"

Chuza blinked and smiled a fraction too late. "Yes, my lord."

Antipas sighed. Chuza would get over his homesickness as soon as he had a ledger under his nose.

They rode through the city, and Antipas made sure to wave at the curious citizens who looked their way.

51

After dismounting at the stables and handing the reins to the groom, Antipas strode into his winter palace. He drew up short as an unwelcome figure stepped forward with his arms spread benevolently.

Agrippa.

Antipas' lip curled, but Herodias hurried past, eager to greet her brother.

Agrippa kissed Herodias' cheek. "You look lovely, as always."

Herodias glowed under his affection. The siblings were a handsome pair, and very aware of it.

Agrippa inclined his head to Antipas. "Welcome back to Tiberias."

Antipas bristled at being welcomed to his own city, but Agrippa was as oblivious as ever.

"I'm eager to go over the city accounts with you," Agrippa said. "I think you'll be pleased with the revenues."

"You report to my steward." Antipas' words slid like ice from his tongue. "Chuza will bring any relevant information to me."

To his satisfaction, Agrippa wilted. "Of course."

Antipas couldn't help grinding the point a little deeper. "Make sure you're thorough in your report, considering your…struggles… with money."

Agrippa stiffened at the barb, but he couldn't deny it. If his sister hadn't wrangled him a position in the city, he'd still be languishing in some out of the way fortress.

Herodias shot Antipas a disapproving frown but then smiled at her brother. "How is your wife?"

Agrippa's expression relaxed. "Cypros has given me another son. I have named him Drusus."

Another baby. That made three. Antipas ran his tongue over his teeth to cover his jealousy.

"A good name," Herodias said, her expression softening. "Your friend would be honored."

Antipas sniffed with dark amusement. Agrippa had depended on his friend Drusus, the emperor's son, to give him a notable position—

perhaps even a crown. But Drusus' untimely death cast those foolish ambitions to the wind. Agrippa had tried to buy his way back into the emperor's inner circle, but the only title he earned was One of the Greatest Debtors in Rome.

"Cypros is nearly recovered," Agrippa said. "I came to invite you to a feast in our son's honor." Agrippa inclined his head to Chuza. "You must come as well."

Chuza's brows rose in surprise. "Me?"

Herodias' smile faltered and Antipas blinked. Why Chuza?

"You are the steward, are you not?" Agrippa said. "A powerful man, as my dear uncle just reminded me." He shot Antipas a cutting smile.

Chuza glanced over, and Antipas begrudgingly nodded.

Chuza inclined his head to Herodias' brother. "I'm happy to attend, my lord."

Agrippa bowed to his sister and finally took his leave. Antipas watched him go through narrowed eyes. Agrippa had never paid Chuza any heed before. What was he up to?

On the day of Agrippa's feast, Chuza dressed with care. Something was going on, and he needed to find out what. He and Agrippa were nodding acquaintances only, despite their months together in Rome. So why had Agrippa invited him?

Chuza stepped through the palace gate and watched Antipas' largest carriage roll up. He sighed at the needless pride.

Antipas strode to the gate with Herodias on his arm.

"Ah, Chuza. I'm glad we caught you," Antipas said. "You must ride with us."

Herodias' smile stiffened, but she said nothing as Antipas handed her into the carriage. Antipas stepped in next, the cart jostling as he found his place. Chuza climbed in after them, wishing he had lingered a few more minutes in his room.

The carriage jerked forward.

"I foresee a pleasant evening," Herodias said, a little too brightly. "My brother Herod is bringing Mariamne and their son, Aristobulus."

"How nice," Antipas said while checking his fingernails.

Chuza gazed over the city as he arranged the family tree in his mind. The number of men named Herod exceeded practicality.

They drove up to an expansive villa, two stories tall with a plain facade facing the street.

Chuza knocked on the door, and a servant swung it wide to admit them into a portico with doors leading in three directions. A maid-servant washed their feet and hands before offering them a cup of wine.

The maid led them toward the sound of pleasant voices and into a courtyard, golden in the afternoon sun. Two small children played with a ball. The boy, about four years old, rolled it toward his younger sister. She shrieked with delight, picked it up, and pelted her brother with more enthusiasm than aim. Their nurse hovered nearby, her braided hair frizzy, and the smear of someone's meal on her simple tunic.

Agrippa's youngest child was sound asleep in his mother's arms. Cypros reclined on a couch, her delicate face pale beneath her freckles. Mariamne hovered over her shoulder, cooing. Herodias hurried to join the women, making all the appropriately eager noises. Cypros smiled serenely and tipped the infant so Herodias could get a better look.

Antipas strode over to the men. Chuza followed, though he wouldn't have minded a look at the child. The bundle in Cypros' arms seemed impossibly small.

"Antipas!" Agrippa's brother Herod lifted his cup in welcome. "It's been months."

"How have you fared?" Antipas asked.

Herod gestured to his son. "We purchased some property. It was in poor condition, but we will turn it into a vineyard."

"You have a sharp mind for business," Antipas said. He lifted his cup to his lips, but instead of taking a sip, he muttered, "Not everyone in your family is so fortunate."

Herod glanced at his brother, and Chuza smothered a sigh at this needless antagonism.

Agrippa glared at Antipas. "I heard you've made a large order of armor. Expecting trouble?"

Antipas sneered. "I wouldn't expect you to understand, but it is better to prepare for war than pray for peace."

"The emperor knows you're amassing weapons and armor?"

"The numbers are so negligible there's no need to trouble him."

"What do you think, Chuza?" Agrippa turned suddenly to face him.

Chuza stiffened. He had his concerns, but Agrippa couldn't seriously expect him to contradict his master in public. He tossed about in his head for a polite response, but he was saved from answering as a servant approached.

"The meal is ready, my lord."

Agrippa stepped away from Antipas and smiled at his guests. "Let's move to the triclinium."

Herodias and Mariamne joined their husbands.

"I'll just be a moment," Cypros said.

The others strode into the house, but Chuza lingered in the courtyard with the hope the conversation topic would move on before he went inside.

Cypros smiled as he approached.

"You are well, my lady?" Chuza asked.

"Very well." She shifted so he could see a little pink face crowned with black hair.

Chuza tucked the blanket gently under the baby's tiny chin. "What a handsome boy." He was surprised by the surge of emotion that filled his throat.

"Would you like to hold him?" Cypros asked.

Chuza stiffened. "I don't know how."

"Nonsense. Sit beside me."

Chuza obeyed, and she passed the swaddled bundle into his arms. The child hardly weighed more than a scroll.

"He's so small," Chuza said, awed. The baby wiggled and yawned, revealing a pink tongue tinged with milk. He glanced at her. "My wife Joanna is pregnant."

Cypros smiled. "How wonderful! When is the baby due?"

"In only a few months." Chuza hesitated. "I am excited—and afraid."

"That's only natural. Birth is dangerous." A deepness shone behind her eyes, a hint at the travails she had endured. "A child changes his parent forever. You will be something more. A father."

"I have an adopted daughter already," Chuza said. "But she was nearly grown when I met her. I didn't have to worry about dropping her."

Cypros chuckled. "You seem like a natural to me."

The baby let out a sudden cry, and Chuza looked at Cypros in alarm.

"He's only hungry," she said.

Chuza handed the baby over, and as Cypros loosened her robe, he averted his gaze.

The ball rolled into his path, and the little girl raced to catch it. She froze, staring up into his face. He picked it up and held it out. She hesitated before grabbing it, clutching it to her chest as she ran back to her brother.

"Three children," Chuza said. "You and Agrippa have been blessed."

"If only Agrippa was content with children."

"What do you mean?" Despite his crippling debts, Agrippa was settled and safe, with a good wife and three children. What more did he need?

Cypros bit her lip. "You'd know better than most." She looked down at her son, and her voice was tight. "Agrippa's position, this house… it is all thanks to Antipas, and he could snatch everything back. You can guess how that makes Agrippa feel."

Antipas had made no secret of his disdain for his wife's brother.

Cypros turned her honey-brown eyes to his. "Even if we live in luxury for the rest of our lives, it will not stop my husband from feeling inadequate. And Antipas is always ready to kick Agrippa in the teeth about money."

Chuza studied his cuticles. "Yes, I've seen that."

"Would you..." She hesitated, her eyes searching his. "Would you speak to Antipas on my husband's behalf? I am afraid of what will happen if they continue to quarrel."

"I'll try." Though he had no idea what he would say.

Cypros' expression eased. "Thank you. I've been afraid of where we'd live if anything—"

"Nothing will happen. This family has weathered its share of quarrels." Chuza stood with a confident nod. "And I know Antipas likes and respects you."

"Perhaps you're right. But I appreciate you talking to him all the same."

He bowed to her and strode into the house, wondering what he could say that would help.

As he entered the triclinium, Agrippa rose. "Chuza, there you are." Chuza blinked in surprise as Agrippa took the cup from his hand and refilled it himself. "I am glad you could join us tonight."

Antipas' suspicious gaze followed Chuza as he sat on a couch. Chuza sighed. If Agrippa wanted his help to manage Antipas, he was going about it the wrong way. At least Cypros had been discreet.

Chuza took a deep drink of his wine. He had done his best to avoid the tempestuous sea of family intrigues, but Agrippa and Cypros seemed determined to pull him in over his head.

# EIGHT

"Taking a little nap?" Leah asked.

Joanna blinked out of her reverie. She was supposed to be washing dishes at the long table in the courtyard. The brisk strokes of Dalia's sweeping mingled with her instructions to Little Mary, who clutched her own small straw broom. Miriam had left to take Samuel to school.

Joanna swiped her cloth around the bowl and passed it to Leah. "Sorry. I guess I'm a little nervous."

Peter had asked her to share her testimony today, and not just among the believers, but in the temple courts. Her hands trembled.

She plunged another dish under the warm water and rubbed it with her cloth. She held the dripping bowl out to Leah.

Leah hesitated before taking it. "Is it safe? Speaking to the people, I mean."

"The disciples have been undisturbed for weeks."

Leah tilted her head. "But would Chuza approve?"

"I'm not sure," Joanna admitted. Chuza had always supported her, even when it meant they had to be apart. But that was in the Galilean

59

hills and rural villages. This was Jerusalem—the heart of the priestly class.

Leah smirked. "That's why you don't want to delay, isn't it? Because he'll be back soon and you're worried he'll stop you."

Joanna shot Leah a glare, though her words rubbed too close to the truth. "Peter asked, and it felt cowardly to refuse."

"To refuse what?" Dalia said.

Joanna winced. She hadn't realized Dalia was close enough to overhear.

"We're going to the temple today," Joanna said. "Peter asked me to share what I experienced during Passover week."

Dalia's forehead creased. "You mean the empty tomb."

Dalia still believed Jesus' followers stole the body and invented the resurrection.

Joanna washed another dish. "My friends Maryam and Mary Magdalene have already spoken to the people. As a fellow eyewitness, Peter wants me to share."

Dalia's gaze flicked to Leah. "But you didn't see… any of this?"

"I saw the crucifixion." Her cheeks pinked. Calvary was no place for a young woman, and she had gone without permission. "But I wasn't at the tomb."

Dalia opened her mouth, but Leah wasn't finished.

"I saw Jesus alive, risen from the dead. He ate a fish I prepared. I watched him ascend to heaven as angels declared he was coming back."

Joanna's pulse fluttered with the memory.

Dalia put a fist on her hip and fixed Joanna with a stern gaze. "You'd let your daughter proclaim that story throughout Jerusalem? Run the risk others would call her insane, or worse, a blasphemer?"

Joanna stiffened as she pictured Leah dragged before the Sanhedrin.

Dalia's voice softened. "If you wouldn't want Leah to do something so risky, why would you do it yourself?"

"Because I feel God calling me to speak."

Dalia stepped closer and spoke softly. "It doesn't need to be you."

Joanna was touched by her sister's concern, but fear wasn't a good enough reason to keep quiet.

She picked up the basin and poured the dirty water into the pots of herbs. The imperfect water was enough to sustain these plants. Perhaps her imperfect testimony would be enough to quench the deep thirst in her people's hearts.

Dalia opened her mouth to continue the argument, but Joanna set down the basin and hugged her sister close. At first Dalia stiffened, but then she softened and returned the embrace. Joanna squeezed her eyes shut. Not so long ago, she feared they'd never be friends again.

Joanna murmured in Dalia's ear. "We'll leave right away if there's any trouble."

"You'd better."

Joanna stepped back and gazed into her sister's eyes. "You could come, you know."

Dalia pressed her lips together, and Joanna was grateful she didn't immediately refuse.

Joanna turned to Leah. "We should go. Fetch your palla."

Leah hurried into the house, and Joanna collected her own palla, winding the long cloth around her torso and creating a hood for her hair. She smoothed a hand down her growing middle and a nudge answered her touch. She didn't share her testimony for herself, but for those she loved. The good news of Jesus' resurrection would change the whole world.

Joanna and Leah walked to the temple and climbed to the second floor of Solomon's Colonnade. A rabbi sat on one of the teacher's seats with disciples at his feet. Joanna and Leah slipped past, Joanna's nervousness increasing.

They paused to watch a man roar a prophecy of doom as spittle collected in the corners of his mouth.

Leah stared in alarm, and Joanna nudged her. "Have you heard about Anna the prophetess?"

Leah pulled her eyes from the ranting man. "Who?"

Joanna tucked Leah's arm under hers, and they kept walking.

"She was widowed young," Joanna said. "But instead of remarrying, she stayed in the temple every day, devoted to prayer. My father heard her speak when she was an old woman. She claimed she saw the Messiah."

Leah's eyes widened. "Had she?"

Joanna liked to think so. "We could ask Jesus' mother."

Leah peered down the long colonnade, where a large group was gathered. "We saw the Messiah too. Sometimes I forget how amazing that is."

Joanna swept her arm toward the temple courts below. "One day, everyone will know the truth. When Jesus returns, no one will be able to deny that he is Lord." Longing thickened her throat. "Until that day comes, we'll share the good news with anyone who will listen."

They reached the disciples. Peter sat in the teacher's seat, and the audience at his feet listened raptly. A large gathering stood nearby, their expressions a mixture of doubt and curiosity. A few men pulled their cloaks high on their heads, as if afraid of being seen.

Joanna's pulse quickened, but the priests hadn't been able to keep Peter and John imprisoned. God was on their side.

Peter noticed Joanna's approach, and he rose to his feet. He extended a hand toward her, and for a moment, her feet were pinned to the ground.

"This is our sister, Joanna," Peter spoke to the crowd. "She ministered to Jesus while we were in Galilee, and she was with Jesus at the cross and his resurrection." He nodded at her and gestured to the teacher's seat.

Joanna stared at the simple, wooden chair. She had always dreamed of being called by God like the prophetesses of old, but this felt unreal. She sat, and her cheeks warmed as she faced a sea of eyes.

Sending a silent plea to God for wisdom, Joanna folded her hands and smiled.

"My friends," she said, "when I came to Jerusalem at Passover, I was afraid for Jesus. As a member of Herod Antipas' court, I knew Antipas longed to see Jesus for himself, to watch him perform a miracle." Joanna continued her story, telling the people how Jesus had been brought before Antipas. "Antipas sent him back to Pilate, who found Jesus innocent." She drew a pained breath. "But the priests accused Jesus of blasphemy, and they insisted he be crucified."

A few listeners shifted at her accusation, and Joanna flinched as she remembered where she was. Fear numbed her tongue. Needing reassurance, she searched the crowd for Peter's face. But instead, she stared straight into her mother's eyes.

# NINE

J oanna stared at her mother and Dalia. Dalia had brought her daughter, and the little girl waved. Joanna forced herself to smile as the weight of this moment pressed on her shoulders. What if she said the wrong thing, and her family never accepted Jesus as their messiah? Seconds slipped by as Joanna's tongue refused to move.

A breath of warm wind blew a strand of hair across her face, and she remembered how the Holy Spirit had come upon her in power.

Finally, the words came.

"Jesus died upon that cross. I watched him take his last breath." Tears burned the back of her eyes as she remembered her horror and disbelief in that moment. "Our brother, Joseph of Arimathea, asked Pilate for the body, and I saw it laid in the tomb."

She shared how they returned after the Sabbath to mourn and anoint Jesus' body, but the stone was rolled away, and the tomb was empty. "Angels told us that Jesus had risen, just as he said he would. They sent us back to the disciples to share the good news."

"Why you?" a man called. He stood on the edge of the small crowd, his arms crossed.

"What do you mean?" she asked.

"Why women?" He thrust out his chin. "Why would an angel appear to you first, and not to his closest followers?" Other men nodded, muttering about the weak testimony of women. Peter stepped forward, but Joanna wanted to answer.

"Because we were there," she said. "We came to honor Jesus, and it seems God wished to honor us in return." Joanna spread her palms, trying to be peaceable. "Who am I to question the way God relayed his good news?"

Peter stood beside Joanna. "When the women brought us this astonishing account, I ran to the tomb to see for myself."

"But I beat him there!" John shouted gleefully, and the crowd laughed.

Joanna rose from the teacher's seat. Leaving Peter to continue the good news, she slipped back into the crowd, trying not to blush as eyes followed her. She had done it. She had shared her eyewitness testimony with boldness. Maryam reached up and squeezed her hand as she passed, and the admiration in Leah's eyes filled Joanna with joy.

Joanna tried to read her mother's face as she joined her on the fringe of the crowd. If she had feared her daughter was flouting tradition before, what must she think now? Dalia's expression was inscrutable. Little Mary lifted her hands to be picked up. Joanna set the girl on her hip, her pulse racing as she turned to face the teacher's seat.

Peter told the rest of the story, how Jesus ascended to God's right hand and promised to return. "If any of you are ready to repent of your sins and accept Jesus as your Lord, come speak to us."

Peter stood, and the curious onlookers dispersed.

Joanna turned to her mother and sister. "I'm glad you came."

Miriam flicked her chin toward Peter. "He was arrested?"

"And John with him, the one who beat him to the tomb." Joanna chuckled, and Dalia smiled.

Miriam was silent for a long moment, studying the tall fisherman. "Do you think your father would have believed?"

Joanna's pulse fluttered. More than anything, she wished her father could have met Jesus. "Do you remember how he would tell us about the prophetess, Anna?"

Dalia's posture softened. "He loved to tell that story. He said it made the Day of the Lord seem near."

"It was near. Well, pretty near, considering." Joanna laughed. She took her mother's hand and gave it a squeeze. She knew, deep in her soul. "Papa would believe."

Miriam's eyes shimmered. "Perhaps you could tell us more."

Joanna was sure her heart would leap from her chest and soar to the heavens. She glanced over and saw the rest of the disciples were preparing to leave.

"Will you come to the disciples' house and meet some of my friends?" Joanna asked.

Miriam glanced nervously at Dalia. "Sure. For a little while."

Leah hurried over, her large hazel eyes flicking between Dalia and Miriam's expressions.

They left the temple complex and headed into the Lower City. Maryam and Naomi walked with them, giving Joanna a chance to introduce her mother to these women who had traveled with Jesus in Galilee.

Miriam took an instant liking to Naomi, and they were talking earnestly as they walked through the courtyard gate. Dalia looked with curiosity at a pair of disciples measuring grain for a line of women.

"None are in want here," Joanna told her sister, pride filling her chest. "We all share what we have."

The disciples gathered in the courtyard for a simple midday meal. Joanna led her mother and sister to a thick mat where they could sit comfortably. Dalia and Miriam glanced around at what was becoming a loud gathering of pleasant chatter and laughter.

Little Mary tumbled into Leah's lap, and looked around herself.

"Is it a feast?" the little girl asked.

"It feels like a feast, doesn't it?" Leah said. "But it's like this every day."

James, the son of Zebedee, blessed the bread. He held up the loaf. "As we share our daily bread, we remember the bread of life."

"The bread of life?" Miriam asked as Naomi passed around a basket of small loaves.

Joanna explained. "On the night before he was killed, Jesus blessed the bread. He told his disciples to eat it in remembrance of him."

Dalia froze. "He knew he was going to die?"

"Yes."

"And he didn't try to escape, to go back to Galilee?"

"No."

"Why?"

Joanna's chest contracted with painful memories. "The forces of evil had gathered against him, but he knew God would help him overcome."

"By raising him from the dead," Miriam said slowly.

Joanna bobbed her head, excited that her mother understood. "Exactly."

Dalia turned her bread over and over. "But why did he have to die? Was that what God wanted?"

Joanna hesitated. "God knew it would happen and he planned for it, even if it wasn't what he wanted." Joanna drew a deep breath. "Even knowing what was coming, Jesus did not hesitate to follow God's plan to turn us back to him. And because Jesus was obedient to the very end, God raised him up to his right hand."

Joanna looked at Leah and saw her hope mirrored in the younger woman's eyes. "Jesus died because sin demanded it. But when evil thought it had won, Jesus burst from the tomb, the firstfruits of the coming kingdom."

Dalia looked at her small daughter. "If what you're saying is true, and the priests and the elders killed a man of God..." She trailed off and looked back at Joanna. "What do we do? What hope is there for our people?"

"There is every hope." Joanna leaned closer. "We must turn to Jesus as our high priest and follow his ways. Through Jesus, we are saved."

Dalia stared into Joanna's eyes, and Joanna saw yearning in the brown depths. Dalia wanted to believe.

"Shalom!" a well-dressed man called as he approached Peter, beaming and nodding.

"I know him," Miriam said. "That's Ananias. He lives just down the street from us. I didn't know he was one of you."

Ananias bowed and set a leather purse in front of Peter. "I have sold a field and brought all the money to you."

The people murmured at his generosity, but Peter held up one hand. Everyone fell silent, and Ananias' smile faltered.

Peter regarded Ananias gravely. "Why has Satan so filled your heart that you would lie about keeping some money for yourself?"

Ananias' face reddened, and his gaze flicked to the purse. He stammered an incoherent reply.

Peter shook his head. "The field and the profits were yours to use however you wished, so why this deception?" Ananias' face grew redder yet. Peter's voice held a weight of sorrow that rippled through the courtyard. "You have not lied to men, but to God."

Time seemed to stretch as Ananias' eyes rolled back in his head. He crumpled to the ground, his arms sprawling. His hand bounced on the ground before growing terribly still.

Women cried out in alarm and men jerked to their feet. Dalia gasped and turned her wide-eyed daughter away from the scene. Maryam's son Joses rushed forward and laid a hand on Ananias' chest.

He stared at Peter. "He's dead."

Stunned silence filled the courtyard and Dalia scrambled up, holding her daughter and tossing her palla to cover Little Mary's face. Dalia stared at Joanna with accusatory eyes. "We have to go. Now."

Joanna's mind spun. Joses swung the cloak from his back and over Ananias' body. As the cloth fluttered into place, Joanna and her family hurried into the street.

Little Mary pushed aside her mother's palla. "What happened, Mama?"

Dalia refused to answer as she walked so quickly Joanna struggled to keep up.

What had just happened? And why did it need to happen now, when Dalia was so close to believing?

Chuza rode through Jerusalem's busy streets, his pulse increasing with anticipation. His two weeks in Tiberias had dragged by, but now he was coming home. Curious eyes watched him pass.

At the palace stables, he slid from the leather saddle and passed Celer's reins to the groom.

"Pleasant journey, my lord?"

Chuza patted Celer's ruddy neck. "Every journey that brings me home is a good one."

The groom grinned, and Chuza swung his bag over his shoulder. He hurried to Alexander's house, straining to keep a respectable pace.

He pulled the door open and stepped inside, calling out a greeting.

Joanna came running from the courtyard and threw herself into his arms. Her belly pressed against him, and the scent of lavender filled his nose. Leaving her side was becoming harder and harder.

He realized she was gripping him too tightly. He set his hands on her upper arms so he could peer into her face, and his stomach plummeted to his feet.

"What's wrong?" he demanded, a dozen terrible scenarios running through his head.

"Everyone is fine," Joanna said, then winced. "Well, not Ananias and Sapphira, but—"

"Who?"

"They live—well, lived—on this street." Her eyes held his. "They're dead."

He blinked in confusion.

She folded her arms against herself. "Peter discerned they were lying to the Holy Spirit and they just... died."

"You mean they—"

"Just dropped to the ground. One second Ananias was giving Peter money from the sale of his land, and the next..." She shook her head, and tears welled in her eyes. "Dalia and my mother had just come to the temple and heard me share my testimony, and—"

"Share your what?" he interrupted, louder than he intended.

She waved away his concern. "Dalia was starting to believe, but now they fear the apostles. So does most of Jerusalem." Her brow furrowed. "Alexander is upset that Dalia and Little Mary were there at all... Oh, it's such a mess, Chuza." Her shoulders sagged.

What was happening among the believers that men and women could just drop dead? Chuza gripped his wife's hand as guilt twined a cord around his chest. While he had been overseeing budgets, answering correspondence, and arranging meetings, Joanna and Leah were left to grapple with this situation alone.

"I should have been here," he said.

Joanna cupped his face and peered into his eyes. "You have a duty to Antipas. We all know that." Her fingertip brushed against his earring.

He caught her hand and held it in both of his. "We'll talk more about your public speeches later. Is Leah alright?"

"She's full of questions," Joanna said. "We all are. I mean, nothing like this happened when Jesus was here." Pained frustration filled her face and echoed in his chest.

"Have you talked to the other disciples?"

"Not yet. My mother insisted I stay away from them, and I thought it best to comply. But if you say it's alright..."

"We'll talk with them tomorrow," Chuza said. "I'm sure we can figure this out together." He smiled to cover his anxiety. Surely nothing bad could happen to Joanna among the disciples. She was one of them.

Joanna went into his arms again. "I'm so glad you're here."

"Me too." He held her closer. Something nudged his stomach, and he pulled back.

"You felt that?" she asked, her eyes wide.

"Was that…?"

"Our baby."

He set his palm on her belly and stared at her middle, waiting. Another kick hit his hand, and suddenly Joanna's pregnancy became startlingly real. Joanna was carrying his son or daughter. His chest glowed with joy, but it was chased by the chill of anxiety.

Joanna led him into the courtyard, but even as he greeted the others, his mind roved through the future. Spending a few weeks apart four times a year had seemed like an ideal compromise. But how could he leave his little family when strange events were happening among the disciples?

If only he was a free man, then he— Chuza cut that thought off. It would only lead to discontent. He had to trust that God would watch over them. If his worries interfered with his duties, Antipas would never let this arrangement continue. And this back and forth to Jerusalem was the best Chuza could hope for.

# TEN

"Ready to go?" Manaen called.

Leah glanced up. "Almost."

She poured the last cupful of flour into a sack and bound it closed. It had been a quiet morning at the palace mill as she listened to the rhythm of Balaam's hooves, the creak of the harness, and the massive mill-stone crushing the grain. Work that should have taken days to complete was finished in hours.

Grunting, she hefted the bag with the others on Balaam's back. The donkey's ears flicked in annoyance, but Leah patted his shoulder. "No fussing now. You should be happy we have a good use for you." Chuza was too practical to keep an animal as a pet.

Leah looked up at Manaen, who watched her with a kind smile. These days he treated her more like a young woman than a child, but part of her missed how he used to muss her hair. Leah gripped Balaam's lead. "We're ready."

They made their way from the kitchen area into the lush central courtyard. Chuza had walked Leah up to the palace this morning, but Manaen offered to escort her—and the flour— back to the disciples' house. His familiar presence was soothing. So much had changed in the past few years, but Manaen remained the same.

Manaen peered around the massive courtyard. It was quieter than Leah was used to. "Do you miss living in the palaces?" he asked.

Leah firmly shook her head. "No, not at all. But I miss cooking with Michael." She missed the cheerful banter among the staff, the rich fragrance of spices the disciples could not afford, and creating dishes fit to serve a king. Preparing simple bread and lentil stew was worthy work, but it didn't stretch her abilities.

She glanced at Manaen. "Do you think everyone will go back?" He looked at her in question, and she added, "To work, I mean."

"Would you like to?"

Guilt twinged in Leah's chest. Was it wrong that she did?

"I'm happy to cook for the disciples." It didn't sound as convincing as she intended, and her neck heated as Manaen studied her profile.

Leah stroked Balaam's neck to hide her emotions. Joanna wanted to spend every day with the disciples. Leah loved the close-knit community, and she wanted to help the poor, but ever since her first day in Michael's kitchen, she had dreamed of becoming a master cook with apprentices, a well-stocked kitchen, and the budget to plan menus fit for royalty.

They approached the servant's gate and a familiar guardsman nodded at her. Leah ducked her head.

"What?" Manaen noticed her expression and eyed the guard.

Her cheeks warmed. "Nothing." She picked up her pace.

The guard had done nothing wrong. He only reminded her of someone else.

Chuza spoke about Jovian Titus all the time, worrying about him and wondering where he had gone. He didn't know why Jovian left, but she did.

It was her fault. She had convinced Jovian to go with her to the crucifixion, sure that Jesus would miraculously escape. Instead, she forced Jovian to witness a brutal, torturous death.

"Slow down, Leah. Are you alright?"

She lifted her face and was surprised to feel a tear slipping down her cheek. Her face flamed as she swiped it away. Manaen's concern only made her feel worse. He reached for Balaam's lead, and she reluctantly handed it over.

"The palace is full of memories," she said vaguely.

"And not all of them are good ones."

It wasn't a question, but she nodded.

"I feel the same way about Jerusalem. I've been coming here since I was a boy, but now..." Manaen sighed. "Jesus suffered here. I find myself searching the cobblestones for dried drops of blood."

Leah shuddered. "I expected him to live," she admitted. She turned her face away, her voice barely above a whisper. "If I had known, I never would have taken him there." Somehow, she needed to undo the damage she caused.

"It's too bad Titus left before he heard the good news."

She jerked to look at him. Did everyone know she had feelings for the Gentile soldier?

Her hands clenched as she remembered how she had turned to Jovian for comfort and exposed her feelings for him. She hadn't cared that he was Greek, not when he shared her faith. Her immaturity was humiliating to recall.

Manaen spoke kindly. "Perhaps he will hear about Jesus' resurrection and return."

"I hope he hears soon," Leah said. "I couldn't imagine believing that was how it all ended."

Manaen reached over to tussle her hair. She glared at him, but her heart sang.

"The truth of the resurrection still overwhelms me sometimes," Manaen said. "We can't keep this good news to ourselves. We need to tell the world."

"The way Joanna talks, I think she's ready to stand on the temple steps like a prophetess."

"What about you?"

Leah's knees wobbled. "I could never."

"You don't know what you can accomplish with the Spirit's help." His eyes grew bright. "We stand where heaven and earth meet, as a priest does, and intervene for the nations."

She raised her eyebrows doubtfully. "We're like priests?" Manaen often said things beyond her understanding, but this was bizarre, even for him.

"Yes, including you."

Leah barked a laugh. Perhaps bold women like Joanna or Maryam could be priests, but not her.

"I think that is why Ananias and Sapphira died," Manaen said. Leah's eyes snapped to his. "Although they were called to be priests, they were more concerned about gaining for themselves than caring for the people. They were like the sons of Aaron, who brought unholy fire into the temple and were burned up."

Ananias' death still haunted her thoughts. Flustered, her voice came out more sarcastic than she intended. "So we'll push Caiaphas out of the way and take over the temple?"

"No, Leah." Manaen gripped her shoulder. "We *are* the temple."

Now he had really lost his mind.

Manaen chuckled at her expression. "Jesus said a day is coming when we will not worship in Jerusalem, or on a mountain like the Samaritans, but in spirit and truth. On the day Jesus died, the veil to the Holy of Holies was torn. God's presence is not contained in a single room, but it is within us. Just like the Spirit descended on the Tabernacle in the days of old, it descended on us back on Pentecost. Don't you see? We are the temple and the priesthood."

Leah's pulse jumped. He might be right about everything else, but she couldn't be a priest. "I'm just a cook, nothing more."

Manaen tipped his head. "You know, there are priests who bake bread for the temple."

He really wasn't going to let this go. She drew a breath to retort, but they had reached their destination.

They led Balaam into the courtyard of the disciple's house, and Manaen helped her unload the flour near the kitchen.

"I'll water Balaam and tie him up for you," Manaen said. He leaned toward her. "You can begin your priestly baking."

Leah pressed her lips together. Manaen meant well, but his attempts to give her confidence made her feel inadequate instead.

Pushing Manaen's strange words out of her mind, Leah turned to what she knew. She measured out the flour, oil, salt, and water, and stirred in the leaven until she formed a sticky dough. She turned it onto her kneading board, sprinkled the dough with flour, and worked it with her hands. In Michael's kitchen, the lowest maids made the bread. It was repetitive, uninspiring work, but bread was essential for every meal.

Some of the other women joined her, kneeling at their own kneading boards. Leah let them talk around her as she set her dough on a shelf to rise until tomorrow.

She fetched a batch of yesterday's dough. Instead of simple round loaves, she twisted the dough into braids, taking pleasure in creating beauty. Leaving the dough to rest, she built a fire in the clay oven.

Everyone knew she loved to cook, but no one knew how high her aspirations flew. And now, with the kingdom coming, it felt selfish to let her dreams soar. Did Jesus even need cooks in the coming kingdom? He could multiply bread to feed thousands.

She banked the coals and slid the loaves into the hot oven. Joanna's voice caught her attention, and Leah watched her discuss important matters with the twelve. Joanna might be like a priest, but Leah was just… Leah.

# ELEVEN

Leah walked close behind Maryam, Naomi, and Joanna as the women wound their way through narrower and narrower streets. The sky was only a thin strip of blue between rooftops. She clenched her jaw and hitched the heavy basket of food on her arm.

They arrived at a large, ramshackle house divided into small apartments. The disciples had heard about a poor widow who needed help.

Maryam stopped at a door with peeling green paint and leaned her ear toward it, her brow furrowed in confusion. Something was causing a steady banging.

Maryam knocked, and the noise stopped. A little boy, three or four years old, opened the door. He held a broken copper pot in one hand, and a stick in the other. Leah chuckled. So this was the source of the noise.

Maryam smiled at him. "Is your mother nearby?"

"She's with baby," the boy said, turning to point. His neck was dirty, and his patched tunic bore the evidence of his last meal. He ran into the house, leaving the door open. Maryam glanced back at the others, then followed him into the dim room.

Leah's nose scrunched as she entered. The stench of an overflowing chamber pot and sour laundry saturated the air.

A young woman sat on a rumpled bed, a tiny baby in her arms. She stared at them in alarm. "What do you want?"

"We came to help you," Maryam said cheerfully.

"Oh," the woman said, and exhaustion crept into her voice. "I'm sorry I can't rise to greet you. I'm trying to feed the baby, but he just won't settle." To punctuate her words, the baby let out a pitiful wail.

Leah flinched and glanced at Joanna. Where was this woman's family, or her husband's family to care for her?

Naomi crouched. "May I see your baby?"

The woman hesitated, but she let Naomi take the infant.

The little boy banged his pot and marched around the room.

His mother pressed both palms to her forehead. "Jed, please!"

The boy thrust out his lower lip, but a stern glance from Naomi was enough to make him obey.

As Naomi rocked the baby, the woman's weak hand fluttered over her lank hair in embarrassment. "I'm sorry I have no food to offer you." Leah detected tears in her voice.

"Don't worry," Leah said. "We brought lots."

Joanna stepped to the window and threw open the shutters. The fresh air was welcome, but it was going to take more than that to clear the stench.

Leah set her heavy basket on the table. Holding her breath, she took the chamber pot outside, cringing as she dumped it into the sewage pipe that wound its way down the hill and outside the city walls.

When she came back inside, the room was already smelling better. Naomi sat beside the woman, asking her questions. Leah checked the small oven. There was plenty of fuel, but it was stone cold. She began kindling a fire.

Naomi came over, her face serious. "They're both feverish and very weak. There's an infection in the baby's mouth, and Keturah's breasts are inflamed. I know a poultice that will help, but I must purchase ingredients."

"I'll go with you," Maryam said.

As soon as the older women left, Jed started banging on his pot again.

"Jedediah!" his mother scolded.

Leah recognized a child who needed a distraction. "Jed, can you help me?" she asked. "We can sweep the house for your mama."

Jed brightened as she handed him the broom. It was too large for his small hands, but he set to work. As he swept, Leah worked around the room, setting things right by straightening floor mats and cushions and stacking dirty dishes on the table. She felt Keturah's eyes on her and hoped the poor widow was more grateful than embarrassed.

Joanna warmed the stew by the fire and dished up two portions. She called Jed over to eat. He ran to the table, dropping to his knees and stuffing his cheeks full.

Keturah watched her hungry son wolfing down the food and burst into tears. "I'm a terrible mother."

Leah glanced at Joanna in alarm. What was she supposed to do?

"Go offer to hold the baby while she eats," Joanna whispered.

It took everything in Leah to cross the room.

"You don't need to feel ashamed." Leah twisted her fingers in the opposite hand. "You're sick."

Keturah shook her head, releasing another volley of tears. "I've been telling myself that if I just get some sleep, I'll be able to take care of my boys again. But I'm too achy to rest, and the baby won't settle."

"I'll hold him for you," Leah said. "And then you can eat with Jed."

Keturah looked wistfully at her son. "He was my baby until this one came along." Her eyes flew to Leah's, full of guilt. "Not that I don't love my baby, it's just that I miss the snuggles with Jed."

Leah held out her arms, and Keturah relinquished the child, biting her lower lip. Leah began to rock back and forth, cradling the infant. He couldn't be more than two or three months old.

Leah flicked her chin toward Jed. "Go ahead."

With a pained groan, Keturah rose and padded across the room, straightening her tunic. She knelt beside Jed and pulled him into her lap. Joanna pushed the bowl of stew closer.

"I'm not hungry," Keturah said.

"Try to eat anyway," Joanna said. "It'll help with your milk."

Keturah took a mouthful of stew and dabbed her lips with the back of her hand. "It's good," she admitted, and Leah smiled.

The baby started to cry again. Leah paced the floor, trying to settle him. She ran a hand over his downy head and swallowed hard. The soft spot was sunken. He was dehydrated, and if he didn't eat soon, he would die.

He opened his mouth wide, letting out a mewling cry. Leah flinched. His tongue was coated in white, and the same sores covered the inside of his cheeks and lips. Swallowing hard, Leah turned the baby and laid him on her shoulder. She rubbed his back until he quieted.

Keturah pressed her lips together. "Why are you here? My neighbors ignore us, except to holler at Jed to be quiet. You don't know me at all."

Joanna knelt at the table with Keturah. "Where is your family?"

Keturah kissed the top of Jed's head. "Jarada. It's in Syria." Emotion colored her voice. "I never thought I'd live in the Holy City."

Joanna leaned her elbows on the table. "What brought you here?"

Keturah fiddled with her bowl. "A rabbi told my husband that if we wanted the messiah to come, God's people needed to return to Israel. My husband believed him, though our families thought he was crazy. The two of us moved to Jerusalem, and my husband found work as a carpenter. We had Jedediah. And then, when I was pregnant the second time, my husband—" Tears sprang to her eyes, and she held Jed closer. "Now I am trapped here in Jerusalem, far from my family, and my husband never found his messiah."

Keturah's pain stirred up Leah's dormant grief, like a pool of tears waiting to overflow.

Leah blinked rapidly. "I think I'll get some water. We can tackle that laundry." She passed the baby to Joanna, who looked at her with concern.

Jed wriggled out of his mama's lap. "Me come too!" Leah glanced at Keturah, who nodded.

Leah gathered up the tall water jug and stepped outside. She had to hurry to keep up with Jed, who had spotted a cat trotting down the dirty street. The boy seemed carefree, but without a man to shelter them, Keturah and her children were at the mercy of strangers. Jed's entire future had darkened with the loss of his father. He just didn't know it yet.

A tear dripped off Leah's nose, and she twisted her neck to wipe her face on her sleeve. If Joanna and Chuza hadn't welcomed her into their lives, her future would have been just as bleak.

She blinked, and her mind filled with the memory she tried so hard to forget—She stood in a threadbare tunic, her shaved head stinging with cuts and itchy from lice bites, and peered into the leering faces of men waiting to buy a skinny eleven-year-old girl. She'd be a house slave if she was lucky, working from sunrise to sunset. If she was unlucky—a shiver ran down her spine at the terrifying alternative.

She reined in her emotions. One woman's pity had saved her, and that same woman's love had changed her whole life.

They arrived at the busy pool of Siloam, and Jed enthusiastically helped her fill the jar with water.

Could she, in some small way, help Keturah like Joanna had helped her? Leah had no money, but she could advocate for the widow, and make sure she and her children were safe, fed, and warm. Keturah needed to know there was at least one person in Jerusalem who cared about her.

Determination settled in her core, and she turned to Jed. "How about a wash, little man?"

Half an hour later, Leah returned with a full water jar and a happy little boy with pink cheeks and freshly washed hair.

She poured the water into a large pot to warm by the fire.

"We're back," Naomi called. She stepped into the house with Maryam. "And we brought someone with us."

Stephen ducked under the door frame, and Leah blinked at him in surprise.

Keturah eyed the man in confusion. "Are you a physician?"

"No," Stephen said, smiling. "The Spirit sent me."

Keturah's gaze flitted around the room in confusion and landed on Leah. "The Spirit?"

Leah stepped closer. "Jesus left the Holy Spirit to be our helper until his return."

"Jesus," Keturah said flatly. "You don't mean that pretender?" Her eyes grew round and she shrunk on the bed. "I'm sorry. I don't mean to insult you." She blinked back tears and looked at Leah with panic, as if afraid they would all storm from the room.

Leah's heart turned over, and she sat beside Keturah. "Your husband was right. By bringing you to Jerusalem, you were here when the Messiah came."

Keturah's brow furrowed. "But Jesus is dead. What good is a dead messiah?"

"No," Leah said. "He's alive. God raised him from the dead. I saw him."

Keturah stared at her. "You did?" She held her baby closer. "My husband was right? The messiah did come?"

The women all nodded, and Stephen smiled.

Keturah's shoulders sagged. "I don't understand."

"We will explain everything," Stephen said, "but first you need help. Do you believe God can heal you and your baby?"

Keturah picked at a frayed thread in her robe. "Well, if he wanted to. But God doesn't work like that."

"I believe he wants to help you," Stephen said. "And his son, Jesus

Christ, has a special love for those who are suffering. If you believe, he will heal you."

Keturah's eyes widened with desperation. "What if I don't believe enough?"

"All it takes is a mustard seed of faith," Stephen said. "Will you pray with me?"

Keturah nodded. Stephen began the Shema, and after a moment, she joined him. Leah added her voice, and as they worked down the familiar lines, peace stole over Keturah's features.

Keturah wiped her damp cheek. "It's been so long since I prayed with others."

Stephen set his hand on her shoulder and lifted the other one to heaven. "Jesus, Lord of lords, we ask that you heal this woman and her child."

Keturah trembled as if a shiver ran down her spine. Leah watched in amazement as the shadows lifted from beneath her eyes. Her skin returned to a normal color. Keturah raised a hand and rubbed her chest. With a trembling finger, she tipped her baby's mouth open. Leah leaned closer. A pink tongue and cheeks.

Keturah stared into Leah's eyes. "Thank you," she whispered. She looked at Stephen, and tears flowed down her cheeks. "Thank you."

Stephen's smile was warm. "Don't thank me. Thank God."

Leah wrapped her arm around Keturah's shoulder as Stephen slipped from the house. Keturah loosened the neck of her tunic and brought the child to her breast. The baby nuzzled and began nursing, his little hand fluttering over her smooth skin.

"It doesn't hurt." Keturah looked at Leah with wide eyes. "I've never seen him eat like this."

"Once his tummy is full, he should sleep deeper," Naomi said with confidence. "And you'll be able to sleep as well."

Maryam beckoned Jed over and began combing his hair, keeping him still by telling him stories. Keturah hummed to herself as she fed her baby.

Leah stood and gathered up the laundry to scrub it outside. Joanna carried the hot water, and they found a laundry tub beside the house.

"She's healed," Leah murmured to Joanna. "But she is still alone."

Joanna poured the water into the tub as Leah hitched up her robe and stepped in, agitating the laundry with her feet.

Joanna said, "You two must be close in age. I'm sure she'd appreciate your friendship."

Leah hoped so, and not just for Keturah's sake. Visiting her cousins in Alexandria had reminded Leah what it was like to have a friend her own age.

Once the laundry was washed and hung to dry, the women gathered their things to go.

Leah was the last to leave, and she paused at the doorway. "If it's alright with you, I'll come back tomorrow."

Keturah's jaw dropped in surprise. "Really?"

Leah grinned and raised an eyebrow at Jed. "Just no more drumming, alright?"

Jed giggled.

The sky was dusky by the time the women entered the courtyard of the disciples' house. Leah was more than ready to fill her belly and rest. Manaen was talking with the other men, but he strode over with a smile.

"I hear you've been about your priestly duties," he said with a twinkle in his eye.

Leah twisted her brows. "Stephen healed them, not me." It felt foolish to even contemplate having such a gift.

He set a hand on her shoulder. "Jesus' love for others had as much of an impact on their lives as his healing touch."

Leah tried to brush off his words, but they wrapped around her like a warm blanket. Maybe she couldn't teach or heal like Jesus, but she could love like him.

# TWELVE

Jovian heaved up the last sack of grain. Husks poked through the rough cloth, scratching his bare shoulder and clinging to his sweat. Striding over to the waiting wagon, he hoisted the sack in the back and gave it a slap for good measure. He lifted his tunic at the shoulders in a futile attempt to shake the chaff free.

His father's hired man had sprained his ankle, but Jovian was more than willing to haul cargo if it gave him a reprieve from calculating losses and profits. His older brother Sergio could tally in his head, but when Jovian tried, the figures and rows became a jumble. His father insisted he just needed more practice, but Jovian knew better.

But no matter how Belen felt about Jovian slinging sacks like a dockworker, someone needed to haul this grain into the city. If they didn't fulfill their orders, another merchant would be more than happy to steal their customers.

Belen strode out of the warehouse, holding a ledger close to his chest. "You're sure you can handle the deliveries?"

"Of course." Jovian pushed down his annoyance. He knew the city better than most.

His father looked doubtful. "Bato will drive the cart. He can rest his ankle and help you with directions."

Bato limped out of the warehouse, leaning on a crutch. His foot was tightly bound. Jovian helped the servant climb atop the wagon and turned to his father.

"I can do this."

His father still looked uncertain. "I can send your brother with you, just to make sure."

"I've got it." Jovian held out his hand.

His father hesitated before setting the ledger in Jovian's calloused palm.

Jovian smiled ruefully. "You sure know how to boost a man's confidence."

Belen grimaced. He turned to go, but then paused. "Please invite Flavius Horace and his family to dine with us tomorrow."

The name tickled the edge of Jovian's memory. "Is that the family with all the daughters?"

His father looked pleased. "You remember them. Horace has four daughters, and the older two have grown into beauties."

Jovian raised his brows and tucked the ledger into the cart. "Have they now? I remember them as squalling, skinny little girls."

"A lot can change in five years."

Jovian ignored the intended barb and climbed aboard the cart with Bato, setting the ledger in his lap and bracing himself with his feet. "I'll pass along the message."

With a flick of the reins, Bato drove the oxen forward, and Jovian gripped the side of his hard, wooden seat.

"Your father is happy you're home," Bato said, and Jovian looked at him in surprise. "He was worried about leaving your brother to handle the business alone."

Jovian scoffed. Sergio could take inventory while riding a horse bareback and backward. "My father told you this?"

"No." Bato lifted his chin. "But I have eyes, don't I?"

Jovian shook his head and consulted the wax tablet. Five different stops. Three bakeries, a brewery, and then Horace's shop. Again Jovian tried to recall Horace's gaggle of daughters, but all he remembered was a pack of noisy girls arguing over who took the last sweetbread. Jovian chuckled to himself.

They rumbled up to their first stop, and Jovian stepped down from the cart. The proprietor came out of his shop and handed over his payment.

Jovian double-checked the coins. The baker crossed his arms, his fingers tapping on his opposite bicep.

"Looks good," Jovian said, and the baker grunted.

Jovian lugged the wheat and barley sacks to the baker's storeroom. A cool wind blew over him as he stepped back outside, and he tossed his cloak over his sweaty frame.

The deliveries went smoothly until only Horace's remained. His shop encompassed the lower level of a two story home in a pleasant neighborhood.

Eager to be done, Jovian leaped out of the cart.

"Careful," Bato said. "That's how I twisted my ankle."

"Ah, but you had farther to fall." Jovian winked at the shorter man.

Bato rolled his eyes good-naturedly.

Jovian took his ledger and money bag and hurried into Horace's shop.

The mingled fragrance of cloves and cardamom filled his nose. Jars of oil, bundles of dried herbs, and vats of pickled olives filled the shelves like a treasure trove. Massive ceramic jars lined one wall, carefully labeled, and a polished set of scales and weights sat on the counter.

Horace emerged from a back door. He was round in the middle, with long sideburns that added distinction to his soft cheeks.

"Jovian Titus!" Horace clasped Jovian's wrist. "It's been years since I saw you."

"I'm glad to be back." The polite half-truth slid easily off Jovian's tongue after weeks of practice. "I have your delivery here."

Horace rubbed his palms together. "Let's see the quality, shall we?"

Jovian brought in a sack.

Horace slit open the top and scooped a handful of wheat kernels. He weighed and sniffed them, and then popped a few in his mouth. After chewing, Horace nodded. "Excellent."

He fetched the payment. Jovian marked the ledger and added the coins to his purse before bringing in the rest of the grain.

Jovian set the last sack in the storeroom and straightened, brushing off his palms. "My father asked me to invite your family to dine with us tomorrow."

Horace accepted with pleasure.

Half an hour later, Jovian and Bato rumbled back up to the warehouse. Jovian reached for the purse and ledger under his seat.

They were not there.

Jovian forced himself to speak calmly. "Bato, did you grab the tablet and purse?"

Bato stretched out his hands. "You had them last."

"Yes, I did." Jovian dragged a hand through his hair, picturing his father's face. He checked the cart again, but it was definitely empty. Sighing with frustration, he thought back. He had filled out the ledger at Horace's. The coins and ledger had to be there.

Jovian unhitched the oxen and hurried them to their stalls, tossing them hay and sloshing water into their trough. He retraced his steps into the city, jogging as he wove through the busy road. What if the purse had bounced out of the wagon? It would be a hefty prize for whoever picked it up, but it would cost Jovian his father's respect.

Anxiety climbed up his throat, and he broke into a run.

Finally, he charged through Horace's door. He drew up short. The smell was right, and the room was right, but this was definitely not Horace. A young woman with reddish-brown hair was rearranging jars. She turned, revealing an oval face and brown eyes. Her left eyebrow was split by a small, white scar.

She folded her hands and smiled. "How can I help you?"

Jovian blinked at her, overcome by his confusion.

She tried again. "My father stepped upstairs for a moment. Do you need something for your wife or—"

"Uh, no," Jovian stammered. "I forgot something here. Something … important."

"You must be Jovian Titus," she said knowingly. "I almost didn't recognize you. My father said you'd be back."

"So they're here? My purse and ledger?"

"You left them on the counter. By the time my father noticed, you were long gone. I'll call him now, shall I?"

"Yes, please," Jovian said.

She slipped through the back door, and Jovian waited. It felt strange to be recognized when, in his memory, her face was little more than a blur. But she had been a child then, perhaps twelve years old, and he had been more than twenty.

The young woman returned. "My father's coming." She stepped behind the counter but leaned toward him.

"Do you remember me?" she asked.

Jovian was caught off guard. He wracked his brain. "Julia?"

She shook her head, her expression falling. "That's my younger sister. I am the eldest, Persephone."

"Ah."

He wandered toward a display of dried herbs, but her brown eyes followed him. He was suddenly very aware of the dust and sweat that coated his face and arms.

He cleared his throat. "Do you often help in the shop?"

Persephone smiled. "When I can."

Silence filled the room as his heart pounded. He hadn't spoken with a young woman since Leah.

He glanced around the room, searching for something to say. "Do you like the work?"

"I do."

"Well, you're luckier than most," he muttered, and then wished he could take the words back.

"You don't enjoy working for your father?"

He swung his arms back and forth awkwardly. "It's not... what I envisioned for my life."

To his relief, her warm eyes held no judgment.

She drummed her fingers on the counter rhythmically. "Resolving to like something is always the first step to actually enjoying it. Our circumstances are what we make of them."

"A pleasant way of looking at life."

"It is the way of women. But I will let you borrow a little of our philosophy." Her eyes twinkled.

"How generous," he said dryly, and she laughed.

Horace stepped into the room. He glanced between his daughter and Jovian, and a pleased smile teased the corner of his mouth. It made Jovian pause. He hoped Persephone didn't think he was flirting.

Horace held out the ledger and purse. He winked. "I think we can keep this little mishap from your father, hmm?"

"Thank you," Jovian said sincerely, and tucked both items securely under his arm. He nodded at Horace, and then at Persephone. "I'll see you tomorrow."

Persephone's cheeks turned pink.

"We look forward to it," Horace said.

The warmth in his tone was disconcerting, but Jovian bowed his head and hurried out the door.

As Jovian rounded the street corner, he opened the purse to count the coins. Even wealthy men couldn't resist the allure of easy money, and Jovian had made it far too easy.

An hour later, Jovian whistled to himself as he entered his family villa, his steps light. He strode to his father's tablinum. Belen was at his desk.

Jovian set the ledger and purse down with a flourish. "All finished."

"Very good," Belen said, but his fingers twitched toward the purse. The light feeling in Jovian's chest dissipated.

"I'll be at the baths," he muttered. He stepped toward the door but then glanced back. "I invited Horace, as you asked. He's pleased to attend."

"Excellent. I hope you will be attentive to his eldest daughter... what was her name?"

"Persephone," Jovian blurted.

"Ah, yes, that's right." Belen spun his pen and grinned.

Jovian hastened away from his father's knowing glance. He grabbed a fresh robe and a coin before heading for the nearest bathhouse.

He might be useless at figures, but he was no fool. It was clear his father was interested in securing a second marriage for the Titus family. Belen and Horace were connected by both business and friendship, so he could see why his father would choose one of Horace's daughters for his son.

Persephone seemed pleasant, but Jovian wasn't ready to fall in love. Though he was finding a new routine, painful memories wedged themselves between his ribs at the most inconvenient times. He had left Israel, but Israel had not left him.

He gripped his coin until the metal edge dug painfully into his palm. He hoped Leah knew he hadn't left because of her. She wasn't to blame for the false facade of the priests, their outward piety uncovered as nothing more than rote tradition and a grasping for power.

Antioch had its own temples to various gods, with priests that charged steep fees to buy the gods' favor. Jovian had believed the Jews were different. He thought he found unadulterated faith, a way to access the divine that was unpolluted by greed.

How wrong he had been.

He arrived at the bathhouse and paid his fee. He strode into the men's side and tossed aside his dusty tunic. Maybe it was better to worship no gods at all. If he was forced to trust in his strength and his wit alone, then at least he knew who he was leaning on.

He plunged into the pool.

Abandoning faith was the logical choice, but something deep inside would not let go. He had sensed a holy presence years ago. In that overwhelming moment, he knew there was a real God who called to him like a homeland calls to a weary traveler.

He burst out of the water, sucking a breath and shaking water from his hair. If only he could go back to when faith was certain. He would stay there forever.

# Thirteen

Jovian joined his family in the triclinium. His parents sat on one couch, and Sergio and his wife Cassandra claimed the other. Jovian bobbed his head cheerfully at them all. After his first dreamless sleep since Judea, his mind was sharper than it had been in months.

"You look well today." Thea smiled. He was freshly shaved and had donned his favorite tunic. "Looking forward to tonight?"

Jovian wanted to say 'no' out of spite, but he was looking forward to seeing Persephone again. She had been like a breath of fresh air in his mind.

He settled for a shrug, and Thea raised her eyebrows knowingly.

They quieted as they heard a brisk knock at the gate. Cheerful voices filtered in from the atrium as Tomas offered to wash the guests' feet.

Jovian smoothed his tunic as his mother shifted her position so she appeared at ease. They all looked toward the doorway.

Horace strode into the room with his wife, and the Titus men rose to greet them.

"My friends!" Horace said, expanding his arms.

Belen clasped Horace's hand. "Welcome to our home."

Horace beamed. "A dinner with old friends is just what we needed. It's been too long!"

Thea rose to kiss Horace's wife Lyra on both cheeks.

The four daughters filed into the room in a flutter of colorful cloth and perfume. Jovian sat back down, blinking at the sudden jolt of femininity. He shot a stunned glance at his brother, and Sergio grinned.

The two eldest girls were of marriageable age, with the same reddish-brown hair. Persephone was slender and graceful, but Julia was tall and expressive, her laughing eyes sweeping the room as her presence filled the small space. They were far different than the bickering children he remembered. The two younger girls giggled at each other, ignoring the adults as they shared secrets of their own.

At last, everyone took a seat. Persephone smiled at Jovian, and his pulse jumped.

Though they were all in one room, the conversation was divided, the women talking on one side, the men on the other. Jovian couldn't help glancing at Persephone now and then, but when she caught him sneaking a peek, he kept his attention firmly averted.

The servants brought in the food. Jovian thought his mother had outdone herself in choosing the menu. Browned quail glistened with a sweet sauce, and fish lay in a neat row on a bed of roasted wheat. There was bulgar wrapped in grape leaves and a plate of pungent cheese. Stacks of soft pita bread sat next to olives, dried figs, pickled eggs, and leafy herbs tossed in vinegar and oil. The guests exclaimed over the delightful array, and Thea blushed at the praise.

Jovian ate with gusto. As he bit into one of the grape leaf rolls, he couldn't help but feel it was missing a certain spice. Coriander. Leah had always added coriander. Against his will, his mind returned to Antipas' palace kitchen.

*Leah's brow pinched with concentration as she measured spices into her bowl. She glanced up, catching him watching her. He blushed, expecting her usual frown, but she smiled instead.*

"Don't you agree, Jovian?" Belen said, and the palace kitchen disappeared.

Jovian blinked at his father. "I'm sorry, what?"

Belen's smile stiffened. "I was just telling Horace how we plan to bring in a shipment of Galilean wool this spring."

Jovian nodded with more enthusiasm than necessary. "Right. Wool. Yes, we are."

Horace chuckled and nudged his host. "I think his mind is on something more pleasant than wool."

Belen shot his son a questioning glance, but Jovian looked at his hands. The memory of Leah wasn't exactly pleasant. More like bittersweet. A reminder of a life he gave up months ago.

When they had all eaten their fill, the servants cleared the table.

Thea rose. "Ladies," she said, "I'm trying a new weaving pattern. Come tell me what you think."

The women followed Thea from the triclinium. The two youngest girls sneaked into the atrium to play. Their giggling voices echoed in the space.

Jovian rose to refill his cup of wine. When he turned, the other men were leaning toward one another, deep in conversation over their shared trade. His insides shriveled at the thought of joining.

He slipped from the room and into the empty courtyard. Voices filtered from all corners of the house, but here, it was peaceful.

Persephone's voice drifted toward him. "It seems we both needed some fresh air."

He turned and watched her walk toward him. Her open expression squeezed the air from his lungs. Had she sought him out, or did her mother send her to speak to him? He was ill-prepared to face the schemes of mothers and daughters.

He took a step sideways, ready to retreat back to the triclinium, but her gaze shifted past him.

"She's always been a favorite of mine," she said.

Jovian followed her gaze to the small fountain. A bronze statue poured water from her jar. Her clothes wrapped around her lithe frame, billowing with realistic detail. His eyes flicked back to Persephone, who stood with her arms clasped behind her, her head tilted to the side. The ease in her posture captivated him. How could she be so quietly self-assured?

"Did you work today?" he asked.

Persephone shook her head. "My mother and I took my uncle up to Aesculapius' temple for treatment."

"Did he recover?"

"The priest says if he has faith, he will become well."

Jovian took a sip of wine. He had seen a prophet heal terrible afflictions with a touch of his hand. The results had been immediate.

"You disagree?" Persephone's brows slanted in confusion.

She was too observant.

"Let's just say that I am more inclined to trust physicians than priests."

"But a physician can do nothing without divine guidance. A person can't be healed if they have angered the gods."

He made a noise in his throat and wished she would choose another topic.

Again, she seemed to sense his emotions. "Mother says religion makes for uneasy conversation." She chuckled. "So tell me, what are your plans now that you're back in Antioch? If you don't enjoy working for your father, will you join the army?"

He answered without thinking, as if his tongue had a mind of its own. "I'm considering becoming a guard again."

"Really?" she said. "Why?"

He hesitated. Unlike his father, she seemed genuinely interested in his answer. He had truly enjoyed working for Antipas, protecting the tetrarch in his palaces and along his routes. It was the one job in which he both excelled and experienced a sense of pride. But that was too difficult to explain.

"The adventure," he said at last.

She pursed her lips.

"You disapprove of adventure?"

She circled the bronze figure to admire it from another angle. "Not at all. But there are many types of adventure. Not all pull us far from home." Her gaze met his as if trying to convey some greater meaning. His feet shifted, unsure what she wanted from him.

Again, she smiled that confident, secret smile, and admired the sculpture. A curl of red-tinged hair escaped from her braid to float along the soft skin of her neck.

He blinked, realizing Persephone had stopped studying the statue and was instead watching him. His ears burned. Her eyes were soft and inviting and his chest stirred unexpectedly.

He cleared his throat, suddenly uncomfortable with being alone. "I think we should go back in."

Disappointment flickered in her eyes, but then she smiled and strode back inside without saying a word.

After the guests had gone home, Jovian wandered back into the courtyard. Stars hung brightly in the dark sky.

His mother came to his side. "Persephone is a lovely girl."

Persephone was lovely. He could not deny it. She was also kind and sensitive.

Thea hooked her arm into his and leaned her head against his shoulder. "Your father and I want you to be happy."

"I am happy."

"Are you?"

Jovian drew a frustrated sigh. "As happy as I can be."

Thea settled on a bench, and patted the place next to her. He sat and leaned his elbows on his knees, toying with his fingers.

"I've heard you prowling the house at night, unable to sleep," Thea said.

He winced. He had hoped his restless nights had gone unnoticed. "You're going through the motions of life, living without purpose."

"Isn't working for Father my purpose?" He gave her a crooked smile.

She smacked his arm. "Don't be glib. Now tell me, why did you leave Judea?"

Jovian stiffened. "There was nothing for me there."

"There must have been something, or you wouldn't be fighting against your father and me at every turn. You've come home yet you are not fully here."

"Is that how it looks?"

"It's how it feels. You are lost, my son."

Jovian scoffed deep in his throat. "And a wife would keep me safely home. Is that what you're getting at?"

"A wife could bring you peace. Give you safe anchorage in the storms of life."

He shot her an amused glance. "Do you consider yourself an anchor, mother? A great weight hanging off father's neck?"

She shoved him. "You know what I mean."

They both peered at the stars. His mother's perfume hung in the cool air. The familiar fragrance made him homesick, though he was home. The division within himself was exhausting—the questions, the doubts. Perhaps it was time to be done with them.

He studied his palms as his heart pounded against his ribs. Somehow the words slid from his dry mouth. "I found faith in Judea."

Thea stiffened. "You mean—"

"The Jewish faith, yes," Jovian said. "I was learning so much. I even met a prophet and saw him do miracles." Thea studied him silently. "But just when I was beginning to understand, he was crucified."

Thea made a pained noise in her throat. "I see."

Jovian turned and grasped his mother's hand, willing her to fully understand the confusion that tore up his chest and made it hard to breathe.

"It was so terrible, so wrong. It haunts me. I dream of him on that cross, bleeding—" His words failed him as a sob shook his shoulders.

Thea's face crumpled in sympathy and she wrapped him in her arms. Jovian leaned into her, desperate for the warmth and comfort she offered.

After a few minutes, Jovian sat up. He threw back his head to scoff at the stars. "Do you want to know how insane I am? I still believe in the God of the Jews. But he is as unjust and cold as the gods I grew up with." His hands turned to fists. "What is the point of faith? What is the point of prayer, of sacrifices, of any of it?"

"Your father says the gods are fickle. They do as they will, whether or not we pray."

"So why do you pray?"

"Because it comforts me."

"But if your goddess won't help you, why worship her?"

Thea cupped his chin. "I don't think you're seeking a god. You're seeking a being who grants your every wish."

His cheeks warmed. "Maybe I'm being childish, but I want to worship a just God. I thought I had found him, but then—"

"I know very little about the Jewish faith, but I have seen their strictness. They don't join in our festivals or participate in our guilds. Their beards, their clothes, their food—all of it is regulated. What free man would bind himself to that?" She looked Jovian in the eye. "I'll admit, it's not the life I want for you. Would you still be able to eat with us if you converted to their faith?"

Jovian hesitated. "Perhaps not."

"See? Would a just god cut you off from your family?"

He roughly wiped his cheeks. He couldn't talk about this anymore.

"You're right, Mother." His voice was scratchy with emotion. "It's time for me to move on."

"You will find peace again, I'm sure of it."

He nodded, though he did not believe her.

Thea leaned her head on his shoulder. "If I could take away your pain, I would."

"I know." He kissed the top of her head. "Could any woman take your place in my heart?"

"I hope not, but I'm willing to share."

She surely imagined a woman like Persephone, not like Leah. Persephone was Greek. She would fit in with Jovian's family and his life in Antioch. Persephone would make no demands on his faith, or ask him to change.

Jovian was tired of wrestling with the past, of trying to make sense of senselessness. Antioch was his home. He was a Greek man, not a Jew. He would put Judea and its God behind him for good.

# FOURTEEN

J oanna glanced over her shoulder and ensured Leah was in her wake. The sky above the temple courts churned with the promise of rain. Joanna drew a deep breath of the sweet air as she followed Chuza through the crowds. The people prayed for a good, heavy downpour, enough to refill their cisterns and revitalize the fields and hills.

They joined the line heading up the stairs into Solomon's Colonnade. Chuza broke a path for them, and Joanna's chest warmed with contentment at being together. If her husband struggled with stewarding Antipas' lands from a distance, he hid it well.

They wove their way down the long colonnade to join the other believers—a large group of men, women, and children. An invisible fence surrounded them. The whole city knew about Ananias and Sapphira, and the invisible line required a leap of true faith to cross.

A drizzle began and the shofar blew, calling the people to prayer as the priests began the morning sacrifices. All around her, men and women lifted their hands in supplication, praise, and thanksgiving. The prayers mingled as the altar smoke rose sluggishly through the rain.

In the humid air, Joanna's hair released the faint scent of lavender, and she coiled a strand around her finger. The perfume had been a gift from her brother-in-law. If only Alexander would accept the gift she tried to share in return—the good news of Jesus Christ. But Alexander was on the other side of the invisible fence. He spoke respectfully about the apostles, but he would not let his wife visit them again.

Joanna blinked, realizing the prayers were over and the apostles had begun their lessons. Chuza, Joanna, and Leah joined the believers. John, the son of Zebedee, shared stories about their time around the Sea of Galilee, how Jesus filled their nets with fish, and how he walked on water.

The rain stopped before John finished his teaching. The crowd dispersed, heading to work or chores.

Chuza rose and held out his hand. Joanna accepted his help, awkwardly standing around the bulk that had become her middle. Two whole months until her time, yet it seemed impossible that she could grow any larger.

As Chuza led them toward the western gate, Leah spoke up. "Can I spend the day with Keturah?"

Chuza glanced at Joanna, and she nodded. They turned for the southern gate and emerged near the public mikveh. Men and women lined the temple steps, some with bandages, others were borne on litters by friends. They waited for Peter, hoping he would heal their afflictions.

"How is Keturah?" Joanna asked Leah.

Leah's lips pressed together with concern. "She worries. She knows she must remarry, but she has no dowry or family to arrange a betrothal. Plus, she still grieves her first husband."

Joanna squeezed Leah's arm. It would be best if Keturah could rejoin her family in Syria, but getting her there would be difficult.

They reached Keturah's home and Leah knocked. The young widow opened the door. Her cheeks were fresh, and the bright-eyed baby in her arms sucked his thumb.

"Leah!" Keturah beamed and held out her free arm so Leah could step into a half-hug. "I was hoping you'd come." She looked at Joanna and Chuza. "Can you come in as well?"

Joanna shook her head. "I'm helping Dalia and my mother today." Miriam had bought a large basket of olives, and Joanna had offered to prepare them.

The two young women stepped into Keturah's house, already deep in conversation before the door closed.

Chuza walked Joanna to Dalia's house. Glancing around for nosy neighbors, he wrapped his arms around her and kissed her soundly.

"Work hard and hurry home." Joanna tugged on the front of his robe.

"Always." He chuckled.

As he set off for a day in his palace office, Joanna let herself into Dalia's house and unwound her palla. She strode into the courtyard kitchen and unhooked a long apron from its place, tying it around her bulky frame. She smiled at Alexander's unmarried sister, who was building a fire in the bread oven. Jael was the assigned baker in the family.

"Good morning," Joanna said, and Jael nodded. The young woman still treated Joanna like a stranger—an odd and potentially dangerous stranger. Joanna tried not to let it bother her.

Joanna uncovered the cistern and drew up a jar of water. She peered into the plastered depths. The cistern was low. They needed more rain, but sunlight broke through the clouds and filled the courtyard with warmth.

While Jael baked her bread, Joanna washed the olives, sorting out any that were bruised, and carefully slicing each one. Pleasant voices broke the silence as Dalia and Miriam walked in, each holding one of Little Mary's hands.

"Why can't I go to school with Samuel?" Mary thrust out her lower lip. The little girl doted on her big brother, and to be separated from him, even for half a day, was torture.

Joanna beckoned to the little girl. "Why don't you come help

Auntie?"

Curious, Mary came over.

Dalia mouthed 'thank you', and Joanna smiled in response. Miriam brought her basket of mending to a seat in the sun, and Dalia settled at her loom. Easy conversation passed around the courtyard as they discussed local news and their neighbors.

Joanna and Mary dumped the glistening black fruit into a large vat in the storeroom.

"Stand back," Joanna warned the little girl as she measured out the poisonous lye and stirred it into a jar of fresh water. She poured the mixture over the olives so the lye could break down their bitterness. After a few days, Joanna would wash the fruit many times before setting it to soak again, this time in brine.

Joanna stepped out of the storeroom, but she stiffened as someone pounded on the front door. Little Mary ran to her mother's side. The other three women froze in fear.

Joanna forced herself to march to the door and pull it open. Her heart stopped.

A rabbi held Samuel's limp body in his arms. A cluster of boys surrounded the teacher, all of them distraught, and a few of the younger ones were crying.

"Dalia!" Joanna screamed. She clutched her nephew's hand. It was cold. The boy's face was deathly pale, emphasizing a swollen abrasion on his forehead.

"Is he alive?" she gasped.

The rabbi's panicked eyes met hers. "Barely."

Dalia came running, and her blood-curdling wail seared a scar on Joanna's soul. Jael grabbed Little Mary's hand and rushed her upstairs, away from the horror.

Dalia took her son into her arms but struggled to support his weight. "Wake up, my love!" she begged.

Miriam grabbed the rabbi's sleeve. "What happened?"

The rabbi wrung his hands. "We were going up to the temple.

He was rough-housing. Before I could correct him, he tripped and tumbled down the stairs."

Joanna shuddered at the thought of those long stone steps. Her sister sank to the ground, cradling her son. Miriam crouched and cupped his face while Dalia coaxed Samuel to open his eyes.

Joanna forced herself to focus. "We need to tell his father." She turned to the oldest student. "Run to the market. Find Alexander the perfumer. His booth is yellow and red. Hurry!"

The boy nudged his companion, and they raced away.

Dalia's mother-in-law Patara hurried into the room with her serving girl, both gasping as they beheld Samuel.

Joanna gathered up a mat and cushions and laid them out.

"Here!" she said, beckoning to her sister and mother. "Lay him here."

The women laid Samuel down, and Dalia's mother-in-law turned to her servant. "Get my physician!"

The girl raced past the rabbi and his students.

"Has he not woken up at all?" Patara asked the rabbi.

He shook his head, and Patara pinched her lips, looking at Dalia's weeping form with pity. She set her hand on her grandson's chest. After a few moments, her shoulders sagged. "His pulse is weak."

Dalia rocked back and forth, tears pouring down her face. "God help him. Please help him."

The rabbi stepped forward and prayed aloud, his voice filling the room. His students gathered around him like a flock of chicks.

Joanna squeezed her eyes closed and sent her own plea to God. What should she do?

The image of the people lined up outside the temple filled her mind, as clear as day.

Her eyes snapped open.

"The apostles will heal him," Joanna whispered, then repeated herself, louder.

Dalia and Miriam stared at her, but Joanna knew this was the

107

right choice. "We can bring Peter here." She looked at Samuel again. His chest was hardly moving. "No, we must bring him to Peter. Hurry!"

Patara scowled at Joanna. "He should not be moved!"

Joanna stepped around Patara to crouch in front of Dalia, and prayed her sister would trust her. "This is his best chance. We must go."

Dalia stared into Joanna's eyes, searching. Finally, she wiped her face and nodded.

The rabbi stood in stunned silence as Miriam helped Dalia pick up her son, his thin arm dangling by his side.

Miriam and Dalia hurried into the street with the lifeless boy cradled between them. Those passing stopped to stare.

They reached the end of the street before Alexander came running. He cried out in alarm as he saw his son. Dalia passed Samuel into his arms.

"We're going to the apostles," Joanna said. "Go to the temple. Go!"

Alexander stared at her, his face a mask of anguish. She feared he would refuse, but he turned and jogged down the street, his firstborn in his arms. The women ran after him. Joanna prayed they were heading the right way. If the apostles had already left the temple, they could be in the Lower City.

They reached the temple steps, and Joanna sagged with relief as she saw the ill and injured were still waiting. She peered up the staircase just as Peter emerged through the doorway.

Alexander bounded up the steps, charging ahead of the women. He fell to his knees in front of Peter and held up his son as his chest heaved.

Peter immediately crouched and laid his hand on Samuel's head. "In the name of Christ Jesus," Peter said, "be healed."

Samuel's foot twitched.

Dalia cried out and stumbled up the steps after her husband.

Samuel straightened, sitting upright as Alexander clung to him, weeping. Samuel looked around himself in confusion as his mother pulled him into her arms. Miriam dropped to her knees next to Dalia and brushed the hair off her grandson's forehead and kissed him again and again. Samuel squirmed, embarrassed at this overflow of affection.

Joanna stood at the base of the stairs. She realized tears were streaming down her face as relief flooded her like a river. "Thank you, Jesus," she whispered. "Thank you."

Peter gripped Alexander's shoulders and spoke quietly before he continued on his way.

The sick stretched forward, reaching for Peter's shadow. Where it fell, they drew gasps of relief or cried out in wonder.

Joanna pressed her hands over her lips. The touch of Peter's shadow was healing them.

Peter passed Joanna, and he grinned, some of his familiar boisterousness showing through.

Joanna's heart fluttered as she remembered Jesus' words. *Truly, truly I say to you, the one who believes in me…greater works than these he will do; because I am going to the Father.* Jesus had promised it, but she hadn't realized what he meant.

Alexander, Dalia, Miriam, and Samuel picked their way down the steps. Dalia gripped Samuel's hand in both of hers.

They wound their way back through the city, all of them dazed.

Dalia looked up at her husband. "What did Peter say to you?"

"He said, 'Your faith has healed your son.' I honestly didn't think I believed, but when Samuel's life was on the line, I was willing to believe anything." Alexander stopped and turned toward Joanna. His heart was in his eyes. "I believe Jesus is the Christ."

Joanna's pulse leaped as Dalia gripped her hand.

"Your faith saved my son," Dalia whispered tearfully. "I believe in your Jesus too."

Miriam ran a hand over Samuel's hair. "What do we do now?"

Joanna struggled to speak around her joy. "You can be baptized to wash away your sins and declare your decision to follow Jesus."

Alexander wrapped an arm around his wife's shoulders. "We will.

But I need to tell my family first."

Alexander led the way into the house.

Patara gaped at her grandson as he strolled through the doorway. With trembling hands, she cupped Samuel's cheeks. Besides a few smudges of dirt, his face was perfect.

"What's for lunch?" Samuel asked.

Patara burst into tears and clung to her grandson.

Alexander turned to Dalia. "I think a feast is in order. Invite all our friends and neighbors to come tomorrow night. We will offer a sacrifice in thanksgiving to God."

Little Mary hopped down the steps, towing Jael. "We're having a feast?"

Alexander scooped Mary up and spun her around. "Yes, my love, with good food and music!"

Alexander turned to his mother, who finally released Samuel and wiped her face with the corner of her shawl.

"How?" Patara gasped.

Alexander shared a glance with Joanna. "I will explain everything."

# FIFTEEN

"Chuza, come and sit with us!" Alexander waved him over. Chuza blinked at this exuberant welcome. He smoothed his best robe and wove through the packed courtyard to join Alexander's friends. When Joanna said there would be a feast, Chuza had not expected a crowd this size.

The courtyard was awash in light despite the night sky, with brightly colored scraps of cloth tied anywhere available. Long tables were decorated with sprigs of greenery and fragrant herbs. Hired musicians played the lyre and flute as dozens of guests held cups of wine and stood in groups, chatting.

Samuel and Little Mary, also dressed in their best, ran about with the other children, weaving through the indulgent adults. The boy seemed completely unfazed by his near-death experience.

Nodding at his brother-in-law, Chuza sat among the men.

Alexander clasped his shoulder and introduced Chuza to the others. With a grin, he added, "He saw the risen Messiah."

Alexander's friends studied Chuza, not with the usual disdain reserved for Antipas' steward, but with curiosity.

Flushing, Chuza glanced over at Joanna. She sat among Dalia's friends and neighbors as they leaned close to hear her speak. She seemed to sense Chuza's gaze, and their eyes met across the courtyard.

A hired servant approached and bowed his head to Alexander. "The meal is ready, my lord."

Alexander stood and held up his hands. The courtyard fell silent. "My friends and family, join us for the feast!"

With a cheer, everyone found places at the many tables.

Chuza's mouth watered at the array of tantalizing trays. Delighted with the chance to use her skills, Leah had been in the kitchen since before dawn. Chuza's chest puffed with fatherly pride as everyone exclaimed at the sumptuous food.

The guests ate with gusto. Wine flowed and conversations grew louder. Alexander spoke eagerly about the apostles, extolling their good works and Jesus' teachings.

The guests, softened by good food and wine, were willing to listen. Heads nodded. Lips curved in gentle smiles. If not everyone believed that Jesus was the Messiah, they were at least willing to accept that Alexander's family had received a miracle.

When the guests groaned with full bellies, the servants cleared the tables and refilled the cups. The musicians began their music again, and the men reclined.

Chuza was warm and sleepy, his stomach pleasantly stretched, when one of the servants approached him. "My lord, there's a man at the door for you."

Chuza's languid mood dissipated. His eyes flicked to the starry sky above. Who would come at this hour?

He stepped into the dim house, and stiffened when he saw Manaen's somber face. "What's wrong?"

Manaen gripped Chuza's shoulder. "The temple guards arrested the twelve."

Chuza's knees wobbled as if the floor shifted beneath him. Perhaps they should have expected this. With people pouring in from neighboring towns to lay their sick before Peter, it had only been a matter of time before the priests felt threatened enough to act.

Chuza cleared his throat. "All of them?"

Manaen nodded and dragged his hands down his beard. "I would've come sooner, but Maryam is distraught." He gestured toward the courtyard, where laughter and music drifted on the air. "I'm sorry to ruin your celebration with bad news."

Chuza closed his eyes and gave his head a shake. "What are the charges?"

"Blasphemy. And this isn't their first warning, so it's not likely they'll just walk away."

Chuza drew a sharp breath through his nose. "I'll go to the temple in the morning and find out what's happening."

"I thought you'd say that. I'll meet you there."

The men clasped arms before Manaen slipped back into the dark streets. Chuza walked toward the courtyard. He leaned on the door frame and watched Alexander's face glow with the flush of a new believer. What would happen to Alexander, and those like him, if the twelve were executed like Jesus?

A shiver ran down his back. "God, you must protect your flock," Chuza whispered. "Don't take our shepherds away."

Joanna detached herself from the women and came to his side. "What is it?"

Chuza stepped into the shadows of the house, and she followed. "I'm afraid I have bad news."

Chuza rubbed his gritty eyes as he, Joanna, and Alexander hurried up the quiet streets to the temple, wearing warm cloaks over their best robes. The feast had gone till dawn. He and Joanna had kept the worrisome news to themselves until the last guest departed, so they wouldn't spoil the celebration.

Alexander's shoulder bumped against Chuza's. "If we gather enough people to stand as witnesses, the priests would have no option but to let them go."

Joanna glanced at Chuza, and grim understanding passed between them.

Chuza sighed. "I'm not sure it would make any difference. The Sanhedrin has absolute power in matters of blasphemy. If they vote against the apostles..." He left the rest unsaid, but they quickened their pace.

A small group of early morning worshipers waited outside the closed temple gate. Pink tinged the gray sky, painting a flush on cold cheeks. A flock of sparrows flew overhead, and an ache spread in Chuza's chest. Not a sparrow fell to the ground without God's knowledge. God knew his apostles were in danger. He had to intervene.

At last, Chuza heard the clunk as the gates were unbarred, and they swung inward on oiled hinges. While the worshipers strolled toward the inner courts, Chuza, Joanna, and Alexander found a place to stand near the Sanhedrin door. The trial would not be for at least an hour, but they hoped to catch sight of the apostles beforehand, to give them encouragement with their presence.

The temple grew busier as the sun rose. Priests went about their routines and the Levites made their way to the inner courts, carrying their instruments. The shofar blew, and men crowded into the inner courts to pray. But Chuza and the others hung back.

Before long, Manaen and Joses joined them with Maryam. Her red-rimmed eyes were dark on her pale face. Joanna took her arm, and the women leaned on one another.

Money changers and those selling sacrificial elements opened their trade, and the chink of coins in collection boxes punctuated the air.

Sunlight shifted across the elaborate tile floor, marking an hour before the elders began to arrive. The large door was held open by a young scribe, and Chuza caught a glimpse of the tiered seats, arranged in a semi-circle so all seventy-one men could look down upon the accused. His shoulders crept toward his ears, picturing those glares beating down upon him.

"Chuza, do you hear that?" Joanna gripped his arm.

He strained his ears and heard a faint, familiar voice.

His heart jumped. "Is that…?"

Joanna whirled around to peer up at Solomon's Colonnade. "It's Peter!"

Without pausing, Maryam rushed for the stairs, and the others followed in her wake. Chuza's pulse pounded in rhythm with their sandals smacking the stone. They rushed down the long colonnade. Chuza's jaw dropped. Twelve familiar figures stood among a little crowd, teaching.

Abandoning all dignity, Maryam ran up to her son James and gripped his face with both hands. "How are you here?"

James' eyes were alight. "An angel opened the prison door and led us out. The guards didn't see a thing." Chuza's stomach swooped. He would never grow used to these miracles. James gestured to the others. "The angel told us to speak here in the temple."

The crowd around the twelve was growing. Chuza's initial astonishment rapidly drained away. The priests were about to discover their prisoners had escaped. Surely James and the others realized it too, but they were boldly speaking God's word.

Chuza's mouth dried as half a dozen guards marched toward them. The captain of the guard led the way, with the emblem of his office emblazoned on his armor. Chuza reached for Joanna's arm and drew her a half-step behind him.

The apostles grew quiet, and the captain stomped to a halt, his face mottled with embarrassment.

"You must come with me." The captain's voice was quiet but commanding. "We don't want trouble." He glanced around at the watching crowd.

Alexander opened his mouth to protest, but Peter inclined his head. "As you wish, Captain."

The rest of the twelve fell in with Peter as they strode down the colonnade, and men stopped to watch them pass. Chuza and Joanna shared a worried glance.

Chuza, Joanna, and the others followed until they were stopped at the Sanhedrin door. It closed with a thud of finality.

Joanna held her head in her hands. "A moment of dazzling hope, and now we're back here again."

The others said nothing, but their anxiety hung in the air like a storm cloud.

Minutes crawled by as they waited, saying little.

After an hour, a scribe came out of the Sanhedrin and hastened away. On his return, a group of men stopped him. The Herodian party.

"I'll be right back," Chuza muttered to Joanna. He strode across the courtyard. The young scribe slipped away as Chuza approached.

Chuza inclined his head to the leader of the Herodians. "Do you know what's happening with the trial?"

Omri regarded him with one brow raised. "Your master must be quite concerned about these men. Whenever they are arrested, here you are."

"We share a mutual curiosity, it seems."

Omri inclined his head, seceding the point. "The priests are tired of these Galileans. They want them killed."

Chuza gripped his hands behind his back and forced his face to remain calm. "If they kill them, the people might revolt."

"The people are fickle."

Omri's gaze drifted over Chuza's shoulder, and Chuza turned. Peter led the way out of the Sanhedrin, flanked by guards. The sons of Zebedee whispered to each other, but the other men were silent. The door shut behind them.

"Apparently, the elders need to deliberate," Omri said.

Maryam stepped toward her son James, but the guards tightened ranks. Joses drew his mother back.

Omri and his companions discussed possible outcomes, but Chuza only half-listened.

The same young scribe opened the Sanhedrin door and ushered the twelve men back inside. He glanced about himself before hurrying across the courtyard to join Omri. Chuza caught the glint of a coin passing into the young scribe's hand.

"What news?" Omri asked.

"They will live," the scribe said, and Chuza drew a relieved breath. "The teacher Gamaliel warned the rest of the Sanhedrin to be careful, lest they find themselves fighting against God. He said if the apostles are not of God, they would end up like Theudas, or Judas of Galilee, whose followers scattered and came to nothing."

Chuza shifted his feet. Judas of Galilee was dead, but his followers still lingered on the fringes of society, like Joanna's brother Amichai.

Chuza stepped closer. "So the priests are letting them go?"

The scribe scanned Chuza from head to toe. "They will be flogged and released."

Chuza's mouth dried. His gaze shot to the Sanhedrin doors. "Are they being flogged now?"

"As we speak."

Chuza walked in a daze back to the others. Flogging was done with a short whip or thin rods, striking the chest and back. If the embarrassed captain was dealing the blows, the apostles' skin would likely be broken.

Chuza's ears strained for the sound of the punishment, but no cries permeated the thick Sanhedrin door.

He had the awful task of explaining to the others. They drew closer together, and Maryam's eyes overflowed with tears.

Naomi approached, and she and Maryam tearfully embraced. Chuza gripped his fingers until his knuckles protested. Naomi had two sons among the twelve. Two sons who were now suffering.

Finally, the door to the Sanhedrin swung open. Peter and John led the rest outside. Their stiff arms revealed their pain, yet their faces were radiant with joy. How was this possible?

Naomi rushed to her sons, and John set his hand on her shoulder, his damp eyes gleaming. "We have been considered worthy to suffer in Jesus' name."

Andrew sang the first few lines of a psalm of celebration, and the rest of the twelve joined in or laughed.

Chuza glanced at Omri and his party. Their expressions were confused. The high priest Caiaphas and his father-in-law Annas came to the Sanhedrin door, their faces stony as they beheld the rejoicing apostles. Shaking their heads, the high priests strode away, their pace clipped.

Everything in Chuza ached to get Joanna out of the temple courts.

"All right, settle down," Naomi said to her exuberant sons. "We must tend to your bruises."

The twelve strode through the temple courts, ignoring the whispers as men and women drew away. Thomas patted Bartholomew's arm and spoke quietly. Matthew glanced over his shoulder and met Chuza's gaze with a calm nod. Chuza could not imagine such inner peace in the face of grave injustice.

Alexander followed them, awe on his face. But exhaustion swept over Chuza as he walked beside Joanna. They had been awake for more than twenty-four hours, and he couldn't imagine how tired she must be. He offered her his arm, and she leaned gratefully on him as she supported her belly with her other hand.

She sighed. "I guess we shouldn't be surprised."

"What do you mean?"

"Jesus warned us that this would happen. That we would be whipped in the synagogues in his name." Her eyes tightened. "He said some would even be killed."

Her words punched Chuza in the gut. "Maybe it's time we leave the city."

Joanna's chin jerked toward him. "I need to stay here. Dalia and Alexander just joined the believers. They have so much to learn. And I'll need my mother for the birth." She looked down at her large middle. "We have to stay in Jerusalem."

Chuza's need to keep her safe wrestled against his desire to give Joanna everything she wanted. "If things get worse, I need to get you and Leah out. I can't lose another family." His throat closed over his words, and Joanna clutched his arm.

"God will keep us safe."

Chuza looked behind them. The temple complex loomed over the Lower City. Jesus promised many things, but never physical safety.

Weeks passed, and there were no more arrests. The others began to relax, but as Joanna drew near her time, Chuza's anxieties increased. Jesus had promised to return, but he hadn't said when. What kind of world would greet their innocent, newborn child? He began to end all his prayers with a plea—Come, Lord Jesus. Come Lord.

# SIXTEEN

## 32 AD
### WINTER

Joanna tried to ease away from the cramp that wrapped around her belly, but it followed her movement. In the pitch dark of the stable loft, Chuza snored gently. As the pain faded, she pushed the blanket aside. The winter air raised the hair on her arms. She groped for her wool shawl on its hook. Wrapping herself, she stepped toward the one small window and opened the heavy curtain. The moon hung high in a starry sky, its pearly glow interrupted by streaks of clouds. The windows in the neighbor's house were dark. Dawn was hours away.

Joanna watched the clouds drifting across the moon, massaging her belly in a circle. Her baby shifted at her touch, and she rocked side to side, humming. As another cramp gripped her, her humming turned into a low groan. Was it time? Dalia had given her signs to watch for, and told her that sometimes labor was false—though still painful.

Jesus had given them signs to watch for as well. Famine. Wars. Jesus' lament over Jerusalem was seared into her mind.

"Better the breasts that never nursed," Joanna whispered.

Her own breasts were full, ready to sustain this child in her womb. Jesus prophesied that great trials were coming. But when?

Another pain spread across her middle, and she pushed down her anxiety. With the Holy Spirit as her helper, she could face the future without fear.

As the pain slipped away, she looked down at her huge belly. "I can't wait to hold you, little one."

A whisper of wind slipped through the window and a shiver ran down her limbs. She closed the curtain and crawled back into bed. Chuza's warmth was soothing, and she snuggled closer.

When the room lightened, Joanna rose and dressed. She climbed down the ladder into the stable below, moving carefully around her ungainly figure.

Balaam flicked his long ears at her, and she let herself into his stall. He nudged her with his nose, his liquid eyes blinking at her in question. She spent a few minutes stroking him. As another contraction gripped her, she drew comfort from his calm presence.

She left the stable and shut the door.

The courtyard was still. Hoping for a few quiet minutes, she padded under the awning where her loom sat next to Dalia's. The dim light was enough to see the strands, so she nudged her basket of threads closer with one foot and sat on the low stool, shifting awkwardly around her cumbersome belly.

Joanna took her time and enjoyed the familiar motions. Phasaelis had taught her embroidery in Antipas' household, but growing up she had spent countless hours weaving with her mother. It had brought peace to her busy mind, smoothing away her many quarrels with Amichai. She picked up the comb and tightened the weave. Her brother didn't even know she was giving him another niece or nephew.

"Where are you, Amichai?" Had he heard about Jesus' resurrection? Surely not, or else he would have returned. Unless he had rejected it as impossible.

Joanna glanced toward the upper room where Leah slept. Perhaps

Titus had rejected the resurrection too. Thankfully, Leah was not pining after the Greek soldier. Between the outpouring of the Holy Spirit, their trip to Alexandria, and her work among the believers, Leah didn't have time to mope like a lovesick girl.

Joanna ran the shuttle through the vertical threads. She liked the Greek soldier, but not as a husband for Leah. Chuza had been confident that Titus was ready to become a proselyte, but Joanna doubted. And even if Titus began the process, it would be years before he could lead a Jewish household. Would that be fair to Leah?

Another pain gripped her. Joanna swayed side to side, her brow puckering. This one was the strongest yet.

"Good morning!" Her mother's voice sang across the courtyard. "You're up early."

Joanna puffed out a slow breath, and the pain flowed with it.

She half-turned on her stool. "I couldn't sleep."

Miriam's gaze swept over her younger daughter. "You're having labor pains, aren't you?"

Amused at her mother's discernment, Joanna nodded, and Miriam came forward to cup her cheeks, her eyes glowing. "I will make you some breakfast."

Joanna wasn't at all hungry, but she let her mother bustle around the courtyard, building a small fire in the oven and measuring out crushed grain for porridge.

With sudden clarity, Joanna saw her mother with fresh eyes. Only a few years ago, Miriam had servants to do everything for her. She had lost her husband, her vineyard, and her son. Yet, as she worked in Dalia's kitchen, Miriam seemed at peace. Gratitude for her mother's presence surged up Joanna's throat.

Dalia emerged from the house. After giving Miriam a half-hug, she set the table with dried fruit, bread, and pomegranate syrup. Leah strode into the courtyard kitchen, humming. She opened the pot of porridge and added a few spices before Miriam shooed her away. Grinning, Leah disappeared into the stable and emerged fifteen minutes later with a steaming pitcher of goat's milk.

Chuza shuffled into the courtyard, yawning and disappearing into the privy. When he returned, he washed his face in the cold water that sat overnight, sputtering and puffing out his lips.

He strode to Joanna, his beard still dripping. Joanna protested, but he leaned in to kiss her anyway. She giggled and pushed him away, just as a pain caught her off guard. She gasped, and Chuza stiffened. Leah turned to look, and Dalia froze with a cup halfway to the table.

Miriam chuckled and brought the pot of porridge to the table. "She's in labor."

Joanna smiled wryly at her mother.

Chuza dragged his hands through his hair. "How do you feel? Do you need anything?"

Joanna shook her head but held out her hand so he could help her stand.

"It'll be hours and hours yet," Dalia said knowingly.

Joanna did not find that comforting. Chuza walked her over to the table and helped her sit. Leah hovered nearby, her eyes wide.

Miriam waved Chuza away. "Sit down, man." She clicked her tongue. "All will be well." She poured Joanna a tall glass of milk. "But you will need your energy. Drink up."

Leah sat at her usual place at the table, watching Joanna too closely. Joanna sipped the milk as Dalia woke her children and brought them down to eat. Dalia poured each of her children foaming cups of milk as Alexander came downstairs, his forehead pinched with calculations, tapping a wax tablet with his stylus.

He sat at the table and passed Chuza the tablet. "Check these figures for me, will you?"

Dalia shot her husband a scolding glance. "Working before breakfast?"

Alexander grinned and pulled her closer to kiss her wrist.

Joanna tensed as another contraction rolled over her, and her belly stiffened with pain. Alexander's eyes flicked to hers. Understanding dawned, and he looked at Dalia, who nodded.

Alexander nudged Chuza's arm. "Why don't you come with me to the booth? My father is giving me more responsibility, and I can't let a little bookkeeping make me look bad."

Chuza looked at Joanna, uncertain.

"Yes, go," she said with mock annoyance. "I can't have you underfoot all day, twitching whenever I move."

Alexander's family came from their side of the house to join the meal, and easy chatter swirled around Joanna. She ate slowly, scooping her porridge with her bread, trying not to draw attention.

After the meal, everyone drifted away. Miriam took Samuel to school and the men walked into town.

Dalia washed the dishes as Leah swept the courtyard. Joanna cleared the table. She had to pause halfway to the storeroom, and closed her eyes against the pain.

"Getting worse?" Dalia said. "That's a good sign."

Leah shook her head doubtfully. "I don't see how."

Dalia patted her arm. "Her body is making itself ready."

Once the courtyard was tidy, Dalia prepared the birthing space, inviting Leah to help.

"I gave birth in this same stable," Dalia said. "It saves blood stains on the floor."

Leah's lips parted in shock, and Joanna's knees trembled. Dalia tied her donkey and the nanny goat in the courtyard.

"Leave Balaam," Joanna said. Dalia shot her a strange look, but Joanna lifted her shoulders. "His presence is soothing."

Dalia shook her head but obliged. She cleaned out the other stall, piling the soiled straw and manure on the side street where it would be collected and made into fuel. Dalia asked Leah to spread fresh straw as she attached two ropes to the loft above. "For you to hang onto," she said to Joanna.

This whole birthing idea was feeling like a mistake. Perhaps it wasn't too late to change her mind. Joanna pressed her knuckles into her lower back.

Dalia seemed to sense her misgiving. "You'll be fine. We are all here for you, and we'll call the midwife soon. Sarah has birthed almost every baby in the Upper City."

Joanna's anxiety would not dissipate. Women died in childbirth. She couldn't leave Leah to grieve again. Her pulse quickened, and she returned to the courtyard to fill a cup of water. She drank it all, but it only made nausea climb up her throat.

She looked at Leah. "Will you fetch Maryam, please?"

Leah raced for the door.

Joanna squeezed her eyes closed. The pains were coming stronger and closer together. Her mother had said it was not uncommon to labor for days. How could she sustain this pain for so long?

Chuza returned from the longest day of his life. No matter how many accounts and lists Alexander pushed under his nose, he could not stop thinking about his wife. There was nothing he could do to protect her or their unborn child. Helplessness wrapped around his ribs like bands of iron.

Chuza hurried into the courtyard where Leah prepared the evening meal. He barely registered the delicious aromas over the quiet hum of women's voices in the stable. A low groan twisted his gut. Joanna was in pain. In three steps he was at the stable door and cracking it open.

Joanna sat on a low stool, her eyes closed and her sleeveless tunic hitched above her knees. She rocked from side to side, her face flushed and damp with perspiration. Miriam, Maryam, Dalia, and the midwife were gathered around her, speaking soothingly.

Balaam stuck his head over the stall gate.

Chuza blinked. "What's the donkey doing here?"

The women turned to frown at him, and Joanna opened her eyes to smile. "Keeping me company. What are you doing here? I thought you were helping Alexander."

"The booth is closed for the day."

She seemed surprised. "The whole day is gone?"

Before he could answer, Dalia coaxed Joanna to take a sip of water. The midwife opened a jar of oil, and the spicy fragrance permeated the small space. The women responded to Joanna as waves rocked her body and her limbs shuddered like leaves on an olive tree. The women breathed with her, drawing her into their calm.

He was completely out of his depth.

Miriam noticed him. "Out," she said, and pushed him out the door.

He blinked in the courtyard, dazed.

Leah set dishes on the table. "Eat something, Chuza. You'll feel better."

Chuza ate mindlessly. After delivering a tray of food to the stable, Leah sat opposite him, her chin in her hands, her eyes unseeing.

Alexander and his family joined them. Samuel and Little Mary argued about who would hold the baby first.

Time moved slowly, yet before he knew it, it was time for the children to go to bed.

Chuza and Leah sat alone in the courtyard and listened as the women sang songs, low and rhythmic. Sometimes Joanna sang too, other times she groaned.

Alexander circled the courtyard and lit the lamps. Chuza faced the stable door, incapable of moving. Whenever the door opened, he saw his wife on the birthing stool, and her swollen belly pulled the universe toward the promise and travail of creating life. Ropes tossed over the beams gave Joanna handles to grip, but the women encouraged her to lean on them, to use their strength.

As the moon rose over the courtyard, the sounds within the stable changed. Chuza stood, his legs trembling as Joanna's cries became primal, and the women's voices were eager.

Joanna gasped, and a baby cried.

It was the most glorious sound he ever heard. Chuza sank to his knees with tears in his eyes. The women spoke softer, full of praise and joy.

The crying stopped, and Chuza tensed.

Miriam opened the door to peek out. Her face beamed with pride. "Everything is fine. The baby is nursing, and Joanna is well." She shut the door and Alexander clapped Chuza on the shoulder and offered his congratulations.

Chuza rose to his feet and exhaled a prayer of thanksgiving. He had been powerless, but God had watched over Joanna and brought her safely through.

Miriam came out of the room, holding a bundle. His child. Chuza jerked forward.

"Would you like to help me?" Miriam asked.

Chuza nodded, unable to speak, and Miriam set the baby in his arms. His child weighed nothing at all. The baby's eyes were open, though unfocused. Chuza kissed his child's forehead, his chest so full it was close to bursting.

"Hello, little one," he said. "I'm your papa." His throat closed up, and he couldn't say more.

"You have a beautiful daughter," Miriam said. She hesitated, as if afraid he would be disappointed his firstborn wasn't a son.

"A girl." Chuza's heart expanded. He blinked back tears as Leah approached, her eyes glowing as she beheld her little sister. "Two beautiful daughters. Could I be more blessed?"

Leah's gaze softened, and he kissed her forehead.

Together they anointed the baby with oil and salt to prevent infection, gently working around the infant's scrunched legs and arms. Miriam wrapped the baby in clean linen and passed the child back to him.

Maryam opened the stable door. "Joanna is resting now, if you'd like to see her."

Holding his new daughter, Chuza went into the stable. The warm air was rich with scented oils and the tang of blood. It reminded him of the temple.

The soiled straw was cleared away and replaced by a low bed. Joanna reclined, exhaustion in every line of her figure. She wore a clean tunic and her hair hung in a simple braid on her shoulder. Her eyes shone with love as she beheld her daughter.

She was the most beautiful woman in the world.

"I can pass the baby." Miriam reached for the child.

Chuza stiffened. He knew Joanna was ritually unclean because of the blood of birth. It was the way of Torah. Yet, Jesus had touched those who were unclean. Chuza stepped past Miriam and set the baby in Joanna's arms himself. Joanna's eyes flew to his as he cupped her cheek, and she leaned against his palm as if understanding.

If the women were surprised by his actions, they said nothing. Chuza sat beside Joanna and they cooed over the baby together.

"She's a miracle," Chuza said. "You are a miracle."

Joanna's lips quirked to the side. "I'll remind you of that when she's crying in the middle of the night and I'm cranky and exhausted."

That moment seemed impossible. The other women slipped out of the stable, leaving Chuza and Leah to watch over Joanna.

"What will we call her?" Chuza asked as Joanna traced their daughter's ear with her fingertip.

"Nadia." She looked up at Chuza. "Because of our great hope."

Leah came to Joanna's other side and the four of them nestled together in the small, warm space, lit by the lamp's golden glow. Chuza's throat thickened with unspeakable love for his little family. He would give everything to keep them safe.

# SEVENTEEN

The crowd lunged forward in their seats and screamed as one. Jovian flinched as bony knees jabbed into his back, but he could not take his eyes off the careening chariots. The white charioteer had the inside corner, and he leaned with all his weight as his team of horses circled the spina. Another fish-shaped marker tipped on top of its soaring column. It was the last lap now.

Jovian and Galen were crammed together, hip to hip. Galen wore their team's color in a tunic of blazing red. The roar of the crowd drowned out his shouts, and Jovian's pulse hammered against his ribs.

The races were all anyone could talk about the past two weeks, and now the Antioch Circus was packed with fifty-thousand spectators dressed in white, blue, green, and red, yelling until they were hoarse.

The blue chariot inched forward, but the green driver would not give way. Chariots bashed together, drawing screams from the women and making the young men clap their hands, half-hoping for a grand crash.

The chariots turned the corner and tore past the spectators with breathtaking speed. Jovian tasted the plumes of sand behind their wheels.

The red charioteer lashed his four gleaming black horses to greater speed, but it wasn't enough. Jovian groaned as the victor's trumpet blasted through the circus. A pair of slaves waved massive white flags on either side of the stadia.

The spectators in white leaped up and down while the blue, red, and green sat sullenly. Money passed from hand to hand and women fanned themselves with their programs.

"Well, that was humiliating." Galen sat back and crossed his arms. "Let's hope the next race is better."

A wine seller strolled through the crowd below. A rope was slung across his chest, carrying half a dozen small amphorae.

"You there!" Galen beckoned the young man over. The boy, not quite old enough to shave, climbed the tiered seats. Galen glanced at Jovian and then held up two fingers and passed over a coin. The boy untied his rope and passed them each an amphora.

Galen drank deeply and wiped his lips with the back of his hand. Jovian took a sip of his. It was passable, but the wine couldn't match the Galilean vintages he had enjoyed with Chuza.

The whites cheered again, and Jovian leaned forward to peer at the royal box at the far end of the long oval. Flaccus, the new governor of Syria, had sponsored the games, and he gave the winner a wreath and a heavy purse.

"Look," Galen said, elbowing Jovian in the ribs and gesturing down the row. "You have an admirer."

Doubtfully, Jovian turned. A young woman twirled her necklace as her eyes spoke an invitation that made Jovian's cheeks burn. He looked down at his wine. Galen chuckled and teased, but a familiar accent stole Jovian's attention.

Two rows down and a dozen spectators over, four bearded men conversed in Aramaic, debating who would win the next race. Aramaic was common enough in Antioch, but by their clothes and beards, it was clear they were Jews, and by the blue bands tied around their biceps, they were fans of the races.

Galen shoved him and flicked his chin at the men. "You have a problem with Jews?"

"No," Jovian said. "Of course not. I lived with them for five years."

Galen frowned as he watched them. "My father says more Jews are coming to Antioch all the time. The city is full of them and their synagogues." A bitter sentiment shared by many, but it was hard to hear from Galen's lips.

Jovian took a long drink from his amphora, and a sudden headache stabbed at his temples.

"I think I'll go home." He stood.

"Already?" Galen's eyebrows pulled down in disappointment. "We've been looking forward to this all week."

"I think I've had too much sun." Jovian shaded his eyes and squinted at the sky. "You stay. You can tell me all about it tomorrow."

Galen frowned but nodded. Jovian picked his way down the stands. A cheer announced the next round of chariots were lining up in their starting posts, but Jovian turned under the arched doorway that led him back into the city.

The street was just as crowded. Vendors lined the road selling souvenirs, food and drink, parasols, hats, clothes in team colors, and pleasant company. Jovian wound through the wide road until he reached the bridge.

He leaned on the railing with his elbows and watched the Orontes River flow toward the sea. A breeze lifted his short hair and cooled his brow. Galen was right, the races were a bright spot after days of taking inventory in his father's warehouse. So why had he let thoughts of Judea ruin his fun?

Jovian pushed off the stone railing and strode for home.

Tomas let him into the house. Surprised to hear his father's voice in the triclinium, Jovian stepped into the room, and Belen and Horace jerked in their seats to stare at him. An awkward silence hung in the air. Jovian had the distinct impression they had been talking about him.

"You're home early," Belen said.

"Headache," Jovian said, though it had faded during the walk.

Horace glanced at Belen. "Perhaps it's better he's here, now that we have decided."

Jovian crossed his arms, suspecting what was happening. His father gestured toward the empty couch.

As Jovian sat, Belen said, "I invited Horace here to discuss an important matter. A betrothal between you and his daughter."

Jovian's gaze flicked back and forth between the two men. He tried to find the right words. "Persephone is a lovely woman. But I hardly know her."

Belen waved his hand as if this was nothing. "I had never met your mother before we were wed. But our parents knew we were suited, just as Horace and I know you and Persephone will be happy together."

Jovian's lip quirked, and his humor came out dry. "Expanding your trade to matchmaking now, are you?"

Belen allowed a smile, but he reached over and patted Jovian's knee. "You are twenty-six. Let your mother and I arrange a good marriage for you. We want to assure you will be content after we are gone."

"After you're gone?" Jovian said. "You are hardly on death's door."

Belen's smile faded. "It is time."

Jovian's annoyance grew. He leaned back, scowling. "I thought it was customary to discuss with the prospective groom first, before approaching the bride's father."

"I am doing what I believe is best for my son. You find the girl pleasant, do you not?"

"I've seen her twice in five years."

Belen held out his hands. "That is an easy fix. You and Persephone will spend a day together."

Horace nodded. "I'm sure Persephone would enjoy that as well."

Jovian opened his mouth to protest, but his father's stern glare glued his tongue to his teeth.

Belen said, "If you and Persephone find each other agreeable, we will draw up the betrothal contract."

A single day to decide his fate.

"And if we don't?" Jovian challenged.

Something flickered in his father's eyes. "I'm sure everything will go perfectly."

"Ready for a turn-by-turn on the races?" Galen asked as he strode into the courtyard the next morning.

Jovian snapped the wax tablet closed and stuck his stylus behind his ear. He smiled wryly. "Ready to be a groomsman at my wedding?"

Galen blinked twice. "Honestly? My idea sounds better."

"I am meeting with Persephone and her mother tomorrow. If we don't stab one another, we'll be marched up to the registrar's office to file the betrothal."

"You don't sound pleased."

Jovian sighed and stretched his legs out in front of him. "I've talked with her twice, not counting a few encounters as children. Now we're supposed to spend the day together with the threat of marriage hanging over us. What are we supposed to talk about?"

"Hmm." Galen shot him a commiserating look. "Why don't you take her to the races? There's very little talking there."

"Somehow, I don't think that's what my father has in mind."

"So, what are you going to do?"

Jovian sighed. "I have no idea."

"Mother thought we should ride out to the Grove of Daphne."

Jovian blinked up at Persephone as she sat in the open cart, and she blushed. It was not a destination he expected.

Her voice wavered. "If that is pleasing to you?"

Persephone's mother, Lyra, held up a basket. "We have packed a picnic."

A picnic with two women he barely knew. This wouldn't be awkward at all.

Jovian climbed aboard, sitting opposite the two women and feeling self-conscious as both the mother and daughter smiled at him.

The driver flicked the reins. The sorrel horses set off slowly, but as they passed through a city wall and joined the main road through the suburb of Heraclea, they broke into a smooth trot.

Persephone was straight across from him, but Jovian couldn't bring himself to look at her. He was making a terrible impression, but part of him didn't care. This was their fathers' idea after all.

They trotted past beautiful villas, gardens with splashing fountains, public baths warmed by natural hot springs, and a multitude of shady trees. They were not the only ones heading for the famous grove. Other carts whisked by for a day of pleasure—and for those who knew where to go, a little debauchery.

Jovian knew he ought to make conversation. He cleared his throat, drew his courage and aimed a smile at Persephone. She looked as nervous as he felt.

"Do you like the races?"

"Oh yes!" she said, her eyes lighting up. "I thought we could go together but—" Lyra cleared her throat sharply, and Persephone paused. "But a picnic is nicer for talking." She met his gaze for a moment, and understanding passed between them.

She smiled. "What team are you?"

"Red. What team are you?"

"Green, of course." She tugged on the green shawl draped over her pale blue peplos. She leaned back in her seat. "Did you enjoy races in Judea?"

He shook his head. "There's a hippodrome near Jerusalem, at Herodium, but there haven't been races since King Herod. I can't envision Pontius Pilate doling out the necessary funds." Especially when those who opposed Roman entertainment would delight in the chance to protest.

Persephone pursed her lips. "Judea sounds like a backward place."

"It differs greatly from Antioch, especially these parts." He waved his hand around at the elaborate architecture. "But it has its own beauty and an ancient culture. You can walk into the hills and hear a shepherd sing a song written a thousand years before." Persephone seemed to be taken aback by his enthusiasm, and he quickly covered. "But the dust is terrible, finding its way into the most inconvenient places."

Persephone chuckled, but her gaze probed past his flippant words.

The road passed through a massive archway of carved limestone. The driver parked the cart along the road, and Jovian helped the two women down. He picked up the picnic basket with a surprised groan. They clearly had high hopes for his appetite.

Manicured paths wove into the groomed woods where men and women strolled. Jovian allowed Persephone to choose their route. They wandered under the dappled light, and Lyra adjusted her pace until Jovian and Persephone walked side by side.

"Are things getting better for you at your father's warehouse?" Persephone asked.

Jovian shifted the basket to his other arm. "I'm getting better at keeping track of the figures and inventory."

"But you're still not enjoying it?"

Jovian lifted his shoulders and made an uncommitted sound. "I am resolved to accept my role." He tossed her a grin. "It is the first step to actually liking it. Or so I'm told."

Persephone looked pleased he remembered. "Wise words, I'm sure."

"Do you think it is a wise lesson to apply to marriage as well?" Jovian teased, then hastily added, "Not that marrying you would be —I'm not saying—you know what I mean."

Persephone regarded him archly. "You make jokes when you're uncomfortable, don't you?"

"And also when I'm perfectly comfortable."

She laughed, and he liked the sound. She was so different from Leah. Self-assured and at peace with herself. Perhaps some of that inner peace would rub off on him.

They emerged in an open area where flower gardens spread around a large temple of white stone. Behind the soaring columns, a massive statue of Apollo was painted in bright colors. Persephone strode forward, expressing her admiration, but Jovian hung back.

He hadn't visited a temple since returning from Judea. The size and splendor of the massive figure was meant to illicit awe and draw the worshiper into the proper mindset for supplication. But Jovian felt nothing.

Braziers flanked the temple door, and the powerful scent of incense wafted into the air. The cloying smell urged Jovian to spin around and walk the other way, but he couldn't be rude.

He paused at a row of stone markers that surrounded the entire temple.

Persephone followed his gaze as he examined the white stones. "Those are the borders of the sanctuary." She smiled mischievously. "If you find the day unpleasant, you can throw yourself down and declare the need for refuge. No one can make you leave."

Jovian chuckled. "Good to know. I may need to claim it soon, before my arm falls off." He wiggled the heavy basket, glad to use it as an excuse.

"Oh!" Persephone blushed. "Of course. I should have brought the servant to carry it." To Jovian's relief, she turned away from the temple. "Let's find a place to sit. Perhaps if it's in your belly rather than your arms, the load will be easier to bear."

"If I eat everything in this basket, I'm afraid you will have to roll me back to the cart."

Persephone laughed again.

They laid out a blanket in the shade and ate the sumptuous picnic feast. After a while, Lyra rose to admire the nearby flowerbeds, leaving the prospective couple to talk alone. Jovian leaned on one elbow and stretched his legs out long, while Persephone sat upright, her graceful figure displayed for his admiration. They chattered about inane topics, learning nothing that would answer the question pressing on both their hearts—if they would make a suitable match.

At last, Jovian couldn't take it anymore. Keeping his tone light, he asked, "What do you think about this betrothal?"

Persephone looked down at her hands and spun a small ring on her finger.

He may have been too blunt. He searched for words that wouldn't convey more than he felt. "You are kind and sweet," he said. "I like your laugh. We seem to enjoy many of the same things. Though you are a Green."

She chuckled and looked up, her expression both shy and vulnerable. "I like your humor. You are kind and attentive. And we know each other's families."

"No evil mother-in-law, you mean." He winked.

"Is that a concern of yours?"

"Not at all." He waved a hand. "As the first son in your family, I would set the standard your sisters' husbands must strive to reach. An ideal situation, if I say so myself."

She shook her head at him, her lips curving. "See, I was right. You use humor when you feel uncomfortable."

He smiled around his pounding pulse. "I'm sorry. It's just that it feels so overwhelming. Our entire lives hang on the choice we make today."

She looked into the distance. "So, how do we decide?"

Jovian had no answer.

His father and mother were both waiting in the triclinium when the cart deposited Jovian back at home.

"Well?" Belen asked.

Jovian smiled through the panic fluttering in his chest. He had loved two women he could not have. Perhaps following tradition was the best way, but he wasn't about to admit that to his father. He kept his face neutral.

"It went well."

His father bristled at Jovian's nonchalance. "So we can prepare the betrothal contract?"

Jovian looked between his parents, stretching the moment.

"Yes."

Thea clasped her hands, delight shining on her face. "You will both be so happy!"

Belen thumped Jovian on the back. "Marriage will change everything for you. Just wait. You will have purpose again."

Jovian prayed both his parents would be right.

# Eighteen

32 AD
SPRING

Spring arrived, blowing away winter's frosts and rain and bringing balmy temperatures and clear nights. Joanna recovered, excused from all chores as she healed and cared for Nadia. Chuza threw a feast to celebrate Nadia's safe arrival, inviting their friends to join the family in the Upper City. Joanna watched her spiritual brothers and sisters mingling with her family, delight shining in her eyes. Peter blessed Nadia, anointing her with a dab of oil on her forehead as Chuza beamed.

It was a time of turning inwards, of late-night whispering as Joanna breastfed Nadia, of slow walks around the courtyard as Chuza patted his daughter's back to relieve gas pains. Before they knew it, it was time to prepare for Passover and the anniversary of Jesus' death.

It was also time for Antipas to return to Jerusalem.

Chuza set down his pen. He pinched the bridge of his nose and squinted his tired eyes. He missed the days when Joanna acted as his scribe.

Leaning back in his chair, he studied the letter. It was another message for King Aretas of Nabatea. The king was amenable to peace, and Antipas was offering to send an emissary to discuss the matter in person.

He drummed his fingers on the desk. This could be a suitable task for Agrippa, a way to show his usefulness to Antipas.

Chuza cut the papyrus scroll and set the letter aside. He picked up his pen and rolled it between his fingers. The women were preparing for Passover, when the believers would celebrate their bridged history between the Exodus and Jesus' death. It was also an anniversary for something more troubling. Titus had been gone for a year without a single word.

Chuza dipped the pen in ink, bowed over his desk, and wrote.

*To Jovian Titus of Antioch, from your friend Chuza, Herod's steward.*

*I pray you are well. I must tell you the good news. Jesus of Nazareth is alive! He rose from the grave and has been exalted to God's right hand. There is so much I want to tell you. Please, my friend, answer my letter and let me know you are well.*

Emotion surged up his throat, and Chuza tossed aside his pen, splattering ink. It was impossible to send the letter, but if he could, he would demand answers for Titus' heartless silence. How could he leave without a word or a hint of his well-being?

Crumpling his letter to Titus, Chuza heaved himself to his feet and picked up the letter to King Aretas. He strode to Antipas' room.

Antipas was alone, lounging on a couch as he perused a sheet of papyrus.

"Ah, Chuza!" he said, waving the papyrus. "I'm invited to a feast in Tyre after Passover."

"By who?"

"Bacchus. You remember him, the city official who negotiated the contract for our grain. Pointy beard, large belly."

Chuza smothered a grin at the description. "So you plan on attending?"

"Of course. He probably invited my brother Philip as well, and I can't shut myself out of any important opportunities."

Perhaps Antipas' excursion to Tyre would mean Chuza could delay joining him in his summer palace in Sepphoris, which meant more time with his family. His pulse jumped, but he kept his face calm.

"Speaking of opportunities," Chuza said, "I have finished the letter to King Aretas." He handed it to Antipas, who barely scanned it before setting it aside. "I thought you might send Agrippa as your emissary."

Antipas snorted. "That idiot?"

Chuza shifted his feet, remembering Cypros' anxious eyes and her fear that Antipas could cut them off at a whim. "Agrippa has done well managing the markets in Tiberias. I have been over his accounts, and they are meticulous."

"Hmm," Antipas said, unconvinced. "At least if I sent him, he'd be gone from my sight for a few weeks. I'm sick to death of his cold eyes, and his sneers behind my back. I wish he had stayed home this festival."

The door behind Chuza opened and Herodias swept in. "A message arrived for Agrippa. He's invited to a feast in Tyre." She froze under Antipas' sudden scowl. "What?"

"Agrippa?" Antipas said in disbelief. "Why him?"

Herodias blinked in confusion. "He is Herod's grandson. My brother has friends all over the world. "

"Ah, yes." Antipas sneered. "The all-popular Agrippa, sought by all, including his creditors."

Herodias bristled. "He's made something of himself in Galilee."

"I have made him something," Antipas corrected.

Herodias frowned but thankfully did not push her point.

Antipas thrust the invitation at Chuza, seeming less impressed with it now. "I was invited as well."

"Will you and Agrippa travel together then?" Herodias asked.

"I suppose we must." Antipas scowled at Chuza, his gaze laden with frustration. "Reply to the invitation and let Bacchus know I am pleased to attend."

"And the letter to King Aretas?"

Antipas waved his hand. "Yes, yes, send it too." Chuza stepped toward the door, but Antipas's voice drew him up short. "Oh, and about Bacchus' feast. I want you to come with me."

Chuza's stomach sunk, all hope of spending more time with Joanna and his daughters fading fast. He smoothed his face and turned back to Antipas. "To Tyre?"

Antipas fixed him with a stern glare. "Is that a problem, Steward?"

He and Joanna had enjoyed five uninterrupted months together, for which he was grateful. But he still had responsibilities to his master. "No, my lord."

Antipas' expression eased, and he flicked his wrist in dismissal.

Chuza stepped into the hall and looked at the letters in his hands. An invitation to a feast, and a discussion of peace with a neighboring nation. It was clear which issue Antipas cared more about. Was Antipas blind, or just stubborn? He sighed and stormed away.

Chuza shoved open his office door more roughly than he intended and cringed as it banged against the wall. Perhaps Antipas' misaligned priorities were his fault. He had left the tetrarch to Herodias' influence. If only he could divide himself in half. Father, husband, and follower of Jesus on one side, and loyal slave of Herod Antipas on the other.

Chuza tossed the letters on his desk and poured himself a cup of wine. A tray of dates stuffed with goat cheese sat on the sideboard. He sat heavily in his chair and pushed one into his mouth as he swirled his wine.

How long would he be gone this time? If only he could bring his family with him, but he couldn't make Joanna go back to living in the royal household. In Jerusalem, she was surrounded by friends and family, supported and encouraged, with opportunities to share her faith through her testimony and service to the poor. Leah had integrated into their new household, happy to cook and care for the children. She had grown close to that young widow, Keturah.

And Chuza had finally learned what it was like to be part of a large family that shared their whole lives with each other. His throat thickened, and he swallowed the date with difficulty.

There was no way he could rip Joanna and Leah away from all of that. But that meant he had to leave alone, to go with Antipas for weeks at a time. Nadia would grow while he was gone, and he would miss it all.

Antipas' retinue announced their arrival in the fertile Galilean valley with the rumbling of covered carts and clop of hooves. They dominated a road dotted with families returning home after the Passover feast and Week of Unleavened Bread. The people not only took home good memories, but they carried the wares they had purchased in Jerusalem—new pots, cloth, or perhaps a scroll.

Despite everything, it felt good to be back in Galilee. The valley overflowed with flocks, herds, and grain crops. Gardens and vines filled the terraced hills. The farmers swung sickles through the golden wheat as women bound the sheaves and propped them upright to dry. A young woman with a yoke on her neck brought jars of water. The workers stopped, wiping their brows and chatting as they sated their thirst. It was a pastoral gathering, far different from Antipas' retinue.

Patting Celer's neck, Chuza glanced over his shoulder at the carts trundling behind the mounted riders. The canopies were closed, shutting out the bright sun and the dust, but also the pleasant views.

Chuza turned to face the front again. They should reach Sepphoris by nightfall. The court would be left behind as Antipas and Agrippa continued on to Tyre in the morning, and Chuza must go with them.

A baby cried, and Celer's ears flicked backward. Chuza's heart gave an extra beat, but it wasn't his daughter demanding attention. Agrippa and Cypros' children rode in a covered cart with their mother.

The baby wailed again, and this time Agrippa spoke to Antipas. Antipas hesitated before turning to call, "We'll stop here for a few minutes."

The caravan ground to a halt and the sound of insects and bird calls filled Chuza's ears. Agrippa dismounted to check on his wife. A maid stepped down and led the older children to a nearby scrub of brush to relieve themselves.

Chuza unhooked his wineskin and took a deep drink. The wine tasted faintly of resin, but it quenched his dusty throat.

Agrippa walked back to the front of the procession, and when his eyes met Chuza's, he was apologetic. "A family does slow things down."

"We are still making good time," Chuza said.

"Kind of you to say so, but I know this is taking longer than my uncle wishes." He glanced ahead at Antipas. "I told Cypros she should have left the children at home with their nurse, but she refuses to be parted from them." He smiled wryly at Chuza. "Does your wife know how to get her way too?"

Chuza chuckled. "I find it's better to trust her judgment."

Agrippa tipped his head. "She must be a worthy woman. It's a shame I haven't gotten to know her. Will she join the court?"

"She prefers to stay with her family in Jerusalem. We have a young daughter, you know."

"Ah, I see. She likes to stay safely at home."

Chuza's lip twitched as he thought of all the months Joanna had spent canvassing Galilee, Samaria, Perea, and Judea. She had been to the cities of Tyre, Petra, and Alexandria.

Chuza glanced back at Cypros' cart. "If I remember correctly, Cypros' father was often away from home. Perhaps she wishes to keep your family together. ”

"Perhaps. My own father was gone so often, I hardly knew him." Agrippa's eyes grew distant. His father had been executed as a traitor when Agrippa was very young.

The maid boosted Agrippa's oldest son back into the cart. Drawing a sigh through his nose, Agrippa said, "I'm a lucky man. I don't always feel like it, but I am." He patted Celer's neck and strode back to his own horse.

Agrippa mounted and they set off once again. After a few minutes, Antipas slowed his mount to ride beside Chuza, leaving Agrippa to lead the way.

Antipas gave Chuza a long, narrow look. "What were you and Agrippa discussing?"

"His wife and children," Chuza said. "Cypros appreciates your friendship. You have given her a good life by helping Agrippa."

"I wish her every happiness. Enough to outweigh her bad luck at being married to my nephew."

Chuza shook his head in frustration. "Nagging Agrippa benefits no one. Isn't it time you built a friendship with him?"

Antipas pretended to look affronted. "Haven't we been riding side-by-side this entire journey? Though he rides like a sack of grain, I have hardly mentioned it at all." Antipas chortled and trotted to catch up to Agrippa.

Chuza puffed out his breath with frustration. Unless it involved business, Antipas never listened to his counsel. He feared Antipas was breeding trouble—inside his palace walls and without.

# Nineteen

The three men rode into Tyre on the main road, flanked by guards and trailed by a servant driving a two-wheeled cart. Chuza did his best to ignore the tense conversation between Antipas and Agrippa as he swept his gaze over the city. Modern and ancient architecture blended with temples, three-story insulae, private houses, and government buildings. The structures completely obscured the view of the Great Sea, but its salty scent bathed the city.

Agrippa and Antipas bickered over directions until Chuza asked a local, and they turned down a wide street into a wealthy district.

They arrived at a large villa and dismounted. Antipas and Agrippa strode past the doorman, each trying to look the most impressive. Chuza sighed and prayed they could keep the peace until they returned to Sepphoris.

A man shuffled toward them, leaning on a cane. Chuza blinked in shock as he recognized Philip. The tetrarch had lost considerable weight. Rather than basking in the glow of married life, it was clear he had been ill.

Antipas twitched in alarm, and he hesitated before clasping Philip's hand.

"It's been too long, brother," Philip said. "They've put us three in a room together. It will be like old times."

Antipas' smile was thin. "How wonderful. Why don't you show us the way?"

Philip inclined his head, and Agrippa followed his uncles into the house.

A servant stepped toward Chuza. "Welcome, Steward. I will show you your room."

He led Chuza through an atrium with marble floors and an elegant fountain. The house was built around a central courtyard, with the upper floor doors opening on a railed balcony. The servant led Chuza into a narrow room arranged with several couches. Someone's belongings already claimed one.

Chuza washed in the basin before he exchanged his dusty riding clothes for a clean tunic and robe. Smoothing a few drops of scented oil over his curls, he leaned closer to the small mirror. A gray hair glinted in the light, and he studied it ruefully. He remembered when his youth used to startle people. Those days were long gone.

His stomach rumbled, and Chuza opened his door. On the far side of the balcony, another man emerged from his room.

Chuza's breath caught in his throat. Pontius Pilate. Chuza should have realized he would be here.

Pilate strode for the stairs as Antipas stepped out of his room.

"Pilate!" Antipas called. "Let me walk down with you."

Pilate turned with a smile, and Antipas' words from the previous year rang in Chuza's ears. *If I can't be rid of the governor, I will make him my friend.*

Chuza's hand tightened into a fist. No good could come of this friendship.

Chuza walked into Bacchus' central courtyard. Lit with lamps and warmed by braziers, wide couches bordered a central table. Less than a dozen men reclined on their sides as servants filled silver cups with wine. Antipas chose a place near Pilate. Philip leaned on a bolster, and his eyelids were already drooping.

Agrippa strode past Chuza. He bowed to Bacchus and started a conversation, charm seeping from his handsome frame like perfume.

Chuza took the lowest place at the table and accepted a cup of wine. He peered over the rim at the mixed company. Jews eating in a Gentile's house. The priests would have a fit, but Antipas had been educated in Rome and ruled a land governed by Caesar.

Chuza had learned to walk the fine line of Jewish purity in a Gentile world—a line that was growing more and more blurred as years passed and cultures mixed.

Bacchus held up his cup. "My friends, let us toast the Emperor, Caesar Tiberius, the Son of God."

Chuza's pulse skipped a beat. The men around him echoed the toast, but Chuza's tongue clung to the roof of his mouth. Thankfully, no one noticed, and Chuza prayed the rest of the evening would pass as easily.

The night went long. Bacchus treated his guests to culinary delights and stimulating conversation, but Chuza couldn't relax. Antipas drank cup after cup of wine. His face grew florid, and his humor increasingly brash. The other guests frowned at him, but Pilate seemed amused, and Antipas grew even louder under the governor's influence.

Chuza shot Pilate a dark glare that went completely unnoticed.

In a lull, Antipas' voice filled the courtyard. "Agrippa is a pauper, you see."

Chuza's heart jumped into his throat.

Antipas' voice slurred. "If not for me, he'd be on the street with his wife and children, poor things."

Agrippa reddened, and the other men stared, but Antipas wasn't finished. "He thinks he has such good friends, but they mock him behind his back. They would rather throw him in debtor's prison than invite him to a feast." He took another gulp from his cup, and dribbled wine down his robe.

Chuza's cheeks burned with shame for his master. He began to rise but then hesitated. He couldn't drag Antipas away without humiliating him further. He shot their host a pleading glance.

Bacchus spoke loudly, "So, who follows the races?"

But Antipas was oblivious. "I am my nephew's salvation, you see," he said to Pilate. "Without me, he is nothing. You'd think he'd be more grateful, hmm?" He finally noticed Agrippa's glare. He thrust his cup toward Agrippa, jabbing with one thick finger. "You should be more grateful, boy!"

Heavy silence blanketed the courtyard.

Philip cleared his throat. He leaned on his cane as he rose from his couch. "I'm ready to retire. Perhaps my brother would care to join me?"

Grateful for Philip's tact, Chuza hurried to Antipas' side. "Come with me, my lord."

Antipas was too muddled to protest. With a heave, Chuza helped him stand and pulled his arm over his shoulder. Gritting his teeth under his master's weight, Chuza half-carried him up the stairs to the second level.

Antipas giggled as Chuza opened the door to his room. His body slave rushed to help Chuza lay him on the couch.

"You tell him, Chuza," Antipas slurred. "I used to drink my friends under the table and then go for a roaring ride." He aimed a finger in Chuza's general direction, his gaze unfocused. "Getting old is miserable. Don't do it, if you can help it."

Chuza made an uncommitted sound in his throat.

"Agrippa can get old though." Antipas' eyes drifted shut. "He can rot for all I care."

Shaking his head at Antipas, Philip sank onto his couch with a sigh.

Antipas was snoring before Chuza left the room.

Chuza leaned on the balcony railing and peered at the feast below. Bacchus had resurrected the conversation, but Agrippa sat like a statue.

Pilate was poised, contributing with eloquence. Chuza gripped the railing with white knuckles. Pilate may have been encouraging Antipas for his own amusement, but Antipas should have known better.

Antipas had ruled for more than thirty years. He could rule another thirty, but only if he stayed in favor with powerful men. Chuza sighed and made his way to his bed. There would be headaches and bruised egos to manage in the morning.

Chuza dreamed he was in a boat being tossed by the waves.

"Steward!" a voice hissed, and Chuza realized he was being shaken awake. He opened his gritty eyes. It was still dark.

"What is it?"

"Agrippa is preparing to leave," the servant said. "He is demanding his horse, but the grooms aren't sure if they should give it to him."

Chuza groaned. Whatever was going through Agrippa's head, the servants were pouring salt on his wounded pride.

The servant hesitated. "Perhaps you could sort it out?"

"Right." Chuza yawned hugely as he sat up. The floor was chilly under his feet and the other couches were mounded with sleeping figures. By the light of the servant's lamp, Chuza pulled on his outer robe and dragged his fingers through his hair.

The servant led him around the balcony. The courtyard below was dark, the air cold and still. It had to be an hour from dawn. Why was Agrippa trying to leave now?

Chuza followed the servant out of the house. It was so quiet he could hear the sea washing against the shore. A single lamp inside the stable cast a soft glow on the cobblestones.

Agrippa whirled around, his shoulders easing as he saw who had come.

"Chuza, make this man see sense," Agrippa said. "I simply want my horse."

Chuza turned to the head groom. "Prepare the horse. I will handle everything with Antipas."

The groom hurried into the stable.

Agrippa folded his arms across his chest. His voice was petulant. "Perhaps I should ask permission to leave with the clothes on my back."

"Antipas was drunk. He said things he didn't mean."

"Did he?" Agrippa's voice was razor thin.

Chuza cleared his throat. "Things will be better in the morning. Why not go back to bed?"

"If I stay, I will only be humiliated further." He peered at Chuza in the dim light. "You will smooth things over with Bacchus, won't you?"

Chuza was grateful that the shadows hid his frustrated expression. "Of course."

Perhaps this was for the best. With any luck, Agrippa's sudden departure would embarrass Antipas, and he would act better toward his nephew.

"I will send a guard with you," Chuza said. He turned to the servant, who hastened to fetch one of Antipas' men.

Agrippa clasped Chuza's hand. "Thank you for your help."

Chuza pressed his lips together. Agrippa lived far beyond his means, but he was still a man with feelings and a family.

Chuza nodded. "I will see you in Sepphoris."

"I can't stay in Sepphoris. Or Tiberias. I have to get as far away from Antipas as possible."

Chuza hesitated. "You can't return to Rome."

"I'll go to Syria. The new governor, Flaccus, is a friend, and my brother Aristobulus is there too. They will help me without shaming me further."

Before Chuza could formulate a reply, the groom led the horse out, saddled and ready. Agrippa took the reins.

Chuza gripped the bridle. "What about your wife? Your children?"

Agrippa stroked the horse's neck. "You're right. Cypros will want to go with me. I will stop and collect her and the children. But I will need carts for travel. Supplies. Guards. More money than I have on hand."

Chuza dragged a hand through his hair. Agrippa would ask for the moon next.

Agrippa seemed to sense his reluctance. "I'm going either way. Cypros will manage without me."

For Cypros' sake, Chuza needed to help him.

"Take whatever you need from Sepphoris to provide a safe and comfortable journey for your family. I will handle Antipas."

Agrippa clapped a hand on Chuza's shoulder. "You're a good man. I won't forget your help."

The guard arrived. Another horse was brought, and the men mounted and adjusted their robes. Chuza gripped his hands tightly behind his back and prayed he wasn't making a huge mistake.

He peered up at Agrippa. "Cypros is a capable woman. She could be your greatest ally, if you let her."

Agrippa grinned, his old humor returning. "I'll pass on your kind words." With a nod, Agrippa dug in his heels and the horses trotted away, hooves clattering on the cobblestones.

Chuza stood on the street and watched until Agrippa and his guard were out of sight. Antipas was finally free of Agrippa's presence, but Chuza feared it would come at a hefty price.

# TWENTY

Jovian hesitated outside the shop door and looked down at the spring blossoms. Did Persephone even like flowers?

Straightening his shoulders, he stepped into the shop and was bathed in the enticing aroma of exotic spices. Persephone's father was working near the back.

Jovian cleared his throat. "Good day, Horace."

Horace turned and saw the flowers. Jovian's neck heated.

Horace smiled in welcome. "I told you to call me Flavius." He shook his finger.

"Of course. Flavius." The name felt strange on his tongue. "Is Persephone home? I thought we would take a walk. It's a beautiful day." He gestured unnecessarily to the doorway where sunlight painted a glowing square on the tile floor.

"I'll fetch her for you." Horace disappeared through the back door.

Jovian rocked back and forth on his toes. He hid the flowers behind his back but then thought better of it. He hadn't seen Persephone since they signed the betrothal agreement, and that was three weeks ago. Work had kept him busy, but he had put off seeing her again, afraid it would be awkward. Now, awkwardness was all but guaranteed.

The minutes stretched, and Jovian began a slow circle of the room. A jar marked "cassia" caught his attention. He lifted the lid. The sweet and heady fragrance wafted to his nose, and Leah's face filled his mind. He clattered the lid back into place.

"Doing a little shopping?" Persephone's teasing voice made him spin around. She wore the lapis lazuli necklace and earrings he gave her at their betrothal, along with the gold ring that encircled her third finger.

Her gaze was drawn to the flowers, and he flushed again, holding them out.

"These are for you."

Persephone smiled, and the anxious knot in his chest loosened a fraction. Her eyes closed as she inhaled the bouquet, and her dark eyelashes fanned on her smooth skin.

She lifted her gaze to his. "Thank you."

His heart back-flipped.

Julia and one of the younger sisters approached wearing cloaks and curious expressions. Julia scrutinized his clothes, and he forced himself not to look down and check for stains on his front.

Persephone said, "Mama couldn't come, so she sent these two."

A captive audience to watch his every fumble. Wonderful.

Jovian gestured to the door. "Ready?"

Persephone nestled the bouquet in the crook of her arm and led the way with a contented smile. The girls followed, and Jovian glanced back at Horace, who nodded his approval.

The city felt drab after the sweet scents of the quiet shop, but Persephone took charge of their direction, strolling down the busy street and occasionally lifting the flowers to her nose. Her sisters kept right on her heels. He moved into position beside Persephone and glanced over his shoulder. Julia raised her eyebrows as if enjoying a private joke at his expense. He hastily faced front.

Persephone walked purposefully, and after a few turns down quieter streets, they arrived at a public garden. It was a green oasis amid the busyness of Antioch, with leafy trees, shrubs, and a huge, spraying fountain. Large cages held an assortment of colorful birds. Persephone approached them and exclaimed over the creatures with delight. Jovian studied the preening birds. They were pretty, but he would rather see them flying freely in the trees.

Persephone's sisters were distracted by the colorful feathers and playful antics. With a wink at Jovian, Persephone led him a few steps away, and they sat on the fountain's edge.

"Now we can talk," she said with a smile.

He cleared his throat, unsure of what to say. "How are you?" he asked, then immediately hated the mundane question.

"I've been busy. Mama and I have been finishing my marriage chest." A blush painted her soft skin like the sunrise on a sandy shore.

Jovian smoothed his tunic over his knee. "The carpenters have expanded my—our room. We will have a sitting room and bed-chamber."

Persephone brought the bouquet to her nose, and her fingers trembled. He berated himself for his insensitivity. They hadn't even touched, yet he spoke of sharing a room.

He hesitated only a moment before taking her hand. Her eyes flew to his, but she did not pull away. Her thumb brushed against his, and her eyes shone.

In five months she would be his wife. He needed to know more about her. "What do you enjoy doing at home? Do you like to weave?"

"I weave." Persephone wiggled her brows. "Though I wouldn't say I enjoy it. I like teaching my younger sisters to read."

They were soon deep in conversation, trying to see what histories and poems they both knew. Jovian's anxiety eased as they talked. If this was a peek into their future, he would be content.

Her sisters grew tired of watching the birds, and Persephone rose. The four of them wandered around the garden, but Jovian and Persephone struggled to converse with additional listening ears and the occasional whisper and peal of giggles in their wake. Jovian did not want to learn what was so funny.

Finally, Persephone turned back to the garden entrance and they rejoined the street.

They walked side by side as they passed a simple building and a harmony of voices spilled into the road. "... the Lord is one. You shall love the Lord your God with all your heart ..."

Jovian stumbled.

"Are you alright?" Persephone reached out to steady him.

He pulled a trembling hand through his hair. "I'm fine," he stammered. "I was just caught off guard." He gestured to the synagogue, his pulse racing. Memories of Calvary crawled up his spine and he shivered.

Persephone tilted her head to the side. "Is that Hebrew? It's so... guttural."

"This is one of the Jewish synagogues?" Julia's derisive tone brushed like brambles over Jovian's skin. She didn't understand. None of these sheltered girls could comprehend the complex political and religious world of Israel.

He faced the synagogue's doorway, his chest too tight.

With the rise and fall of the prayers, Israel returned to him—the sand on his lips, the smell of incense and sacrifices, good Galilean wine, unleavened bread, the tramp of his hobnailed sandals, the rolling gait of his horse, the thrilling call of the shofar, the murmur of thousands in prayer, the voice of a prophet speaking in the hills —

"Where are you going?"

He blinked and realized he had stepped up to the open door. The three girls stared as if he had lost his mind.

"Come on," he said, drunk on the past and desperate to be free from the questions that haunted him. For a reason he could not explain, he knew this synagogue held the answers.

Persephone paled. "We can't go in there! It's for their people."

"I've been in many synagogues." Chuza had led him into this world, translating Hebrew when needed, and explaining the stories.

Jovian took another step forward as Persephone hissed at him. "No!"

He barely heard her over the pounding of his pulse. He stepped inside, and the words of Torah rolled over his mind like waves, pounding on his soul. The entrance was at the back of the room, and he slipped in unnoticed. The girls followed him with hunched shoulders. They all slid onto a bench.

The reader switched to Greek. Jovian blinked, coming back to himself. His tunic clung between his shoulder blades and he shook as if he had not eaten in days. What was the matter with him?

Persephone whispered in his ear. "We should go."

Jovian hesitated. Whatever had pulled him through the door had dissipated. But if he wanted to learn how the Jews could call their God 'good', even after everything God had done to them, and everything he refused to do for them, the answers were here.

"Just wait," he muttered without looking at her.

She sat stiffly, crossing her arms and legs.

The rabbi came forward to give the lesson. He walked sprightly, though his beard was gray and deep crinkles surrounded his bright eyes. As he taught, he welcomed questions and carefully considered his answers.

Persephone fidgeted in her seat and her sisters whispered. Jovian's better sense commanded retreat, but the more the rabbi spoke so blithely about God's good plan for the Jews, the more Jovian wanted to lay Jesus' life at the rabbi's feet and show him that God did not care.

The lesson ended and the people sang a psalm. Jovian closed his eyes as the words ground into his wounded soul like salt. It was all lies. God was not a good shepherd, making them lie down in green pastures. He was as fickle and flawed as the gods Jovian grew up worshiping.

After a closing prayer, the congregation rose to go. Persephone jerked to her feet and then groaned as Jovian fixed his eyes on the rabbi and strode toward him.

The old rabbi blinked as a Greek man stormed down the aisle. He looked past Jovian and held up his hand. Jovian glanced to the side and realized half a dozen men had stepped forward, prepared to eject him from the building. He drew a breath, trying to calm himself.

"Shalom, Rabbi," Jovian said in Hebrew. It was little better than a growl, but the rabbi's eyebrows rose in surprise. He scanned Jovian from his short hair and beardless face to his sandals.

"Shalom," the rabbi replied at last. He continued in Greek. "How can I help you?"

"Did you hear what your God did in Jerusalem a year ago?"

The rabbi assessed him a second time. "We've heard rumors. You come from Jerusalem?"

Jovian lifted his chin. "My name is Jovian Titus. I recently returned from Judea. I became a God-fearer there."

The rabbi sat back down on the teacher's seat. "I see. Well, why don't you tell me what happened?"

Jovian's neck strained with the effort of holding back his emotions. This rabbi had nothing to do with what happened to Jesus, but Jovian's pain demanded a target. "I saw a prophet of the Lord handed over to the priests, who called him a blasphemer. They gave him to Pontius Pilate and pretended he was inciting the people to rebellion. The prophet was crucified."

The rabbi's brow furrowed, and he tilted his head. "If he was blaspheming, he couldn't be a prophet of the Lord."

It took everything in Jovian not to step closer and tower over the rabbi. Each word rasped like a blade. "The priests lied."

The rabbi crossed his arms, his expression darkening. "Why are you here, Jovian Titus?" He pronounced the name sharply, reminding Jovian of who he was and where he stood. "What do you want from me?"

All the air whooshed from Jovian's lungs, and he sagged. "I don't know," he admitted. "I just can't understand how God could possibly be good. Not after what I saw."

Embarrassment climbed up his neck like fire as the rabbi's suspicion turned to pity. This whole thing had been a mistake. He turned to leave.

"Wait," the rabbi said, and Jovian hesitated. The rabbi tugged on his beard, his gaze flickering over his congregants who hovered nearby, staring at the crazy Greek man who had invaded their synagogue. Jovian grimaced under their probing eyes and wished the roof would collapse and bury him.

The rabbi folded his hands in a way that reminded Jovian of Chuza. "Come back tomorrow."

Jovian stared at him in shock. "Really?"

"I will listen to your story tomorrow, but right now, I think your companions are waiting." He raised his brows and looked past Jovian.

Jovian winced. Persephone. He had completely forgotten about her. He peeked over his shoulder. Her arms were knotted across her chest and her eyes burned with anger. He would have a lot to explain.

"I will see you tomorrow, Rabbi," Jovian said, his voice subdued.

"My name is Rishon. I will look for you, Titus."

Jovian's shoulders tensed as he rejoined Persephone. Her nostrils flared, and her two sisters stared as if he had grown another head.

Jovian's cheeks burned. "Let's get you home."

They didn't need a second invitation.

Persephone walked in icy silence. She had misplaced her bouquet, perhaps on purpose. Guilt twined around his ribs, but he couldn't seem to apologize. He didn't know what had come over him, but something deep within insisted this was the right path. He needed answers if he was ever going to move past what had happened in Judea.

When they returned to the shop front, Persephone gestured for her sisters to enter, but she turned to face Jovian.

"What was that?" she demanded. She stared into his face, but he looked down at his hands, kneading his palm. "What were you thinking, taking us into a synagogue and then shouting at their teacher? How could you submit us to that kind of embarrassment?"

His shoulders hunched. "I couldn't help myself. The prayers grabbed hold of me, and I had to go in."

She studied him, her jaw working. "Do you believe in the Jewish God?"

The answer was complicated. "I did. Part of me still does. I've seen his power. But he is as heartless as the other gods. I don't know if I can worship him."

Persephone waved her hand. "Then don't. There are a dozen other gods you could choose." He hesitated, and she stepped closer. "Perhaps you should count yourself blessed. You saw the Jewish people for who they really are."

Jovian had seen the Jewish people. He had seen Chuza's loyalty, Joanna's faith, and Leah's fragile heart. He had seen the people celebrating harvests, breaking bread together, and mourning their dead. He had seen them working hard to provide for their families, determined to find peace while the world around them battled for power. He had seen them bowed in prayer, confident that God heard them.

Persephone would never understand. He still visited Judea in his dreams and walked the roads of Galilee, hearing the call of a murdered prophet.

He could not make her understand, so instead, he bowed his head. "I'm sorry. I won't do that to you again."

Her demeanor shifted, and she brushed his arm. "I'm not blind, you know. I can see that something happened to you in Judea. I thought perhaps you left a woman behind." Her lips curved. "Am I petty for being relieved that a god broke your heart, and not a woman?"

Jovian looked away, but she cupped his cheek and turned his face back to hers. "I just wish you'd share your pain with me, instead of pretending. We're going to be married. Your burdens are my burdens." Her hand slid down his arm to weave her fingers in his. Her warm hand was comforting, and Jovian leaned toward her.

She whispered, "You can put it all behind you. I will help."

Guilt dug under his ribs. What she offered was impossible.

"Thank you." He gave her what he hoped was a passable smile. She smiled in return, and he stepped away. Her hand stayed in his until he turned and strode down the street.

He would return to the synagogue tomorrow. He needed answers.

# TWENTY-ONE

Joanna kissed Nadia's soft hair as she approached the disciples' house. The four-month-old was wide awake in her sling, her large round eyes taking in the usual bustle in the courtyard.

Joanna passed Stephen on his way out. "Where are you off to?"

"A synagogue," he said, grinning. "I've been debating with some Hellenistic Jews. I'm trying to show how the scriptures foretold the suffering Messiah."

Joanna chuckled. "You seem eager for an argument."

"I'm always up for a good debate." He clapped his hands and rubbed them together. "Rachel is here, if you'd like to say hello." He gestured with his chin toward a group of chatting women.

Joanna liked Stephen's wife, who was always ready to offer encouragement or advice as needed. Stephen strode jauntily into the city.

Joanna made her way to the women sorting through articles of clothing. She stopped to squeeze Rachel's shoulder in greeting, and laughed at Rachel's daughter who was dressed up in a man's too-large robe and showy turban.

"Ah, good." Maryam beckoned to Joanna. "We received a donation of used clothing from a new believer. He has a booth in the market. You can help sort out what needs repair."

Joanna picked up a tunic in a sickly shade of green. "Was this what he couldn't sell?"

Maryam made a face and snatched the tunic back. "The poor will be grateful." She held up the ugly tunic and shook her head. "Though this might serve better as rags." They all laughed.

Joanna helped the women examine the clothing and set aside anything that needed mending. The clothing was a generous gift. Despite the apostles' flogging, their numbers had increased. Even some of the priests had come to believe in Jesus. Nadia squirmed, growing restless, and Joanna patted her back with one hand as she sorted with the other.

Joanna turned at a tap on her shoulder, and smiled at Ananias. Though he shared a name with the man who lied to Peter, Ananias of Damascus was a devoted follower of Jesus.

"Can you help us for a few minutes?" he asked. "We have a new believer here with his wife. I think she'd feel more at ease with a woman present."

Joanna's chest warmed. "Of course."

Ananias led the way over to a middle-aged couple. The woman seemed nervous, but when she saw Nadia, she relaxed and reached out to brush Nadia's cheek. Joanna smiled to herself. The infant was already part of The Way, creating connection between strangers with her bright eyes, rosy cheeks, and sweet smile.

"Shalom," Joanna said. "I hear you want to learn about Jesus."

Joanna returned home as the sun dipped low, invigorated by her day. There was always so much to do and shared history to discuss. Their three years with Jesus were relived again and again, the parables retold and explained until even the children understood. Joanna learned about moments she had missed and shared stories that others had not heard. For the first time in her life, Joanna knew she was exactly where God wanted her to be.

She let herself into the house. "I'm home!"

"It's nearly time for supper," Leah called from the courtyard.

Joanna strode in and grinned as Little Mary ran up, bouncing on her toes to see Nadia.

"Hold on and I'll untie her." Joanna loosened the sling and felt the loss of warmth as she freed Nadia from her cozy nest. The front of Joanna's tunic was damp.

"Hmm," Joanna said. "Nadia needs to be changed." She grinned at her little niece. "You can handle that, can't you?"

"Ewww, no!" Mary squealed and plugged her nose. But the little girl did not leave Joanna's side as she unwound the thick wool and linen padding on the baby's bottom. Joanna added the soggy cloth to the laundry pile. She sighed at her evening chore. The amount of soiled laundry one baby created was staggering.

The courtyard was bathed with sunshine, so Joanna laid out a blanket and let the baby stretch her arms and legs. Mary dangled a toy over Nadia's face, and Nadia made clumsy attempts to grab it.

Dalia rose from her loom with a hand pressed against her middle. She was pregnant again. Another child to join the family and bring more happiness to their lives.

Leah brought the food to the table and the family emerged from all over the house. Joanna sat Nadia on her lap, and the child reached at everything and everyone.

The meal was nearly over when a cheerful voice called out. "Save any for me?"

Chuza strode into the courtyard, his traveling bag slung over his dusty clothes.

Joanna rushed to him, holding Nadia in one arm. His strong arms came around them both. The little girl beamed at her papa, and Chuza stared.

"How did she grow so much?" His brow puckered as if he was torn between delight and pain.

Joanna's chest twinged. Chuza had been gone a month, and Nadia was growing in leaps and bounds. She tipped Nadia into Chuza's arms and prayed the baby would not be shy.

"We missed you," Joanna said. "How did it go with Antipas?"

Chuza made a wry face as he bounced Nadia. "He's settled in Sepphoris for the summer, but in a few weeks I need to go to Tiberias and check on the new mayor."

"New mayor? What happened to Agrippa?"

Chuza sighed. "That's a long story. One that can wait until after I've eaten, if you don't mind."

Joanna took Nadia back so Chuza could wash. As he sat at the table, the rest of the family called out greetings. Alexander asked for news, and Leah slid the food closer. While Chuza talked and ate, he wrapped an arm around Joanna's shoulders.

Joanna sighed with happiness. If only every day was like this.

Chuza woke early, surprised by the dusty scent of hay and warm animals. He blinked in the dimness, disorientated for a moment before he remembered where he was. Home. Warmth spread through his chest and he rolled on his side. Joanna was asleep with her arm curled around Nadia. He lay still, taking in the precious sight.

As the room brightened, Nadia wiggled and woke, letting out a short, demanding cry. Joanna's eyes fluttered open, and she adjusted her tunic and brought Nadia close to nurse. She looked at him, her lips and eyes soft with sleep.

He lifted himself on one elbow and leaned forward to kiss Joanna's forehead.

"Want to come with me to the disciple's house today?" Joanna asked.

He trailed his hand down her hair. "Sure. But first, I want time with just my girls."

Joanna smiled, and Chuza rose, eager to see Leah.

The morning passed swiftly. Chuza held Nadia as much as the baby would permit, trying to make up for the time they had lost.

After a midday meal, they prepared to visit the disciples. Joanna tied Nadia into her sling and Leah gathered up a basket of bread she had baked to share.

They walked side-by-side, and Chuza surveyed his little family proudly. Everything was perfect.

Leah tugged his sleeve. "What's that sound?"

They all stopped. Chuza strained his ears. A man—no, many men were shouting. His muscles tensed with foreboding. He strode toward the sound, his steps lengthening until they emerged on the main road beneath the temple mount.

A mass of angry men dragged a lone figure down the temple steps. He tried to speak to his captors, but their shouts drowned him out.

A Roman soldier stepped toward the mob and pulled his sword free from its scabbard. "What's going on here?"

"This is Sanhedrin business," one man sneered. "He is a blasphemer and this stoning is sanctioned by the high priests."

Joanna gripped Chuza's arm. "Did they say stoning?"

The soldier eyed the angry mob and weighed his options. Chuza held his breath, hoping the soldier would put an end to whatever this was.

But the soldier stepped back. "Outside the city," he commanded. "And I will be informing the governor."

The men ignored him, intent on their business. As they pushed forward, their victim tossed his head and revealed his face.

Chuza's blood turned to ice in his veins.

"Stephen!" Joanna cried out.

Hearing her voice above the crowd, Stephen turned, and he and Chuza locked eyes before he was jostled away.

Joanna and Chuza stepped forward together, meaning to follow, but at the same moment, they looked down at the baby bound to Joanna's chest.

"Go home," Chuza said firmly.

Joanna pressed her lips together. "We'll tell the others." She gripped his hand, her heart in her eyes. "Be careful."

Leah was frozen in shock, but Joanna pulled her away from the street.

Chuza hurried after the mob, his mind racing with his pulse. What was he supposed to do?

The guards at the gate eyed the angry crowd, but they let them leave, happy to have the trouble move outside the city walls. By the time Chuza followed the mob into the open, they had formed a circle. Stephen was flung to the ground, and he landed with a grunt. The men picked up rocks.

Chuza's panic spiked. "No!"

Before he knew what he was doing, he lunged at the nearest man's back. An elbow struck Chuza's lip. He stumbled backward, tasting blood. Chuza gathered himself to try again, but a powerful arm caught him around his throat, pulling him several steps backward. Fear punched his gut as he scrambled to get his feet under him.

A grim voice spoke in his ear. "Unless you wish to join your friend, I'd step back."

Chuza gripped the man's steely arm with both hands, trying to break free. The guard squeezed tighter, cutting off Chuza's air.

"Think, man!" his captor hissed. "If you defend a blasphemer, they'll stone you too."

"But it's not right." Chuza gasped as his pulse hammered in his ears. "You can stop them. Please!"

Through the circle of men, Chuza saw a rock soar through the air. It struck Stephen's chest and the disciple jerked with pain.

Chuza twisted, but he could not get free. Darkness pressed on the corners of his vision and his legs wobbled.

As the executioners drew bravado from one another, they hurled larger rocks. Panting, they stripped off their coats, tossing them toward a small man with a Pharisee's shawl draped around his neck.

Time seemed to slow as rock after rock flew through the air, spiraling with deadly force. All Chuza could do was fight for air while the city guard gripped his throat like a vise.

Stephen hunched under the rain of stones. Blood seeped from his cheek, his arm, and his neck. He clutched his ribs as dust coated his face. A rock knocked him onto his side. With effort, he dragged himself to his knees.

Tears burned in Chuza's throat as he realized Stephen had accepted his fate.

"No," Chuza croaked, tears streaming down his face to dampen the arm that held him captive.

"Lord Jesus, take my life," Stephen cried out. He held his arms wide. "Lord, forgive them for this sin."

A large rock struck him in the head with a sickening crunch, spraying blood. Stephen collapsed to the ground.

Chuza stared, unable to comprehend.

Blood spread in a pool, staining the sandy soil.

Silence fell. The executioners stood with heaving chests, sweat dripping from their brows and soaking through their tunics. They drifted away, not looking at each other.

The Pharisee watching the coats slowly turned his head until his piercing pale eyes locked with Chuza's.

Chuza's pulse skipped a beat. Who was this man?

The guard finally released him. Chuza stumbled forward, tripping over rocks stained with Stephen's blood. Questions stabbed at his mind. Why had this happened? Why hadn't God intervened? Helplessness pulled Chuza to his knees next to Stephen's body.

The scrabble of footsteps made Chuza whirl around. Joses came forward, along with some of the other young men.

Chuza stood, shame filling him like poison. He was safe, and a good man was dead at his feet.

Joses' eyes were full of tears. "Joanna said there was trouble, but we hoped…"

He had to make them understand. Chuza gripped Joses' sleeve so tight his knuckles protested. "I couldn't stop them."

There was no blame in Joses' eyes. "I know. There was nothing you could do."

His words were both a balm and a burning coal.

The men shifted rocks off Stephen's body, the stones clattering in the silence.

A man swung off his cloak and they knelt to roll Stephen's body onto the cloth. Stephen's head lolled as his eyes stared into the world beyond.

The city guard joined them, gripping his spear. "Will you bury the body, or do I need to have my men do it?"

Chuza's chest burned. "We'll do it."

Joses sighed heavily. "I'll get his wife."

While Joses went back into the city, Chuza helped the young men carry Stephen's body to the nearest graveyard. Lines of raised soil marked the graves of the poor in silent rows.

The gravediggers sat under a canopy, and one slowly rose from his stool.

"This way," he said. He led them to a long, open trench, six feet deep, but tapered at the end so they could walk in. Rocks and dirt were piled to the side.

They waited until Rachel came from the city with her two young children. Tears streaked her dusty cheeks as she knelt beside her husband's body and tenderly uncovered his face. She leaned forward to kiss his brow, lingering for a long moment as she trembled.

Chuza wiped his face on his sleeve.

While Stephen's family looked on, the men carefully placed his body in the trench.

Joses prayed aloud, though Chuza hardly heard him. His throat burned as if he had swallowed a blade. Stephen was leaving behind a wife. Children.

At last, Joses picked up a stone. He placed it gently on Stephen's body. The men worked together to cover Stephen, but each stone was baptized with tears and sorrow instead of hate.

Chuza blinked rapidly as he set the last rock down. "Until you rise again, brother."

They stood back, and the gravedigger picked up his shovel. As he pushed the dirt back over the grave, Rachel let out a keening wail that pierced Chuza's soul.

Who else would lie beside Stephen before Jesus returned? The Sanhedrin might hesitate to kill the twelve, but Stephen had not escaped the priests' wrath.

"There was a Pharisee," Chuza told the others. "I didn't recognize him." The memory of the man's approving nod was like vinegar in his stomach. He met Joses' eyes as Rachel's lament echoed over the hills. "We may have a new enemy."

# TWENTY-TWO

Chuza slowed his pace as he entered the Upper City. Stephen's death would shock the believers, but Chuza had to know if they were all in danger.

He had to speak to Omri.

The Herodian party leader lived in a lavish house only a few streets from the palace. The most direct path would take Chuza past Caiaphas' house. Chuza took a longer route, and it was dark by the time he stood at Omri's gate.

He rapped on the door.

After a long moment, a servant pulled it open. "Yes?"

"Tell your master that Chuza, Herod's steward, wishes to speak to him." He used Antipas' official name for emphasis.

The servant opened the door wider. "Very well. You may wait in the courtyard."

Chuza stepped in, and the gate shut solidly behind him. The servant walked away, his feet whispering on the stone path. Lamps cast amber circles on the ground.

Chuza looked down at his hands. A smear of Stephen's blood

marred his finger. He froze, staring at it. He was unclean.

The law said Chuza must wash and avoid touching others for a week. He must be sprinkled for purification by a priest before he could enter the temple complex. A dark laugh bubbled up his throat. Those who were supposed to purify were soaked in the blood of innocent men.

As the servant returned, Chuza put his hands behind his back.

"My master will see you now." He led Chuza to a waiting basin.

"I will wash my own feet, thank you," Chuza said.

The servant's eyebrows rose, but he said nothing as Chuza slipped his sandals off and washed his dusty feet. He made sure he cleaned his hand as well.

When he was done, the servant led him into the house. Thick mats softened the floor, and lamps hung behind ornate screens, splaying delicate patterns over the plastered walls. The house smelled like a meal had recently been served.

The servant showed him into another room, modeled after a Roman triclinium. Omri was eating with his household, and a dozen eyes turned as Chuza entered.

"Welcome, my friend." Omri rose and beckoned. "Come and eat with us."

Chuza flushed. "I can't. I've just come from a funeral."

Omri glanced at his wife, and then inclined his head. "I see. Then perhaps we can talk in my office?"

He led the way deeper into the house and they entered a small room full of color and ornamentation. Chuza wondered how Omri could concentrate in such a space.

Omri sat in a cushioned seat, but Chuza stood, worried he would offend his host by sitting when he was ritually impure.

Omri leaned back in his chair, his expression sympathetic. "Who died?"

Chuza swallowed hard. "A friend. A follower of The Way."

Understanding dawned on Omri's face, and he rested his elbows on his chair arms, tenting his fingers. "I heard about that."

"Do you approve?" Chuza asked before he could stop his tongue. He clenched his hands, willing himself under control.

Omri wobbled his head back and forth. "The Way is of little threat to our party. If they would just hold back from blasphemous claims about a mortal man being something akin to—" his lip twisted sardonically "—divine, the priests would probably not care either." His expression softened. "I must admit, I was a little surprised they stoned him."

"Brutally."

Omri winced. "And this man was your friend?" His gaze roved over Chuza. "Is that a wise choice for... Herod's steward?"

Chuza ignored the question. "There was a Pharisee overseeing the execution. He was in his early thirties, perhaps, small in stature, with pale eyes and thick eyebrows."

Omri leaned back. "Ah, yes. Gamaliel's pupil. I believe he was just ordained as a full Pharisee. His knowledge of the Law is quite impressive."

Chuza stiffened. Gamaliel was the grandson of the famous Gamaliel, a man of great wisdom and discernment, whose teachings were carefully recorded and taught. This Pharisee would have powerful friends.

Chuza said, "What do you know about him?"

"Not much. He was born in Tarsus but moved to Jerusalem as a boy. He's a Roman citizen, apparently." Chuza's eyebrows rose, and Omri held up a finger. "Don't let that sway your opinion. He is more committed to Torah than many born within this city."

Chuza nodded grimly. "He would not pick up a stone himself, though he clearly approved."

"Probably keeping himself pure so he could return to the temple."

Chuza pressed his lips together to smother a bitter comment.

"His name is Saul." Omri tipped his head to the side. "If you meet him, I would avoid mentioning you are friends with those who follow The Way."

Or mentioning that he was a follower himself.

Chuza inclined his head. "I will not keep you from your meal."

Omri rose, and Chuza turned to go.

"I am sorry for your friend. It's a terrible way to die."

Images of Jesus' mangled body flared in Chuza's mind. "There are worse."

Chuza waited in the hushed courtyard while the other disciples went about their chores in a subdued manner. Leah shaped loaves of bread near the oven. He wished she and Joanna had stayed at home, but they insisted they needed to be here with the others.

Chuza plucked at his robe. He had washed his clothes and his whole body as was ordered by Torah, but the idea of kneeling at the temple gate for a priest to sprinkle him with holy water turned his stomach. He needed to ask Peter if that was still required. So much about his faith was changing in light of Jesus' death and resurrection. Sacrifices, ritual cleanliness, the role of the priests—all had shifted. It was disorienting, but at least he wasn't facing it alone.

"Chuza?" Matthew beckoned from the upper room.

Chuza climbed the steps with heavy legs.

The twelve sat around a table. Matthew gestured for Chuza to join them.

"What have you learned?" Peter asked.

Chuza told them what he had heard from Omri. James and John shared glances, though they did not look afraid.

Chuza drew a deep breath. "It sounds like this man is zealous. If we continue as we are, Stephen won't be the last to die."

"We must be shrewd," Peter said, and looked at his brother, Andrew. "We should spread ourselves around the city. We can meet in various houses instead of gathering together here, a place that has become well known."

"Won't that still be risky?" Thomas leaned forward. "Perhaps it's time to leave Jerusalem."

Peter hesitated. "I don't wish to go where we haven't been sent."

The others agreed, but Chuza hoped the Spirit would send them soon—before it was too late.

"We grieve for our brother Stephen," Peter spoke to the group. "But take comfort. He died full of faith and in the Spirit. He is with Jesus now. There are still many in Jerusalem who need the good news. We can't abandon them because we are afraid of mere men."

Mere men who could imprison them, whip them, and stone them.

Peter smiled at Chuza in encouragement. "Do not fear this Saul. He can't stand against Jesus."

Chuza nodded with his hands gripped in his lap.

Joanna hitched Nadia on her hip as she wove through the eerily empty courtyard. The long tables were wiped clean. All personal belongings had vanished, and the oven was cold.

She climbed the steps to the upper room, trailing her hand on the wall. She had raced up these steps to declare Jesus' resurrection. This was where Joses broke the news that Stephen was dead. Rachel's wail had echoed down the street.

Joanna shivered as she stepped into the upper room. She closed her eyes and let her imagination roll back to the day of Pentecost. Her arm lifted to the sky as she remembered the tongue of fire resting upon her. She had declared the glory of God in a language she never spoke before.

She let her arm drop and opened her eyes. She had witnessed countless heavenly miracles, yet the priests still held the power on earth.

Joanna kissed Nadia's head as a tear tracked down her cheek. Peter said they would gather in homes throughout Jerusalem. The good news could not be stopped.

Joanna straightened her shoulders and stepped back outside, latching the door behind her.

Chuza waited at the foot of the stairs. He took her hand, and they joined Leah. The young woman's face was pinched with stress. They walked home, none of them speaking.

They arrived at the house, and Joanna ushered Leah inside. She turned to Chuza. "You want us to leave Jerusalem, don't you?"

Chuza shifted his feet. "It's not safe here."

Frustration rose up her throat. "But this is our home. We can't leave my family and flee for safety. They are believers now, too."

Chuza took her hand. "They aren't as well-known as you. You've spoken in the temple courts. Witnessed to dozens and dozens of believers. You've been seen with the twelve since the first day. You are a target."

Joanna stiffened. Was that true? She gave her head a shake. "You are Antipas' steward. You can protect us."

Chuza looked pained. "I can only do so much."

Joanna shifted at that uncomfortable thought and rested her palm on the mezuzah fastened to the door frame. Everything felt uncertain, but surely they just needed to trust in God.

She prayed aloud, "God, protect this house and all who dwell within."

Chuza set his hand on the opposite doorpost. "Amen."

# TWENTY-THREE

Leah wrapped the warm bread in a cloth and nestled it in her basket. She glanced furtively around the vacant courtyard and hurried up the stairs to the empty sleeping room. Snatching her yellow palla off the hook, she tossed it around her head and shoulders as she jogged back down the steps and into the courtyard. She drew up short as she found Joanna examining the basket.

"What's this?" Joanna crossed her arms.

Leah slid past her adoptive mother and gripped the basket handle. "I thought you were lying down with Nadia."

"I came down for a drink of water." Joanna scanned the empty courtyard. "Where is everyone?"

"The market." Leah's cheeks heated under Joanna's gaze.

Joanna rubbed her forehead and sighed. "You were going into the city alone? After what happened to Stephen?"

Fear flickered in Leah's chest, but she lifted her chin to meet Joanna's eyes. "We can't just hide away."

"I agree," Joanna said, and Leah's lips softened in surprise. "But we must be wise. If something happened to you, no one would know where to look."

Leah hooked the basket on her arm and prayed Joanna would not forbid her to go. "You'd have a good guess." There were few people she visited, and Keturah and her two little boys were at the top of the list.

"You can't go alone, but I will go with you."

"And who will we tell?" Leah asked sarcastically, unable to help herself. "Balaam?"

"Just let me get Nadia, alright?"

Leah tried to hide her relief. If Keturah didn't need her, she wouldn't even consider going into the city alone.

Joanna returned a few minutes later with Nadia in her sling and a wax tablet in her hand. She propped it on the table.

Leah squinted and sounded out the words. "Gone to Keturah's. Be back soon." She glanced at Joanna. "Hmm. Why didn't I think of leaving a note?"

"Because your writing is illegible," Joanna said dryly.

Leah shrugged. She read well enough for simple lists or to decipher a recipe.

The women let themselves out of the house and walked toward the Lower City. Despite her bravado earlier, Leah stuck close by Joanna's side.

They entered the narrow streets where the crowded houses captured the mingled scents of cooking and refuse. It was a path Leah had trod many times before, but something felt different.

"It's quiet for this time of day," Joanna said.

She was right. Usually, there were children playing in the streets. A knot of men walked with their eyes cast down, their pace clipped.

Leah shivered as a tingle ran down her spine. Maybe this was a mistake. She opened her mouth to suggest they turn back just as Joanna rounded the corner and jerked to a stop.

A pair of temple guards stood at the end of the street, their spear tips glinting in the sunlight. They flanked the doorway of a simple house.

"What are they doing here?" Leah whispered.

A man was pushed from his house. His hair and beard were mostly silver. He looked at the armed guards without fear and Leah blinked, recognizing him. He had been friends with Stephen.

"Oh no," Joanna groaned.

As Leah and Joanna stepped backward, half-hiding behind a house, guards dragged two more men and a handful of women into the street. One woman was crying, and her tears stabbed at Leah's heart. A neighbor stuck her head out the door to see what was going on, then jerked back inside.

The believers were bound with chains as a man strode from the house, his hands gripped behind his back. His thick eyebrows tilted fiercely over pale eyes. He joined the guards and they led their prisoners away.

Joanna leaned against the house, her eyes wide. "They're arresting believers in their homes?"

Leah ached to go back, but her basket hung heavily on her arm. Keturah needed this food.

The two women hastened down the street, the basket banging on Leah's hip. She jerked in alarm as a man ran past, and her head swiveled in fear.

Joanna shot her a glance. "You're going to draw attention. Relax."

The next few minutes felt like hours. They arrived at Keturah's apartment and Leah knocked once before pushing the door open and rushing inside. Joanna shut the door behind them and Leah sagged with relief.

"Leah!" Keturah rose from where she played with her sons. "And Joanna! How wonderful you both came."

Leah bolted the door, and Keturah stiffened. "What's going on?"

"Have you heard about Stephen?" Joanna asked, and stepped to peer out the window.

Keturah's gaze flitted between Joanna and Leah. "No." Her thin arms wrapped around her middle. "What happened?"

Joanna pulled the curtain closed. "The priests killed him for declaring that Jesus is the Son of God."

Keturah gasped, and her hand covered her mouth as tears pooled in her eyes. She turned to stare at her youngest child, the baby Stephen healed.

Joanna held Nadia closer. "We just passed a house where more believers were arrested."

All three women refused to say what this might mean. Imprisonment. Flogging. Perhaps even death.

Leah set her basket on the table. Jed ran to it, eager to see what special treats she had brought.

Keturah stood stiffly, watching him. "What happens to The Way?" Her anxious eyes turned to Leah. "What happens to those who need help, or healing?"

Leah took Keturah's hand and squeezed it. "We'll make sure you and your boys are alright. Perhaps you should come back with us."

Joanna nodded. "Yes, come stay with us."

Keturah's cheeks grew pink as she looked at Joanna. "I'm just a poor widow with young children. No one will care what I believe."

What she didn't say echoed in the room and sent a shiver down Leah's spine. Joanna was well-known among the apostles. She could be a target.

Keturah gestured at her sons. "I can't put them in danger."

Nadia stirred and let out a hungry cry. Joanna smiled despite her uncertain eyes.

"I'm sorry, Keturah. We came to bring help, not fear." Joanna sat beside Keturah's younger son and adjusted the sling to bring Nadia to her breast. Keturah's baby scooted closer, reaching a pudgy hand toward Nadia.

Joanna grinned at Keturah. "I can't wait until our babies can play together." She picked up one of the small toy animals, making animal sounds at Keturah's baby until he laughed.

The innocent sound broke the spell of fear that filled the house. Keturah sat beside Joanna and asked how Nadia was doing.

Glancing back at the bolted door, Leah sat down as well. Jed finished his sweetbread and plopped into her lap. She picked up a wooden sheep and wiggled it in his face. "Moooo!"

The boy collapsed in a fit of giggles at her joke.

Keturah touched Leah's arm. "I'll understand if you can't come again." Her eyes shimmered with unshed tears. "You have done so much for me, but you can't put yourself in danger. I will find another way." The flicker in her eyes belied her confident words.

Her anxiety bolstered Leah's bravery. "Don't give up on me yet."

Joanna nodded. "Jesus warned us we would be persecuted. This is not a surprise to God. He has everything in hand."

Keturah looked between the two women in confusion. "If you knew this would happen, why join The Way?"

Joanna chuckled. "It wasn't The Way then, it was just Jesus. I was following the one who healed me and changed my life."

"You were healed?" Keturah looked at Joanna with wide eyes. She shot Leah a chastising glance. "You never told me that."

Joanna grinned at Leah. "Really? I thought you'd love to tell how you helped smuggle me out of the palace."

Leah made a face.

Joanna switched Nadia to her other breast and told the widow about her first time meeting Jesus. She made it sound exciting, but Leah remembered the months leading up to that miraculous encounter. She would never forget how thin and pale Joanna became, wasting away before her eyes. Leah had been petrified Joanna would die and she would be alone again. Leah picked at a loose thread in her palla. Stephen's death was a stark reminder that she might have a family now, but they could be taken away in a heartbeat.

Joanna stood, and Leah lurched back to the present.

"We should head home," Joanna said. "But we will come again soon."

The two women walked quickly through Jerusalem, straining their ears for any hint of trouble. Leah could not draw a full breath until they were back at Dalia's house, the door latched securely.

Joanna set her palm on the closed door and they locked eyes. "You must never go into the city alone, do you hear me?"

Leah nodded, swallowing hard.

Sunset descended on Jerusalem and bathed the courtyard in shades of pink. Leah carried a tray of bread, hummus, and olives into the courtyard. It had been three days since her visit to Keturah. Three days of Saul going door to door, arresting anyone who followed The Way. Three days of battling the anxious fear that wound around her ribs, making it hard to breathe.

Maybe, finally, her family would do something about it.

The adults were gathered around the table, and they watched silently as she set down the tray and placed each item with unnecessary care.

Joanna patted the place next to her. Leah sat, and Alexander looked around the table.

"There were five more arrests today," he said.

Leah's stomach flipped. Who else had been taken?

Patara pulled her shawl closer around her shoulders. "What do we do?"

"We should go," Leah blurted, and her cheeks blazed as everyone looked her way. She picked at a crack in the tabletop. "I just want to feel safe again."

Chuza winced.

Joanna glanced around at the others. "The twelve haven't said anything about leaving Jerusalem."

Frustration brushed across Chuza's features before he smoothed it away. Leah's anxiety eased. If Chuza was on her side, he could convince the others it was time to escape the city.

Alexander glanced at his father. "Our home is here. Our business. I don't want to leave unless it's absolutely necessary."

Alexander's parents bobbed their heads and glanced around at their beautiful home. But a house was just a house, and it would be an empty one if they were all arrested.

Chuza cleared his throat. "I know someone who can tell us what Saul is planning. Let me arrange a meeting, and then we can decide what to do."

He glanced at Joanna, who twisted her fingers in her belt, uncertainty playing across her features. She might be hesitant to leave Jerusalem and her new life among The Way, but Leah couldn't get out of the city fast enough.

# TWENTY-FOUR

J ovian strode through his front courtyard and into the empty street.
The sun was barely over the horizon, the air cool and fresh. There
was plenty of time before he was due at the warehouse. He extended
his stride as a tickle of guilt climbed the back of his neck. He hadn't
told anyone about these visits. Not his parents, not his betrothed.

Jovian wove down the familiar streets as the city awakened. He
dodged around a slow-moving family and slipped through the open
synagogue door. A dozen men prayed, and Jovian slid onto the back
bench. His right leg jiggled as he waited.

The prayers ended and he forced himself to wait as the Jewish
men chatted. Finally, they filed out the door on their way to work,
eyeing him as they passed. When only Rishon remained, Jovian leaped
to his feet and strode forward.

"Shalom, Jovian." Rishon's movements were deliberate and un-
hurried as he dusted the altar at the front of the synagogue. "So, you
have come yet again."

"I have more questions."

"Mmm." Rishon studied Jovian for a moment. "Why don't you

let me ask the questions this time?"

Jovian opened and closed his mouth, his brow furrowed. Was Rishon teasing him? He was no rabbi. "What questions could I possibly answer?"

"What you hope to achieve by coming here, for a start."

Jovian flushed. "Do I annoy you?"

"Surprisingly, no." Rishon chuckled. "But every week, you demand to know why God does what he does. Why do you think I hold the answers?"

Jovian gestured to the altar. It was empty now, but Rishon had opened the scrolls for him many times. "Because you know the scriptures."

Rishon turned to wipe the long benches. "And what are the scriptures?"

Jovian crossed his arms. Was this a test? "They are the Jewish sacred writings. Your laws, histories, books of wisdom, and poetry. Your prophecies."

"So they are not God," Rishon said, still dusting.

"No, of course not."

"So God is outside these scrolls, bigger than the ink and papyrus."

"Of course."

Rishon looked him in the eye. "Then why do you restrain yourself to scrolls?"

Jovian furrowed his brow. "What do you mean?"

Rishon sighed and sat down, facing Jovian. "The scriptures are a guide, the tales of travelers who have gone before, seeking God. They show our people's wrestling to understand how God works in a world that is harsh and unyielding." He studied his hands, all knobby knuckles and wrinkles. "Sickness and death come for both Jew and the Gentile. Injustice runs riot."

Rishon gestured to the cabinet where the scrolls were stored. "The scriptures were not written to answer your personal questions like some sort of oracle. Those scrolls give wisdom and discernment so that when God speaks, you can hear."

Jovian sat down. "You mean through prayer."

"Prayer, yes." Rishon folded the dustcloth and set it beside him on the bench. "But also in the laughter of a child, an act of kindness, or the sound of wind in a grove of trees. The sun rising every day without fail. A fresh fig. Love between a husband and wife. The birth of a child. The bond of family."

Rishon leaned toward Jovian. "You come day after day, asking how I can call God good. How I consider him to be omnipresent, just, and loving when you have looked around at the fallen creation and see suffering and pain."

"But there is suffering and pain," Jovian insisted. "What reward is there in following—"

"Reward?" Rishon tilted his head to the side.

Jovian shifted, uncomfortable. "We worship gods so they will give us what we need. Food. Victory. Protection. Answers."

"Yes, that is a common thought, and unfortunately, not just among the Gentiles." Rishon's expression grew sad. "Are we insects before God, something he will trample if we do not remind him we are here? Or beggars, pleading with God to take mercy on us? Or tradesmen, exchanging worship for earthly blessings or eternal life?"

Jovian dragged his hand through his hair. "But isn't that the point? Eternal life?"

"Is it?" Rishon asked mildly.

The man was infuriating. Jovian crossed his arms over his chest. "I don't understand."

Rishon set his palms on his knees and leaned forward. "Let me put it another way. Are God's laws a test? Are the sacrifices and prayers how we appease God's wrath when we fail that test?"

"What else could they be?"

"Perhaps they are less about what God demands from us, and more about what God wants *for* us. You have seen the horrors man works upon man. God does not want that."

Jovian tensed, pushing away painful memories. "So we worship

God because…?"

"Because it is for our good. He is God, creator of heaven and earth. Worship is our natural state." He faced the front of the synagogue. "I am a mere man. By worshiping God I become part of something greater than myself, participating in a purpose that goes beyond my own life."

Jovian felt stupid. He had spent years in Israel, learning from Chuza and sitting in the synagogues. How could he not understand?

"What purpose?"

"To show God to the world." Rishon smiled so broadly that Jovian was jealous of his confidence. "God appointed the children of Abraham to show the world the nature of God. Love, mercy, justice." Rishon's smile faded. "We fail miserably, mind you. God had to correct us more than once, and show us the error of following our own selfish ways. As our morals declined, our governments were corrupted, our society collapsed, and we were defeated and taken into exile. Yet, each and every time, God allowed us to begin again."

Jovian worked the words around his mouth before speaking. "So that's the point of life? Show God's image to the world?"

"You're catching on, my Greek friend."

Rishon made it seem so simple, even if it felt almost impossible to achieve.

But if anyone had presented God's image to the world, it was Jesus. His love for the downtrodden, his call to put aside selfishness for the sake of others, his power to heal. But when God's image burst upon mankind, they had beaten it to death.

Jovian rubbed his forehead. Rishon hadn't answered all his questions, but the rabbi had given him something to think about.

Rishon stood and picked up his broom. Realizing the time, Jovian jerked to his feet.

"Thank you, Rabbi." Jovian inclined his head. He turned to go, but then hesitated. "Would it be alright if I came back on the Sabbath?" Rishon raised his bushy eyebrows, and Jovian flushed. "To participate this time."

Rishon nodded. "I will see you then."

Jovian dashed through the streets, feeling more at peace with God than he had in months.

He skidded to a stop outside the warehouse door and smoothed his hair before stepping inside. His father and Sergio were just coming down from the upstairs office, carrying their wax tablets.

"Ah, Jovian," Belen said. "Shall we begin?"

The three men spent the next few hours assessing their stock, preparing orders for Bato to deliver, and discussing what would be most profitable for their next shipment. Jovian felt utterly useless the entire morning and allowed his mind to wander back over his conversation with Rishon.

"Jovian, did you hear what I just said?"

Jovian jerked back to the present, and his father sighed. "I want you to attend the banquet with your brother and me."

"Banquet?"

Belen frowned. "It's my turn to host our merchant guild, and I want to nominate you for membership."

Jovian kept his face calm, though a chilling realization sliced through him. The guild meal would center around meat offered to an idol.

He cleared his throat, stalling. "Where and when is it?"

"I need to book a private room, and then arrange the food and entertainment." Belen looked down at his tablet. "I'll have to make time this evening to get it done."

Sergio leaned against a stack of grain sacks. "Why not let Jovian plan the banquet?" He grinned as if offering a rare treat. Jovian appreciated his brother's intention, and he tried to look grateful.

Belen looked doubtfully at Jovian. "Have you ever planned a banquet?"

"Well, no," Jovian said slowly. "But I have been to many." He had partaken of sacrificial meals countless times at city festivals and weddings.

Belen glanced at Sergio before he sighed. "Very well. I'll give you the list of guild members. Arrange the feast and give the invitations."

Jovian hesitated. On one hand, he had no desire to partake in this meal or join his father's guild. But refusing to participate would not only anger his father, it could reveal his interest in the Jewish God. He needed more time to decide how far he was willing to go with his faith—without his family breathing down his neck.

"Yes, Father," Jovian said at last. "I'll throw a banquet your friends will talk about for years."

Belen lifted his brows at the double meaning, but he listed off the guests and gave Jovian a purse for expenses.

Jovian bounced the coins in his hand as he strode out of the warehouse and back into the city. He knew he could plan a sumptuous banquet, but what was he going to do about the sacrificial meat? If Jovian refused to honor Mercury, the patron god of merchants, his father could be cast out of the guild.

Jovian winced. The tensions between him and his father were tight enough without Jovian casting aspersions on his family's devotion to the gods. The entire family would be cut off from their social circles. Their business would suffer, perhaps even face ruin. And it would be all Jovian's fault. His stomach roiled at the thought.

His vow to abstain from idol-worship had been easy to follow in Israel, but everything in Antioch revolved around the Roman gods.

He glanced over the nearby buildings, catching sight of an imposing temple. He would ask Sergio to offer the sacrifice at Mercury's altar. Once they were at the banquet, Jovian would do everything in his power to avoid eating the meat, feigning ill if necessary.

It was a satisfactory, if temporary solution. He would tell his family about the synagogue eventually, but he was just getting his feet under himself. Guilt encircled his throat as Persephone's face filled his mind. Once he was sure what he believed, he would tell his betrothed.

Just not yet.

# TWENTY-FIVE

Chuza drew the scratchy cloak higher on his head and smoothed his dark curls over his earring. He picked his way through one of the oldest portions of the city, where a man could walk from roof to roof without trouble.

He glanced sideways before he ducked under the low door frame. Dingy light hesitated to touch the rickety furniture, and the air was steeped in garlic. It was not the sort of place Chuza would have chosen, and the numerous empty tables shared his sentiment.

The proprietor swept his narrow gaze over Chuza. He pursed his lips as he examined Chuza's feet. Chuza cringed with realization. Fool that he was, he had bought a rough-spun cloak but wore his expensive leather sandals. There was no help for it now.

"Wine?" the man grunted.

Chuza slid into a chair and gingerly rested his wrists on the stained tabletop. A chipped cup was set in front of him. Chuza sipped and his tongue curled in his mouth. It was practically vinegar. He placed a small coin on the table, and it disappeared faster than he could blink.

The door opened, illuminating dust motes in the air before dimness overtook the few patrons once again.

Chuza did not turn his head, but shuffling steps warned him the moment before a man slid into the chair opposite.

He studied the young scribe who worked in the Sanhedrin building. They waited as the barkeep poured another cup of wine. The scribe sipped it and shuddered.

Chuza set a small purse on the table.

The scribe's eyes flicked to it, and he pushed the cup away. "What do you want to know?"

"Tell me what Saul is planning."

The scribe ran his tongue over his teeth. "Why does Herod's steward care about a motley group of blasphemers?"

Chuza lifted one shoulder. "It's my job to know what's going on. Now tell me, how far can Saul reach?"

"You mean, how many of the so-called Way will die before he's finished?" His eyes narrowed, probing Chuza for a reaction.

Chuza's fingers twitched, but he forced his face to stay calm. "You'd know better than I."

The scribe leaned back with his chin lifted. "Saul insists he will keep going until he has purified the city. And his reach is long. Caiaphas even allows him to vote with the Sanhedrin." He grinned cruelly. "He has voted for death every time."

Chuza's chest burned. Good men and women had been killed for their faith. Perhaps Pilate would put an end to the Sanhedrin's reign of stones, but he was away in Caesarea Maritimea.

Chuza cleared his throat. "If Saul's reach is so long, why hasn't he arrested the twelve who lead The Way? Cut off the head, so to speak."

"They are too popular among the gullible." He leaned across the table and lowered his voice as if sharing a secret. "See, you have the analogy all wrong. It's like dismantling a crooked house. You start with the bricks. One by one, we will remove them, and when they're gone, we can dismantle the support beams and foundation."

Chuza's lip twitched. "You do know Jesus called himself the corner-stone the builders rejected?"

The scribe retreated into his seat. "I guess."

Chuza spun his cup and considered the scribe's report. The twelve were safe for now, but there were a thousand others in Jerusalem, including Chuza's family. "How is Saul finding the followers of The Way?"

The scribe shrugged and picked at a splinter on the table. "There are faithful Jews willing to give up those who preach a crucified messiah. Turn on their neighbors. Maybe even their families."

Chuza's mind rolled back to the banquet when Alexander told all his friends and neighbors about Jesus. Anxiety dug under his ribs, but he kept his face calm.

He stood and tossed the purse across the table. The scribe caught it with a wide grin and pulled open the strings to peer inside. As Chuza turned for the door, the scribe called, "See you soon, Steward."

Chuza's back tensed, but he did not stop walking. He strode outside and marched up the street. The scribe might suspect he was one of The Way, but he was also Antipas' slave. His position was a shield, but he did not wish to test its strength until absolutely necessary.

He shook his head. He needed to meet with Manaen tonight and plan how to get their loved ones out of the city. Before it was too late.

Joanna laid Nadia down and brushed her rosy cheek with one finger. Nadia's lips pursed as if suckling, then grew still. She should sleep soundly for the next few hours. Leah sat nearby, illuminated by a single lamp. Her face was pinched with the same worry that ached in Joanna's chest.

"We'll be back as soon as we can." Joanna rose and smoothed

her robe.

Leah studied Nadia's sleeping form, then lifted her face, squaring her shoulders. "Be careful."

Joanna wrapped her palla around herself and hurried down the stairs. She was relieved to see Chuza hadn't left without her.

His brow creased with worry. "You don't need to come."

She knew he would prefer she didn't. "I need to see my friends. We're in this together."

They slipped from Dalia's house and latched the door behind them. Joanna glanced at the neighbor's shuttered windows. Lamplight slipped through the cracks. Only a few months ago, Alexander had invited these neighbors to celebrate his son's miraculous recovery. Any of them could inform the priests.

Joanna shivered and slipped her hand into Chuza's. Her mind was a mess of problems and unsatisfactory solutions, but her analytical husband would have a plan.

They hurried through the dark streets of the Upper City. Joanna's pulse hammered as their sandals scuffed the cobbled road. Every shadow concealed a guard, every glint was a spearhead. Chuza slowed his pace and muttered to himself, counting buildings and streets. At last, they reached a three-story dwelling.

A narrow strip of light shone under the door, accompanied by voices joined in song. Chuza knocked and the voices cut off raggedly. After a moment, the door cracked open to reveal a sliver of Manaen's face. He sagged and held the door open so they could slip inside. He barred it behind them.

Joanna strode into the main room of the house. It was large and well decorated, with soft matting and couches, and brightened by lamps hanging in front of bronze mirrors. Maryam sat on one couch with her son Joses. Susanna sat near Jaban and his parents. Susanna's two sons, tall young men, were next to their father.

"Joanna," Maryam breathed in relief, rising and holding out her arms.

Joanna wrapped Maryam and then Susanna in an embrace.

Manaen and Chuza came into the room. Chuza scanned their worried faces. "Saul has the full backing of the Sanhedrin and no intention of stopping."

Susanna looked at her husband. Her voice was resigned. "We need to leave the city."

Joanna winced. The same conclusion was circling in her head like a whirlpool, trying to pull her into despair.

Jaban looked at his parents. "You should come with us. Close up this house until the threat has passed."

His parents shared a long look, and Jaban's father squared his shoulders. "I agree."

Maryam crossed her arms tightly. "I can't go. Not when my James is staying." Joanna stared at the floor, biting her lip. Part of her wanted to side with Maryam, but staying in Jerusalem could mean imprisonment or death.

Chuza crossed the room to stand before Maryam. She looked up at him, and a tear followed her crescent-shaped dimple to land on the floor.

Chuza said, "My source says Saul will not target the twelve. Not until those who follow The Way are completely scattered."

Susanna stepped closer to her sons.

Maryam shook her head. "I still can't go."

"And I won't leave you." Manaen patted Maryam's shoulder, his gaze soft.

Chuza pulled a hand through his hair. "Jesus told us to preach to the nations. We don't need to wait in a city that has rejected him and his message."

Manaen glanced at Maryam again, then back at Chuza. "We're staying."

Joanna touched her husband's back. He couldn't make them go. Chuza met her eyes, and his shoulders sagged.

Joanna looked at Maryam. "Why don't we get everyone some

wine?"

The two women moved deeper into the shadowy house. The kitchen was dim, illuminated by moonlight shining through a single window.

Maryam arranged cups on a tray. "I'm afraid," she whispered, and Joanna's stomach twisted. "I'm afraid to go, and I'm afraid to stay."

Joanna's throat ached as she swallowed back her tears. "I'm worried about what will happen to those who just started to believe, like my sister and her family. What if this scares them away from following Jesus?"

Maryam clutched Joanna's hand like a lifeline. "We just need to hold on. Our circumstances do not surprise God. Jesus will return soon. I have to believe that."

Joanna's chin sank, frustrated by her fear. "Sometimes my faith is so weak."

Maryam lifted Joanna's chin and peered into her eyes. "Faith is perfected in weakness. Hold onto God, leaning not on your own understanding."

"In all your ways, acknowledge him."

"And he will make your path straight."

Maryam pulled Joanna into a hug.

A harsh knock broke the silence. "Open up!" a man shouted. "By order of the Sanhedrin!"

# TWENTY-SIX

"God protect us." Joanna choked the words through her tight throat. The sound of rushing footsteps paralyzed her, and she flinched as Chuza burst into the kitchen.

"Is there a back door?"

Galvanized by his voice, Maryam led them deeper into the house, but Manaen cut them off. "We can't go that way."

The others scurried to join them as the door hammered again.

"What do we do?" Susanna gasped.

Joanna's mind sharpened. "Follow me!"

As the door creaked and splintered, Joanna bolted back into the kitchen. She threw her head and shoulders through the window. Raised voices filtered into a narrow alley, but no one was in sight. She scrambled outside.

Joanna helped Susanna crawl through. The other two women followed, and Susanna's sons hopped out easily. The seconds rushed past as Joanna willed the men to hurry.

The narrow space between the two houses grew crowded as the men folded themselves through the window. The door inside the house crashed open, and Susanna whimpered as shouting voices filled her home.

Chuza was the last one out, and Joanna exhaled with relief. But they were not safe yet.

Susanna's son Asher beckoned. "This way!"

They hurried after him. Their steps whispered on the packed dirt as he led them into the neighbor's courtyard and shut the gate behind them. The windows glowed through closed curtains.

"We can't stay here," Jaban whispered.

"We won't," Asher whispered back. "Come on."

He led them up a set of exterior stairs to the roof, where planks bridged neighboring houses.

Jaban eyed his boys. "I'm not even going to ask."

His sons hurried across the narrow bridge, their arms stretched wide for balance. Joanna's mouth dried as she watched the boards bounce and shake.

Jaban crossed and held his hand out to Susanna. She recoiled, and Joanna couldn't blame her.

Angry voices spilled into the street. Saul knew they had escaped.

With a whimper, Susanna hurried across the bridge and collapsed into Jaban's arms.

Joanna waited as the others crossed, sick with fear. Finally, it was just her and Chuza.

"Hurry," he whispered in her ear.

Her knees trembled as she stepped onto the board. It bowed beneath her weight and her stomach plummeted. Staring at her waiting friends, she set one foot in front of the other, holding her breath until she was on the other side. She whirled around to make sure Chuza followed. He crossed as easily as if he did this every day. They filed down another flight of stairs and into a side street.

They took off running.

A stitch pulled at her side. She tossed glances over her shoulder, making sure everyone stayed together. Chuza pushed forward until he led the way, and after a few twists and turns, Joanna realized where he was taking them.

"Why are we here?" Maryam panted.

The guards at the palace gate stepped forward, gripping their weapons. "Halt!"

Chuza stepped into the light of their torches and the guards flinched in surprise.

"Steward!" they exclaimed in unison. The guards straightened and squinted at the panting men and women.

Manaen and Jaban stepped forward, two regular visitors to the palace.

"My guests will stay the night," Chuza said.

The guards relaxed their weapons, and one bowed his head. "Of course, my lord."

"Fetch the housekeeper," Chuza said. "Tell him to provide my guests with beds and anything else they require."

Chuza gestured for the others to continue up the stairs, but he hung back. Joanna met his eyes, and torchlight flickered in the brown depths.

"Let's go home," he said.

They clasped hands and walked quickly through the streets, too spent to run.

"Do you think Saul knows about Alexander and Dalia?" Joanna asked. "If they refuse to leave—"

Chuza jerked to a halt, and Joanna stumbled into him. He gripped her forearms, and his voice was thick with suppressed emotion. "We're leaving. You hear me? No matter who stays, we have to get our daughters out!"

Joanna's pulse fluttered at the depths of his fear. "Of course. We'll get them to safety."

Chuza wilted, and she went into his arms. They embraced for only a second before rushing up to the house. Chuza rapped on the door, and Joanna shivered until Alexander slid the bolt back.

"Well?" Alexander scanned their faces as they stepped into the safety of the house.

Dalia came into the room, her arms folded across her chest and her brows contracted with worry. Joanna turned for the stairs. She needed to know that her daughters were safe. Chuza's voice followed her.

"We're leaving Jerusalem as soon as we can. I hope your family will come with us."

Joanna could not hear Alexander's reply as she hurried into the sleeping room. She passed Little Mary and Samuel slumbering on their beds, their innocent faces untouched by fear. Leah sat cross-legged, and her hazel eyes searched Joanna's face.

"What happened?" Leah asked.

A tremble ran from the top of Joanna's spine to her feet. The night felt so unreal. She knelt beside Nadia.

"Saul nearly arrested us," Joanna whispered.

Leah's eyes widened. "What about the others?"

"Chuza took them to Herod's Palace. We're leaving as soon as possible."

Leah said nothing for a long moment. "Where will we go?"

Joanna struggled for an answer. If only they still had the vineyard. "I don't know. Maybe Tiberias. Or Sepphoris. Chuza still needs to serve Antipas."

Leah wrapped her arms around her knees, her eyes wide. "But what about everyone else? The believers who can't leave?"

"Your father will come up with a plan." Joanna said. But there was no guarantee anyone could escape. Saul might have posted guards at the city gates.

Leah rose to her feet as Chuza slipped into the room. He wrapped her in a hug and kissed the top of her head. "We'll stay here tonight. In the morning, we pack our things."

Joanna darted a glance at her niece and nephew. "What about Dalia's family?"

"Alexander is discussing it with his father. I don't know what they'll decide."

Joanna's throat burned, but she refused to cry.

Picking up Nadia, she followed Chuza down the stairs and through the shadowy courtyard. Alexander sat at the table with his father, and both men grew quiet as Joanna and Chuza passed. Miriam came out of the storeroom with a tray of wine and cups. Guilt pressed on Joanna's shoulders. If she hadn't convinced them to follow Jesus, then—

Then what? They had needed the good news. They had needed to accept Jesus as their savior.

Chuza pulled open the stable door and Balaam stuck his head over his stall. Chuza shut the door, closing them in darkness. Joanna stroked Balaam's long nose as Chuza climbed up to the loft. She passed Nadia up to him. The baby woke and let out a short cry.

Joanna climbed up the ladder and lay on her mat, adjusting her tunic so she could nurse her daughter.

Chuza lay facing her. Moonlight shone through their window, and in the dim, silvery light, they stared into each other's eyes. Love for her husband beat back her fear. Whatever happened, they'd face it together.

Chuza reached for her hand, and in the darkness, they knotted their fingers together.

# TWENTY-SEVEN

Chuza swallowed an ache that would not go away. He stood in the busy street holding Balaam's lead. Burdened with their belongings, the donkey's long ears flicked back and forth. Leah patted the beast, her gaze distracted. Joanna came out of the house with Nadia tied to her chest.

Dalia followed. Dark shadows camped beneath her eyes.

"You and the children can come with us," Joanna said. Worry tinged her voice. "The men can follow later."

Dalia shook her head and folded her arms tight across her chest, over the swell of her pregnancy. "I need to stay with Alexander."

Chuza understood her reluctance to leave her husband behind, but it could take Alexander weeks to close his business and let out the house.

Joanna gave her sister a one armed hug. "We'll see you in Sepphoris."

Dalia's lips curved in a sad smile. "Remember how we used to go with Papa to sell wine at the palace?"

Joanna glanced at Chuza, and her expression softened. "How could I forget?"

Dalia twisted her fingers. "Do you ever miss the way things were? You, me, and Amichai? Our quiet life on the vineyard?"

"Sometimes. The vineyard still feels like home. It's the place I go most often in my dreams."

"Me too. Strange, isn't it?"

Chuza cleared his throat. He didn't like standing on the street, no matter how ordinary it felt in the daylight.

"We'll see you in a few weeks." Joanna smiled through the quiver in her voice. Dalia slipped back inside.

Chuza prayed the next step in his plan would go as smoothly.

They found the others gathered in the palace kitchen, eating a simple meal of bread and fruit. Responsibility pressed on Chuza's shoulders. He had to get them away from Saul.

Leah clicked her tongue. "Is this the best the staff could do?"

Maryam waved her hand. "The staff have their own responsibilities."

Leah set down her bag and snapped an apron off a hook. She tied it around herself, nodding once. "I'll have a proper meal ready in no time."

As Joanna slid onto a bench beside Maryam, Chuza slipped from the room to gather important documents from his office.

An unopened scroll sat on his desk, and the ornate seal was inscribed with King Aretas' signet. Chuza broke the seal and scanned the letter. Aretas had agreed to receive an envoy.

With everything happening in Jerusalem, he had forgotten about his letter to the Nabatean king. Chuza sighed and rubbed his temple. He would sort this out in Sepphoris.

Tossing the letter with the rest, Chuza packed his important scrolls and documents in a small chest. With a pang, he realized Jaban's parents would be forced to leave their house abandoned, all their family heirlooms and belongings at the mercy of their neighbors. He clenched his fist. Saul had a lot to answer for.

Chuza returned to the kitchen. The warm scent of cinnamon drained some of the tension from his neck.

Leah set bowls in front of everyone. "You'll feel better with something hearty in your bellies."

Chuza nodded at Leah in gratitude and slid onto the worn bench between Joanna and Manaen.

Once they were all served, Manaen lifted his palms to bless the meal. After the usual blessing, he continued, "Our Father in heaven, holy is your name. Your kingdom come, your will be done—"

"That's the Nazarene's prayer," a voice said sharply.

Manaen fell silent as everyone stared at the doorway.

A gray-haired slave gripped the door handle, his narrow shoulders stiff beneath his simple tunic. Chuza shifted in his mind for the man's name. Namir. A slave who fell out of Antipas' favor because of his belligerent attitude.

Namir worked his stubbly jaw. "You speak the prayer of a blasphemer?"

Chuza rose to his feet, and Namir jerked with recognition.

Chuza forced himself to speak calmly. "Allow me to finish it for you. 'Your will be done on earth as it is in heaven. Give us this day our daily bread, and forgive us our sins, as we forgive those who sin against us. Lead us not into temptation, but deliver us from evil.'" He held the slave's gaze until the man looked at the floor. "There is nothing blasphemous about that, is there?"

Namir's chin lifted. "The priests say that man was dangerous."

"Antipas permits us to believe what we will."

Namir hesitated, then spun to leave.

Chuza turned back to the others, and his chest ached at the nervousness in their faces.

Leah tried to smile. "Don't let my fine porridge grow cold."

Susanna's son reached for a jar of pomegranate syrup and drizzled it in his bowl. He took a huge mouthful and grunted with appreciation.

Chuza's lip curved in amusement. Nothing suppressed the appetites of young men.

Chuza sat back down and tore a piece of bread to scoop his own porridge. He cleared his throat and looked at the other men. "My family is going to Sepphoris."

Jaban said, "I thought you might. My family will return to my house in Tiberias."

Joanna's face scrunched before she smoothed it away. Chuza patted her hand. He disliked this situation as much as she did.

Manaen said, "Maryam still wishes to stay in Jerusalem." Chuza opened his mouth to argue, but Manaen held up his hand. "We have a plan. I am Antipas' foster-brother. If I keep my head down, the priests will avoid arresting me. I believe they will extend that same immunity to my family."

Chuza blinked. "Your family?"

Manaen leaned past Chuza and Joanna to look at Maryam, and the pair shared a knowing smile. Manaen grinned. "Maryam has agreed to marry me."

Joanna cried out in surprise and turned in her seat to embrace her friend.

"So you will stay here, in the palace?" Chuza asked.

Manaen nodded, and some of Chuza's worry faded. Even Saul wouldn't dare to storm the palace gates.

Chuza slung his arm over Manaen's shoulder. "I'm glad you have found happiness again."

Manaen beamed.

Chuza turned to Jaban. "We will leave together this afternoon. I'll arrange carts and ride Celer. If the city guards see a wealthy retinue, they will hesitate to question us at the gate."

Jaban and Susanna shared a look of relief. "Thank you," Jaban said. "I don't know what we'd have done without you."

Leah spoke up. "But what about Keturah?"

Manaen bobbed his head at her. "Don't worry. We'll watch out for her."

Leah's brows tipped in worry. "I think she should come with us. There is nothing for her here. Perhaps if she comes to Sepphoris, we can send her on to Syria, to her people."

Chuza couldn't allow any more delays. "I'm sorry, but there's no time."

Leah folded her arms and stared at the tabletop.

Chuza promised himself he would come back someday and collect the young widow, for Leah's sake. But for now, they had to go.

Leah glanced over her shoulder and her pulse fluttered. The palace courtyard was empty save for the grumpy, gray-haired slave. He glared as she strode to the palace gate.

The guards said nothing as she trotted down the stairs. On the bottom step, she hesitated. Jerusalem seemed to grow in size before her, a maze of streets, alleys, and houses. She straightened her shoulders and lifted her palla to cover her head like a hood.

"Leah!" Joanna's voice called.

Leah flinched and glanced back. Joanna stood in the palace gate with Nadia in her sling.

"I'm sorry!" Leah called. "I need to get Keturah!" She launched herself off the step and took off running.

Guilt dug under her ribs as her feet pounded on the cobbled street, but there was no way she would deny Keturah the chance to leave Jerusalem and its danger behind.

Leah was panting hard by the time she made it to Keturah's street. She skidded to a stop at the chipped door and banged on it with her fist. No one answered. She pushed the door, but it wouldn't open.

"Keturah, it's me!"

The bolt slid back, and Keturah cracked the door open.

She scanned Leah with wide eyes. "Get inside. Hurry!" Leah

slipped inside, and Keturah shut the door behind her. "You shouldn't have come. I've seen temple guards in the street."

Leah gripped her wrist. "Get your things. We're leaving the city."

Keturah stared. "You'd take me with you?"

"Of course! You're my friend."

"Your father said it's alright?"

Leah hesitated, and Keturah's lips pressed together. "I see. Leah, you must go without me."

"You don't understand. If you come to the palace, he won't be able to say no."

A knock made them both jump.

"Leah! Keturah!" Joanna's voice came sharply.

Leah yanked open the door. Joanna's face was flushed and hair clung to her damp forehead. Both her arms cradled Nadia in her sling. She frowned and pushed her way inside.

Joanna shot Leah a frustrated glance and turned to face the young widow. "Are you coming?"

Keturah stood dumbfounded.

Jed tugged on Leah's robe and Leah bent to scoop him up, resting him on her hip.

Finally, Keturah smiled. "I guess we are."

Joanna spoke briskly. "Hurry, gather what you need. We need to get back. No one even knows we're here."

Keturah jerked into action, grabbing a tall basket and shoving articles of clothing and personal effects inside. Leah set Jeb down and helped him gather up his few toys. Joanna shifted her weight from side to side, patting Nadia's back as her eyes flicked around.

Leah helped Keturah tie her baby on her back, and Keturah picked up the basket.

"Let's go," Joanna said.

The women filed outside, Leah gripping Jed's hand.

A man's voice speared the air. "You there! Stop!"

Leah's mouth turned to dust. A Pharisee strode toward them, small of stature and with piercing pale eyes under thick brows.

Saul.

Behind him marched a trio of guards, led by the gray-haired servant from the palace. Leah's mouth turned to dust.

Somehow, Joanna spoke calmly. "What do you want?"

Saul stopped right in front of her, and Joanna drew up to her full height, forcing him to look up at her. He scowled. "I've been informed you are followers of The Way, spreading lies and blasphemy throughout the city."

Joanna's voice was icy. "I'm the wife of Chuza, Herod's steward. You would detain me and my family?"

Saul pointed at Keturah. "She is your family?"

Keturah shrank, and Joanna put herself between Saul and the younger women. "She's a family friend."

"Admit it," Saul said, and stepped so close he nearly trod on Joanna's toes. "She is an innocent widow you coerced into declaring a crucified messiah. You offered to feed her in exchange for this confession, didn't you?"

The walls of the neighboring houses hemmed them in. The air was too close. Jed tried to yank free from Leah's grip. Even he could sense the danger they were in.

Joanna lifted her chin. "We did not."

Saul sneered. "Do you believe Jesus of Nazareth was raised from the dead?"

Leah's breath evaporated in her lungs, but Joanna did not hesitate. "I saw him raised from the dead and into heaven."

Saul's satisfied grin was chilling. His hand snaked out to grip Joanna's arm, and he pushed her toward a guard. Joanna stumbled and wrapped her arms protectively around Nadia.

Leah opened her mouth to protest, but Saul's hard eyes captured her like a mouse before a hawk. "And you," he said. "Do you believe the same?"

Leah's pulse filled her ears with a rushing sound as her lips parted.

She could lie. She could tell Chuza what had happened and he would free Joanna. Her gaze drifted past Saul's cruel face and met her adoptive mother's eyes. They had both seen Jesus alive. He had eaten the fish she prepared.

The words came from deep within her soul. "I believe."

Accepting her fate, she released Jed's hand. He bolted for his house.

Without waiting for Saul to push her, Leah stepped beside Joanna, her pulse galloping like a deer.

Keturah quaked before Saul. Before he opened his mouth, she gasped. "I don't believe. It's just like you said. They tricked me."

Leah's stomach sank, but part of her understood.

Saul turned back to glare at Joanna and Leah. He motioned to his armed escort. "Take them."

Joanna stiffened. "I am a nursing mother. You can't do this."

Saul seemed to notice the baby for the first time. He considered only a moment before he turned and pointed at Keturah.

"Leave the child with her."

Joanna opened and closed her mouth in dismay, but Saul's expression was like stone. With shaking fingers, Leah helped Joanna untie the sling. Saul reached for the baby, but Joanna recoiled. Stepping around him, she kissed Nadia's head and handed the child to Keturah. Keturah took Nadia in shock, unable to speak.

As Joanna turned away, tears streamed down her face. Guilt threatened to pull Leah to the ground. This was her fault. She had left the palace without permission. She had made Joanna chase her into the city. And Chuza had no idea where they were.

Saul led the way. Guards surrounded the women and pushed them forward. As they passed the gray-haired servant, Leah leaned toward him, ready to spit at his feet.

Joanna gripped her arm. "No. We do as Jesus did."

Leah shivered. Jesus had not fought his accusers, and he had died.

Faster than Leah believed possible, Saul marched them to the public jail near the temple. The building was imposing on the outside, but inside it was dim and dank with fear. The women stepped closer together in the sparse room. Doors dominated the far wall, reinforced with bands of iron. Leah stared at them as her knees quivered.

After speaking with the guard, Saul left and didn't look back.

The jailer pushed Joanna and Leah to a thick door. He unlocked it and the door screeched on rusty hinges. A putrid stench wafted up to Leah's face, and she took an involuntary step back. The jailer shoved her forward. She nearly fell down a flight of narrow steps. Joanna was pushed in after her and caught herself by gripping the stone wall. The door slammed shut, and the bolt slid into place with awful finality. They were in total darkness.

"Go down," Joanna said, her voice echoing.

Leah dragged one hand on the rough wall, finding her way one step at a time. Panic rose the further down she went. The stairs ended on a slick floor, with straw scattered thinly over the stone.

"Is anyone here?" Joanna called.

No one answered, and Leah shivered with cold and fear. Joanna tugged on Leah's arm, and they groped around the room, looking for a place to sit. There wasn't one. They pushed the dirty straw into a paltry pile and huddled side by side.

"Chuza will get us out," Joanna said.

Leah prayed she was right.

Chuza inspected the three covered carts. The canopies would shield the women from view, and he would ride Celer at the front. He had ordered four guards to accompany them, giving them not only protection but an imposing air. He hoped it would be enough to get them out of the city.

A palace guard marched into the stable courtyard. "Steward, there's a woman at the gate asking for you."

Chuza furrowed his brow. "Who is it?"

He shook his head. "I've never seen her before. She has children with her."

Chuza hurried past the guard, relieved. It must be Dalia or Miriam. They had changed their mind and were moving the children to safety.

But as he approached the gate, he saw Keturah. Disappointment rose, but at least the widow could come with them. Leah would be relieved.

Keturah clutched her little boy's hand as tears streamed down her face. She carried a chubby baby tied to her back, but held a smaller baby on her hip. Chuza slowed. Keturah only had two children. Chuza's heart turned over as he recognized the third.

"Why do you have Nadia?" he demanded.

A sob burst from her lips. "I'm so sorry."

# TWENTY-EIGHT

Chuza's nightmare had come to life, and he couldn't make his mind work.

His hands trembled as Keturah sat on his couch and tearfully explained. Her baby slumbered in the sling on her back, and Nadia squirmed in her lap. Her little son stood beside her, his eyes wide and confused.

A cloud of unreality kept Chuza from understanding. How could Leah go into the city after everything that had happened?

"Chuza, do you hear me?" Keturah's voice cut into his thoughts.

Nadia let out a cry, galvanizing him into action. He took his daughter from Keturah's arms, holding her close and bouncing her up and down.

He whispered in her tiny ear as hot tears burned his eyes. "I'll free them. Somehow."

Nadia's cries persisted. She sounded hungry. Joanna should be here. Despair lanced through him.

"Give her to me," Keturah said.

Chuza hesitated, but as Keturah loosened the neck of her robe, he reluctantly handed over his daughter. Nadia cried, not wanting to nurse from a stranger, but hunger took over.

Chuza strode to his window and dragged his hands through his hair.

"What do I do?" he whispered.

Manaen's voice rose in his mind. *Do the most powerful thing of all. Pray.*

Chuza closed his eyes, but instead of a prayer, Stephen's bloodied body filled his mind. Fear rose like a wave and surged from him in a groan. He leaned both hands on the window frame and bowed his head. "God, help me."

Omri's face came to him. The Herodian leader might be able to help, but he was also closely connected to the Sadducee party. Could he be trusted?

Chuza had no choice.

He turned to Keturah. "Stay here. You'll be safe in the palace. Just stay here. Please."

Keturah nodded with wide, damp eyes.

Chuza found a servant and commanded him to send Maryam to his office. At the palace gate, he spoke to the guard. "The woman who just arrived must not leave this palace, do you understand? Not without my permission."

"Yes, my lord."

"If I'm not back by tomorrow, send word to Antipas. Tell him to speak to the priests."

"The priests?" the guard repeated, his brow furrowed.

There was no time to explain. Chuza strode for Omri's home.

He knocked on Omri's door, and the doorman hurried into the house. Omri himself returned, his expression concerned. He took one look at Chuza's face and dismissed his slave.

"Good God, Chuza! What happened?"

Chuza stiffened his back to keep from crumpling. "Saul has arrested my wife and daughter."

Omri paled. "Does he know they're your family?"

"Would that make a difference?"

Omri gripped his shoulder. "You are Antipas' steward. It counts for something."

"Will you speak to the priests on my behalf?" Chuza said. "See if they'll give me an audience without—"

"Without arresting you too? Of course." Omri took his arm and led him to a bench. "I will return with news." Chuza tried to rise, but Omri pushed him back down. "Wait."

Chuza sat as an hour went by, each minute trickling like blood from a wound. His mind spun, and every scenario was worse than the last. Finally, the gate opened and Omri came in.

"The priests will hear you out." Chuza jerked to his feet, but Omri lifted a hand. "Tomorrow."

"Tomorrow?" Chuza croaked.

Omri shook his head. "It's the best I could do. Now go home. Rest. I'll meet you at the temple after morning sacrifices."

Chuza drifted back across the city, trying to be grateful he had an audience. But the thought of Joanna and Leah cold and afraid haunted him. No matter what he said, the priests could crush Chuza's family like grapes in a winepress.

Joanna crossed her arms over her chest and pressed hard, trying to stop the letdown. She groaned in pain as her tunic was slowly soaked.

"What's wrong?" Leah's disembodied voice said.

"My milk. It's time to feed Nadia."

"I'm so sorry."

Joanna's insides writhed, wanting to shout at Leah and hold her close at the same time. "I know."

They sat in silence, leaning against each other until they fell into an uneasy sleep.

Chuza slipped into the temple complex as the sun rose. He stood behind a column and waited. The courtyard slowly filled and the constant hum of voices muffled Chuza's tight breathing.

Omri entered the courtyard and stopped to scan the crowd.

Chuza strode to his side. "What are the chances I'll be immediately arrested?"

Omri's lips softened in compassion. "Small, but not impossible."

Chuza's hands trembled, and he clutched them behind his back. If he was arrested, there would be no one left to save his family.

"Have you changed your mind?" Omri asked.

Chuza shook his head.

Omri strode toward the Sanhedrin building and went inside. He came back a moment later. "They're ready for you."

As Chuza stepped inside, he pushed back his hair to let the glint of his earring show. He was Antipas' slave, his right-hand man. It counted for something.

The Sanhedrin milled, but as Chuza strode to the center of the semi-circular seating, the elders and priests found their seats. A familiar scribe sat at a little desk near the front with a stack of wax tablets. He regarded Chuza smugly.

Alone before a mountain of piercing eyes, Chuza's mouth was dry as bone.

"Chuza, Herod's steward," Caiaphas said. "Why have you come?"

Chuza cleared his throat. "Saul of Tarsus has arrested my wife and daughter."

Silence answered his words, and a few men darted glances at one another.

Chuza kept going. "My wife is a nursing mother, and my daughter is an unmarried maiden. They don't belong in prison."

Saul rose from his seat and strode into the center of the room, stopping a few feet from Chuza. He coldly scanned Chuza up and down, and recognition flickered in his eyes. "You were there when that blasphemer was stoned." He lowered his voice so only Chuza could hear him. "Was he your friend?"

Chuza knotted his fingers behind his back to keep from grabbing Saul by his collar and shaking him until his teeth rattled out of his head.

Saul twisted his lips in perverse satisfaction and faced the Sanhedrin. "I arrested two women who claim they saw Jesus ascend to heaven. They are blasphemers."

Chuza ignored Saul and spoke to Caiaphas. "The followers of The Way are peaceful. This man—" he shot a glare at Saul "—is reduced to arresting mothers and young women."

Saul scoffed and shot Chuza a patronizing look. "I have witnesses who will testify that your wife sat in a teacher's seat in Solomon's Colonnade and spoke boldly. You did not stop her then, and now you try to downplay her role in spreading dangerous lies throughout the city." He swept his gaze around the room. "I beg the council, do not be fooled."

Caiaphas' father-in-law Annas leaned forward. "We are not fools. And you are not a full member of the Sanhedrin."

Hope flickered as Chuza studied Annas' disgruntled face. If Saul's welcome was wearing thin with the priests, Joanna and Leah had a chance.

Saul spread his hands wide. "I am the one who caught these blasphemers."

Caiaphas raised his brows and scoffed. "A woman and her daughter."

Saul's face darkened. "Who claim to be eyewitnesses!" He lifted his chin. "These women are leading the people astray. They are liars and corrupters. They have made a mockery of God and of our great hope for a messiah." He turned to Chuza, his eyes blazing. "They deserve death."

Chuza's chest tightened as a few elders nodded at Saul's words.

He drew up taller and faced the Pharisee. "So you think the people would follow my wife, rather than these powerful priests?"

The men on the benches shifted.

Saul glared as he folded his arms. "You speak like a politician, covering truth with clever words." His eyes narrowed. "But what about you? Do you believe Jesus of Nazareth is the messiah?"

Panic climbed up Chuza's legs like heat, and his heart beat out a frantic prayer. Saul had baited the trap. If Chuza said the wrong thing, he and his family could be dead by tomorrow.

Against all logic, a wave of peace washed over him. God was in heaven, with Jesus at his right hand. All Chuza needed to do was speak the truth.

"I do." His answer echoed around the room.

Saul blinked in surprise, and a malicious grin spread over his face.

"He admits it," Saul spoke to the room without taking his eyes from Chuza's face. "We should throw him in prison with his wife."

Panic rippled through Chuza's chest, but he turned to the gathered men. "The steward, the slave of Herod Antipas believes in Christ Jesus." He let that hang for a moment. "My master knows."

Caiaphas shifted. He had a vested interest in keeping peace with the tetrarch. He glanced at his father-in-law, Annas. "If we arrest his slave, we challenge Antipas' authority."

Men muttered in agreement.

Saul's expression flickered with annoyance. "Fine, let the slave go. But we must make an example of his family. Show the people of Jerusalem the futility of this so-called Way."

Fear and anger coiled around Chuza's throat, but something told him to keep silent.

Caiaphas stroked his beard and turned toward his father-in-law. The men around them leaned closer and joined the hushed debate.

Finally, Caiaphas stood and addressed the Sanhedrin.

"There's merit to Saul's words. I say we punish these women and let them go."

Chuza's heart twisted with mingled relief and trepidation. Anything was better than death. His hands were cold as ice as the Sanhedrin voted. Only a few were in favor of death, Saul included.

Caiaphas sat down and peered coldly at Chuza. "The prisoners will be flogged. Then get them out of my city."

# TWENTY-NINE

Chuza's hands turned to ice as he realized what was about to happen. His brief moment of relief was quickly replaced by a sense of failure that dragged on his shoulders like a millstone, threatening to pull him to the ground.

Saul spun to go.

Omri waited outside the Sanhedrin door, but Chuza stumbled after Saul, his pulse roaring in his ears. They left the temple complex and strode toward a stark building. Chuza's legs seemed to move of their own volition. This couldn't happen. It was impossible.

Saul yanked open the prison door, and Chuza numbly followed him inside.

"Bring out the mother and daughter and bind them with chains," Saul commanded.

The jailer unlocked a door. As it swung open, a stench like an overflowing latrine made Chuza gag. Joanna and Leah had been forced to endure that all night?

Carrying manacles, the jailer lumbered into the darkness.

A few minutes later, Joanna and Leah emerged, scrunching their eyes against the daylight. Joanna was hunched in pain with her arms drawn against her chest. Her wrists were bound with chains.

Chuza rushed to her. "Are you alright?"

The jailer glared but did not stop him from supporting her.

"Nadia," she gasped. "Is she alright?"

"She's safe. Keturah's been feeding her."

Saul's voice rang through the crowded room. "The elders and priests show you mercy. You will be flogged for your blasphemy. Learn your lesson and sin no more."

Chuza gritted his teeth as a man like Saul preached repentance.

The jailer pushed Chuza aside and led the women toward a side courtyard. Two armored men sat along the wall, playing dice. They rose, abandoning their game and picking up spears as they eyed Chuza.

With practiced motions, the jailer hooked Joanna and Leah's chains on a rough wooden pole in the center of the courtyard, hauling their arms over their heads.

Chuza's hands shook. It was all happening too fast. His mind scrambled for a way to stop the madness.

"Go, Chuza." Joanna twisted to face him. "Don't watch."

Leah let out a sob.

Staring at these two women he loved, Chuza's mind finally cleared and he knew what he had to do.

He stepped toward the jailer. "I will take their punishment. I will take it for them both."

The jailer hesitated and looked at Saul.

Saul's lip twitched as if amused. "I can't order Antipas' prize slave to be beaten," he said dryly. Chuza had never felt such a strong urge to strike a man. "But, I can release them if you deny Jesus is the Christ."

Chuza's breath caught as Saul gestured to the women, the jailer, and the two armed guards. "Tell them that Jesus is dead and rotting, a false messiah rejected by God, and your wife and daughter will go free."

Chuza trembled. He could just say the words and recant later.

Yet, after Jesus had suffered and died to save them, they were far more than mere words.

Chuza looked at Joanna, his lips parted in a silent plea. But she shook her head at him, pity gleaming in her eyes.

Saul grinned cruelly as Chuza turned to face him.

"Jesus is Lord."

Saul's mouth pressed into a thin line, and he jerked his head at the guard. "Do it."

As the bundle of rods whistled through the air, Chuza fell to his knees.

Joanna's back arched as the flexible rods struck, but she did not gasp. She was trying to be brave for him. Another blow and her head flew back, her mouth open to the sky, her eyes wide. The third strike elicited a cry of pain, and Chuza cried out with her. Leah wept as she watched her mother beaten, knowing her turn was coming.

He had failed to keep his family safe. Every blow seared that message deeper into Chuza's mind, flooding his limbs with despair.

Saul was not content until Joanna received the thirty-nine blows. Sweat shone on her face and soaked the back of her tunic, mingling with a few stripes of blood.

Chuza shook as his knuckles screamed from being clenched into tight fists.

And it was only half over.

Joanna found her footing and turned to Leah, nodding once. Leah trembled, and her hazel eyes were wide with fear. Chuza jerked to the side as his empty stomach heaved, bringing up bile.

The first strike made Leah cry out, and she sobbed as the blows fell. Each strike on her back tore into his soul as she wailed. "Jesus! Help me!"

Saul gazed down at Chuza with cold accusation.

Finally, the jailer unhooked the women's manacles and they collapsed on the sand. Leah fell forward into Joanna's lap.

Chuza stumbled forward as the jailer unlocked their wrists. He ached to wrap Joanna in his arms, but she gasped as he touched her shoulder. As carefully as he could, he helped the women stand.

Saul held the courtyard door open. "Leave the city," he said with cold authority. "Don't return until you are ready to come before the priests on bended knee."

Chuza's chest boiled with anger, but he refused to speak. He supported a woman on each arm as they stepped onto the street.

Those passing by stopped to stare.

"I can't seem to smile," Joanna said.

Chuza blinked, his mind like sludge. "What?"

"Remember the apostles? They left the Sanhedrin rejoicing."

Chuza grunted. "Let's just get you safe."

Joanna jerked to a stop. "No."

Frustration spiked his chest, but she stood in the street, her eyes closed and her brow furrowed in concentration. After a moment, her lips curved.

She smiled.

Chuza stared in disbelief.

Joanna opened her eyes and reached for Leah's hand. "Rejoice! We have suffered in Jesus' name, just like the others. We will be rewarded in the coming kingdom and honored for our faith."

Leah's face crumpled. "I can't. It's my fault. Because I went to Keturah's." Guilt swamped her eyes. "I couldn't just leave her behind. I had to do something. But I never meant for this—" She gestured toward the jail, but pain cut off her words and she sucked a breath between her teeth.

Chuza blinked as guilt drove deeper than he believed possible. This was his fault. He could have collected Keturah, but his mind had been too full of getting his own family out of the city.

Joanna took Leah's hand. "Saul did this, not you. I forgive you, Leah."

Tears slipped down Leah's face, and she looked at Chuza. With dismay, he realized she was waiting for him to forgive her too. He ached to wrap her in his arms, but he feared hurting her. He reached for her other hand.

"I'm the one who should be sorry. I couldn't stop Saul."

"We will heal," Joanna said, with a bark of tense laughter. "I was expecting to be stoned."

Leah drew a deep breath, and then, somehow, she smiled.

Chuza was nearly overcome.

"Rewards and honor, hmm?" Leah said, lifting a brow.

Chuza's heart eased a fraction as the two women grinned at one another, but he fixed his eldest daughter with a stern glare. "Don't you ever do anything like that again."

She nodded sheepishly.

Their journey through the city was slow. As he broke a path for them, Chuza ran a checklist through his mind. There was no time to let the women recover. They had to leave Jerusalem as fast as possible.

The palace guards and servants stared as Chuza took the beaten women to his office.

Chuza pushed open the door, and Keturah cried out. "What happened?"

Nadia squealed with delight to see her mama, and Joanna reached for her.

Chuza took Joanna's arm. "You're too weak."

Joanna batted his hands away and growled. "Not for my daughter."

Ignoring her protests, Chuza led Joanna to the bed in the back room, and helped her lie on her side. Keturah laid Nadia against Joanna's chest. Joanna groaned in pain as Nadia nursed.

"I'm so sorry." Keturah sobbed. "I do believe in Jesus. I just panicked. I was afraid for my children. I'm alone, and…"

Joanna reached to grip Keturah's wrist, and their wet eyes met. "You are not alone."

Keturah stared, her mouth opening and closing as tears flowed down her face. "But, I denied Jesus."

"You're forgiven." Joanna let her eyes flutter closed, humming as she stroked her daughter's back.

Chuza swallowed hard. Keturah had denied Jesus to save her children. Why was she forgiven so easily when he was forced to endure? He turned and strode woodenly into his office. Leah sat on the couch, her face in her hands. Keturah's little boy stared at her, his round eyes trying to understand.

Chuza's ribs were too tight around his lungs. "I'll fetch lanolin for your wounds, but we need to go soon."

Leah nodded without lifting her head.

Chuza found the others praying in the kitchen. As soon as they saw him, they jerked to their feet.

His voice sounded flat in his ears. "We need to leave."

Within the hour, everyone was bundled into carts hitched behind pairs of mules. Susanna rode with Joanna and Leah to help them on the difficult journey ahead.

Manaen, Maryam, and Joses came to the stable courtyard to bid them good-bye.

Maryam lifted her hands toward them. "The Lord bless you and keep you. The Lord cause his face to shine on you and be gracious to you. The Lord lift up his face to you and give you peace."

Chuza's throat was too thick for words as the believers prepared to split. They would divide even further when Jaban and Susanna took their family to Tiberias. It felt like an era was ending.

He gave his foot to the groom and swung onto Celer's back. The guards moved into position. Chuza nodded at Manaen once, understanding passing between them. He led the procession out of the stable courtyard and into the city streets. Curious bystanders watched as the carts trundled past, searching for a hint of who rode inside.

A little girl bounced up and down. "Is it a princess, Mama?"

Chuza's mouth twitched, and then, somehow, he smiled. Heirs of the kingdom, Jesus called them. And one day Jesus would return, and everything they endured now would be worth it.

# THIRTY

Men drifted in from the dark streets. They ignored the Greek who claimed a seat on one of their benches. After a handful of Sabbaths among them, Jovian had become an accepted presence in the synagogue. They did not speak to him, but neither did they exude suspicion or bitterness.

The meeting was small, a dozen men gathered to pray and read the Torah.

As the men took their seats, Jovian glanced at the doorway, sensing a presence. A bearded figure was half-illuminated by the lamplight. His palm rested on the mezuzah fastened to the doorpost, and he peered into the room uncertainly. Jovian half rose, prepared to welcome him, but remembered his place.

Rishon set the scroll on the altar and cleared his throat. "Come in, brother."

The man jerked out of his reverie and stepped forward. "Forgive me. I was gathering my thoughts."

The others bobbed their heads at the newcomer in welcome.

Rishon smiled. "Where are you from?"

"We just came from Jerusalem."

Rishon encouraged the man to come deeper into the room. "What news can you share?"

The newcomer strode forward and faced the men in benches, nervousness flitting over his features. "My name is Micah. I can tell you that a prophet of the Lord came to the Holy City."

Jovian's mouth dried as Micah described Jesus of Nazareth's visit to Jerusalem, and how he had taught and healed in the temple courts. The other men glanced at Jovian, no doubt remembering his outburst during his first visit to the synagogue . Jovian glanced at the doorway and considered a hasty escape.

"Jesus was killed." Micah said, and silence hung over the room.

Jovian squeezed his eyes shut as months of nightmares rolled over him. His back dampened with sweat. He didn't want to remember, but memories clawed their way to the front of his mind.

"But three days later, he rose from the dead."

Jovian eyes flew open. He stared at the newcomer.

A man scoffed. "That's impossible."

Another man shook his head. "I did hear a rumor, but it was too far fetched to believe."

Micah spread his arms. "Jesus appeared to his disciples many times. Hundreds saw him."

Jovian stared in shock and doubt. Did Chuza claim to have seen Jesus? Did Leah?

Rishon gripped Micah's shoulder, his knuckles white. "The priests affirm this?"

Micah pressed his lips together. "No."

Rishon stepped back, and men muttered, but Micah plowed on. "Jesus' disciples can also perform miracles. They teach the people, even though the priests arrested them and had them flogged. A man was stoned. But they still insist Jesus lives."

Anxiety and confusion wrapped around Jovian's chest. What was going on in Jerusalem?

He leaned forward. "Do you know Chuza, Herod's steward? Or Joanna, his wife? She traveled with Jesus in Galilee." He bit back Leah's name.

Micah glanced at Jovian with surprise. "I know them by sight, Joanna in particular."

Jovian's chest squeezed. "Are they safe?"

"Most of the believers were forced to flee Jerusalem. Some went to Damascus. Others, like me, came here. I don't know where Joanna and Chuza went."

Jovian shifted, his mind spinning. Even if Jesus hadn't risen from the dead, it sounded like Chuza and Joanna were in danger. Probably Leah too. And Jovian had not been there to help. Guilt weighed down his shoulders like a sack of grain.

Conversations broke out in the room as the men digested the new-comer's claim.

Rishon patted Micah's shoulder. "Perhaps we could talk tomorrow, and you could tell me more."

Micah bobbed his head. "Of course."

As he took a seat, Rishon and Jovian locked eyes.

After prayers, the rest of the men went home, muttering about the strange news.

Jovian rose as Rishon locked up the scrolls.

"What do you think?" Jovian asked.

"I think you'd better come for supper."

Rishon extinguished the lamps, casting the room in darkness. Jovian stepped into the balmy summer evening and waited while the rabbi locked the door. Rishon gestured toward the street, and the men walked side-by-side.

They arrived at an insula and climbed the stairs. A man going down spoke to Rishon. "Good Sabbath, Rabbi."

"Good Sabbath," Rishon answered absently.

Rishon pushed open the door to his home. A lamp illuminated a pot and basket of bread laid on the low table.

"My daughter leaves a meal for me," Rishon explained. "I don't think she trusts me to feed myself.

Jovian shut the door behind them. "She doesn't live with you?"

"They have their own place, just downstairs. I spend much of my time there, but I enjoy a quiet evening." He leaned closer and spoke in an undertone. "She has five young children."

"Ah." Jovian grinned.

Rishon washed up in the basin, then gestured for Jovian to take his turn. Jovian hesitated. He had eaten with Chuza many times in the palace kitchen, but this felt different.

"It's alright," Jovian said. "I can sit apart while you eat."

Rishon's smile softened. "I appreciate your thoughtfulness, but I think we can eat together in my house, as friends. The Lord commands us to welcome the stranger, for we were once strangers in Egypt."

Jovian washed his hands before kneeling across from Rishon. Though his hands were clean, he still worried he was tainting the rabbi's table.

"Are you sure you're permitted to eat with me?"

Rishon studied him beneath his thick brows. "You have kept the seven laws?"

"I have."

Rishon nodded once. "Some rabbis disagree, but I say a God-fearer can eat with a Jew—in a clean home, and with clean foods only, of course. And there are some foods we cannot share, like the Passover lamb." He shook his head sadly. "Though of course, none of us here can sacrifice to the Lord. Perhaps next year, we can go up to Jerusalem."

Rishon began the Sabbath prayers, and the rolling rhythm brought back Jovian's days in Jerusalem. He could hear the sounds of the city, taste the dust and wine, and smell the incense at the temple.

Rishon ended the prayer and picked up a small loaf of bread. He tore it and offered half to Jovian.

Jovian's heart swelled with gratitude as he accepted the simple token of community.

"So," Rishon said, taking the lid off the pot. He wafted the steam to his face and sniffed appreciatively. "Tell me what you think of the news. You saw this prophet killed, and now we hear he was raised from the dead. Can it be true?"

Jovian scooped a mouthful of the delicious lentil stew, rich with cumin, date syrup, garlic, and leeks.

"I'm not sure," he admitted. "I mean, I was there when Jesus resurrected a little girl, but—"

"You were?" Rishon's brows rose and he leaned closer. "I think you need to tell me everything you saw this prophet do."

Jovian tipped his chin back and let the memories wash over him. "The first time I saw Jesus was when an unclean woman touched him and was healed. She admitted what she had done, but instead of being angry with her, he praised her faith."

Rishon's lips pursed in disapproval, and Jovian held up his hands. "The local elders were not happy about it either. But then a little girl died. The mourners were already gathered, but Jesus brought the girl out of the house, alive."

Rishon looked troubled. "But did you actually see her? You're sure she was dead?

Jovian raised his shoulders. "Her family was certain."

"Hmm." Rishon leaned his elbows on the table and peered at Jovian over his knobby fingers. "What else?"

Jovian sifted through his memories. "Jesus was always teaching. He often talked about the coming kingdom, but he spoke in parables, which confused the people—including me. But though his parables could be debated, his miracles were undeniable."

He told Rishon how Jesus fed five thousand men from a few loaves and fish. Rishon stared doubtfully, but Jovian had seen it with his own eyes.

"So, after all the healings and the miracles," Rishon said slowly, "the priests found him guilty of blasphemy."

"Jesus didn't even try to defend himself. He just stood there as they abused him, lied about him, and then crucified him." Tears pushed at Jovian's eyes as his throat burned. "Even in his last moments, he forgave them."

The words hung in the air, saturated with Jovian's painful memories.

"And after that, you left the city."

"That same day." Jovian swallowed his shame.

"And now, this newcomer arrives in Antioch, saying that Jesus of Nazareth rose from the dead."

Jovian pursed his lips. "Do you think he's lying?"

"I think he believes it's the truth."

"So he's deluded?"

"Perhaps."

"But if three thousand Jews believed?"

Rishon shook his head, muttering to himself. "Three thousand Jews."

Jovian took another mouthful of stew. "Isn't the messiah foretold? Shouldn't there be prophecies about this?"

Rishon tipped his head from side to side, his lips pursed. "Some texts allude to the messiah, but they are vague and much debated. There are passages in Isaiah and Jeremiah, among others. Some say the seer, Daniel, had visions of the coming kingdom."

"The people used to say Jesus sounded like Jeremiah."

"Did they?" Rishon drew a hand down his beard. "This man certainly sounds intriguing. He was charged with blasphemy, yet by your account, he had the hand of God upon him. Crucified, yet those who knew him say he rose from the dead."

Rishon began to eat, his eyes distant. Jovian scooped another mouthful and wondered if there had ever been a stranger discussion between a Jew and a Greek.

Jovian swallowed his stew and wiped the corner of his mouth

with his thumb. "So what do we do?"

"We must pray about it."

Jovian flushed. His private prayers were dismal things, not the sort of prayers that God would answer. Every time he tried to open his heart to God, it was as if he stood in the outer courts of the temple in Jerusalem, forbidden by the pain of death from drawing near to where God's presence dwelt.

Rishon seemed to understand. "God speaks to Gentiles too, you know. Once via a donkey, but make of that what you will." His brows waggled. Jovian chuckled, but Rishon leaned closer. "God presented signs to the kings of Babylon and Persia. God can hear you, and even speak to you, young Jovian Titus."

# THIRTY-ONE

Jovian stepped into his recently expanded bedchamber, carrying a lamp. Worries for Chuza, Joanna, and Leah crowded his mind. Was Jesus truly alive? Micah was a stranger, and it was possible he was lying. But why would he lie about something like this?

Jovian set his lamp on the table and began to undress. As crazy as it sounded, he wanted Micah to be right. The idea that God had not abandoned his righteous prophet to a shameful death was deeply comforting. But on the other hand, Jovian was interested in facts, not rosy feelings. So what was he supposed to believe?

Rishon said God could speak to a Greek. With all his heart, Jovian wanted that to be true. He knelt, and the soft matting pressed its pattern into his knees. He closed his eyes and drew a deep breath, then another, willing himself to feel a brush with the divine. But he only felt a cool draft from the window.

"God, if you would listen to a mere Greek who is too insignificant to even speak your name, I ask for wisdom. Help Rishon and me discern the truth." He paused, then added, "Amen."

He stayed on his knees for a long minute, but no voice answered.

Sighing, Jovian rose and sat on his narrow bed. His room had more than tripled in size, and a new doorway led into a small sitting room. The expensive renovation had consumed all his wages. For now, the room was starkly empty. He was supposed to furnish it before bringing Persephone to live with him as his wife.

Jovian flopped sideways, and his head landed on the bolster. He still hadn't told Persephone about his regular visits to the synagogue. She, along with most of Antioch, would not understand what pulled a Greek man to the Jewish God.

He blew out the lamp and loneliness rolled over him like a wave. Those who would understand were far away and facing trouble of their own.

"There's a man at the gate, asking for you."

Jovian blinked sleep from his eyes. "What?"

Tomas stood in the doorway. "He won't come inside."

Jovian groaned and pulled himself upright. He peered out the window. The sky was still pink. He grumbled to himself as he pulled on his clothes and plodded through the house, trying to smooth his hair as he walked.

He crossed the front courtyard and pushed open the gate. Rishon stood there, his face illuminated like the rising sun.

"Jesus is the Messiah!"

Jovian blinked at him. Rishon wore his clothes from the night before, and dark shadows deepened his creased eyes.

Jovian leaned one arm on the door frame. "Did you sleep at all?"

Rishon waved away such trivial concerns. "Come, I will show you!" He seized Jovian's hand with surprising strength and pulled him into the street.

"Hold on!" Jovian yelped. "Let me get my sandals."

Once Jovian was dressed, the two men hurried through the city, and Rishon muttered the whole time. "I can't believe it! He has come!"

Jovian glanced sideways at his friend. If a man like Rishon could accept Jesus was alive, did that mean it was true? His chest fluttered with a whisper of hope.

Rishon led Jovian into the synagogue. Jovian blinked with surprise as the newcomer from yesterday rose from a bench. He rubbed his tired eyes and smiled.

Rishon hurried to the front of the room. "I found Micah and brought him here to talk. Now come and see what we discovered!"

The scrolls were piled on the altar. The great, thick Pentateuch lay open, as well as many smaller scrolls. One lay on top of the others, and Rishon tapped it with his finger. "Read!"

Jovian looked at the elderly rabbi with concern, but he leaned over the Greek text and read aloud.

*"He was despised and abandoned by men, a man of great pain and familiar with sickness;*

*And like one from whom people hide their faces, he was despised, and we had no regard for Him.*

*However, it was our sicknesses that he himself bore, and our pains that he carried;*

*Yet we ourselves assumed that he had been afflicted, struck down by God, and humiliated.*

*But he was pierced for our offenses, he was crushed for our wrongdoings;*

*The punishment for our well-being was laid upon him, and by his wounds we are healed.*

*All of us, like sheep, have gone astray, each of us has turned to his own way;*

*But the Lord has caused the wrongdoing of us all to fall on him.*

*He was oppressed and afflicted, yet he did not open his mouth;*

*Like a lamb that is led to slaughter, and like a sheep that is silent before its shearers, so he did not open his mouth.*

*By oppression and judgment he was taken away; and as for his generation,*

*Who considered that he was cut off from the land of the living for the wrongdoing of my people, to whom the blow was due?*

*And his grave was assigned with wicked men, yet he was with a rich man in his death,*

*Because he had done no violence, nor was there any deceit in his mouth.*

*But the Lord desired to crush him, causing him grief;*

*If he renders himself as a guilt offering, he will see his offspring,*

*He will prolong his days, and the good pleasure of the Lord will prosper in his hand.*

*As a result of the anguish of his soul, he will see it and be satisfied;*

*By his knowledge the Righteous One,*

*My Servant, will justify the many, for he will bear their wrongdoings.*

*Therefore, I will allot him a portion with the great, and he will divide the plunder with the strong,*

*Because he poured out his life unto death, and was counted with wrongdoers; yet he himself bore the sin of many, and interceded for the wrongdoers."*

Like a stone thrown into a pool, the implications rippled to every corner of Jovian's mind. "Are you saying this is about Jesus?"

"It lines up with everything you and Micah told me. Look here." Rishon tapped the scroll. "'My servant will justify the many', and 'He himself bore the sin of many.'" Rishon looked expectantly at Jovian, but Jovian scratched his head.

"What does it mean?"

Rishon raised both hands. "For generations, my people have prayed that the Lord would bring his presence among us again, to restore Israel to glory, bring back the lost tribes, and cast off the pagans who rule over us. There's only one way that happens."

Jovian chewed his lip. "How?"

"The forgiveness of sins!" Rishon threw his arms wide. "Throughout our history, when my people sinned, God withdrew from us. We suffered famine, sickness, persecution, and exile. Only after we repented would God forgive us and return. Don't you see? We have tried to live according to the Torah, to show God to the world. But we fall short because our sins still get in the way."

Jovian's mind churned through Rishon's reasoning. He looked at the scroll and a spark flashed in his mind. "So you're saying Jesus showed God to the world, as the perfect Israelite?"

Rishon grabbed Jovian's face as his eyes sparkled with wonder. "Yes, my boy, yes! Jesus did what we could not do! He showed the world God's own heart, even when it cost him his life. And through his sacrifice, we are forgiven."

Rishon set both palms on the altar. "It all makes sense. Because he rendered himself, his days are now prolonged. He lives again!"

Jovian stepped away and sank onto a nearby bench. "So it's true. Jesus is alive."

Rishon nodded rapidly at Jovian, and then at Micah.

Jovian's hope rose but then plummeted. "This is excellent news —for the Jews."

Rishon shook both hands in the air. "Have you learned nothing, Jovian Titus? There are no other gods, no Roman pantheon. There is only One True God, and he sent the Messiah. Isaiah says that the nations will come to God's light. Don't you see? Greeks and Romans, Syrians and Egyptians—all will come to the Lord and worship him."

Rishon's words pierced Jovian's soul with the sharpness of truth. There was only one God. One Messiah, not only for the Jews, but for the whole world.

Jovian rose and paced the room. If it was true, then something spectacular had happened in Jerusalem, and he had left too soon.

Jovian shook his head and muttered, "I was right there, but I missed everything."

"What are you talking about?" Rishon scoffed. "Micah says the Spirit has come among the believers, and they are performing miracles. There is more to be done!"

The idea made Jovian's head spin with wonder, but he could not forget why Micah was in Antioch.

He turned back to Micah. "Jesus' followers are still in danger? Even those who left Jerusalem?"

Micah twisted his lips to the side. "I think so. Yes."

Jovian dragged a hand through his short hair. His friends were in danger. He had to go back. He had to protect them.

Jovian took three strides for the door but then the reality of his decision struck him.

He looked back at Rishon. "My parents. Persephone. They will never understand if I go back."

Rishon came forward and gripped his shoulder. "Tell them the good news of Jesus."

"And if they don't believe?"

Rishon leaned his head closer. "Pray. You will know what to do."

Jovian's lips twisted in a rueful grin. His last prayer for wisdom was already turning his life upside down.

# THIRTY-TWO

## 32 AD
### SUMMER

A slave interrupted the cupbearer. "My lord, a letter arrived for you."

Chuza turned, his stylus poised over his tablet. The wine cellar was cool and earthy, lit by a single lamp that hung from the low ceiling. Chuza accepted the scroll and squinted at King Aretas' seal.

"We'll continue our inventory later," Chuza said and snapped his tablet closed.

The temperature climbed steadily until he emerged in the Sepphoris palace kitchen. Michael stood on one side of a long table, kneading dough with his large hands. Leah stood opposite him with her sleeves tied at her elbows to reveal her thin arms. She held pots of spices.

"Cardamom," Michael growled.

Leah tossed her head. "No. Cinnamon. And cloves."

Michael's nostrils flared as if she had asked him to serve fried eel to the priests. "What rural housewife taught you that?"

"Good morning," Chuza said, striding past them.

"Ha!" Michael scoffed. "No morning is good with this untrained girl ruining my kitchen." But his eyes twinkled and Leah smiled at the burly cook affectionately.

Chuza chuckled as he walked down the long corridor in the servant's wing of the Sepphoris palace. He let himself into his small office and stepped near the window for better light. Years ago, he had peered through this ornate screen and watched Joanna walk with her mother. So much had changed since then, but Joanna's problems were still his.

His cheerful mood faded. Somehow, Joanna had found a smile as she walked away from the prison, but her joy faded with the marks on her skin. And he didn't know how to bring it back.

Chuza broke the seal on the letter, suspecting what it would contain. He was right. King Aretas was frustrated that an envoy still hadn't arrived. He accused Antipas of offering empty words.

Chuza pressed his lips together. Antipas needed to send someone to Nabatea at once. Agrippa had been Chuza's first choice, a man of rank and prestige. But Agrippa was in Syria, driven away by Antipas' derision.

Chuza turned to his desk where a sheet of papyrus gave a detailed inventory of the armor Antipas had ordered. It now filled a huge storeroom in Tiberias—rows of chain mail shirts, bracers, and helmets, plus stacks of spears and short swords. Enough to outfit a thousand men. Enough to make Emperor Tiberius suspicious if he caught word of it.

Chuza's lips pulled into a frown. His sway over his master was diminishing. Worsened, no doubt, by Chuza's continual absences. Perhaps now that he lived in Sepphoris, he could exert a greater influence. And his first task was to remind Antipas of his long-held goal of maintaining peace.

Chuza strode for Antipas' apartment and found it empty. He began to search the principal rooms.

Herodias was entertaining several ladies in the main courtyard. They stood around long tables, tittering as they arranged vases of summer flowers.

Herodias' smile slid off her face as she noticed Chuza. "What is it, Steward?"

Chuza bowed his head. "I'm looking for my lord."

Herodias slid another stem into her vase and shot one of her friends an amused glance. "I thought the steward knew everything. Apparently, he's losing his touch." Herodias looked back at Chuza and flicked her wrist. "He's at the stables."

Chuza bowed again and made his way out of the palace.

The paddock held a dozen fine horses, Celer among them. The bay gelding noticed Chuza's approach and trotted over, lifting his black nose over the fence to bump Chuza's chest.

"I haven't brought you a treat." Chuza stroked his friend's smooth neck. "Next time, alright?"

Celer followed along the fence as Chuza moved into the stone stable. He inhaled the comforting scent of hay, manure, and the sun-and-dust scent of horses. Men's voices drew him to a back stall. Antipas stood with two of his friends, holding a horse's head. The young stallion was nearly perfectly white, but grey points marked his hooves and the tips of his ears.

Hunched at the animal's side, the head groom had a hoof drawn between his legs as he worked with a rasp. The young stallion did not seem impressed with this treatment, but Antipas stroked the horse's nose, murmuring quietly.

As Chuza stepped closer, Antipas grinned. "A beauty, is he not?"

"He's magnificent," Chuza agreed.

Antipas noted the scroll in Chuza's hand and sighed. "Come to pull me away?"

"It's a letter from King Aretas. He awaits your envoy."

"Oh, is that all?" Antipas lifted a shoulder. "Who should we send?"

"I hoped you'd have a suggestion."

Antipas studied his two friends, younger men who enjoyed pleasure more than business. He turned back to Chuza. "Why not go yourself?"

Chuza blinked. "Me, my lord?"

Antipas ran his palm down the horse's nose and the stallion's nostrils quivered. "It's not that complicated. State our terms, bow a lot, and make sure I come out on top." He grinned, and his friends chuckled.

Chuza shifted his feet. Reaching Petra would take more than a week, and then he would have to wait for an audience with the king, perhaps multiple audiences. Then a long ride back. He could be gone for a month. Joanna's drawn face when he left this morning filled his mind. He couldn't leave her.

"What if you send—"

"You," Antipas interrupted. "I've already decided. You're going."

The groom set down the stallion's hoof and straightened his back with a groan.

Antipas relinquished the halter and drew Chuza outside, away from the others.

"Look," Antipas said. "You, among all my other friends, have no reason to turn these negotiations for your own gain." He glanced around for listening ears before stepping closer. "And for that reason, I can trust you to work in my best interest." His gaze intensified. "You will not give a finger-width, do you understand? I would prefer to go to war than lose one mile of territory to Aretas."

Chuza grimaced. The cost of war, both financially and politically, would be staggering. "Isn't it better to concede a mile than risk losing an entire territory?" Antipas frowned, but Chuza pushed on. "The emperor favors peace above all. Continuity."

Antipas twisted the ring on his finger, his head tilted to the side. "Tiberius depends on us to keep the borders he approved. If I let another ruler take my land, we both break the emperor's decrees. I'm sure you can make that clear to Aretas."

Chuza studied his master's face. Unwillingness to negotiate with a more powerful ruler was a difficult way to approach peace talks, especially when there was already ill feeling. It would take great skill to keep from offending Aretas further, and Chuza was practiced in negotiating trade deals, not borders.

252

Chuza licked his lips. "Is there no one else you could send?"

Antipas set a hand on his shoulder. "No one better than my most trusted slave." His words were heavy with meaning, and Chuza gave him a questioning look.

Antipas gave Chuza's shoulder an encouraging slap. "Now, King Aretas is waiting. Prepare to leave. Take an armed escort and gifts."

Chuza inclined his head reluctantly. "As you wish, my lord."

Antipas frowned. Chuza should be grateful for the prestigious assignment, but instead he walked as if he was sent to clean the latrines.

Antipas crossed his arms and drummed his fingers on his bicep. Herodias insisted Chuza's loyalties were divided, that the steward put Joanna and The Way before his responsibilities to his master.

But truth be told, it wasn't Chuza's devotion to his wife or his religion that troubled Antipas most.

Chuza had helped Agrippa leave Tyre by giving him everything he asked for—money, transportation, and protection. Chuza had always shared Antipas' disdain for Herodias' brother—until now. His stomach clenched with the possibility that Agrippa could turn Chuza against him.

Chuza had been by Antipas' side since the beginning, through everything. Antipas would rather navigate the sea on a starless night than rule without Chuza by his side.

Chuza steeled himself as he entered his new home.

He and Joanna had chosen a large house, anticipating the rest of the family's arrival. But Joanna wanted to wait for her mother and sister before choosing furnishings. So while they had lived here for nearly a month, it looked as if they had just arrived.

At least Joanna had arranged one corner of the courtyard with matting and cushions, shaded by a striped awning. She sat there now, watching as Nadia practiced her new skill of sitting up.

Joanna looked over as Chuza approached. "You're home early." She glanced at the cold oven. "I haven't started cooking yet."

Chuza sat beside Nadia. The little girl swung her arms at him, and he picked her up. Nadia tangled her pudgy little fingers in his beard, and he grunted as she gave a sharp tug.

"I said we could hire a servant to help."

Her lips twisted. "There are only four of us. It hardly seems necessary. Maybe when Mama and Dalia move in."

"They'll be here soon."

Joanna's eyes sparked with anger. "You don't know that. We have no idea how our friends are faring in Jerusalem." She looked away. "Or who else has been killed."

He winced, knowing it was true.

Joanna studied her palms. "We should be there with them."

Frustration flickered up his throat. "And put our daughters in danger?"

"Of course I don't want that. But we are so disconnected here. We have no community, no way to work for the coming kingdom."

Chuza tried to remain patient. "I said you could start a charity for the widows in Sepphoris." Antipas gave sums to aid the poor. Chuza was more than willing to let Joanna spend it as she wished.

Joanna's shoulders sagged, and Chuza wished he could give them a good shake. He had hoped she would get to know their neighbors and rebuild their lives in Sepphoris, but she spent all her time in this empty courtyard.

Maybe he was asking too much of her. She had been cut off from her family and her community in one blow. And it was his idea to move to Sepphoris. Maybe they should have settled in Tiberias, so at least Joanna would be near Susanna. But the city was considered unclean by most Jews, and he was confident Alexander's family would refuse to live there.

Nadia tugged on his beard again. Chuza untangled his daughter's fingers and turned her around to sit in his lap.

He got straight to the point. "Antipas is sending me to negotiate the border disputes."

Joanna blinked. "You're going to Nabatea? When?"

"As soon as I can be ready."

Her brow furrowed, and she looked away. "I'm sure you'll do well."

A thought flashed through his mind like light in a dark room.

"Come with me."

Joanna jerked to stare into his face. "To Nabatea?" She looked at Nadia. "You want to take a mother and baby across the desert?"

"No." He grinned. "I want to take my wife and daughter to visit the beautiful city of Petra."

Joanna blinked at him as if he was crazy, but Chuza knew this idea was perfect. Joanna needed a change of scene, and he wouldn't miss another month of his baby daughter's life.

"What about Leah?"

Chuza lifted his shoulders. "She loves working with Michael. She can move into the palace while we're gone."

Joanna looked around the courtyard. "What about when my mother and sister arrive? We won't be here to meet them."

Chuza took her hand. "We don't know when they're coming, and I don't like you sitting here alone day after day. If they arrive before we get back, Leah can show them the house."

Joanna turned to peer into his eyes. "You really want us to come?"

Chuza leaned closer. "More than anything."

Joanna shrugged and nodded. It wasn't the eager agreement he wished for, but he prayed this trip would soothe the pain in Joanna's heart.

Leah hurried down the dark streets, accompanied by a burly male servant holding a torch.

Her clothes and hair were coated with the scent of fresh bread, roasted meat, and spices. She grinned. She couldn't believe she was working side-by-side with Michael again, creating culinary delights that stretched her skills. And she wasn't a mere apprentice anymore. She was a proper cook with a good wage. When Antipas left Sepphoris, Michael would go with him, leaving her in charge of the kitchen here. Sure, she would only feed a dozen staff and an occasional guest, but she would be the head cook.

They turned the corner and her new home came into view. The flower pots flanking the front doorway held only shriveled stems and crisp leaves. Joanna said she would plant some herbs, but weeks had passed and the pots sat lifeless.

Leah bit her lip. It wasn't right that she experienced joy while Joanna struggled. It felt wrong to be at home in the palace kitchen when their friends were scattered to the winds.

Keturah had left last week. Chuza found a trader's caravan that would pass near Keturah's hometown and paid a handsome sum for the widow and her children to ride in a cart, fed and protected. Though Leah missed both Keturah and Jed, she was happy for her friend. But after the widow's departure, the house became even quieter and Joanna withdrew even more. Leah wasn't unsympathetic. Joanna was grieving. But her grief weighed on them all.

Leah let herself into the dark portico, and the faint smell of burnt food made her sigh. She unwound her palla as she strode into the central courtyard.

A simple meal was laid out on a woven mat. Chuza and Joanna had waited for her—or perhaps they were delaying digging into the over-cooked food.

Joanna's cheeks colored as she flicked a hand at the pot. "Sorry, I had a little trouble with the stew."

"I'm sure it'll be fine," Leah lied with a smile.

Joanna needed to find her footing—not just in the kitchen, but in their new reality. The world had shifted beneath all of their feet, but Jesus had not abandoned them. Even far from Jerusalem and the other believers, there must be a way to live in The Way.

# THIRTY-THREE

Joanna supported Nadia in her sling and slid from Balaam's back. The donkey stepped sideways, his little black hooves tapping on the stone floor. The air was thick with dust and heat, and the faint scent of garlic rose from the city below. After enduring the beating sun all day, the shade was welcome.

Joanna patted Balaam's neck, and a puff of fine dust fell to the ground. "You deserve a good rest after lugging us all this way."

Shifting her weight from side to side, Joanna stretched her inner thighs. She was sore, but she'd rather ride a donkey than jostle about in a cart. Nadia kicked against Joanna's hips and reached for Balaam's bristly mane. Balaam turned his long nose to sniff the baby's bare toes.

The two guards hopped from their horses and checked their equipment with practiced efficiency. Chuza dismounted from Celer in one fluid motion, and his gaze turned toward Joanna, making sure she and Nadia were alright.

Joanna did her best to smile. She knew he was worried about her. But it was like a shadow had spread over her mind, a darkness she didn't fully understand. The Way was scattered to escape from Saul, and she had no idea how to serve Jesus alone. Even Chuza's offer to start a charity in Sepphoris was a reminder of what they'd lost. Using Antipas' money was not the same as a community banding together.

A groom took Balaam's lead, and Joanna turned to study the familiar courtyard in Macherus. The palace was a jewel crowning the flat-topped mountain that edged the line between Antipas' lands and Nabatea. The last time Joanna was here, she helped Phasaelis escape Antipas' control. Her lips twitched at the memory.

Chuza strode toward her, brushing off his riding clothes. "I think we could use a bath."

Joanna tipped her head to the side. "We? Are you saying I smell?"

He grinned and rolled his eyes at her. "Let's find our room." He held out his hand, and she slid her fingers into his.

Joanna rubbed Nadia's back with her other hand as she walked. She'd been doubtful about traveling with a young child, but Nadia loved the rocking motion of the donkey and napped for hours. And Joanna was grateful to spend time with Chuza. She gripped his hand a little tighter, and he looked over.

"Perhaps we could eat in our room tonight?" she asked. "Just us?"

Chuza's smile brightened.

The housekeeper bustled forward and bowed to reveal his gleaming scalp. "This way, my lord. Your rooms are all prepared. If you'd like to go over the accounts this evening, I have everything ready."

Joanna's hopes for a quiet evening faded.

Chuza glanced at her. "Not today," he said to the housekeeper. "Perhaps on our return trip."

Joanna exhaled a relieved breath.

The housekeeper led them to a pleasant room on the upper level. North-facing windows welcomed a fresh breeze, and Joanna looked longingly at the wide bed, plump with white and red linens.

"I forgot what it was like to sleep in palaces." Joanna ran her palm over the soft cloth. Chuza chuckled. She untied Nadia's sling as a servant set down their bags.

Eager to be free, the little girl wiggled as Joanna removed her soiled linens. Joanna reached for her bag.

"Don't wrap her back up," Chuza said. "Let's take her for her first Roman bath."

Joanna blinked at him. "Together?"

Chuza grinned roguishly. "Yes, together. We have the palace to ourselves, if you haven't noticed."

Joanna's cheeks warmed, but Chuza was already pulling fresh robes from their bags. He strode for the door. Flustered, she scooped up Nadia and followed him down the wide, cool corridors.

The bathhouse was near the palace entrance. Chuza pushed open the door and the moist air soothed her lungs after their dusty ride. They slipped off their sandals and padded over to a bench.

Chuza shrugged off his coat and unwound his belt. Joanna's pulse jumped as Chuza pulled his tunic over his head. She had seen him undressed many times before, but this was different.

The muscles on Chuza's lean back rippled as he stepped into the waist-deep water. He turned, showing his well-shaped chest. Her core fluttered.

He held out his arms. "Pass me Nadia."

Joanna obliged. As her toes splashed the warm water, Nadia froze, and her tiny arm swung excitedly.

Chuza chuckled. "You like that, don't you?" He held her against his chest and crouched to dip Nadia in the water. She beamed, letting out a squeal.

Chuza glanced back at Joanna. "Coming in?"

Joanna undressed and hastily stepped into the water. As the warm water lapped over her thighs, she sighed with pleasure. She lowered herself to sit on the submerged bench, and the water rose over her shoulders. Her head lolled back as the aches of the day melted away.

She tilted her head to smile at Chuza. "If there is one thing I miss about palace life, it's this."

"I thought you missed the beds."

"Them too."

Chuza chuckled and let her soak. He played with Nadia, pulling his daughter through the water as she splashed him. Nadia stuck out her tongue and spat noisily in delight. Chuza laughed, throwing back his head. Water glistened in his dark beard, and he shook back his curls, revealing the streaks of silver at his temples. He had never looked more handsome.

Chuza came to sit next to Joanna. Nadia splashed one chubby arm and flicked droplets into Joanna's eyes. Joanna giggled and wiped them away.

"I've missed your laugh," Chuza said.

Joanna's shoulders tightened as she took Nadia. She knew her dark mood weighed on him, but she couldn't seem to shake it off.

"Me too," she admitted. "It's easy to forget, here in this big empty bathhouse in the middle of nowhere."

Chuza pushed off the bench and turned to face her as he crouched, swishing his arms back and forth under the water. "Forget what?"

Joanna pressed her lips together. It felt foolish to say it aloud. "To forget that evil is winning."

Chuza's eyes softened with sympathy.

The silence echoed in her ears until she couldn't take it. "Don't you feel it too? Antipas is the same, more interested in pleasure than his own people. Pontius Pilate is still governor, and Caiaphas is still the High Priest. And now Saul wants to see every follower of The Way imprisoned or killed." Tears burned in her eyes. "Why has Jesus allowed it to get this far? Why hasn't he come back?"

Chuza pushed through the water and wrapped both Joanna and Nadia in his strong arms. "I don't know. Jesus conquered death, but the power of evil still holds sway in the world."

Joanna squeezed her eyes shut, wishing with all her heart that it wasn't true.

Chuza kissed her damp shoulder. "Those who believe will shine like lights in the darkness." He pulled back and looked her in the eye. "We cannot let the darkness overtake us. Take heart, for Jesus has overcome the world."

An image of Jesus filled her mind. He stood among them in the Upper Room, inviting them to touch him and see that he was alive. Jesus had faced persecution. He had been tortured and killed, though he was innocent. And he had been raised to new life, a resurrection he promised to all who believed. The believers who had been killed would rise again, glorified for standing firm in their faith.

Joanna shuddered. "I know what you're saying is true, but my heart still hurts. Hope feels so far away right now."

Chuza ran a wet palm over her cheek. "Then I will hope for both of us."

Joanna's pain overflowed as tears, and Chuza wiped them away with his thumbs. The Lord had known what he was doing when he sent her this wonderful man, one who was her equal in faith, who could hold her up when she felt too weak to stand.

The following day dawned beneath a cloudless sky. Joanna packed up their belongings and tied Nadia in her sling, feeling lighter than she had in weeks.

She strode down the stairs to meet Chuza in the courtyard. He was studying a door with a strange look on his face, but he smiled as she approached. "The camels are here."

She looked at the door he had been staring at. "What's behind there?"

"The stairs to the prison."

It took her a moment to realize what was troubling him. She wrapped her arm around his. "John the Baptizer was kept there, wasn't he?"

"But he's not there any longer." His lips curved in a sad smile.

"Now come, we should leave while the day is still cool."

Cool was a relative term in the desert, but Joanna nodded.

A small herd of camels waited outside the palace gates, along with two Bedouin guides dressed in black. The guards loaded the gifts for Aretas onto one kneeling camel. Chuza led Joanna toward a cream-colored beast burdened with a strange contraption. Rather than a fringed saddle like the rest, it bore a dome-shaped frame tightly wrapped in cloth. The frame surrounded a cushioned seat.

"It will protect you and Nadia from the sun," Chuza said.

Joanna eyed the camel nervously, but Chuza helped her climb inside. The walls restricted her view, but she and Nadia would be safe from the sun's glare.

"Hold on here," the Bedouin said in his heavy accent, showing her a leather loop. Joanna gripped it and he tapped the camel, commanding it in Arabian. Joanna's stomach swooped as the camel lurched to stand, and she had to lean back to keep from tumbling over the beast's head. After squat little Balaam, this camel was impossibly high. Joanna smiled nervously at Chuza.

"Don't worry." He passed up a waterskin and Nadia's bag. "The guide says she's the easiest mount in the herd."

Chuza clambered onto his own camel. He looked strange sitting upon the cud-chewing, knobby-kneed beast instead of Celer. Chuza pulled a scarf over his head and wrapped it around his face for protection against the dust and sun. She grinned. Her husband looked like a desert nobleman.

The guards and guides mounted their camels, and their procession made its way down the main road of Macherus and through the wide city gates. They turned toward the desert, where prickly grass grew sparsely on soft hills, and the sky rose in unrelenting blue above them.

Joanna turned Nadia to face forward. There was a chance Phasaelis was still in Petra. Would they meet? Phasa had been her best friend, and unknown to Joanna at the time, her captor. Joanna spent two years trying to teach the Arabian princess the Jewish faith, but it never sank more than skin-deep.

Joanna rocked with the camel as they crossed the unseen border into Nabatea, and her chest ached with the weight of too many emotions. As much as she wanted to know how the princess fared, they had parted on rocky terms. Phasaelis might not want to see her again.

# THIRTY-FOUR

Chuza's grip on the reins slackened as their guides led the camels into a narrow chasm between towering walls of strange red rock. He had never seen anything like these cliffs. They were smooth, scoured by sand and wind into curves and twists, the stone striated in shades of pink, white, rust, and scarlet. Along the road, a deep channel of stone sat empty, but he suspected it would fill with water during the brief rainy season, replenishing the city cisterns. The Nabateans were famed for their ability to collect enough rainwater to maintain a large city in the middle of a desert wilderness.

They emerged in a vast canyon, and Chuza stared in disbelief. He had heard many things about Petra, but nothing prepared him for this view. Buildings were carved into the rock face with elaborate designs, and men appeared as insects compared to their bulk. The people strolled in flowing clothes in bright hues, walking down wide roads lined with leafy palms.

Chuza glanced over his shoulder to ensure Joanna's camel was near. She had pushed back a corner of her canopy, and she smiled in delight at the beautiful city. Chuza's spirit soared. Bringing her along had been the perfect idea.

They rode past a massive, semi-circular theater, and moved deeper into the heart of the city. The valley was filled with buildings built with both sandstone and limestone. Gardens broke up the stonework with bursts of green. Smoke rose from altars with prayers to foreign gods. Chuza had experienced Rome, Alexandria, and various other cities, but they were nothing like Petra.

They rode through a busy market lined with booths, displaying goods from all over the world. Skin of every shade, strange fashions in hair and beards, tattoos, and exotic piercings threw themselves at Chuza at once.

They turned down a wide street and faced the palace. It rose on an imposing hill, reached by at least a hundred wide stairs. The architecture was beautiful, but completely foreign. Chuza's chest tightened. What was Antipas thinking, sending him? Chuza's skill was in Greek, and his familiarity was with Roman customs. None of that would serve him here.

They stopped before the palace stairs, and the guides made their now familiar noises, tapping Chuza's camel until it knelt. Chuza dismounted and waited as the guides brought the other camels to their knees.

Chuza helped Joanna hop down. Nadia was back in her sling, and Joanna straightened her robe and peered up at the enormous palace.

"I never thought I'd be back." She shot him a glance. "It has a way of making you feel incredibly small, doesn't it?"

He couldn't agree more.

Chuza, Joanna, and their two guards made their way up to the massive palace doors. The climb seemed to take forever, the wide yet shallow steps forcing them to take a reverent pace.

King Aretas' guards flanked the enormous doorway, and a man in long robes strode toward them. His gaze lingered on Joanna with Nadia tied to her chest.

Chuza stepped forward. "I am Chuza, Herod's steward."

"Of course. We were expecting you. Though, I was not expecting…"
He trailed off, looking at Joanna again.

"My wife and daughter," Chuza said.

The servant bowed to Joanna before returning his gaze to Chuza.
"My name is Fareed, and I will ensure your comfort during your
stay in Petra. Let me collect your luggage." He snapped his fingers
and a young servant hurried down the stairs.

Fareed turned, and Chuza followed him into the dim, cool palace.
The cavernous entrance hall did nothing to ease his nerves, with stone
pillars supporting a roof so tall it was lost in shadow. The hobnailed
sandals of the guards echoed.

They were led to another door, and Chuza was relieved to emerge
in a more appropriately sized hallway. The air was rich with spicy
incense. Screened windows filtered light and bird song from a courtyard shaded by palms and canopies. The ceiling was elegantly carved,
and the walls were inlaid with glazed tiles in ordered patterns.

They passed dozens of servants busy with their duties. Fareed
opened a door and led them into a large apartment.

Chuza blinked with surprise to find a shallow pool of water dom-
inating the center of the room, lined with tiles of deep blue ceramic
and greenish copper. A fountain shot a continuous spray of water
into the air, cooling the room and adding a pleasant ambiance. Chuza
raised his brows. So much water was a luxury few could afford in a
desert city. Apparently Aretas was eager to impress Antipas' envoy with
his wealth.

Embroidered cushions were piled on the bed, and the floor was
softened with carpets. Floor length windows were hung with bright
fabrics that puddled extravagantly on the floor.

"We can have a separate room made up for your wife, if you
wish," Fareed said. "Use the pool to wash. Please rest and food will
be brought to you. "

Chuza cleared his throat. This luxurious room did not distract
him from his purpose. "When can I meet with the king?"

Fareed smiled patiently. "When the king deems fit. It could be in a day, but perhaps not for a week. We have pleasant gardens and a library you may enjoy in the meantime."

Chuza wouldn't be surprised if Aretas left him waiting for weeks in revenge for Antipas' delay in sending an envoy.

The guards set down the heavy chest of gifts for King Aretas, and the young servant stepped around them, carrying Joanna and Chuza's bags.

"Amud," Fareed said to the servant, "show these men to the barracks."

Amud hastened to obey, and Fareed bowed and followed him out of the room.

Joanna drifted around the apartment. She leaned to look in a mirror and smoothed the hair on her brow.

Chuza sat on the bed to test its softness. "Where did you stay when you were here with Phasaelis?"

"In the women's house, where Aretas' wife keeps her own court. It's pretty much its own palace."

Chuza crouched to trail his fingers in the large pool. The water was tepid rather than heated like a Roman bath, and it was large enough a man could lay flat and not touch either side. He glanced up at his wife. "Do you think Phasaelis still lives in the women's house?"

Joanna sat Nadia down on a plush carpet, and dropped a fringed pillow behind the little girl for safety. "I'm not sure. Perhaps she has remarried and moved away."

"Did you want me to ask the servant when he returns?"

Joanna glanced at him, uncertainty playing in her eyes. "Do you think she's changed?"

Chuza rose and flicked his fingers dry. "I'm sure she's the same as ever. Which means she missed you."

Joanna wrapped her arms around her middle and gave him a crooked smile. "I suppose she won't try to hold me hostage again."

"You know she prefers novelty to routine." He grinned to mask his conflicted feelings. If Phasaelis hadn't held Joanna captive, he never

270

would have gotten to know the vintner's daughter. But that didn't justify Phasaelis' selfishness. But Joanna seemed to have forgiven the princess, even if Phasaelis had never admitted she was wrong.

Joanna nodded. "Alright, ask."

There was a light tap on the door. Amud returned with a tray of refreshments. He arranged the food on the low table, and then unpacked their clothes, hanging them in the cedar closet.

Chuza sat at the table. Joanna set Nadia down near the table and filled the cups as Chuza selected a few pistachios.

Amud closed the closet door and inclined his head to Chuza. "Can I do anything else for you, my lord?"

Chuza cracked a nut. "My wife would like to send a message."

Amud glanced at Joanna in surprise. "I can arrange that."

"I would like to see Princess Phasaelis," Joanna said. "We are old friends." Amud blinked twice, and Joanna hesitated. "I was Phasaelis' companion when she lived in Galilee."

Understanding dawned on the servant's face. "Ah, of course. Phasaelis has remarried, but she lives near the palace. A message will be easy to send."

Joanna glanced at Chuza, and nervousness played in the depths of her eyes.

Chuza smiled at Amud. "Thank you."

Both Chuza and Joanna waited anxiously throughout the next day, but no summons came from either the king or his daughter. Time crawled as Chuza and Joanna wandered the palace courtyard dressed in their best robes. They visited the library and perused King Aretas' impressive array of scrolls. He even had a few clay tablets on display marked with a strange spiky script. They looked ancient, and the librarian proudly explained they were from Persia.

But the next morning, Amud brought news.

"The king invites you to join him for the evening meal."

Chuza's stomach twisted. He was eager to get to work, yet he feared he would fail Antipas and Galilee.

Amud inclined his head toward Joanna. "Princess Phasaelis has also invited you to dine with her tonight in her home."

Joanna smiled at Chuza. "At least I won't be sitting here alone, wondering how your conversation with the king is going." She spoke calmly, but he didn't miss how she twisted her fingers into the ends of her belt. While Chuza was negotiating the future, Joanna would revisit her past.

# THIRTY-FIVE

Her hair refused to cooperate. Joanna scowled at her reflection and let the twists in her hair unravel.

Chuza was already dressed, but he stood at cedar closet and sifted through his clothes.

Her lips quirked in amusement. "You look perfect."

Chuza made a vague noise as he pulled a deep blue coat from the closet and held it against his chest.

Joanna turned her attention back to the mirror and gathered the strands at her forehead. It would be simpler to wear her usual braid, but Phasaelis had always preferred her hair this way.

"Is it strange that I still want her approval?" she asked.

Chuza cast her a sympathetic look. "Is it strange that I still want to please Antipas?"

Joanna chuckled. "Well, at least we can be strange together."

The braid finally came together in a crown encircling her head, and she secured it with a wooden needle and black thread. With a sigh of relief, she dropped her aching arms.

Joanna donned the gold necklace and bracelets she had bought with the reward money from King Aretas. She smoothed her best peplos and adjusted her belt before she checked on Nadia. The baby had already nursed and was growing sleepy.

"Are you sure you don't want to leave her with a servant?" Chuza asked.

"I want Phasa to meet her."

Phasaelis had always wanted children, but Antipas had denied her that as well.

Amud knocked and stepped into the room. He inclined his head to Chuza. "It's time."

Chuza's face was serene, but Joanna could sense his nervousness.

Amud beckoned a servant girl forward. "Pavda will escort your wife to the princess. One of your own guards is waiting at the palace gate, as you requested, my lord."

Joanna picked up Nadia, and the little girl snuggled into the curve of her neck. Joanna stepped around the gleaming pool of water and smoothed Chuza's neckline. "Don't be nervous. You can handle this."

His eyes were distant, his mind already in the throne room.

They walked together, but in the massive entrance hall Chuza veered one way, and Joanna the other. She cast him one last, encouraging smile before he strode away.

As promised, one of Antipas' men waited at the palace entrance, and he fell in behind Joanna as she followed Pavda down the palace steps.

Twilight blanketed Petra as they reached a wide street lined with large houses.

Nadia grew heavy as she fell asleep. Joanna adjusted the baby into the crook of her arm, and the child's peaceful face taunted Joanna's nervous pulse.

Joanna stared as they stopped at a massive home. The servant knocked on an ornate door, and the doorman ushered Joanna into a courtyard, shady with palms and canopies.

"Joanna!"

Joanna's nerves evaporated as Phasaelis rushed from the house, her arms outstretched. She looked just the same, with kohl-lined eyes and glowing skin. Phasaelis threw her arms around Joanna but drew back as she realized there was something between them.

"You have a baby!" Phasaelis sounded accusing. They both laughed and the years between them melted away.

Phasaelis cooed over the child before she wrapped an arm around Joanna's waist and tugged her toward the house. Her voice was playful. "So, Chuza finally worked up the courage to propose?"

Joanna told the story as Phasaelis led her into a large portico and up a flight of stairs.

"I never thought of Chuza as soft-hearted," Phasaelis said. She squeezed Joanna's waist. "But I'm happy to be wrong."

"And what about your husband?" Joanna said.

Phasaelis pushed open a door at the end of the hall. Joanna followed her into a cheerful room.

"He's handsome and powerful, and he's given me two sons."

Two little boys were stacking blocks, helped by a maidservant. The boys were almost identical, with thick, black hair and full lips. They jumped up and raced to wrap their arms around their mother's legs. Phasaelis crouched and held them close, kissing their foreheads.

Joanna's throat thickened with happiness for her friend.

Phasaelis stood and gestured to one of the low beds. "Lay your daughter here. My maid will fetch you if she wakes."

Joanna laid Nadia down and followed Phasaelis from the room.

Phasaelis led Joanna into a garden lit with dozens of golden lamps and lush with greenery and flowers. Couches were arranged around a table, and as Phasaelis sat down, a servant hurried forward to pour the wine. Joanna's nerves returned as she sat opposite her former mistress.

Phasaelis' smile faded. "I'm so pleased you're here." She flicked a hand and the servant left, leaving the two women alone. Phasaelis picked up her cup, and her hand trembled. "I thought about writing you so many times, but I couldn't bear to dictate my shame to a scribe."

Joanna's brow furrowed. "What do you mean?"

She picked at the embroidery on her robe. "I'll admit, after you left, I was so angry. I thought you were selfish to leave me." She winced. "I was a monster, wasn't I?" She held up her palm. "Don't answer that."

Joanna chuckled.

Phasaelis grew serious again. "I thought love justified keeping you by my side. But as I reflected on our time together, I saw things differently. Perhaps it was having a devoted husband or children, but slowly the guilt grew. Even now, it presses on me like a millstone. I'm so sorry, Joanna." Tears shimmered in her eyes.

Joanna moved to sit beside the princess and wrapped an arm around her shoulders. "I only remember the good times we shared. I want you to do the same."

Phasaelis looked at her doubtfully. "Really?"

Joanna squeezed her. "Really. You were in an awful marriage, just trying to survive. I don't agree with your choice to keep me at the palace, but I understand and forgive you for it."

Phasaelis drew a deep breath. "You have no idea what that means to me."

Joanna had forgiven the princess years ago, but hearing an actual apology lightened her heart more than she expected.

A servant stepped into the courtyard with a heavy-laden tray. Joanna returned to her seat.

"So! Tell me everything!" Phasaelis said. "Do you live on your vineyard?"

Some of Joanna's joy was quashed. "It's Antipas' vineyard now."

Phasaelis stared. "What? How?" Her expression grew pained. "Did he punish you for helping me?"

"No, nothing like that." Joanna dipped her bread in seasoned oil. "My brother was arrested, and Antipas demanded the vineyard in exchange for his life."

Phasaelis blinked. "Wait, your brother Amichai? The one who ran away? Go back and tell me everything."

Phasaelis ate as Joanna explained how Amichai had been arrested for bringing weapons into Jerusalem.

"Why on earth would they do that?" Phasaelis' eyes widened.

"They misunderstood the teachings of Jesus of Nazareth. They believed it was time to rise against Rome."

Phasaelis made a disbelieving sound. "Galileans fighting against Pontius Pilate's soldiers? They didn't stand a chance."

Joanna looked away, remembering the riot that killed her father. Phasaelis leaned forward, her brows tilting. "I'm sorry, I should have phrased that better."

Joanna smiled around the grim memory and took a large swallow of the excellent wine.

Phasaelis leaned back. "But who is this Jesus you mentioned? Another revolutionary leader?"

Joanna's mouth dried. This was her chance to share the good news with a woman she had tried to lead to faith time and time again.

As the sky darkened overhead, her years with Jesus tumbled from Joanna's lips. Phasaelis was speechless as Joanna shared it all—the miracles, the jealous leaders, Jesus' death and resurrection.

Phasaelis held up her hands. "You actually saw him raised from the dead?"

"We did," Joanna said. "Me and so many others, including Chuza."

Phasaelis leaned back and shook her head. "You used to say all sorts of strange things, but nothing like this."

"Thousands joined us at the beginning, but now the elders and priests don't want anyone teaching about Jesus. Leah and I were arrested and beaten."

Phasaelis' eyes grew troubled. "You took a beating rather than renounce your claim about a crucified messiah?"

Joanna inched to the front of her seat and willed Phasaelis to understand. "It seems like foolishness, but after what we witnessed throughout Jesus' life, and after he sent his Spirit to us—"

Phasaelis held up one hand. "Wait, his Spirit?"

Joanna explained how the Holy Spirit had descended on the day of Pentecost.

"Fire from heaven?" Phasaelis' lips quirked in amusement. "Joanna, if you were anyone else, I would call you a liar."

"But it is me," Joanna said. "You know how much I love the Lord."

Phasaelis threw back her head with a laugh. "Half our conversations were about you trying to teach me about your God."

Joanna fiddled with her cup. "And here I go again, right?"

Phasaelis tucked her legs beside her and leaned one elbow on a bolster. "So, what now? If everything you said is true, what are you supposed to do while you wait for your savior to come back?"

"The kingdom begins now," Joanna said. "Everything we do is with the kingdom of God in mind."

Phasaelis considered for a long moment. "I'll admit, I hardly know what to think."

Pavda stepped into the courtyard holding a lamp, and Joanna clutched her hands in her lap. She had run out of time.

She turned to Phasaelis. "I wish I didn't need to pile it all on at once. But if your father and my husband finish their negotiations tonight, I could be leaving tomorrow."

Phasaelis' expression fell. "I wish you could stay."

Joanna reached for her hand. "I'm grateful we had this chance."

They stood together under the starry sky. Joanna's chest was bursting with a thousand unspoken words, but there wasn't enough time to say them all.

Joanna collected Nadia from the nursery and hugged Phasaelis farewell.

Phasaelis stepped back. "Well, this was almost the strangest evening we've ever spent together."

Joanna chuckled. "I hope we see each other again someday."

"You can write to me," Phasaelis said. "Perhaps I'll even write back."

Joanna laughed and kissed her friend on the cheek. Her chest ached as she turned and walked away.

Joanna found their guest room empty. Lamplight cast patterns over the walls and danced on the gleaming pool of water. The only noise was the splashing fountain and the song of cicadas drifting through the window.

She nursed Nadia and laid her on the bed. Peering out the window at the starry sky, she repeated the conversation with Phasaelis over and over in her head. Had she said too much, or not enough? Peter had given one sermon and three thousand men and women were baptized. Her lips twisted ruefully. She was no Peter.

She sat at the vanity and unclasped her necklace. Perhaps she asked too much from one conversation, but the past few years had taught her to expect miracles. She leaned her elbows on the tabletop and tipped her face into her palms.

Chuza strode into the room and gave her an exhausted but happy smile. He shrugged out of his coat, and leaned forward to kiss Nadia's forehead before planting a kiss on Joanna's lips.

"The peace will stand. The King agreed to honor the borders. Not because he respects Antipas," Chuza twisted his lips, "but out of regard for Caesar."

"I'm proud of you. I knew you could do it."

Chuza sat on the bed and scanned her face. "How was your evening?"

"Phasaelis asked what I've been doing these past few years, so we talked about Jesus."

"How did that go?"

Joanna lifted her shoulders. "She was interested, I guess."

"All these years, you've been trying to lead her to faith. You can only do so much. The rest has to come from her."

"I know." Though she wished it was possible to drag someone to faith against their will.

Chuza rose and undressed.

"So we leave tomorrow?" Joanna asked.

"Bright and early."

A rapid knock roused Joanna from her sleep. The room was tinted pink. She sat up groggily as the door swung wide, and then her eyes flew open.

"Phasa!" she exclaimed.

Chuza jerked awake as the princess stormed into their room. Joanna scrambled out of bed, and her stomach plummeted when she realized Phasaelis was in tears.

She hurried around the pool. "What happened? Is your family alright?"

Phasaelis shook her head, then nodded.

"Then what's wrong?" Joanna asked.

"I believe you!" Phasaelis burst out. "I believe in your Jesus. But what do I do?"

Joanna froze, staring at the princess. "You believe Jesus is the Messiah? That he died for your sins and was raised up on the third day?"

"I do." Phasaelis dragged her hands down her cheeks, leaving pale streaks on her flushed face. "It sounds insane, but I do."

Joanna's mind spun like a whirlwind. The room was silent except for the splashing of the water fountain. The sound galvanized her into action.

"Then you must be baptized," Joanna said. "In the waters of baptism, we die with Christ, our sins dying with us. We are raised up new creatures, children of God and heirs of the kingdom."

Phasaelis bobbed her head. "Let's do it."

Chuza yanked a robe over his tunic, his eyes wide.

Joanna stepped down into the tepid pool, and the water rose to her thighs. Phasaelis bent to flick off her sandals. Tossing aside her shawl, the princess stepped into the water, and her costly robe bloomed around her.

With her heart in her throat, Joanna took her friend by the shoulders. "I baptize you in the name of the Father, the Son, and the Holy Spirit." She gently laid Phasaelis back until the princess was fully submerged, and then, with difficulty, she hauled Phasaelis to her feet. Phasaelis sputtered, and Joanna pulled her into a hug.

Phasaelis clung to her as water streamed from her hair and face. "I am forgiven?" Phasaelis whispered. "Every sin I ever committed is gone?"

"Yes. You are one of God's children, and nothing can separate you from him. Now you must live in faith, with love and mercy, as Jesus showed us."

Phasaelis' brow puckered. "But I'm alone. How can I be part of God's people when it is just me?"

Joanna's chest squeezed. It was the same question that haunted her since Jerusalem, but Phasaelis was even more cut off.

She ran her hands down Phasaelis' dripping arms to clasp her hands. "Even though we're far apart, we're still family. And this good news will spread. Perhaps you can tell some of your friends. Your husband."

Phasaelis' eyes widened. "I could never explain it the way you did. You were there."

"But you can explain what happened to you. What brought you to be standing in this water at the crack of dawn."

Phasaelis burst into laughter. They sloshed out of the pool, and at that moment, Amud knocked and entered, jerking to a stop as he saw the two dripping women.

"Amud," Chuza said calmly, as if nothing was odd. "Could you fetch a change of clothes for the princess?"

Amud spun around without a word.

Joanna burst into laughter and the two women hugged again. It had taken years, but her prayers for Phasaelis had finally been answered.

Joanna beamed at her husband. They had both found peace in Nabatea.

Antipas strode into his room and found Herodias waiting for him. Something in her manner put him on guard.

He cleared his throat and stepped to the sideboard to pour himself a cup of wine. He took a deep drink before facing her.

"Chuza did it," he said, and satisfaction warmed his chest. "He negotiated peace with Nabatea without losing a finger-width of my territory."

Herodias tilted her head to the side. "He only did his duty as your slave. Do you expect me to sing his praises?"

Antipas sighed and carried his cup to his desk. Herodias might not be convinced, but Antipas was reassured. Chuza was still loyal to him.

Herodias sashayed forward and leaned both hands on his desk, allowing her neckline to gape tantalizingly. "I received a letter from my brother Aristobulus, in Antioch."

His eyes were glued to her cleavage. "Oh?" His voice came out higher than he intended.

"It seems Agrippa got into a spot of trouble. Something about accepting bribes."

The warm feeling in Antipas' belly evaporated, and he leaned back in his chair with a frown.

She twirled a curl around her finger and spoke sweetly. "Agrippa and Cypros have moved to Ptolemais. Perhaps we can send them some money? They do have three children to support."

Her eyes were innocent, but he saw her game.

"Absolutely not."

# THIRTY-SIX

Jovian gazed around the triclinium. The soft couch under his hips was no more welcoming than the hard bench in his father's cart. He had dreaded this conversation for weeks, and now it was here.

His parents' eyes betrayed their intuition. Their son was about to turn their lives upside down. Again.

Horace sat next to his wife, and Persephone was perched next to her mother, her face pale. She sensed it, too.

Jovian's stomach swooped as if he teetered on a precipice. "I've booked passage to Judea."

Thea's face crumpled. "No, Jovian, you can't."

"I have to." He was afraid to look at Persephone.

"What on earth for?" Belen demanded.

Alone in his room, Jovian had tried to formulate an explanation. Everything he wanted to say would sound insane to them, but he had to try.

"The prophet I believed was dead, is alive."

It was as if he threw a bucket of cold water over the room. They stared at him, blinking in confused shock.

"Wait." Persephone leaned forward. "This is what you were talking about in the synagogue."

"Synagogue?" Belen and Thea said in unison.

Jovian turned toward Persephone. After months of secrecy, it was time to come clean. "I've been going back to talk with the rabbi."

"And you never told me?" She leaned away from him, her eyes darkening with pain.

Belen's eyes narrowed angrily. "The rabbi? Are you becoming a *Jew*?" The way he spat the name made Jovian's insides curdle. Thea covered her mouth, and Persephone looked at her parents with panic in her eyes.

Jovian held up his hands. "I just need to learn more. I'm not becoming a Jew." At least, not yet.

Horace blinked like an owl on a sunny afternoon. "So you are leaving Antioch on a religious quest? For the Jewish God?"

"The only God," Jovian said firmly.

The air in the room thickened as everyone glanced at each other and joined forces against him.

Jovian's stubbornness rose. "I saw a prophet crucified." The women gasped at the word, but Jovian wouldn't retreat. "Three thousand people believe he rose from the dead."

"Three thousand Jews in a remote city in the middle of nowhere." Belen threw his hands in the air. "For this, you go on some pilgrimage to their holy land?"

The others all began speaking at once.

Jovian folded his arms across his middle. He had been right. They'd never understand.

Horace raised his voice to speak over the others. "Alright everyone, let's calm down. We were all young once." He turned to Jovian. "How long will you be gone?"

Jovian hesitated. "I don't know."

Horace's voice sharpened. "And my daughter is just supposed to wait for you?"

Jovian's pulse quickened. He had wrestled over this question for weeks, trying to see it from every angle, and he came to the same conclusion every time. He didn't want to marry a woman who did not share his beliefs.

But he had made a promise, so the choice was up to her.

"I don't expect her to wait. If Persephone wishes to be released from our betrothal, I will understand." He tried to look like he wanted the opposite, but his face must have revealed the truth.

Persephone jerked to her feet. "I should have ended things the moment you dragged us into that synagogue." Jovian winced at her tone and the tears in her eyes. She stormed from the room, and her mother hurried after her.

Horace stood, his face dark with anger. "Consider the betrothal ended. Our two houses will not unite, as I had hoped."

Belen jerked as if slapped.

Jovian hesitated only a moment before he sidled past Horace to go after Persephone. She stood in the courtyard with her back to him, staring at the bronze statue pouring water into the fountain. Lyra hovered nearby.

"I am sorry, Persephone," Jovian said. "I had every intention of making you happy. I never wanted to cause you pain."

Persephone whirled to face him. Her eyes burned with dry heat. "You're lost, Jovian Titus. Floundering for meaning in life. I'm only glad you revealed your weakness before you dragged me down with you."

With trembling hands she unhooked the earrings he gave her at their betrothal. Lyra stepped forward to interfere, but Persephone shook her head as she unclasped the lapis lazuli necklace.

"No, Persephone," he whispered around his aching throat. "Those are yours."

"I don't want them," she said tightly, and tried to twist the ring off her finger. It was stuck.

"Then sell them."

Her hands stilled as she closed her eyes, pain and resignation flickering over her face. Finally, she met his gaze, her eyes dry. "Good day, Titus. I wish you every happiness."

With the remnants of their betrothal in her fist, she strode from the room. Her mother rushed after her.

Jovian dragged both hands through his hair, tipping his face to the sky and groaning. This was harder than he expected.

After gathering his nerve, Jovian returned to the triclinium.

His parents cut off their conversation as he sat back down. Thea wiped her cheeks, and Jovian steeled himself. He would not back down.

Belen leaned forward, his palms outstretched. "Explain it to me, son. Make me understand why you're abandoning your family, your betrothed, and even your gods."

Jovian swiped his damp palms down his thighs. "The world is changing, and it starts in Judea. Jesus announced a kingdom that will affect everyone, including Antioch. Perhaps even Rome."

Belen scowled. "Nothing can change Rome. Especially not a small kingdom like Judea." He jerked to his feet and paced the room. "Admit it. You're running away again. The first time you were running from your patron's daughter. Now you flee Persephone. Or is it me you are running from? The life of a merchant?"

The pain in his voice tore at Jovian's conscience. "You have Sergio to help with the business."

"I wanted you too!" Belen threw his hands in the air. "All my life, I worked to provide you with everything. And you throw it back in my face."

Jovian dropped his gaze, guilt lancing through him. "It isn't like that."

"Isn't it?" Belen said.

Thea's quiet voice filled the room. "When do you leave?"

"In two days."

Thea turned her face away as Belen stomped from the room.

Jovian studied his palms, shame and doubt twining around his chest. It would have been better for everyone if he'd never come home.

Thea came to sit beside him. She leaned against his shoulder, and he wrapped his arm around her. They sat side-by-side as the minutes slid past. Jovian turned to kiss the top of her head, closing his eyes as he drew in the fragrance of her perfume. Guilt weighed on him, but this was what he needed to do.

"You must come back," Thea said. Jovian hesitated, but Thea peered into his face. "You will return to this house. Promise me."

Jovian hesitated to make the vow, but as tears trickled down his mother's face, he nodded. "I promise."

She sagged against him and tears burned in his eyes. The last time he left home, he only thought about himself. Knowing that he was hurting his family only made his choice harder. But he needed to know if the God of Israel was everything he claimed to be.

"I almost envy you." Galen peered around at the bustling port. Wind stirred their hair with the scent of adventure.

Jovian hitched his heavy bags on his shoulder. One held his armor and sword, the other his changes of clothes and some food. He had spent nearly all of his money on boat passage to Joppa. The two men stood on the quay as small waves rocked the waiting ship. Sailors shouted to one another, loading the last of the merchandise into the hull.

"You could come with me," Jovian said. He was not surprised when Galen shook his head.

"I can't. My father needs me. And besides," he grinned, "I said I *almost* envy you. If you need to run from a woman, at least pick someplace you can watch a race."

Jovian bristled. "I'm not running away from Persephone. She would have made a lovely wife."

"Right." Galen slapped Jovian's back. "Just like you would have been content as a merchant."

Jovian shot him a disparaging look, but Galen gripped his shoulder and leaned closer. "Just don't lose yourself in Judea, alright?"

Jovian tried to smile, wishing he could explain this aching call on his heart.

"Come aboard!" a sailor bellowed from the ship deck. Passengers climbed the gangplank.

Jovian's heart jumped into his throat, and he hauled Galen into a crushing hug. "I'll miss you."

"Good. Then maybe you'll come back." Galen's voice was rough with emotion.

He gripped Galen's shoulder. "May God protect you."

Galen smiled crookedly. "Which god?"

Jovian didn't answer. His pulse quickened as he climbed the gangplank. He wove his way to the ship's railing and dropped his bags. Galen was still waiting, watching from shore.

The sailors hoisted the gangplank and the sail unfurled, snapping to catch the wind. Galen put his hands on either side of his mouth and shouted, "Which god?"

Jovian grinned as he leaned against the railing to shout back. "The only God!"

Galen seemed to laugh, but Jovian couldn't hear him as the ship slid from its berth. Behind him, the other passengers hastened to choose prime spots on the deck, but Jovian gripped the railing, watching the city until the ship turned its prow for the mouth of the river and joined the current that would draw them to the sea.

Jovian licked his lips and tasted the dust of the promised land. His shoulders ached beneath the straps of his bags, but he was back.

He reached the height of the hill and his pulse skipped a beat. Jerusalem spread before him, just as he remembered it. The towers of Herod's Palace rose over the bulky city walls. Someone at the palace would know where Chuza had gone.

It was more than a year since Jovian had left. Was Chuza angry with him? Leah had surely moved on. She might even be married. His insides squirmed at the thought, but he stamped his rebellious heart down. He would be happy for her. Not only was Leah a Jew and he a Greek, Persephone's dry, angry eyes still haunted him. He wasn't cut out for a relationship.

Jovian made no claims on Leah's heart, but he did need to speak with her. She, better than anyone, would understand the questions that plagued him. She knew what it was like to doubt God's goodness.

Jovian adjusted his bags and marched to a city gate. He ignored the suspicious glances as he joined the busy main street. The temple mount dominated the eastern side of the city and Jovian's pulse fluttered with a mixture of good and bad memories. He turned toward Herod's Palace, and his eagerness to find Chuza gave strength to his weary legs.

The palace rose ahead of him, and as Jovian reached the steps, he was relieved to recognize the guards.

"Marcus!" he called.

"Titus?" The guard stared in shock. Jovian climbed the steps, grinning as he extended his hand. Marcus gripped his wrist. "What are you doing here?"

"I'm looking for Chuza."

Marcus' expression grew troubled. "The steward isn't here. Have you heard what happened in the city?"

"Some of it."

Marcus puffed his breath through his lips. "I couldn't believe it when I saw the women beaten like that."

Jovian stiffened. "What women?"

"Titus?" a familiar voice called from within the palace courtyard. Jovian turned as a bearded man strode forward, his tzitzit bouncing as he walked. Manaen grinned widely, his arms extended. "Thank God you've returned!"

Jovian was taken aback at this welcome.

Manaen spoke to Marcus. "He will come with me."

Jovian let Antipas' foster-brother lead him into the palace courtyard.

"You must be looking for Chuza," Manaen said as they walked.

"What was Marcus talking about? Women beaten?"

Manaen sighed. "I will explain everything."

He led Jovian into a suite of rooms. A woman rose as they entered, and Jovian recognized her crescent-shaped dimples. She was one of Joanna's friends who had followed Jesus. What was she doing in the palace?

"My wife, Maryam," Manaen said, and Jovian blinked in surprise. Manaen chuckled. "And her son, Joses."

A man rose from behind a desk with a smile. "I remember you."

Jovian slid his bags to the ground. Maryam poured wine, and Manaen gestured to a soft seat.

But Jovian didn't sit.

"What women?" he asked, though he feared he knew.

Manaen sat heavily. "A lot has happened. It'll be easier if I start from the beginning."

Jovian clenched his jaw, and Maryam shook her head at her husband. "We should ease his mind first." She offered Jovian a cup of wine, but he refused.

Maryam set the cup aside. "Joanna and Leah were flogged, but they're alright now. They're safe."

Jovian's legs wobbled and he sank into his seat.

Manaen propped his elbows on his knees as he explained what had been happening in Jerusalem. The first months of excitement after Jesus' resurrection were chased by months of uncertainty. Arrests. Death.

Jovian scanned their faces. "So how were Joanna and Leah…"

Maryam's lips pursed in sympathy. "We were planning to leave.

Leah sneaked into the city to collect her friend, and Joanna went after her."

Memories pushed into Jovian's mind. He remembered chasing Leah into the city, the way her braid bounced between her shoulder blades, the flash of her sandals. But this time, Jovian wasn't around to protect her.

"They spent a night in prison." Manaen shook his head. "We feared the worst, but Chuza petitioned the Sanhedrin to spare their lives."

Jovian jerked upright and paced the room. He should have been here. "So, what about the others? Has everyone left Jerusalem?"

"The twelve are still here," Manaen said. "Saul won't arrest them for fear of inciting a riot."

"But everyone else—"

"Most have left the city."

Jovian tried to wrap his head around it all. "But I thought the kingdom was coming."

"It has, and it is," Manaen said. "Jesus beat sin and death, but the powers of this world haven't given up."

Jovian looked at his bag of armor. "There will be a war?"

The other three tensed.

"The war is being raged on the spiritual plane," Manaen said firmly. "The twelve insist we are not to raise arms."

Maryam stepped behind Manaen and put her hand on his shoulder. "Our ancestors did not have to fight their way out of Egypt. God can free us from Rome without us lifting a single weapon."

Jovian sat back down. Hunger and weariness rolled over him like a smothering wave. "So everyone is just waiting around for Jesus to return?"

"We are teaching the people the good news of Jesus Christ," Maryam said.

It made sense. The people needed to know who their Messiah was.

Manaen peered into Jovian's face. "What about you? Do you believe?"

Jovian nodded. He believed, even if he didn't know what to do with his belief. It was like he had jumped onto a wild horse and was galloping with the wind, with no idea where he was headed. The best he could do right now was keep from tumbling to the ground.

# THIRTY-SEVEN

Wind blew through Chuza's hair as he rocked with Celer's smooth lope. The pounding hooves were like a second heartbeat as Celer's powerful muscles stretched and contracted beneath him with every stride. Sunlight danced over the tall grass that rippled like an inland sea, and grasshoppers leaped out of Celer's way.

The grape harvest would be underway by now, including the harvest at Joanna's childhood home. His memories of her vineyard were bittersweet. Joanna had traded the property for Amichai's freedom, but the young man hadn't stuck around to appreciate the family's sacrifice.

Celer's ears flicked backward, attuned to Chuza's frustration.

Chuza reined in Celer and leaned forward to pat his neck. He scanned the valley and looked up to the hills where Nazareth was concealed. Jesus had grown up there. He surely walked these same paths.

Jesus had been a man just like him. He had known loss, frustration, and responsibility. Somehow, that was comforting.

Chuza nudged Celer's side with his heels, and they turned back toward Sepphoris. A traveler marched down the main road with heavy bags slung over his shoulder. His hair was short, but his stride was familiar. Chuza's pulse skipped a beat. It couldn't be. He trotted Celer closer, and the man lifted his face.

Chuza's jaw dropped. He leaned forward and swung his leg over Celer's back to land with both feet in the dust.

"Am I seeing things?"

"If you are, then so am I." Titus grinned. Chuza walked forward as if in a dream, his gaze sweeping over Titus' familiar brown eyes and crooked nose.

Before he knew what he was doing, Chuza hauled Titus into a fierce hug. "You came back!"

"I shouldn't have left."

Months of worry thickened Chuza's throat as he stepped back. "You're right."

Titus' brows tipped. "I wish I could do it over. All I can say now is that I'm sorry."

"I just wish you stayed long enough to know that—"

"That Jesus rose again?"

Chuza blinked at him. "How did you find out?"

"It's a long story." Titus tipped his head toward the city. "Perhaps we can talk about it on the way?"

Chuza helped Titus tie his bags together and balance them over Celer's saddle. He led his mount as the men walked side by side up to the city.

Chuza studied Titus' familiar profile. It was hard to believe this was real. "What happened to you? Why did you leave without saying goodbye?"

Titus sighed heavily. "I couldn't reconcile what I saw Jesus do in Galilee with that broken body on the cross." Pain flickered over his face, and Chuza's heart twisted in sympathy. "I didn't tell you I was leaving because I was afraid you'd convince me to stay."

Of course he would have tried to make Titus stay. He was his friend.

"So what made you come back?" Chuza asked.

As Titus explained, Chuza blinked in realization. Saul had inadvertently sent the good news all the way to Syria. He pushed that thought away. He wasn't ready to credit Saul with any good deed —even accidental.

"So, you believed Micah?" Chuza asked as they passed the city guards and joined the main road that led up to the palace.

Titus smiled ruefully. "I didn't at first. But a friend convinced me. He told me that the coming kingdom is not just good news for the Jews, but the Greeks too."

"Because the Greeks—and the rest of the world—will come under the covenant of Abraham." His pulse leaped. Was Titus ready to take the rites and become a proselyte?

Titus seemed to read his thoughts. "I can't be bound by that covenant."

Chuza swallowed back his disappointment. "Why not?"

"My family. I'm not ready to cut myself off from them."

"You wouldn't have to."

"You know I would."

Frustrated, Chuza scanned the busy street. As people went about their business, Jews and Gentiles intersected, but it was like an invisible wall kept them apart. Titus could enter the Court of Gentiles, but he couldn't pray with Chuza in the inner courts. They could eat together, but only in Jewish spaces, with food prepared by Jewish hands.

Part of him was glad that Titus was taking the decision seriously. But as long as Titus refused to become a proselyte, he could never fully join the chosen people. He would be stuck halfway between his Greek roots and his faith in the Jewish God.

They stopped at the palace gate. Chuza slid Titus' gear off Celer's saddle and handed it over. He forced himself not to look back as he led his horse into the stable courtyard and passed Celer off to a groom.

He was relieved to find Titus waiting for him, leaning on the palace wall with his arms crossed.

"Come on," Chuza said. "Joanna and Leah will want to see you." He did not miss the nervousness that spread over Titus' face as the soldier hefted up his heavy bags.

"I can't wait to show you my new house," Chuza said with a chuckle, "but it might be a little more crowded than you expect."

Jovian steeled himself as Chuza led him through the doorway and into a large portico. Familiar voices beckoned him into the central courtyard, and he stared in surprise at Joanna's extended family.

Miriam and Dalia were setting the table, and Dalia's middle was round with pregnancy. Alexander and his father sat around the table and compared sheets of papyrus. Two children, a boy and a girl, knelt on the ground, playing a game with colorful sticks.

Joanna's relationship with her sister was tense, so why was Dalia's extended family acting like this was their home?

His breath caught as Leah strode toward the table with a large clay pot, her hands protected by a thick cloth. As if sensing his presence, she turned.

Their eyes met.

Jovian fell into those hazel depths, forgetting to breathe. Then embarrassment hit him like the flat side of a sword.

Leah turned scarlet. Without a word, she plunked down the pot and fled into the house. The others noticed Leah's hurried retreat, and they stared at Jovian with surprise.

"Perhaps I should have warned her." Chuza cast Jovian a sheepish look. "I almost forgot you two were..." Now it was his turn to flush. "That you two were friends," he finished lamely.

Jovian's neck heated with guilt. He had not treated Leah like a friend when he left without a word.

Joanna hurried out of the house with a baby on her hip. She stared at him in shock. "I can't believe it!"

The child reached for Chuza, and Chuza took the baby into his arms as naturally as if he did this everyday.

Jovian gaped at him. "You had a baby?"

"This is Nadia," Chuza said, and his chest puffed with pride.

Jovian crouched to see the child better. The little girl had her father's eyes, but Joanna's smile.

"You must be starving," Joanna said, and without waiting for him to answer, she steered him toward the low table. "Come and sit down."

Jovian hesitated. He expected Alexander and his father to frown at the idea of a Greek man joining them at their table, but they both nodded in welcome. Dalia smiled as she offered him a cup of wine. Slightly dizzy from this unexpected welcome, Jovian set his bags down and sat cross-legged on the soft mat.

Dalia brought more food to the table, familiar dishes that resurrected years of memories. Leah didn't reappear until everyone was gathered. She kept her gaze averted and chose a spot far down the table.

Chuza cleared his throat and the others fell silent. "Let's give thanks to the Lord for bringing our friend back." Jovian flushed as Chuza prayed, uncomfortable with being the center of attention.

As "amens" floated around the table, Chuza grinned. "Jovian has heard and accepted the good news."

Joanna looked at Titus in surprise, and he smiled awkwardly. Glancing around at all their smiling faces, Jovian realized that every single member of this family believed. His shock mingled with a thread of jealousy as he remembered his bitter farewell back home.

"So that's why you came back?" Alexander asked.

Jovian accepted a platter of flatbread from Joanna. He took a piece and passed the dish to Alexander. "I'm actually not sure why I came back," he admitted. "When I heard my friends were in danger, I—" he cut himself off. He flushed and lifted his shoulders. "I wanted to be here. Where it will all begin."

"Begin?" Joanna asked.

"The kingdom of God," Jovian said.

The others around the table shared knowing smiles, and Leah cast Jovian a curious glance. His stomach swooped as their eyes met.

Alexander's father asked Jovian about his journey, and conversation flowed around the table. Jovian sneaked glances at Leah, tracing the changes on her face. She had matured in his absence, growing even more beautiful. He drew that thought up short. There was no future for him and Leah besides friendship—if she would allow even that.

Chuza insisted Jovian spend the night. A bed was prepared for him on the roof, overlooking the city.

Jovian bedded down under the stars and listened to the rumblings of the city and the rhythmic song of cicadas. Folding his arms behind his head, he stared up at the sky. He had made it. He expected a sense of satisfaction, but instead, a question spiraled in his mind— what now?

# Thirty-Eight

Leah entered the courtyard, smoothing her hair and straightening her robe. The pale sky hinted at sunrise, and the air was sweet with dew. A cook's day began before dawn, but this was early, even for her.

"Good morning."

Jovian's voice turned Leah's stomach inside out. It wasn't fair that he still affected her like this.

He stood across the courtyard at the bottom of the stairs.

"I'm off to work," she said. Thankfully, her voice sounded normal.

Jovian's eyebrows rose. "You don't wait for Chuza?"

Chuza wouldn't leave for hours yet. Leah crossed her arms. "Antipas might object to eating his breakfast at noon."

He fidgeted with his hands as he took a few steps closer. "May I walk with you?"

Leah hesitated and glanced at the sky. A palace servant came each morning to escort her, but he wasn't due yet. It was either stand here and make awkward conversation, or walk as fast as possible to the palace.

She nodded once, and Jovian followed her through the portico and into the empty street. He walked silently by her side, and Leah began to hope they could make it to the palace without either of them saying a word.

But then he cleared his throat. "I wanted to say that I'm sorry. I shouldn't have left the way I did."

Her cheeks flamed. "I'm sorry too. I should never have made you witness the—" her tongue tripped over the word "—crucifixions."

When he didn't answer, she dared to peek up at his face. Pain flickered over his features as he dragged a hand through his hair. "I'll admit, I had nightmares for months."

Guilt surged up her throat. She walked several paces before she realized Jovian had stopped. She squeezed her eyes shut, and tension radiated down her limbs. As much as it hurt, she deserved his bitterness.

She turned to face him.

He said, "It's not your fault, you know. I don't blame you."

That couldn't be true. She wrapped her arms around herself. "Would you have left if you hadn't seen… that?"

Jovian winced, and Leah whirled back around and strode for the palace. He left because of her. She was the reason he was plagued with nightmares. If she had just gone back to the palace when he asked, he would have been in Jerusalem when Jesus rose from the dead. She had ruined everything for him.

"Leah, wait," he said and jogged to catch up. "Leaving was my choice. I fled rather than face the truth."

She couldn't look at him. "What truth?"

"That even with faith, the world is cruel."

She had learned that lesson long ago. Painful memories climbed up her throat and burned her eyes. She needed to get away. She couldn't cry in front of him, not again.

But he lengthened his stride to keep up. "Before I left, we, uh, shared a moment."

Leah's cheeks burned. Now? He wanted to discuss this now?

Jovian reached for her arm but let his hand fall. "I want you to know I cared for you. I would never have held you... like that... if I didn't."

Leah wished the earth would open beneath her feet and swallow her up. She had believed herself to be in love and even hoped for a betrothal. She recoiled from the memory.

"That was a long time ago." She flicked her wrist. "We both moved on." Her heart squeezed painfully as his silence spoke his agreement.

They reached the palace gate, and she forced herself to face him and smile. "Thanks for walking me, Titus." She purposefully used his family name.

He winced. "Don't do that."

"Do what?" she asked, feigning innocence.

"I want to be friends."

It wasn't so simple. "How long are you staying in Sepphoris?"

"Until I know what I'm supposed to do with my life."

Her chest heated. This was just some pilgrimage to him. "I hate to break it to you, but it's not like God is handing everyone assignments."

Jovian leaned toward her, and her breath caught at the earnestness in his gaze. "I just need to be with people who understand. Back in Antioch, I was with my friends and family, but none of them believe in God. The way they talked about Jews..." He trailed off. "I guess I just felt alone."

He felt alone? He had left her to deal with the guilt and grief over his disappearance for more than a year.

Her emotions overflowed like a boiling pot. "You came here to feel accepted?" She scoffed. "You may be a God-fearer, but you're not one of us."

His jaw slackened. She shoved open the door and escaped into the palace, tears blurring her vision.

Jovian stood stunned as the door slammed in his face. Out of everyone, he'd been sure she would understand.

He gritted his teeth. Well, if she wanted to be left alone, it was fine by him.

His stomach rumbled, but Jovian couldn't return to Chuza's house with Leah's words ringing in his ears. He couldn't face their smiles while wondering if they welcomed him for who he was, and not for who they hoped he'd become.

He wandered down the city streets.

The market booths were just opening. Jovian stopped to purchase a loaf of warm, yeasty bread. He leaned against a building and watched the city come alive as he ate his breakfast. The men striding past had trades—carpenters, bakers, leather workers, beekeepers, perfumers, jewelers, weavers, and scribes.

His hand reached for his sword hilt and grasped air. He had spent years training to join the army as an officer. Another plan that came to nothing.

Persephone's accusation taunted him. Was he lost and floundering for meaning? Returning to Israel and those who shared his faith hadn't brought the relief he hoped for.

He pushed off the wall and strode toward the permanent shops and warehouses. He couldn't stay in Chuza's house forever, but he would need money to rent a room. Someone in Sepphoris must need a Gentile with his skill set.

Chuza peeked into the kitchen and was relieved to find Leah busy at work. But where was Titus? When Chuza went to call him for breakfast, he found Jovian's sleeping mat already rolled and put away. Maybe Leah knew where the Greek man had gone, but the tension in her jaw suggested she was in no mood to talk.

Chuza stepped backward and strode down the hallway. It had

been more than a year since the young people saw each other, and based on the glances across the table last night, things were awkward. He sighed, unsure how to navigate this particular mess.

Chuza turned the corner and paused. The captain of the guard waited outside his office door.

"Can I have a moment?" Eli asked.

Chuza gestured to the door and followed Eli inside. The gray-haired captain had commanded Antipas' guard for decades, choosing which men to accompany the tetrarch, which to leave in specific palaces, and running all of them through grueling drills.

"Wine?" Chuza asked, picking up the pitcher.

The captain shook his head. Chuza poured himself a cup and sat at his desk. Eli stood with a wide stance and his hands clasped behind his back.

Chuza took a drink and set the cup aside. "How can I help you?"

"There's an applicant who wants to join the guard," Eli said. "The thing is, he's worked for me before and I dismissed him."

"Oh?" Chuza drummed his fingers on the table. "Well, I trust your judgment. If he isn't a good fit, send him on his way."

"That's the problem," Eli said. "He was a good fit. He never shirked his duties, trained hard, and was skilled in combat. I would have trusted him with my life."

Chuza furrowed his brow. "Then why did you dismiss him?"

Eli colored. "Because he disobeyed a direct order."

Understanding dawned, and Chuza leaned back in his seat. "You're talking about Titus, aren't you?"

Eli nodded and Chuza frowned. Titus hadn't mentioned coming back to work at the palace.

Eli stiffened. "If you think I was right to let him go—"

"No, it's not that."

Eli's shoulders eased. "I was too hasty in dismissing him, considering what I asked him to do." He looked down at the floor. "I'm not too proud to give him a second chance. If you approve, that is."

Chuza sipped his drink to stall for time. Perhaps Titus wanted to give Leah some space, and moving into the barracks would certainly afford them that.

"Go ahead and hire him," Chuza said.

"I'll get him on the roster right away." He turned to go but then paused. "I remember he was your friend. You must be pleased he came back."

As the captain left, Chuza rose to peer out the window. 'Pleased' didn't even come close. Titus' return was an answer to prayer, a chance to finish what Chuza had started.

The young man belonged with the people of God.

Jovian bounced on his heels as he waited outside the palace gate for Chuza. It took dozens of doors slamming in his face before he accepted Leah was right. He wasn't one of them, and he might never be.

But he had swallowed his pride and went to his old captain. And now he had a job. For the first time in months, his hip felt naked without the weight of his sword.

Chuza stepped through the doorway and Jovian jumped forward. "Did you hear?"

"I did," Chuza said with a smile.

"I'll gather my things right away."

Chuza set a hand on his shoulder. "You can move into the barracks, but you're not getting away that easily."

Jovian blinked and Chuza leaned closer. "The believers meet on the first day of the week in our house, and we share a special meal to remember Jesus. I expect you to be there."

Jovian tensed. Not only would that mean seeing Leah, but there would certainly be other Jews, strangers who would regard a Greek man with suspicion.

He smiled weakly at Chuza. "Do I have a choice?"

Chuza grinned. "Not about this."

# THIRTY-NINE

Jovian stood outside Chuza's house and rubbed his palms over his bristly face. He had decided to grow a beard with the hope it would help him fit in. An elderly couple approached, and Jovian jumped back and allowed them to enter ahead of him. They peered at him in confusion, and his stomach plummeted. Who was he trying to fool? He would never fit in here.

Chuza stuck his head out the door and shot Jovian an impatient glance. "What are you waiting for? Come in!"

Jovian pulled his courage around himself like a cloak and strode into the house.

The courtyard bustled under the twilight sky. Leah was carefully lighting the lamps. He pulled his gaze away from her and allowed Chuza to lead him over to half a dozen men. Jovian inclined his head to each of them as he was introduced, but their names tangled in his mind.

Across the courtyard, the women chatted happily as they laid out a meal on two tables pushed into an L shape. Several children chased each other in a game of their own. It felt like a close-knit community, and Jovian's heart ached with the impossible hope that, someday, this could be his community too.

Once the table was ready, everyone found a seat. Jovian stiffened, not knowing where he belonged, but Alexander beckoned him to sit between him and Chuza.

Leah was almost in arm's reach, with Joanna's baby in her lap. Though she didn't look at him, a soft blush painted her cheeks. They hadn't spoken since their argument at the palace gate. His chest tightened at the memory. He'd been a fool for expecting her to forgive him for leaving.

Joanna came from the house with a tray bearing a large loaf of unleavened bread and a single cup. Everyone grew silent.

Joanna set down the tray and scanned the group. "My friends, on the day before he was crucified, Jesus took the bread and he gave it to his disciples, saying, 'Take and eat. This is my body, given for you.'" She tore a piece from the bread, then handed the loaf to Alexander's father. He tore a piece and passed the bread to his wife. She repeated the action and gave it to Dalia, who took a piece and passed it to Alexander.

Jovian's pulse leaped as he realized it was his turn. But he wasn't a Jew, and he was unfamiliar with this ritual. What was he supposed to do?

His mouth dried as Alexander passed the bread to him. Jovian prepared to tear off a piece, but the elderly man cleared his throat.

"What is he doing?"

Suddenly the bread in Jovian's hand felt like a lump of burning coal. He tried to pass it to Chuza, but Chuza wouldn't take it.

Chuza spoke calmly. "Jovian believes that Jesus died for our sins and rose on the third day."

The elderly man screwed up his mouth and glanced around at the others. "But he is Greek." It sounded like a curse.

Jovian wished he could crawl under the table as men and women murmured, discussing his right to be here. Leah had been right. He might be a God-fearer, but he would never be one of them.

Joanna still stood by the tray with the cup of wine. A deep V cut between her brows as she scanned the group.

"Enough," she said firmly. The others fell silent. "We take this meal to remember Jesus' sacrifice for us. Don't turn it into something contentious." She met Jovian's eyes and smiled. "We should rejoice that one of the Gentiles has come to believe in the Lord. Let's not become a stumbling block to him."

Jovian's palms dampened as a long, silent moment dragged through the courtyard. Finally, the men nodded.

Jovian's hand trembled as he tore off a small piece and passed the loaf to Chuza. He put the bread on his tongue, but his mouth was as dry as the desert.

Leah bounced Nadia on her lap as the other women cleared the table. She sneaked a peak at Jovian. He sat between Chuza and Alexander, his jaw tense. She would have died from embarrassment if someone had stopped the Lord's Supper because of her.

Nathan was the eldest of their little community, and he commanded a lot of respect. If he couldn't accept Jovian, it might mean trouble.

She wished Jovian would turn to her, so she could smile and show him she was on his side, but he wouldn't look her way. She couldn't blame him after what she'd said.

The women gathered to wash the dishes in the courtyard kitchen, and Leah rose to join them.

Nathan's wife, Mara, picked up a towel. "Did you hear about my neighbor? He was repairing his roof when he fell and broke his leg."

The other women murmured in sympathy.

Joanna asked, "Is there anything we can do?"

Mara smiled and the wrinkles around her bright eyes deepened. "I was hoping you'd ask. There's still a gaping hole in the middle of their house. I think we should offer to finish the job."

Dalia raised her brows as she poured hot water into a basin. "You mean, we should offer our men to help."

Mara chuckled. "I think it would sow good feelings among Sepphoris for those who follow The Way."

Leah stepped forward. "We can bring a meal to feed both the workers and your neighbors."

"Excellent," Mara said.

Jovian slowly unstrapped his sword and set it in the chest beside his narrow bed. The captain had granted his request for the afternoon off, removing the last obstacle that Jovian had secretly hoped would keep him in the palace.

Jovian pulled his official tunic over his head and exchanged it for one of his own. He strapped on a plain belt, and ran a hand over his beard. It was still too short to hide him in Sepphoris.

He met Chuza at the palace gate. The steward seemed equally apprehensive about their task, but for different reasons.

"Have you ever repaired a roof?" Chuza asked.

Jovian glanced around at the flat roofs in the city, so different from the sloped and tiled roofs in Antioch. He shook his head. "I'm just the muscle."

They met the others outside a small house near the city wall. Alexander stood beside a young Jewish man whose name escaped Jovian's memory.

Nathan was waiting, and he smiled at Chuza in welcome. Jovian flushed as the elderly man assessed him once again. Was he not even acceptable as a laborer?

They were led into a humble home, where a man lay on a narrow bed with his leg tightly bound. His wife swept the floor. Jovian's gaze was pulled to the ceiling, where sunlight poured through a huge hole in the reeds and plaster.

The injured man gave them a gap-toothed grin. "I'm mighty pleased you came." He gestured at the roof. "I'm afraid I made the hole even bigger by tumbling through."

He gave detailed instructions for them to remove the cracked plaster and weave a thick layer of reeds between the wooden beams. Then they'd have to mix new plaster and spread it over the patch.

Chuza leaned toward Jovian and whispered. "Perhaps we should just pay to have this done properly."

That didn't sound like a bad idea.

They got to work. While the other three gathered the broken plaster into baskets, Jovian was given the task of pounding it back into powder so it could be reused. Sweat beaded on his brow as he worked in the small courtyard, a cloth tied over his mouth to keep from inhaling the fine dust.

The injured man's wife came into the courtyard. She was a small woman, and rather shy, but she instructed Jovian on the proper mixture for new plaster. It was a precise combination of clay, crushed shells, finely chopped straw, and water. She had him pour it all into a trough, and he looked about for something to stir it with.

"You'll need to mix it with your feet," she said.

Jovian hesitated. Was she being serious? He looked at her face, but no hint of humor glinted in her eyes. He bent to untie his sandals.

The goopy mixture slid between his toes, cool and not unpleasant. He began to trod back and forth, working it together. It wasn't so bad. But as his legs began to tire, she instructed him to add the old plaster. The mixture thickened even more. His thighs burned, and sweat trickled down his back and under his armpits. The plaster sucked on his legs, splattering as he pulled his calves free. Soon he was filthy up to his knees, and crusty drops had landed on his arms, tunic, and face.

Female voices came from inside the house, and Jovian stifled a groan. He had forgotten that the women were bringing a meal. They would all see the Gentile covered in muck, just like the pigs they despised as unclean.

Chuza and Alexander came down the exterior stairs and gaped at Jovian. A grin teased at the corner of Chuza's mouth, but Jovian's glare stifled any teasing remarks.

"We're ready for the plaster," Alexander said, his lips twitching.

Jovian unstuck his feet with difficulty and stood in the courtyard as Chuza and Alexander heaved the trough up to the roof.

The woman set a jar of water at Jovian's feet. "Wash up," she said and disappeared back into the house.

Jovian regarded the small amount of water doubtfully. It would take a river to wash away the clay encrusting his legs. With a sigh, he found a stick of kindling and used it as a makeshift strigil.

He glanced up as someone stepped into the courtyard.

"Oh!" Leah said, blushing furiously. She carried a large basket. "I was just going to lay the meal. There's too much dust and plaster inside."

He looked at the mess he had made in the small courtyard. "Not much better out here," he said sheepishly.

She set her basket on a tall, narrow table. "Nothing a little sweeping won't fix."

"Let it dry first," Jovian warned as she reached for a broom. "It'll stick to anything." He extended his leg as a prime example.

She glanced at his feet but quickly averted her gaze, swallowing awkwardly.

With most of the plaster scraped from his legs, along with a good bit of leg hair, Jovian sloshed the water over his feet, rubbing them furiously. For some reason, Leah didn't go back inside.

After a long moment, she broke the silence. "It's nice you came." She leaned her seat against the table and gripped the edge with each hand. "Especially after…"

Jovian grunted. "Chuza didn't give me much choice. He thinks it'll help the others accept me." Nathan, in particular.

Leah scuffed the toe of her sandal back and forth. "I'm sorry for what I said."

"No, you were right," he muttered. "I will always be an outsider."

She furrowed her brow. "Then why come back?"

He smiled ruefully. "I'm a God-fearer. I hoped that would be enough." It might be enough to call him righteous, but it wasn't enough to crumble the walls that stood between him and her people. Or between him and her.

He sighed. "I'm still considering becoming a proselyte, but you have to understand, my parents are against it. And I have done so much to disappoint them already."

Her face was frustratingly neutral. "Will you return to Antioch?"

"Someday. I promised my mother I would come home."

Leah nodded, and Jovian knew she understood. She might be the only person who did.

She looked down at her feet. "Whatever you decide, you're not an outsider. Not to my family."

But what about her? Could he and Leah be friends again?

The sounds of men on the roof made them both look up. The three men came down the stairs, brushing off their hands at a job well finished.

"As good as new," Alexander said.

Jovian met Leah's eyes, and she flushed and looked away. Not everything was so easily mended.

Jovian begrudgingly admitted that Chuza's plan worked. Nathan no longer protested his place among The Way. He joined them once a week to share in the Lord's Supper, pray, and sing a hymn or two.

Joanna shared her eyewitness testimony with them, along with the stories she had gathered from the other believers. But again and again, she took them back to the cross. At first, Jovian resented her for it. Why did they have to remember the day when Jesus was dishonored and rejected? Why must they dwell on his suffering? Even the memories of the cross were enough to sour Jovian's mouth.

But, little by little, Jovian understood why everything Joanna taught spiraled back to the cross. The moment that plagued Jovian with nightmares wasn't a tragic mistake. It had been a choice. Jesus had given up his life because of his love for them. It was a humbling and awe-inspiring realization.

The meetings in Chuza's house also afforded Jovian ample time to observe Leah from a distance. Her laughter often wafted on the warm air, rich and full. In those moments, Jovian looked at her in wonder. Leah was no longer a sarcastic orphan with a tragic past. She was a joyful young woman with a promising career and a bold faith.

The changes he saw in Leah tantalized him. He wanted to get to know her all over again. They could never be more than friends, but he still wanted her in his life.

A single lamp cast shadows over the empty cups and trays. Leah watched as Joanna and Chuza followed their guests to the door, bidding them goodnight as stars emerged in the purple sky. The meeting had gone late tonight.

"Can we talk?" Jovian's voice made Leah jump.

"I didn't realize you were still here," she stammered.

In the darkness, Jovian's presence overwhelmed her. She could smell the oils he used in his hair.

"I'm so grateful your family welcomed me into this community," he said. She was unsure what to say, and he stepped even closer. "But I miss our friendship."

She missed it too. Every time she saw him laughing or talking with one of the guards at the palace, she wondered what they were talking about. When Joanna spoke about their days around the Sea of Galilee, she was reminded of the times Jovian protected them on the journey, always cheerful and open.

She saw the changes in him that went deeper than his new beard. She longed to ask him what had happened in Antioch. She wanted to learn more about his family.

But those were questions one asked a friend.

He pulled a hand through his hair. "Can we be friends again?"

She met his gaze, and his eyes gleamed in the lamplight. Perhaps she was gambling with her happiness, but she was willing to take the risk if he understood the rules.

"That is all we can be," she said. "Friends."

The relief on his face warmed her heart. "I promise I won't run off again without saying goodbye."

She shook her head. "You don't need to promise me anything. Friends trust each other."

"I'd like that," he said, and his sincerity was unmistakable.

Jovian looked ready to say more, but Joanna and Chuza came back to the table. He lowered his voice as he met her gaze. "Can we talk more tomorrow?"

She nodded, afraid to speak when Chuza and Joanna were watching.

He turned to go, and her gaze followed him across the courtyard. Unlike her, he wasn't plagued with unrelenting stubbornness. He was a good man and had been a good friend. It wasn't his fault she fell in love back then, and she couldn't blame herself for admiring him still. But she was older now, with a bright future all her own.

She searched her heart and decided. She could be friends with Jovian. In fact, she was looking forward to it.

# FORTY

Chuza strode through the market, searching for fresh grapes to bring home for Joanna. He hoped they would soothe the homesickness that bothered her this time of year.

He made his selections carefully. As he paid the merchant, his attention was caught by a sprightly man weaving down the busy thoroughfare. He clutched a long staff and wore a dusty linen cloak draped around his head.

An inner prompting nudged Chuza forward. He inclined his head to the stranger. "Shalom! Where have you come from?"

The man paused. "From Bethany."

"What news from Bethany and Jerusalem?"

"Have you heard about that Pharisee, Saul?"

Chuza's pulse skipped a beat. "Yes. What of him?"

"He's on his way to Damascus, pursuing the followers of that prophet." The man grunted. "Perhaps the city can finally have some peace."

The air in Chuza's lungs evaporated. "Saul left Jerusalem? Are others continuing the persecution?"

The man shrugged. "I don't know. But if you ask me, the city is relieved. The constant fear was oppressive."

That Chuza could believe. He fixed a smile in place. "Thank you for the news. Please, take these." He offered a bunch of grapes, and the man beamed as he accepted the gift.

As the man continued on his way, Chuza wracked his brain, trying to remember which of the believers had gone to Damascus. Ananias had been determined to bring the good news to his people. Apparently, someone told Saul.

Anger climbed up Chuza's throat. What drove a man to persecute those who did not fight back, who made it their mission to care for the poor?

"Are you alright?" a voice asked. Chuza glanced over at the merchant. "That man's report troubled you."

Chuza looked down at the grapes in his hands. "I just feel so… powerless."

"You are the steward. You're hardly powerless."

"In this, I am. There is only one thing I can do."

"What's that?" the man asked.

"Pray."

The door was unbolted, and Chuza let himself into the portico. Joanna was setting the table.

He strode to her and pulled her against his chest. His throat thickened. Joanna was safe. Their family was safe. But what if Saul came for Sepphoris next? Would Antipas allow targeted persecution within his city?

"What happened?" Joanna asked. She pulled back to look into his face. "Is Leah—"

"She's fine," Chuza said. "She's helping Michael finish supper preparations. But I couldn't wait to see you."

Joanna smiled and set her palm on his cheek. "I missed you too."

He took her hand and drew it to his heart. "I have news from Jerusalem."

Fear flitted over her features.

"Saul left for Damascus. I can only guess he plans to drag believers back to Jerusalem to stand trial."

Joanna's lips parted. "He'd go all that way?" The implications weighed on them both. Was nowhere safe?

That night, after the children were tucked in bed, the small group of believers gathered in the courtyard.

They stood in a circle under the night sky. They took turns praying, pouring out their fears and their hopes. The moment was intimate. Holy. The courtyard did not shake, but Chuza knew that God heard them.

"Protect Damascus," Chuza prayed aloud. "I ask you, Lord Jesus, to stop this man who hunts your followers. I ask for a miracle. Pull Saul back before he can do any harm."

Chuza waited for word of Saul's persecution in Damascus, but none came. He sought news from the caravans passing through Sepphoris, but it seemed the Pharisee had disappeared off the face of the earth.

Chuza could only hope that God had heard their prayers and finally intervened.

Chuza traveled with Antipas to Jerusalem, leaving Joanna safe in Tiberias. As he rode through the city streets with Antipas' retinue, the city seemed normal, as if the events of the past few years had never occurred.

They stopped in front of the palace, and Chuza swung out of the saddle before Celer had fully stopped. Ignoring Antipas' teasing, Chuza tossed Celer's reins at the groom and hurried up the palace steps. The housekeeper strode forward, but Chuza interrupted his welcome.

"Where is Manaen?"

"He's gone," the housekeeper said, and Chuza stiffened.

"What do you mean, gone?"

"He moved back into the city with his wife."

Relief weakened Chuza's knees. "Do you know where?"

"No, my lord. Do you want me to make inquiries?"

Chuza shook his head. Once Manaen learned Antipas was in Jerusalem, he would come to the palace. As the housekeeper moved past Chuza to greet Antipas, Chuza drew a slow breath. If Manaen and Maryam had moved back into the city, it must mean the threat had lifted. Perhaps it was only a temporary reprieve during the fall festivals, but he would take whatever peace was offered.

As Chuza hoped, Manaen came to his office that night.

Chuza rushed from behind his desk. "We prayed for you daily."

Manaen clasped Chuza's shoulders. "Come, the others want to see you."

They wound down dark streets until they reached a large house. Manaen pulled the door open, and light poured into the street, along with dozens of voices. Chuza followed Manaen into the central room, and his jaw dropped. At least a hundred people were gathered. They packed the large room and flowed into the courtyard and side rooms. It was more believers than Chuza had seen gathered in one place for months.

Maryam waved them over, and Chuza and Manaen found a seat as Peter rose so everyone could see him.

"My brothers and sisters," Peter said. "I'm pleased so many of you could make it. These past months have been trying on us all. We have suffered fear, pain, and loss. Hold firm to that which you have witnessed. I don't know what challenges will come in the days ahead, but take heart. Our brother Philip has been to Samaria, and he says the Samaritans are accepting the good news with joy."

Excited and surprised murmurs filled the room.

"John and I are going to join him in Samaria. Pray that the Lord will give us a large harvest." Peter grinned. "But now, let's remember our last meal with Jesus." Peter bent to pick up a loaf of bread. "Take, eat, every one of you. For this is Jesus' body, given for you."

He ripped off a small piece and passed the bread. The loaf circled the room. Chuza accepted it from Manaen, and a sense of community permeated him as he ripped off a piece and passed it along. Peter lifted a cup. "We drink the fruit of the vine as we remember Jesus' blood, given for us."

He took a sip and passed the cup to the man next to him.

Once everyone had tasted the wine, the conversation began, humming in the snug space like a family reunion. Chuza was pressed for news about Joanna and Leah.

"Titus found you, I take it?" Manaen asked.

"He accepted a position as a guard. It is almost like old times."

"With a few notable changes," Maryam corrected.

Chuza chuckled. This was not the future he had anticipated, but he wouldn't have it any other way.

# THREE YEARS LATER

# FORTY-ONE

35 AD
SUMMER

Chuza was forced against the plastered wall as a dozen maid-servants rushed past, their foreheads damp with sweat and their arms piled with a rainbow of cloth.

Salome and Herodias' raised voices carried down the hall. Their sharp tongues dredged up painful memories of Salome's first visit to Jerusalem. Herodias had manipulated her daughter to dance for Antipas and then ask for the Baptizer's head. Chuza winced at the memory.

Salome had moved back into Antipas' household ten months ago. Widowed and childless after her husband's death, Salome had lost her rank and what little power she claimed as a tetrarch's wife. At twenty years old, she was dependent on her mother once again.

The servants disappeared into Salome's room, and both women exclaimed over the beautiful cloth.

"This one!" Herodias said. "It's perfect for your bridal robes."

"No, not the pink," Salome said petulantly.

Chuza shook his head and pressed on, his sandals scuffing the polished floor of the long hallway. He passed a screened window and paused to peer into the courtyard. Despite the gardener's best efforts, the plants wilted under the baking sun. The thick walls of the palace deadened the worst of the heat, but Galilee was in the midst of one of the hottest, driest summers Chuza remembered.

The heat would become nearly unbearable when the royal retinue traveled south to Jericho for Salome's wedding. He pursed his lips as he considered the travel itinerary. Perhaps he should add extra stops, not just for the passengers, but for the poor animals that would convey the bride to her new husband's family.

Herodias and Antipas had arranged for Salome to marry her cousin, Aristobulus. Chuza had only a faint memory of the young man and his scant beard, but he hoped the couple would be happy.

He stopped outside the carved doors to Antipas' room as a bead of sweat trickled between his shoulder blades. Knocking briskly, he let himself into Antipas' apartment. The ruler was stretched out on a couch, his skin glistening with oils as the masseur kneaded his thick back. His body slave doggedly swung a massive fan of peacock feathers.

"Is that you, Chuza?" Antipas asked without lifting his face.

"It is."

"Well? What did you learn?" He groaned as the masseur pressed deeper. Chuza cringed at the pop of Antipas' spine.

"The land is under Syria's trust. But the revenues are being held within the tetrarchy, which suggests Caesar still plans to choose a ruler."

"Well, that's something, I suppose," Antipas muttered. The fate of his late brother's territories was a constant source of conversation between Antipas and his wife. Herodias' scheme to profit off her daughter's fortunes had turned to naught.

Chuza cleared his throat. "Vitellius only offers Syria's protection. I'm sure the emperor will choose a ruler in due time."

"In due time?" Antipas jerked upright, forcing the masseur back a step. He swung his legs over the side of the couch and turned to glare at his steward. He wore only a white cloth around his thick waist. Extra weight softened his once powerful frame, and bags drooped beneath eyes that were bloodshot from too much wine. His cropped hair was more silver than black. Antipas was fifty-six, only a decade younger than Philip.

Antipas swung his arm. "Tiberius would rather do nothing than decide! He prefers to hide on his precious island with his women and wine, leaving the Senate to rule."

Chuza cleared his throat and looked pointedly at the listening staff.

Antipas flicked his hand at the masseur, who bowed and left. His body slave set aside the fan and hurried forward to help him into a robe. Antipas dismissed him as well.

"Curse this heat," Antipas muttered, and swiped his upper lip.

Chuza stepped to the sideboard and poured his master a cup of watered wine. Antipas accepted the cup and drank deeply.

Chuza sat on a chair nearby. "I understand your impatience, my lord, but—"

"You think I want his land for myself, don't you?"

Chuza hesitated. What else could his master intend?

Antipas dragged a hand through his hair. "I have no interest in more responsibility. Another palace to visit, more disputes to settle, more wealthy landowners to placate, and more taxes to squeeze out of the hard-working citizens."

"Then why—"

"For Herodias. Philip's tetrarchy is all she thinks about. If the land was ours, perhaps she would be content. And we could be happy." His shoulders sagged as he stared into his cup.

The sadness in his voice pulled at Chuza's heart. "I see."

Antipas' voice fell to barely above a whisper. "My brother's death taunts me. In my mind, we are young men just starting our careers as tetrarchs, building cities and laying the foundations of our legacy. I was intent on becoming a good ruler, remember?"

Back then, Chuza had been Antipas' body slave, his closest confidante

327

and attendant to his every need. After witnessing the crowds rejoice at King Herod's death, Antipas had been determined to be loved by his citizens.

Chuza leaned toward him. "I remember."

"And haven't I done it?" His eyes probed Chuza's, craving approval. "We've been at peace. I have secured trade with our neighbors and ensured safe roads. Sure, there will always be a little frustration over taxation—" Antipas rolled his eyes "—but the people are content, aren't they?"

Chuza chose his words with care. "The emperor could find no fault in your rule." The Galilean people would never be content living under Roman occupation, but Antipas had at least softened the iron grip of a foreign power.

"Then why can't I enjoy it?" Antipas demanded. "I should be basking in the fruit of my labor, but Herodias wants me to plow new fields."

"I see your struggle."

"I'm sure Vitellius is working against me." Antipas glared into the distance. "He is pouring poisoned words into Tiberius' ears, because he wants the land for Syria."

Chuza didn't know the new governor's intentions, but Vitellius had as much claim to the land as Antipas, maybe more.

Antipas groaned as he stood. He padded to the back of the room where his trunks were packed for travel.

Chuza stood as well, and he clasped his hands behind his back. "Everything is prepared for the journey. Titus has outfitted the lead riders with new standards. You will arrive at Jericho in style."

Antipas glanced back at Chuza. "You must be pleased that your recommendation has done so well."

Chuza inclined his head. His influence had ensured Titus was re-hired, but Titus had done the rest. The Greek zealously took on more responsibility whenever he could. Learned in both Roman and Jewish ways, he excelled in his position. The proof of Titus' skill came when Eli retired last autumn and recommended Titus to replace him as captain.

Antipas sighed. "The emperor has the power to do as he wills, even if that means doing nothing at all. I do not have that luxury." He shot Chuza a long-suffering look.

Chuza hoped, for all their sakes, that Herodias could let Philip's former tetrarchy go.

Antipas swiped his brow. "By the stars, this heat! Where did that fool go with the fan?"

Chuza sent the slave back in to attend the tetrarch and made his way through the halls. As he stepped into the servant's courtyard, the heat smacked him in the face, sucking the breath from his lungs. Sweat beaded on his forehead as he passed women pulling laundry off clotheslines and a boy hauling water up from the cistern.

He joined the busy city streets as the sun tipped toward the west and painted Sepphoris in a golden glow. The sour stink of sweat mingled with dust, spices, and the odor of animals as vendors called out, hoping to sell the rest of their wares before closing for the Sabbath. The last shoppers haggled for better deals as they picked over the worst of the day's produce, but both parties gave in quickly, too weary from the heat to argue.

Chuza walked familiar streets to his own house. The door was freshly painted a rich green, with fragrant pots of herbs on either side. He opened the unbolted door and stepped into the portico. As he shut the door behind him, the noise shifted from the busy street to the sounds of his family. He flicked off his sandals to add to the others piled near the door. The cool, tile floor was comforting as he strode through the quiet portico to the heart of the home.

Little Mary, now eight years old, set two pitchers on the table, and her little helper was placing clay cups. They turned as he strode forward, and Nadia's eyes lit up.

"Papa's home!" she cried out, running for him.

This was the best moment of his day. The three-and-a-half-year-old girl threw herself at him, and he caught her and tossed her in the air, his chest glowing as she squealed in delight.

He kissed her cheek, tickling her with his beard until she giggled. "Were you good today?"

"Yes," she said, and looked at her cousin. "I help Mary set the table."

She had probably been more hindrance than help, but Mary was patient with her little shadow.

Chuza gave Nadia another squeeze. "Where's your Mama?"

"In the house," Nadia wiggled to be set down. Chuza set her on the floor, and she ran off, her bare feet flying as she called, "Mama! Mama! Papa's home!"

Joanna came out of the house with a rueful grin, one hand cradling her round middle. "I can only hurry so much."

Chuza met her halfway, kissing her before he tucked a stray hair behind her ear. "Long day?"

"I had a nap, but I'm still exhausted," Joanna admitted. "I don't remember being so tired when I was pregnant with Nadia."

"Just wait until it is your fourth," Dalia said as she came out of the house with an armful of cushions. Their pregnancies were only a month apart, and the rest of the family was treated to a lot of playful comparisons and teasing.

Joanna glanced up at the sky. Daylight was fading. "I should help finish supper," she said, and turned back to the courtyard kitchen where Miriam was pulling loaves of bread out of the oven.

"Alexander is the one who better hurry." Dalia shook her head as she dropped cushions along the table.

Chuza turned as he heard footsteps behind him.

"What is she saying about me?" Alexander asked innocently. His satchel was slung over his shoulder, and the key to his shop hung in his hand.

Chuza grinned. "Just that she's been longing for your company all day."

"Oh, has she?" Alexander held his arms straight out as he trotted toward his wife. Dalia scowled and threw a cushion at him, protesting that he needed to wash. But as he pulled her into his arms, she melted, giving him a quick kiss and a smile.

Alexander's father and mother came from the house with Dalia's other two children. Samuel, now ten years old, was looking more grown up by the day. Patara held Dalia's youngest, Little Alex, a laid-back toddler who was happy to be toted about by his devoted grandmother. The only one missing was Alexander's sister Jael, who had moved to her new husband's home in Cana.

It was a noisy gathering as the women laid out the bread, stew, baked fish, dried dates, and summer herbs tossed in oil and vinegar.

They were just sitting down as Titus and Leah hurried into the courtyard. "Sorry," Titus called out. "I had a little situation at work."

"I almost left without him," Leah said wryly. They went straight to the basin, and Titus gestured for Leah to wash first. She splashed water on her face, sighing with relief at its coolness.

They gathered around the table as the sun set. Tonight, the task of lighting the Sabbath lamp and saying the blessings fell on Joanna. She stood at the head of the table, her face glowing as she used a cinder to light the wick.

Chuza's throat tightened as his wife recited the prayers and blessings. He pulled Nadia into his lap and kissed the top of her short curls, the exact same shade as his. He glanced over at Leah. Her brown braid fell over her shoulder, and her hazel eyes were soft in the fading light. All his life, he had longed for the family he lost when he was a boy. God had answered him in unexpected and wonderful ways.

He blinked rapidly as Joanna took her seat, and he shook his head at her questioning look.

Miriam passed the basket of bread.

"How was your week, Titus?" Alexander asked.

Titus pressed his lips together as he took a warm loaf and passed the basket on. "A troubling report came in just as I was leaving."

Chuza glanced up sharply. He hadn't heard anything.

"Nabateans attacked a watchtower. No deaths, but Antipas needs to decide how to react."

Chuza stiffened. It had been over three years since he and Joanna traveled to Nabatea. Three years without a problem.

"Are they sure it wasn't just brigands?" Chuza asked. "Highwaymen trying to seize the watchtower's supplies?"

Titus lifted his shoulders. "Apparently their armor was Nabatean. It sounds like they were strategic, testing our strength with small numbers before withdrawing." As he scanned the anxious faces around the table, he held up his hand. "I didn't mean to worry all of you. I just think we should pray for a peaceful resolution."

Everyone still looked worried, and Chuza couldn't blame them. King Aretas had nursed his grudge against Antipas for too long. If Antipas didn't do something quickly, it could mean war.

"We leave tomorrow for Jericho," Titus said. "I'm sure Antipas will consult with his family, and they'll decide what to do."

Joanna said, "Can you deliver a letter to Susanna on your way through Tiberias?"

Titus nodded and the conversation moved on, but Chuza let the words slide past him, focusing instead on the trouble brewing along the Nabatean border. Antipas had managed thirty years without engaging in war. Chuza needed to make sure it stayed that way.

# FORTY-TWO

Jovian's armor hung heavier than usual as he strode toward the palace kitchen. His belief in Antipas' diplomacy had been too optimistic. The tetrarch was sending for a general. Which could only mean one thing—Antipas wasn't interested in peace talks.

The faces of his men rose in Jovian's mind. Thanks to grueling practice and constant drills, they were all accomplished guards, ready to fend off highwaymen, quell a riot, and maybe even defend a city until help arrived. But engaging an army was a completely different scenario.

He turned a corner and delightful smells wafted from the kitchen, beckoning like the scent of home. He stepped into the large room. The tables were wiped clean and most of the staff were gone, save two.

Swathed in a large apron, Leah leaned against the long table, her arms crossed and her lips quirked in amusement. Michael was dressed for travel, and he paced back and forth.

"We're almost out of barley," he said. "And you need to keep an eye on those cheeses."

"I know." Leah smacked his thick arm as he strode past her. "I could recite our inventory with my eyes closed." To demonstrate, she began rattling off ingredients at lightning speed.

Michael held up his hands. "Alright!" He chuckled. "It's good to know that when I retire these old bones, you'll be here."

Leah's humor fled, and she straightened. "That's years away."

Michael noticed Jovian waiting in the doorway, and he gestured with his chin. "Ah, the strapping young captain."

Jovian grinned. Michael liked to tease him about his promotion, insisting it would keep him from getting a big head. Jovian didn't think he needed the help. Though he was honored to be captain of the guard, he was now responsible for two hundred men spread over multiple locations.

Leah put her hands on her hips. "You're late for lunch. Lucky for you, I saved some." She gathered a tray from the counter and set it on the table. He eyed it appreciatively, and Leah tossed a grin at Michael. "We can't have the—what did you call him?—dashing young captain fainting on the road."

"I said strapping. But you can call him 'dashing' if you prefer." Michael winked and strode for the door. He paused at the door frame to nod at Leah. "I'll see you in a few months."

Leah's expression softened. "May God keep you and bless you."

Michael disappeared, leaving Jovian and Leah alone.

Leah drew a deep sigh as she peered at the empty doorway. "Do you think he really means to retire?"

Jovian slid onto the bench and pulled his meal closer. "He is getting up in years." She sat opposite him and leaned both elbows on the table. He ripped a piece of bread. "Worried you couldn't manage as the head cook?"

Leah shot him a disparaging look. "That's the least of my worries."

He couldn't fault her confidence. Everything she cooked was amazing.

She frowned. "But I would have to travel from palace to palace, instead of staying in Sepphoris with my family."

"You'd have me." Jovian shrugged to hide the jump in his pulse.

He left Sepphoris with Antipas every winter, and it would be wonderful to have her along.

Leah drummed her fingers on the tabletop. "These days you barely have time to eat, never mind talk."

She wasn't wrong. And if Antipas was contemplating war, Jovian's duties would become much more complicated.

She scanned his face, reading him easier than one of his reports. "What's the matter?"

He sighed and dug his thumbnails into a dried date to rip it in two. "Antipas doesn't have an army."

Leah blinked at him. "I thought he wasn't allowed. Isn't that why Syria has to help whenever there's trouble?"

"Right. But now, he's not asking Syria to help. He's summoning a general to advise him." His shoulders tightened at the thought. Antipas had enough armor for a thousand men stored in Tiberias. But who did he expect to wear it? Worry pressed on Jovian's shoulders.

Leah furrowed her brow. "But wouldn't Antipas need Caesar's permission to fight Nabatea?"

"Technically, yes. But a messenger means weeks of delay, and the borders are being attacked now."

"But if he doesn't have an army, who…" She trailed off, her eyes widening. "You? Your men?"

Jovian's throat squeezed, and he looked down at his tray.

"What about Pilate?" Leah asked. "He has a whole garrison of soldiers."

"Antipas might ask him, but Nabatea isn't threatening Pilate's borders."

Leah wrapped her arms around her middle and scanned her kitchen. "Food is how I do battle."

He raised his eyebrows at her. "I can picture you slinging an overcooked loaf."

She made a face. "I'm serious. When there's a problem between the staff, I cook something delicious and make them eat together. You'd be surprised how food can bring people together."

Jovian grinned. "You'd stop a war with a sweetbread?"

She blushed and stuck her tongue out at him. "I would try."

Jovian wished it was so simple.

Leah leaned forward. Her hand lay on the tabletop, outstretched toward him. He fought the sudden urge to take it.

"What will you do if Antipas sends your men to war?" she asked.

Jovian's stomach roiled. "I'll lead them." And God willing, he would lead them all home again.

"You'd risk everything for Antipas?"

"For Israel. If Nabatea invades, it'll mean trouble for everyone."

She hesitated. "But is this really your war?" He tensed, and she held up her hand. "You could resign. Return to Antioch and your family."

He understood what she meant, but it hurt all the same. "I may not be a Jew, but this is my home."

Her hazel eyes regarded him seriously. "You can have more than one home."

Didn't he know it. For three years he had walked among The Way. When he was in Sepphoris, he worshiped with the believers in Chuza's house and shared their table. When he was in Tiberias, he met with Susanna's people. At Jerusalem, Manaen would bring him into the circle of believers. Everywhere Jovian went, a community waited for him—even if he could not fully participate.

Sometimes, when he saw someone filled with the Holy Spirit, Jovian was sure he was ready to become a Jew. To actually feel God with him was a powerful pull. But every time he considered becoming a proselyte, something held him back. He knew that if he put this wall between himself and his family, his parents would never forgive him.

He smiled ruefully. "I can't just run back to Antioch. If I left now, I'd never be able to face myself."

She picked at a fingernail. When she finally spoke, her voice wavered. "How soon will Antipas send men to fight?"

"Hopefully never," Jovian said. But he suspected it would be soon. Perhaps right after Salome's wedding. Which meant Jovian might not see Leah again before he was sent into battle.

He smiled to cover the tension in his gut. "I'm a guard. I live with risk every day."

"This is different."

"I've trained for war since I was a boy. I'm not afraid." It wasn't completely true, but true enough.

Voices filtered down the hall. Leah and Jovian locked eyes. For three years, they had remained friends. There had been many times he wished they could move past friendship into something more, but never had the urge been as strong as now.

Hoping he wasn't pushing their friendship too far, he set his hand on hers. "I'll miss you."

The voices were just outside the kitchen door.

Her hazel eyes softened. "I'll pray for you."

As a handful of servants entered the kitchen, laughing and talking, Jovian stared into Leah's eyes and wished he could say so much more.

"Isn't it impressive?" Antipas swept out his arm.

Jovian strode down the center of the massive storeroom. The shadowy space was lit by high, barred windows, and a beam of light fell on neat rows of chain mail and padded leather vests. Chain mail took longer to make than the plate armor Jovian wore, but it could more easily fit men of differing heights and weights.

Swords lay in stacks, and Jovian pulled one from its sheath. The perfectly honed edge gleamed as he turned it before the light. He slid it back.

"My men aren't trained in the sword," Jovian said. He faced the tetrarch and his new general. "They use Jewish weapons. Spears. Slings. Knives." Not only was Antipas denied a standing army, but Rome did not allow Jews to own swords.

Antipas looked at his general. Linus was about fifty, clean-shaven, and with an aquiline nose. His age hinted at experience, but few generals would agree to lead a tetrarch's men to a border skirmish.

"We will run a few training sessions," Linus said with a shrug.

Jovian pressed his lips together. He had anguished over lists of his men, deciding who would stay to protect Antipas' holdings, and who he would lead to the border. He would take one hundred men. The general had somehow found another nine hundred, though Jovian doubted their capabilities.

"How soon can they be ready?" Antipas asked.

Linus tucked his thumbs in his belt. "Two weeks."

Jovian frowned. Two weeks of training might keep the new recruits from lopping off their own limbs, but not much else.

Antipas looked pleased. He glanced at Jovian and chuckled. "Don't worry, Captain. The general knows what he's doing. The battle will be quick. Once Aretas realizes we won't give way, he'll retreat."

Linus nodded in a stuffy way Jovian found infuriating. "I am confident of it, my lord."

The two men strode out the door, leaving Jovian to scan the cold and empty armor. The general's cockiness worried Jovian more than anything. His ludus teacher had warned him about overconfidence, citing far too many real-life examples to let Jovian forget.

"Are you coming, Captain?" Linus called.

"Coming," he replied. If he wanted to bring his men home again, they had to begin training at once.

Antipas peered across the courtyard and into Herodias' quiet chambers. She had redecorated her Tiberias apartment when she took the rooms over from Phasaelis. Yet, if Antipas closed his eyes, he could see his Nabatean wife sitting on her couch, talking with Joanna.

Women. Nothing but trouble.

Antipas stiffened as familiar footsteps came up behind him.

"It's not too late," Chuza said.

Antipas turned slowly and glared at his steward. "Too late for what?"

Chuza glanced around for listening ears and lowered his voice. "Send another envoy. Renegotiate the peace. We don't want war with Nabatea."

Antipas regarded him coldly. "We?" When had Chuza become a tetrarch?

Chuza spread his hands. "Antipas, please."

The steward's lack of confidence was insulting. Antipas had lost hours of sleep discussing options with Herodias, and she was right. King Aretas would not invade a client state and risk his alliance with Rome. He was just posturing, hoping to humiliate Antipas for divorcing Phasaelis. Antipas needed to stand up to Aretas, or he risked shame in the eyes of the world.

Antipas scowled at his presumptuous steward. "I'm not afraid. I will protect what God and the emperor have granted me."

"My lord, I'm begging you. Wait for word from the emperor. You have no army."

"I do now." Antipas glared at him. "One thousand men."

Chuza pressed his lips together, but Antipas would not be swayed. General Linus insisted the new recruits were ready.

"If we go to war with Nabatea, your people will suffer. Think of them."

Antipas' neck reared and Chuza took a step back. "I am thinking of them! If we let Nabatea bully us, who will try next? If I want to protect my people, I must show my strength."

He waited for Chuza to cave, to bow and admit he was wrong. But the steward set his jaw.

"We can evacuate those close to the borders while we wait for orders from Tiberius," Chuza said. "If Nabatea is antagonizing you, we must ask why."

Heat surged into Antipas' face, and he grabbed a silver platter and flung it across the room. It clattered to the tiled floor, sending fruit tumbling under furniture. "Why? You know why!"

A servant dropped to the floor, scrambling to clean up the mess.

Antipas jabbed a finger in Chuza's face. "If your wife hadn't helped Phasaelis escape, none of this would have happened."

Chuza blinked. "You would have leveraged your wife as a hostage?"

"I would have kept Phasaelis from telling stories to her father. I had a plan, but somehow she figured it out and fled before I could do anything about it!"

Something flickered across Chuza's face. Guilt? All of Herodias' accusations against Chuza poured into Antipas' mind. He stepped closer, until he and Chuza were nearly nose to nose.

"Tell me, Steward," he spat the title, "how were my plans uncovered when the only ones in on the secret were Herodias and you?"

He gritted his teeth as Chuza's face went frustratingly blank. "Are you accusing me, my lord?"

Antipas huffed through his nose and ran his tongue over his teeth. "Are you conspiring with Agrippa to humiliate me? I saw how you two talked when you thought I wasn't watching.

"Of course not. I haven't seen Agrippa for years."

"You're sick of serving me, aren't you?" Antipas hissed, his gaze flickering between Chuza's wide eyes. "You want to be with your little wife, trouncing about the countryside with your fellow fanatics, declaring a crucified messiah." He flung his hands in the air and shook them mockingly.

He wanted Chuza to shout back. To defend himself. But instead, the steward bowed his head.

"I serve you to the best of my abilities." He sounded maddeningly sincere. "I only work for your good."

Antipas twisted the ring on his finger. Chuza had mastered his face the way other men trained their dogs. How could he trust a man with so much self-control?

He strode away but then spun back around. "You are my slave. You swore to serve me, remember?"

Chuza inclined his head.

Antipas shook his finger at him. "Don't mistake the years we've spent together as friendship between equals. I come first. Always."

The breeze cooled his flushed face as Chuza strode through the streets of Tiberias and toward the makeshift camp on the outskirts of the city. Antipas' confidence would be his undoing. He was tetrarch over a client state, while the Nabatean king was an independent ally with Rome that boasted a well-trained army of career soldiers.

Emerging from the city gates, Chuza clenched his jaw as he surveyed the military camp. Most of the tents were down and packed into carts. The roped-off practice area stood empty, save for six tattered straw men hanging limply on their poles.

A group of new recruits waited near the carts, discussing their promised pay. They spoke as if they were going on a march and then coming home. Chuza pressed his lips together. The general had done an incredible job of instilling confidence in his men. Hopefully he had done as good a job at training them to wield their weapons.

Finally, he spotted the man he was looking for. Titus stood apart, examining a wax tablet with a sharp crease between his brows. He wore his own armor and a blue cloak pinned with a bronze brooch. The Roman armor was a strange contrast to Jovian's shoulder length hair and beard.

The soldier glanced up as Chuza approached and tucked the wax tablet under his arm.

The men clasped hands.

"Ready?" Chuza asked.

"Of course," Titus said, but his voice was strained.

Chuza scanned the camp. "God has used a small number of his people to strike down a larger army before."

Titus twisted his brows. "Our general is hardly Gideon."

"Maybe not, but this is still the promised land. God helped King Ahab triumph over his enemies, even though he wasn't a righteous king. Linus may be over-confident, but he's seen battle." He clapped Titus on the arm. "And he has you."

Titus winced. "I'm afraid I'll let my men down."

Chuza had seen the way Titus' men looked at him, full of confidence and trust. That had to be a heavy burden to bear.

Titus dragged a hand through his hair. "If I don't come back, will you tell Leah something?"

Chuza wanted to protest, but he nodded.

"Tell her…" Titus weighed his words. "Tell her that her friendship means so much to me." He hesitated, as if he wanted to say more. "Your whole family has blessed me beyond measure."

"I'll tell her. But I expect you to come back. If I had any authority over you, I'd say that was an order."

Titus scanned the camp, his expression distant. "I promised my mother I'd come home." He grinned. "I wouldn't dare disobey her."

# FORTY-THREE

Antipas' army sprawled across a brown plain only a few miles from the Nabatean border. It had taken two days to cross the Jordan River and march into Antipas' territory of Perea. Jovian ducked out of his tiny tent and tightened his belt an extra notch as he looked up. Fat clouds hurried across the pale blue sky, blown by a cool wind. A hawk screamed as it flew overhead, searching for prey.

Jovian scanned the rows of tidy tents and absorbed the mood of the camp. The men seemed optimistic, almost cheerful. He wished he felt the same.

He set off for the general's tent in the center of camp. Jovian was ready to fight—if only to have it done and over with.

Eyes followed his progress through the camp, and he straightened his shoulders and smoothed his beard. It was important he look confident. The success of this venture depended on them intimidating the Nabatean army. Jovian needed to set an example.

The general was conferring with a scout, and he turned as Jovian approached.

"Good news," Linus said. "The Nabatean camp is poorly situated, and they have a mere five hundred men."

"You plan to attack?"

"At dawn. By midday, we will celebrate our victory."

The morning dawned overcast and unseasonably cold. Rain threatened to fall as wind whipped through the short grass and raised goose bumps on Jovian's arms.

Jovian double-checked his equipment, straightening his helmet and gripping his sword hilt. He rolled his shield arm and bounced on his toes to warm his leg muscles. He could almost imagine he was back at the ludus with Galen at his side. Just another day of training.

A horn blasted twice, and Jovian's stomach swooped. He scanned the one hundred guards that stood behind him in loose formation. Lucius had put him in charge of Antipas' guardsmen during the battle, and they would form the spear point of the attack. All their eyes were on him.

"Tighten up," he commanded. "It's time to march."

They tramped forward. There would be no attempt at surprise.

Jovian paced his breath with his footfalls. "God, give me strength," he prayed aloud. "Give us victory today."

His pulse quickened as the Nabatean camp came into view. Jovian furrowed his brow. The scout was right, the Nabateans had chosen a poor camp. They were sheltered from the wind, but the hilltop would have given them better defense and visibility. The Nabatean army was ready and waiting, and Jovian's jaw clenched as he saw the archers. His men were armed with slings, not bows.

"Hey," a voice beside Jovian whispered.

Jovian glanced over and Marcus grinned.

"I've got a special bullet for the occasion," Marcus said. He pulled a lead bullet out of his bag and held it so Jovian could see. Jovian took a quick peek at the small letters cast in the dark metal.

"Ouch," he read aloud. He raised his brow.

Marcus chuckled. "I thought it was funny."

Jovian grinned, but his insides were in knots. Marcus was trusting him to keep them alive, and that trust felt like a millstone in his gut.

When they were in sling range, a dozen ram's horns blasted long and fierce, and a great yell rose from the men. Jovian roared with them. The sound vibrated in his ears, but the enemy did not flee.

Lucius raised his arm. "Slings!"

Hundreds of slings whirled with earsplitting song, flinging rocks and lead bullets like a hailstorm. The Nabateans crouched, holding their shields in front of them. One loud "Ouch!" drew a grin from Marcus.

Jovian gritted his teeth. Slings were deadly from the heights, or when an army had no place to hide. In a valley like this, these stones were little more than a nuisance. He had tried to tell Lucius, but his counsel fell on deaf ears.

The Nabateans were quick to respond. Jovian's shoulders tightened as archers stepped forward in terrifying synchronicity.

The sky filled with a hundred arrows.

Jovian shouted to his men. "Shields!"

Antipas' army dropped to one knee and thrust their shields skyward. Jovian flinched as an arrow lodged in his heavy shield. Screams shattered the air as men were struck.

The general didn't wait for another volley of arrows. "Ready spears!"

The men jerked to their feet and grabbed their spears. Jovian's pulse pounded so hard his shield trembled. He glanced back at his men and gave them a nod. They tensed, ready to follow him to victory or death.

He turned forward and glared at the Nabateans.

"Charge!" the general roared as another spray of arrows was aimed for their position.

They leaped forward, hoping to dodge the deadly bolts raining from above.

The stamp of his feet vibrated up his calves as Jovian led his men, running toward the Nabateans, hoping to render their bows useless by proximity. Arrows sliced through the air, but he somehow made it through.

As he had been trained, he singled out a target. He gripped his spear and at the right moment, he hurled it with all his strength. He saw the fear in his opponent's eyes the moment before it struck true. Other spears shot through the air, piercing armor and tearing through the wall of men. Jovian reached for his sword. It felt at home in his hand and all his fear melted away. He had trained for this exact moment.

When the Galileans were only a few paces away, the Nabatean army charged forward to meet them.

Chaos erupted.

Jovian was jarred by the sudden noise. A scream of agony shot through his skull. A Nabatean lunged at him. Jovian's shield came up, and he stabbed. The man stumbled back, and another replaced him. Jovian's nostrils burned with the scent of blood and gore. He moved instinctively, dodging blows and dealing too many to count.

He couldn't let himself be surrounded. He jumped to stand next to Marcus, and they turned so they were back to back. Sweat trickled down Jovian's face, stinging his eyes.

In a brief lull, he glanced around, panting. Somehow, they were winning. His heart leaped in his chest.

But then Lucius' horn blew discordantly, a shill note of panic. Jovian's short-lived satisfaction turned to icy-cold fear. Undulating cries echoed from the hills. Men in rough armor poured over the crest like a swarm of locusts. The Nabateans had reinforcements. Lots of them.

Fear curdled Jovian's gut as this new wave of men joined the fray. The noise doubled as Jovian battled to stay alive. In the slick grass, he struggled to keep his footing. Exhaustion slowed his strikes as minutes slid past. His lungs burned. He lost sight of Marcus. Blood dripped from his blade, and his arm ached beneath his shield. Ducking under a spear strike, his helmet was wrenched from his head, and he felt naked without its weight.

He stepped backward and stumbled over a fallen body. The cries of the injured stabbed his brain.

They were losing.

He was going to die.

Now that it came to it, he was not afraid. He would be with God, finally understanding, seeking no more.

But what about Leah? Her hazel eyes filled his mind.

The glint of a blade jerked him back to reality. Too late, he raised his shield, but the blade sliced into his upper arm.

Fear returned in force. He heaved his shield up, and to his relief, his arm obeyed. But his opponent was already swinging his long knife again, glaring with a burning hatred—with eyes Jovian recognized.

"Amichai?" he gasped.

Joanna's brother stared at him in shock before the snarl returned. "I should have known you'd fight against us." He swung his blade, but Jovian easily deflected it.

"I fight for Galilee!" Jovian said.

"No, I fight for Galilee!" Amichai shouted. "When Antipas is gone, God's true king will rise!"

Jovian's eyes darted around, realizing the truth. These reinforcements were not Nabatean, but Jewish. His resolve wobbled. He hadn't come to fight God's chosen people. This wasn't right.

Amichai swung his knife again, a hacking strike that Jovian caught on his shield. Jovian instinctively shoved him back and jabbed his sword toward Amichai's exposed neck. Fear filled Amichai's eyes.

Jovian couldn't kill Joanna's brother.

Amichai saw his hesitation and stumbled away. But then Jovian heard a cry of pain. It took him half a second to realize the sound came from his own lips.

Jovian's right knee buckled, the flesh and tendons burning as if they were on fire. Wet heat poured down his calf. Panic lanced through him, and as he lurched, pain seared his side, jabbing up under his armor. Jovian's arms went slack, and spots of black danced before his eyes.

"Die, Roman," the man behind him hissed, and he shoved Jovian forward.

Jovian hit the ground hard, another man's arm trapped beneath him. He waited for another strike, but it did not come.

Blood poured from his wounds. He groaned, his hand fumbling to his side, trying to stave the flow. His right leg burned so badly he feared it was gone. The pain was nauseating, shooting through his whole body and overwhelming all his senses.

Every breath counted down to the moment he would bleed to death. A horrible cold spread through his torso as darkness filled his vision. What was he doing here? He had led a hundred men to their death. Guilt battled with pain for supremacy in his mind. This couldn't be God's plan.

A hand gripped his shoulder, shoving him over. Jovian blinked up into a stranger's face. The man raised a spear for a killing blow.

Tears burned in Jovian's eyes. This would be his last breath. Over the man's shoulder, he saw a familiar face. One with sad eyes that grieved for his suffering. Jovian reached for him. "Forgive me, Jesus."

# FORTY-FOUR

"Wait," another voice said.

With difficulty, Jovian shifted his gaze to Amichai's eyes.

Amichai studied him, a multitude of emotions playing over his face. "Bring him with our wounded."

His companion scoffed. "He won't live the night. And if he does, look at that leg. He will never stand on it again."

His words wrenched at Jovian's mind, but they could not overshadow his primal desire to live. He stared at Amichai, his mouth bone dry. "Please. I helped you. With your father."

Amichai's lips thinned. He looked back at his friend. "This one lives."

The man shrugged and strode away. "His life is yours."

Amichai called for a stretcher. Jovian braced himself as hands hooked under his armpits and grabbed his ankles. He tried to prepare himself, but as he was hoisted onto the stretcher, an agonized scream ripped from between his teeth. His right leg would not obey his commands. He squeezed his eyes shut, reaching out with his soul for Jesus' comforting presence.

"Hold on," Amichai said. He cut a length of tunic from a nearby body and wrapped it around Jovian's knee.

Jovian screamed as Amichai bound the wound, the pain biting like a lion. "Stop!"

"You'll bleed to death if I don't."

Jovian gritted his teeth, trying to bear the pain. He had to go home to Leah. If he made it back to her, somehow everything would be alright.

The stretcher heaved upward, and Jovian clenched his jaw to keep from crying out. He turned his head, and his insides shriveled.

The battlefield stretched out in all directions. It was filled with his men—all of them dead or dying. Anger surged up to combat the agonizing pain. This wasn't right.

A man was propped up against his companion, his eyes wide and unseeing. Marcus. Jovian turned his face away, and hot tears ran down his cheeks.

The men carrying his stretcher found every opportunity to jostle him. Amichai walked by his side like a ghost. Joanna's brother was thinner than Jovian remembered, his beard only partially disguising the angular planes of his face. His knife hilt and leather belt were well-worn with years of use. He looked like a man who had given up everything for his cause. So what convinced him to spare Jovian's life?

They entered a large tent woven of black goat's hair. Jovian was set down next to an injured man who cradled a mangled forearm. Jovian's jaw clenched. Dozens more huddled with gashes to the face, slices on their arms, stab wounds in their torso, and some, like him, on rough stretchers. Jovian didn't recognize any of them. He was alone and at the mercy of his enemies.

A Nabatean army surgeon was working his way through the tent, checking the wounded and giving orders to his assistants. Strong-smelling wine was poured over wounds before flesh was stitched back together amid cries of pain.

Jovian shivered with cold, though the wound beneath his palm pulsed with hot blood. Sweat soaked through his tunic under his armor. Nausea rose, along with a terrifying weakness.

He couldn't see Jesus anymore. "Jesus, stay with me," he whispered.

"Surgeon," Amichai called sharply. "This man needs help now."

The surgeon strode over and frowned at Jovian's armor, his gaze flickering over Jovian's long hair and beard. He spoke in heavily accented Aramaic. "This is one of ours?"

Amichai hesitated. "Yes," he lied. "This man is with me."

Jovian darted Amichai a glance, but the surgeon crouched, muttering in his own tongue. Jovian hissed with pain as the surgeon rolled him onto his side to examine the back of his leg with sure fingers.

The surgeon looked up at Jovian's blood-soaked hand and his brow furrowed further. "Take off his armor."

Amichai knelt to unlace Jovian's armor and slide it off. The surgeon's assistant used shears to open his stained tunic and poured wine on his side.

Jovian's back arched as he clenched his teeth, his breath coming in rapid gasps.

The surgeon probed the wound as Jovian cried out. "That should heal if there is no infection." He nodded at his assistant. "Stitch it."

The assistant nodded. "And the leg?"

The surgeon shook his head. "That will take more time. I will return after I have seen to the others."

Jovian reached for him. "Wait. You can save my leg, can't you?"

The surgeon's gaze was distant but not cold. "I will try."

Jovian sank back, despair filling him. If he lost his leg, his career would be over. Rage against the general's foolhardy confidence rose like bile, along with bitterness. He had been a good soldier and followed Linus' orders, and it had cost everyone their lives.

"Bite this," the assistant said, shoving a thick strap between his teeth. Jovian obeyed, his mind a fog. But as the man stabbed his needle into Jovian's side, his screams were barely muffled by the sour-tasting leather.

Jovian drifted in and out of consciousness. In one lucid moment, he muttered, "I'm thirsty." A hand lifted his head and a cup was held to his parched lips.

He was jarred awake as his stretcher was lifted and borne into another tent. It was dark now, and he stared at one of the bright lamps, trying to figure out where he was. A brazier sat in the corner, and someone had thrown herbs on the glowing coals to cut the stench of blood and bodily fluids. Jovian was laid on a rough table.

"Drink this," a voice said. A cup came to his lips and he sputtered at the bitter taste. "It will numb your pain," the voice said, and Jovian pushed past the taste to drink greedily. Within minutes, his mind spun like he had drank too much wine. His body was blessedly heavy and warm.

He was rolled onto his stomach.

He blinked slowly at a flickering flame that shifted in and out of focus. The surrounding voices muddled together. He was aware of the pain in his leg, but it was in a different part of his mind, distant from him.

"Try to relax," a man's voice said near his ear.

Was that Jesus? Jovian's thoughts moved sluggishly. His eyes were trying to close, but he forced them open. "Jesus, where are you?"

"What's he saying?" a voice said, somewhere far away.

"I think he's asking for his friend."

It was late, but Chuza stood in the courtyard of the Tiberias palace, his arms tightly folded as he stared into a glowing brazier, trying to pray. The flames cast dancing shadows over the stone walls, and stars shone overhead.

They should have had word from Lucius by now.

Chuza jerked at a pounding on the palace gate.

A guard opened the small window. "Who is it?"

"A messenger from the battlefield," a weary voice answered.

"Let him in." Chuza ordered as he strode forward.

The gate was unbolted and a man stumbled through, his hair plastered to his dusty face. "I bring word for Antipas."

"I am his steward," Chuza said. "Tell me what happened."

The man bobbed his head but glanced at the curious guards. Chuza gripped his shoulder and led him away from the others, his heart already sinking. If it had been good news, the messenger wouldn't have cared who overheard.

In the shadows, Chuza pulled the man around. "Speak."

"The battle is lost. A complete rout."

An icy shiver ran down Chuza's spine. "Survivors?"

"They speared the wounded."

Chuza's chest squeezed. "Are you sure?"

"They're all dead, including the general."

Chuza's mind spun. It couldn't be true. He took a step back. The image of Titus in his armor, grinning at him, made the idea of defeat ridiculous. Titus had to be fine.

The messenger stepped closer. "We were winning until men from the north joined the battle and turned the tide. They looked like Jews."

Chuza rubbed his face with both hands and dragged his fingers through his hair. Jews from the north? This didn't make any sense. He looked back at the messenger.

"What about Titus, the captain of the guard?"

The messenger shook his head. "I saw the captain fall."

Chuza didn't want to hear any more. His hands trembled as he led the messenger to Antipas, grief flooding his veins. The tetrarch would need to handle this disaster on his own, because Chuza had to return to Sepphoris—to tell his daughter that Titus was gone.

The chatter in the kitchen fell silent. Leah looked up from her mixing bowl. Chuza stood in the doorway to the kitchen, his clothes rumpled and dusty from travel. The pain in his eyes stole her breath, and she knew.

"I need to talk to you," he said as her insides spun like a whirlwind.

Her staff were watching her with wide, fearful eyes. Icy numbness spread through her limbs. She wiped off her hands and followed Chuza to his office. As he shut the door behind her, she managed to say his name.

"Jovian?"

The look on his face told her everything. She couldn't breathe, couldn't cry out, couldn't move. Her chest burned.

Chuza's voice was hoarse. "The whole army was destroyed."

She blinked at him, heat climbing up her legs as if she was being lowered into hot water. The edges of her sight were turning black. "When?"

"Yesterday. I came as soon as I could."

He was pulling her into his arms, but she didn't feel anything. His voice was anguished. "I'm so sorry."

His words cut through her numbness, and she jerked away.

"No!" She glared at him. How dare he say Jovian was gone? "You're wrong!"

Leah yanked open the office door and raced through the palace halls as tears streamed down her face.

Before she knew where she was going, she was home. She stumbled through the front door, catching herself on the wall. The portico was shadowed. Empty. She pulled herself upright and forced one foot in front of the other.

She stepped into the courtyard. Joanna and the others were eating their midday meal. The ordinary scene was so jarring, Leah stared at them in disbelief.

"Leah?" Joanna jerked to her feet. "What's wrong?"

"The battle is lost," Leah said, and her voice sounded strange in her own ears. They stared at her in stunned silence. Anger rose in her chest. Didn't they understand? "They're all dead!"

Chuza panted as he stumbled into the courtyard behind her, and Joanna locked eyes with him. She paled.

Joanna rushed to her side. Leah was too angry to be comforted. But as Joanna rubbed her back making shushing noises, tears rose in Leah's chest and burst out in a sob. She melted into her mother's arms, gripping her fiercely as she screamed into Joanna's shoulder.

Leah felt a hand laid on her back. And then another on her shoulder. Then one on her head. Her family prayed with her in the center. Their words washed over her, baptizing her and driving calm into her heart. As she clung to Joanna, surrounded by prayers, hope flickered, so faint she feared to truly consider it. What if Jovian had survived?

Jovian woke with a groan. His head throbbed in the dim light, and his tongue was thick. Foggy memories tumbled, and he lifted his head, trying to see his two feet.

"It's still there," Amichai said. "Your leg, I mean."

Jovian turned, surprised to find Joanna's brother sitting cross-legged next to him. Dark shadows had made camp under his eyes. Amichai rose stiffly, shuffled to the end of the tent, and brought back a cup. Jovian weakly lifted himself on one elbow, and Amichai helped him drink the stale water. Jovian collapsed back onto his mat.

He tried moving his right toes and pain scared up his leg. He sucked a breath.

"Pain is good," Amichai said.

Jovian looked at him doubtfully, but Amichai gave him a small smile. "The surgeon said the wound severed tendons and muscles." Jovian's heart twisted, and Amichai gripped his arm. "But if you can feel the foot, at least you might walk again."

*Might* walk again. Jovian closed his eyes as pain shot through his whole body. He refused to cry in front of Amichai.

"You muttered in your sleep," Amichai said.

Jovian opened his eyes and cleared his thick throat. "Nothing too embarrassing, I hope."

"You spoke to a man named Jesus as if he was here with you."

Jovian's cheeks warmed. "Did I?" Jesus had been with him, but he wanted to keep that to himself.

"You were talking to Jesus of Nazareth, weren't you?" Amichai said, inching closer. "The man who was crucified?"

"The stuff they gave me muddled my head."

Amichai leaned even closer. "When you thought you would die on the battlefield, you cried out to a dead Jew. Why?"

Amichai was a hot-headed zealot. He betrayed his family and joined forces against his own people. Jovian wanted to hit him, to shake him, to yell at him. But to his surprise, he heard his voice saying, "Jesus isn't dead. He rose from the tomb, resurrected."

"Resurrected?" Amichai said. He stared into the distance and, to Jovian's surprise, something shone in the depths of his brown eyes. Hope. "You saw it?"

Jovian shook his head. "Your sister Joanna did. And her husband. Leah. The eleven, Jesus' mother and brothers, Cleopas and his wife, Mary Magdalene, Manaen and Maryam, Susanna—"

Amichai held up his hand to stave the flow of names. "Why haven't I heard about this before?"

Jovian waved his hand around the dim tent. "You didn't stick around to find out, did you?" Neither had he.

Amichai grunted. "Barabbas couldn't stay near Jerusalem. We lived in the wilderness until we heard about a city safe for men like us." He opened and closed his fists. "Barabbas was killed a couple years ago. I've been moving from group to group, trying to find some purpose."

Jovian stared at him in disbelief. "How is fighting your fellow Galileans your purpose?"

Amichai looked down at his open palms as if they held the answer. "We can't allow Antipas to work with Rome. We will not be slaves to the empire." Amichai looked at Jovian, his eyes begging him to understand. "Roman supporters are not my people."

The screams from the day before jabbed at Jovian's temples. His pulse quickened as he glared at Amichai. He and his foolish friends had not accomplished some great revolutionary act for Israel. They had helped Nabatea.

"So you won," Jovian said roughly. "That must feel good."

"I thought it would. But now…"

Jovian wished he could get up and walk away from this conversation. The stench of blood and death filled the tent. Every time he closed his eyes, he heard the sounds of battle. And Marcus' empty eyes—

He wrenched his mind back to the present and looked at Amichai. "But now?"

Amichai's eyes were dark pools. "I just feel exhausted. Like it will never end."

Against his better judgment, sympathy fluttered in Jovian's core. Amichai's youth had been spent in revolution, with little to show for it. If Jovian had Jesus' ability to peer into the hearts of men, what would he find inside Amichai? Would he see a man past all hope, tainted by blood and violence, an irretrievable sinner?

Jovian winced as he remembered Jesus hanging on the cross, declaring that those who were killing him were still worthy of forgiveness. The world would look at Amichai and see a brutal revolutionary, but Jesus would know what Amichai could become.

Jovian cleared his throat. "After the crucifixion, I went home to Antioch. A man came a year later and told me that Jesus was alive, but it took a rabbi to make me understand."

"Understand?"

"That Jesus is the Messiah."

Amichai's lips twisted. "A crucified messiah."

"It's in your scriptures," Jovian said. "Rishon showed me. In Isaiah, I think."

Amichai stared at him, then chuckled. "For once I wish I had paid more attention in school."

Jovian tried to shift into a more comfortable position. "The believers have searched the scriptures and found countless passages that Jesus fulfilled."

"The believers? Those people Jesus appeared to?"

"And many others. They have spread far from Jerusalem. Saul made sure of that."

"Saul?"

Jovian groaned as the wound under his ribs throbbed. "I'll tell you everything, but first you need to bring me more water."

"I'll get some broth," Amichai said, and scrambled to his feet. He turned and winked. It transformed his whole face. "Don't go anywhere."

As Amichai hurried away, Jovian scanned the tent. He needed to get out of this camp before someone higher up realized he didn't belong here. But between the stitches in his side and his mangled leg—he wasn't going anywhere.

# FORTY-FIVE

Antipas strode out of the palace gate and stood on the crest of the hill, staring down at Tiberias. The lake was choppy beneath a stormy sky, and the gulls flew low under the wind as they harassed the local fishermen.

He tried to calm his racing pulse. He had lost. No, he had been utterly defeated. Where had those reinforcements come from? He dragged his hands through his hair.

"What are you doing?" Herodias called. She stood in the palace gate as the breeze fluttered her scarlet robes and tugged on her gold earrings.

"I needed to get out," he muttered.

She seemed hesitant to leave the protection of the walls. He scoffed. Were they so cloistered within their palaces that an enemy had risen unseen? If he didn't know who had helped Nabatea, how could he decide what to do next?

Herodias walked to his side. "Cypros wrote to me. They've moved to Alexandria, but Agrippa needs money to—"

"Do you actually believe I care?" Antipas turned to stare at her, and she flinched. "Let him rot in Egypt. I have enough problems without that fool."

He strode back to the palace, gritting his teeth. The weight of the world was crushing him, but his wife only thought about her brother. And his steward was nowhere to be found.

"A message from Lord Antipas," a servant said.

Chuza blinked out of his reverie, coming back to the courtyard where the sound of maids washing laundry hit him with startling clarity. He didn't even remember sitting down on this bench.

The young man held out a small scroll.

Chuza took the letter and broke the seal with his thumb. Another demand for Chuza to return to Tiberias at once.

He crushed the message in his fist, his anger rising. Antipas expected him to clean up this mess, but there was nothing more to do. They must wait for the emperor to decide if Rome would help, and how.

Chuza dropped the crumpled papyrus at his feet and rubbed both temples with his fingers. He rarely experienced headaches, but this one refused to let up. Lack of sleep didn't help.

He lifted his face and stared at the palace. Stacks of correspondence waited to be answered. Ledgers and budgets needed to be balanced. But he couldn't face them. He jerked to his feet and strode out of the palace gate.

He wandered through Sepphoris, ending up in the busy market. He mindlessly scanned the booths of goods, half-listening to conversations.

"—not surprised how it ended. It's what he deserved, after divorcing that Nabatean princess."

"Exactly. John the Baptizer said his marriage was unlawful. What did Antipas think would happen?"

Chuza pressed deeper into the crowd, not wanting to hear more. He rubbed his chest where guilt dug in like a splinter. He should have done more to influence Antipas to righteousness. And not only that, he had helped Titus return to Antipas' employ—a path that led him onto that battlefield. It was all Chuza's fault.

Chuza snapped out of his thoughts and blinked in surprise. He had arrived at the city gate. He stared across the valley to the east. Somewhere out there was Titus' body.

Or not. Inexplicably, hope fluttered in Chuza's chest.

The messenger insisted there were no survivors, but what if he was wrong?

Chuza spun around and aimed for home, a plan forming in his mind.

Joanna rose from her loom as Chuza strode into the courtyard. "You're up to something." Her head tilted to the side. "And you're feeling better."

She was right. The headache was gone. He would take it as a sign.

"I'm going to the battlefield to figure out what happened to Titus."

Joanna's smile fled. "Are you sure that's safe?"

He watched her hand brush over her round middle. This might be the most foolhardy thing he had ever done, but he needed to do it. For himself, and for his oldest daughter.

"God will go with me," he said. "Whatever happens."

She pressed her lips together, but instead of convincing him to stay, she went into his arms and leaned her chin on his shoulder. "I wish I could go with you."

This was far too dangerous, even if she wasn't with child. "I'll leave at dawn. I should make good time if I ride Celer."

She stepped back and pursed her lips. "I wouldn't take your horse," she said. He furrowed his brow at her. "If you run into the wrong people, they might consider Antipas' steward a good hostage."

He hadn't even considered that risk.

She took his hand. "Go as a Galilean searching for his friend, not as the steward. You can take Balaam."

He scoffed. "The donkey?"

"It would make me feel better."

Chuza hesitated, then nodded.

"You're going?" Leah's voice crossed the courtyard.

Chuza turned as Leah came out of the house. She rushed toward them. Her face was pale, but two spots of pink dotted her cheeks. "I'm coming with you."

"No," Chuza said firmly, and when her face fell, he pulled her into a hug, aching for her. She had endured too much pain in her young life. "Stay and help your mother."

Leah pulled back to protest, but Chuza would not be moved. He had no idea what he would find when he approached the battlefield. Whatever dark scenes this journey painted on his mind, he would bear them alone.

Jovian shivered violently. Someone pulled his blanket up higher and wiped his face with a cloth. Every joint ached as if he had fallen off his horse and tumbled down a rocky slope. His head throbbed, and his throat burned no matter how much water and broth was poured down it. Beneath the tight bandage across his chest, his skin was slick with sweat, and his nose burned from the strong poultice that was supposed to be drawing out his infection. His only comfort amid the pain was that his leg throbbed with every beat of his pulse. He could still feel it.

The surgeon frowned and shook his head when he did his rounds.

Jovian's unexpected friend sat with his arms resting on his raised knees, his gaze distant. Jovian didn't know what kept Amichai by his side, but without his careful tending, Jovian knew he'd be dead already.

Why had Jesus helped him survive the battlefield if he was going to die of infection in this tent? Joanna would say it was for a purpose.

That he was supposed to do something or that his death would mean something. He shivered. It all felt pretty meaningless to him.

Chuza would say that Jovian had done his duty, that he couldn't be blamed for the faults of those he served.

Leah would say that life was cruel, and that Jesus came to bring comfort, peace, and purpose, not to shield him from pain. She would tell him to stop looking for meaning. To live, while he lived, as Jesus had.

Jovian glanced at Amichai again. The young man's eyes drifted closed, and his head bobbed as he fought to stay awake. Gratitude coursed through Jovian's veins. If he survived this, he would need to repay Amichai somehow.

Chuza slid from Balaam's back. He smoothed his plain robe and removed his wide-brimmed hat, dragging one hand through his tangled curls before replacing it.

He scanned the camp that spread along the hilltop surrounding the watchtower. To the south, vultures and ravens marked the scene of the battle. Chuza's shoulders tightened with trepidation.

"You there, halt!" a sharp voice cried out.

Chuza tensed as an armed man strode toward him, his eyes narrowed. He was tall and bulky, with a scar running down his cheek.

"Shalom," Chuza said as calmly as he could. "I'm unarmed."

The sentry did not seem to believe him. Chuza held out his arms and let him check his person, gritting his teeth at the rough search. The stench of onions was enough to make Chuza's eyes water.

The sentry turned to Balaam and dug through Chuza's bag, finding nothing but a change of clothes, some food, and a few coins.

Balaam tried to shift away, and the man smacked him.

The donkey's ears flattened against his head. He was unused to rough handling after years as Joanna's pet. Chuza took Balaam's bridle and stroked his neck, trying to calm the beast.

Finally, the large man slid Chuza's coins into his own belt and turned to face him. "What are you doing here?"

"I'm looking for a friend. A man from Antipas' army."

"Your friend is dead." He drew a knife from his belt. "Maybe you'd like to join him."

"Wait!" Chuza cried out, but the man jabbed the blade toward his throat.

Chuza stumbled backward, accidentally jerking Balaam's bridle.

The donkey had enough of this treatment. As Chuza landed on his seat in the grass, Balaam kicked with both back hooves, catching the sentry in the thigh. The man gasped in pain, his eyes white circles, but the donkey wasn't finished. He whirled around to sink his long yellow teeth into the man's arm, and spun to yank him off his feet.

The sentry screamed in pain and terror, and his knife went flying into the tall grass.

"Easy, boy!" Chuza shouted, scrambling to his feet as his pulse pounded.

Balaam released his victim, though his ears were still pressed flat against his head.

Chuza grabbed Balaam's bridle and pulled him toward the camp, wanting as much distance between them and the sentry as possible.

"Fine, go!" the man shouted after him, cradling his bleeding arm. "Let them kill you at the camp!"

After a dozen yards, Chuza slowed and glanced back at Balaam. "You may have saved my life back there."

Balaam's ears flicked toward him, and Chuza patted his neck affectionately. "I always knew you were a bargain."

Chuza's relief faded as he drew up to the tents and an armed man approached, squinting as he searched for the scouts that were supposed to be watching the perimeter. He frowned and turned his attention to Chuza. "What?"

The whole idea of coming here and asking for Titus suddenly

seemed ridiculously foolish, but Chuza had to try. "I'm looking for a survivor from Antipas' army."

The man assessed him, the silence drawing long. Behind him, the sounds of a military camp rose and fell, and smoke from a cookfire wafted on the breeze.

"We took no prisoners," the man said at last. His expression was flat, neither taunting nor cruel.

Chuza's stomach fell at this confirmation. "Can I search for his body?"

The man sighed. "We've already buried most of the dead. Now go home before I change my mind."

Not knowing what else to do, Chuza turned away. But as he took the first few steps, Balaam planted his feet in his familiar way and refused to move. Chuza realized Balaam was right. It was wrong to leave. He didn't know why, but he had to stay.

He set one hand on Balaam's neck and drew comfort from his wife's donkey. He hoped this choice wouldn't take him away from Joanna forever.

Chuza turned back to the guard. "I must speak to your commander."

"Why would he talk to you?"

"Because I am Herod's steward."

"Come on, you need to drink," Amichai said, his voice tinged with frustration. Jovian opened his mouth, but as Amichai trickled in the tepid water, Jovian choked, spraying water everywhere. Amichai set aside the cup with a huff.

Jovian sank into his mat, his body unbearably heavy. "Why do you care?" he whispered. Amichai wouldn't meet his eye. "I'm everything you hate. A foreigner. One of Antipas' men. Your enemy on the battlefield."

"You didn't kill me when you had the chance," Amichai said, but it sounded like an excuse.

Jovian shook his head, and pain shot down his neck. "That's hardly worth sitting with me in this stinking tent for days."

"You helped my family."

"That was years ago."

Amichai bunched his hands into fists and stared at him with angry, red eyes. "I don't know, alright? I have no idea why I care what happens to a filthy Greek!" He sank back. "But it's the only thing I've done that feels right." He bent one leg, wrapped his arms around it, and rested his chin on his knee.

Jovian tried to smile. "Well, whatever happens, I'm grateful you were here."

Amichai wouldn't look at him. "Just live, alright? Maybe if I bring you home, my sister will forgive me."

Jovian furrowed his brow. "Joanna forgave you long ago."

Amichai's eyes flicked to his, disbelieving. But then he looked at the tent entrance and frowned. Heavy steps were striding past.

"What on earth…" Amichai trailed off as he scrambled to his feet. He glanced at Jovian. "I'll be back."

Jovian groaned, wishing he had the strength to go after him. But Amichai was back in a moment, pulling another man with him.

Jovian stared in shock. This was impossible.

"Chuza?" he whispered, his voice cracking. "How…?"

"Balaam helped me." Chuza dropped to his knees and gripped Jovian's arm, concern painting his face as he surveyed Jovian's mangled body.

Amichai knelt next to his brother-in-law and stared at him in shock. "But how did you know he was alive?"

"I didn't. But I knew I had to come." Chuza scanned the tent. The surgeon came over, his hands folded.

"What's being done to treat him?" Chuza demanded in his best steward's voice. Jovian almost grinned to hear it.

"We have done everything in our power," the surgeon said. "His wounds fester, and now it is up to the gods. Perhaps it is good you came, to give him solace."

Chuza's brow lowered and he turned to Jovian. "I didn't come to bring you solace. I came to bring you home."

Jovian's heart turned over at the thought, but the surgeon pressed his lips together and returned to his makeshift desk and camp chair.

Amichai looked between Chuza and Jovian and licked his lips. For the first time in days, hope shone in the young man's eyes. Amichai leaned toward Chuza and whispered, "Are you going to... you know?"

Chuza looked at him in confusion. "Am I going to what?"

Amichai fidgeted and spoke even quieter. "Heal him?"

Chuza looked at Jovian, and a smile teased his lips. "Has Jovian been telling you about Jesus?"

Jovian tried to chuckle, but it sounded more like a wheeze.

Amichai's face reddened. "He said that the Holy Spirit gave some the power to heal. Can you?"

Chuza's expression sobered. "I've never healed anyone. I have done no miracles, besides speaking in tongues on that first day."

"So?" Amichai stared intensely at the steward. "If everything Jovian told me is true, then the Holy Spirit can do anything."

"It's not something we control," Chuza said.

"So you won't even try?" Amichai said, emotion straining his voice. "You're so afraid of failing, you won't even ask God?"

Chuza opened and closed his mouth, pain flickering across his features.

Amichai pressed further. "Are you worried you'll offend God by asking? Would you begrudge Nadia if she asked for something good, even if you had to say no?" Chuza twitched at hearing his daughter's name on Amichai's lips, but Amichai grabbed Chuza's shoulder and hissed in his face. "Do you have the Holy Spirit or don't you?"

Chuza closed his eyes as he bowed his head. "Father, forgive my unbelief."

Jovian's heart leaped.

Chuza rested both palms on Jovian, one on his hand, the other on his chest.

Jovian's weak pulse fluttered as Chuza prayed aloud. Joanna had been healed by Jesus. Her nephew had been healed by Peter. Leah said Stephen had healed her friend.

Jovian closed his eyes. His soul yearned to be close to Jesus, and through Jesus, close to God. His body convulsed with the depth of his longing and then relaxed. Completely relaxed. The pain was gone. He reveled in the ease of lying comfortably, wondering how he had ever taken his body for granted before.

He opened his eyes and stared at Chuza, wonder passing between them. Chuza held out his hand, and Jovian took it.

Together, they stood.

# FORTY-SIX

Joanna's voice drifted up the stairs. "Leah, it's time to eat."

Leah lay flat on her back, her arms folded behind her head. It was the third day since Chuza left, and anxiety was eating her from the inside out. She just wanted to lie in bed, alternating between praying and worrying, but that wasn't fair to Joanna or the children.

With a sigh, she sat up and smoothed her hair. She adjusted her face as she trotted down the stairs, squeezing Joanna's arm as she passed.

Leah strode into the courtyard, trying to smile as Little Mary and Nadia watched her approach.

"We made your favorite." Nadia gestured to the table.

Sweet cakes baked with pistachios. A lump rose in Leah's throat. Unable to answer, she kissed the top of Nadia's head instead.

"Did you love Jovian?" Little Mary asked.

Leah stiffened.

"Mary!" Dalia chided. She strode toward the table carrying Little Alex on her hip, his leg tucked under her large middle. She shot Leah an apologetic look as Miriam came out of the storeroom with a bowl of figs.

Little Mary flushed. "I was just wondering."

The rest of the household came from inside the house, all of them unusually quiet as they found their places at the table.

Leah tried to gather her emotions as she sat in her usual spot. The idea that Jovian would never walk into her kitchen again burned like hot soup in her throat, filling her chest with uncomfortable heat.

Joanna led them in prayer and then reached over to squeeze Leah's hand. "Chuza should be home soon."

Leah picked at a knot in the tabletop. She had been counting down the hours until her adoptive father returned, trying not to dwell on the fact this risky journey might only confirm her nightmare. She blinked rapidly. What if, while trying to find answers, Chuza was captured by Nabatea? Or injured? Or even killed? Guilt pressed on her. She hadn't asked him to go, but she hadn't talked him out of it either.

They heard the front door open and close, and Dalia smiled at Little Mary. "I think your father is home." Little Mary scampered to greet her father.

Joanna set a pistachio cake in front of Leah. "You need to eat something."

Leah broke off an edge. She wasn't hungry, but refusing to eat would only make everyone else feel worse.

"I know it's hard," Miriam said softly. "But take comfort knowing Titus cannot be separated from Jesus, whether in this life or the life to come."

"I'll take this life, at least for now," Jovian's voice filled the courtyard.

Leah whirled around as the other women gasped. This was impossible!

Her eyes roved over him in shock, afraid she was dreaming. But he stood next to a beaming Chuza, and Little Mary was jumping up and down, her hands covering her mouth.

Leah jerked to her feet and ran to Jovian, ready to throw herself into his arms. But she remembered herself just in time. She grasped his warm hand with both of hers, and brushed her thumbs over his knuckles, needing proof he was real.

"Are you hurt?" Joanna hurried forward.

"Not anymore," Jovian said. He turned his leg, and Leah stared at a long white scar behind his knee. It looked like it had been healed for months.

"It's a long story that deserves a proper telling," Jovian said. "But the short version is that I was dying until Chuza came. He prayed over me—after some convincing—and I was healed."

Joanna gawked at her husband, but then she crossed her arms. "Wait, convincing? Jovian had to convince you?"

Chuza smiled sheepishly. "Actually, it was your brother."

Joanna paled. "You saw Amichai?"

"Where?" Miriam cried out.

Chuza reached for Joanna's hand. "He's waiting just outside. He was afraid he wouldn't be welcome in your house."

Miriam picked up her skirt and raced for the portico, Dalia on her heels.

"Amichai is here?" Joanna's hand fluttered to her lips. She stared at Jovian. "*Amichai* helped you?"

"More than once," Chuza said. "Amichai brought me to Titus. The surgeon witnessed Titus' recovery, insisted I was a prophet, and wanted me to teach him how to heal. It was Amichai's smooth-talking that got us out of there." He chuckled as if it had all been a grand adventure, but Leah shuddered. So many things could have gone wrong.

Joanna glanced between the two men. "I will need the whole story later." She hurried after Miriam and Dalia.

"Papa!" Nadia jumped up and down, holding both arms up to her father. Chuza scooped her up and went to talk to Alexander's parents, giving Leah and Jovian a moment of privacy.

Leah realized she was still holding Jovian's hand. She dropped it, her cheeks flaming.

"I prayed for you," she said. She wrapped her arms around her middle. There was so much she wanted to say, but couldn't. "I was so worried."

His expression warmed. "It was thoughts of you that kept me going."

His words brushed against her heart, igniting feelings that had slumbered below the surface for so long. But she tamped those emotions down. They couldn't love each other like that.

He seemed to sense her hesitation and gave her a lopsided grin. "Thoughts of your cooking, I should say."

The tension in her chest eased, and she managed to laugh. "I promise you the best meal you've ever eaten."

He tilted his head, seeming to consider her offer. "I'm pretty picky, but I'll give you a few tries."

She laughed again, but then tears sprang into her eyes. Before she broke down in front of him, she took a step backward and gave him a wobbly smile. "I'm so happy you're home."

He opened his mouth to speak, but she fled back into the house.

She wanted to laugh. She wanted to weep. She wanted so badly to be close to him. Grateful tears mingled with her heartbreak. Jovian was safe, but he couldn't be hers.

Joanna stared at her brother across the table as she ran her hands over her belly, feeling the nudges from her unborn child. It had been years since she saw Amichai. Miriam clicked her tongue and fussed that he hadn't been eating well. But his weight was the least of Joanna's concerns.

She leaned sideways to whisper at Chuza. "Is he safe here?"

Chuza's eyes met hers. Amichai was a highwayman and a rebel. He was fresh off the battlefield where he had fought against Antipas.

"Not entirely," he whispered back.

Joanna scanned the faces of her family with worry.

As if reading her mind, Amichai looked her way. He turned to his mother, setting his hand on hers. "I came because I needed to see you. But I can't stay here."

Miriam's expression fell, and she gripped his fingers. "No! Chuza can make this right."

Everyone looked at Chuza expectantly, but Joanna couldn't share their optimism. Amichai may have experienced a change of heart, but that didn't erase years of lawlessness.

Chuza spread a palm on the table. "I might be able to have Amichai's charges lessened as a reward for saving the captain of the guard." He glanced at Titus. "But he would still need to answer for his crimes. It would mean a sentence of hard labor."

Amichai paled and Dalia covered her mouth with her hand.

"No," Miriam's voice cracked. "Surely there is another way."

Chuza's brow furrowed over his tight eyes. Joanna knew how much he hated holding another man's life in his hands.

"What if he left?" Joanna said. Miriam protested again, but Joanna spoke over her. "If it's a life of hard labor or a life in exile, I think the choice is made."

Miriam's jaw snapped closed, and she looked away, blinking rapidly.

Amichai's expression grew anguished. "What if I returned to the vineyard?" Joanna's eyes widened in surprise. "I will change my name. Work as a hired man."

Chuza said, "Someone would recognize you. The neighbors know you joined the revolutionaries."

"But some would side with me," Amichai said, and some of his old zeal returned. "They would help me hide."

Chuza glanced at Joanna before answering Amichai. "But some would not. I can't ask David and Tirzah to shelter a known criminal."

Amichai's head bowed for a moment as he brought his emotions under control. "Then where do I go? How do I support myself? I have no trade and no skills, other than tending vines."

The table fell silent. Chuza studied his palms, no doubt seeing Amichai's plight as a personal failure. Joanna nudged him.

"It's not your fault," she whispered.

"I know. But I wish I could do more. For your mother's sake."

Miriam struggled against tears as Joanna looked around the table. Someone had to have an idea.

Titus cleared his throat. "I plan to resign my position."

Everyone turned to him in surprise, and Titus flushed. "I've given it a good deal of thought. I trained to fight because I want to protect the vulnerable. I never thought it would be so hard to know if I'm fighting for the right cause." Pain quivered over his face before he smoothed it away. "But, like Amichai, I also have no skills to offer, other than my sword."

Chuza leaned toward him. "You can stay with us. We'll find you a position in the city."

Joanna's gaze flicked to the upper level of the house. She wanted to help Titus, but they needed to consider Leah's needs as well.

"I can't live with you," Titus said. "And no one in this city would hire a Greek."

Chuza opened his mouth to protest, but Titus held up his hand. "No, it's alright. I'll go with Amichai."

Chuza blinked in shock, and Joanna furrowed her brow.

Amichai said, "You don't need to do that. I can find my own way."

Titus grinned. "You kept me alive until Chuza and the Holy Spirit showed up. The least I can do is help you get on your feet."

Chuza frowned. "But where will you go?"

Titus shifted to his usual ease. "There must be a merchant caravan that needs a couple of trained fighting men. We would do a little travel, have some adventure."

Amichai raised his eyebrows at Titus, but Joanna could see the idea intrigued him.

Chuza seemed to struggle inwardly, but finally he wobbled his head from side to side. "A caravan might work. No one pays much attention to the guards, and fewer ask questions. And it would bring you back to us every few months. But is this really the career you want?"

"No, not really," Titus said. "But it will give us time to plan for the future."

Joanna again glanced up to the upper level of the house. Leah would miss Titus if he left again, but perhaps this was for the best.

Chuza folded his hands tightly. "You know, you could return to Antioch. Take Amichai with you."

Joanna knew it wasn't what Chuza wanted, but at least both men would be safe and could find a stable future.

Amichai and Miriam shared a pained glance, but it was Titus who shook his head. "I can't go home yet."

Amichai gave him a crooked grin. "You mean you don't want to show up on your father's doorstep with a tattered career and a fugitive?"

Titus grinned sheepishly.

"Your family would be glad to see you," Miriam said thickly. "No matter how you arrive."

"Maybe so." Titus inclined his head to her. "But I'm not ready to leave Israel." He turned to Chuza. "Will you help us find a reputable caravan?"

Chuza nodded.

Miriam gripped Amichai's hand. "When do you need to leave?"

Amichai looked at Chuza.

"As soon as they can," Chuza said. He turned to Titus. "Let's go to the market and make some inquiries."

The two men stood as Leah came out of the house, her arms wrapped around herself. She looked at Titus and the unmistakable gleam of love shone in her eyes.

Joanna and Chuza shared a pained glance. Some things couldn't be fixed, not even by the steward.

# FORTY-SEVEN

## 35 AD
### AUTUMN

Chuza reined in Celer and squinted over his shoulder, studying the dusty procession that rumbled in his wake. Half a dozen carts, twenty guards, and thirty servants had left Galilee more than a week ago. After marching through Philip's former territory and into Syria, they had arrived in the middle of nowhere.

King Artabanus of Parthia had seized Armenia— all while defending his principality against neighboring armies and internal plots. Noting his military prowess, the Emperor decided Artabanus would be a better friend than an enemy, and so he sent Vitellius, the governor of Syria, to discuss terms for peace and hostages. And, somehow, Antipas was chosen as the neutral host for the peace talks.

Chuza glanced sideways at his master. If there was one good thing about this unusual journey, Antipas was distracted from his recent defeat.

The tetrarch beamed from atop his gleaming white stallion, as eager to begin as Chuza was to go home. Joanna was nearing her time, and he would rather be by her side than watching powerful men grasp for even more power.

Chuza sighed and faced forward again, scanning the glistening Euphrates River. It wound between fields of autumn brown. The sky domed in deepest blue over two large camps, one on either side of the river. Each camp surrounded a large tent flying the banners of their respective countries—Syria on one side, and Parthia on the other. A pontoon bridge spanned the river where the rulers would negotiate terms over the flowing water.

"Set up camp there." Antipas pointed to a grassy field. "Once I've bathed, I'll go meet the governor. I'm sure he's as eager to meet as I am."

Chuza kept his doubts to himself as he led the caravan to Antipas' chosen site. The carts ground to a halt. Blessed quiet spread over the field, filling his weary ears with the calm sounds of water, frogs, and insects.

He hobbled Celer with the other animals and strode past servants unloading tents and furniture. Michael had parked the kitchen wagon downwind from the camp, in easy reach of the river where the air was rich with mud and thick grass. His gruff voice echoed across the field as his staff raised canopies and dug the fire pits.

Leah stood near the supply wagon, checking the inventory as crates, baskets, and amphorae were unloaded at her feet.

Chuza joined her. "How was your day?"

"Fine." Leah gave him a quick smile before she returned her attention to a basket of figs.

Despite her reticence, Chuza hoped this change of scene would give her a chance to settle her emotions. Titus' return from the dead had made her feelings for him even more complicated.

Chuza gripped Leah's shoulder and waited until her eyes met his. He wanted to tell her that her heart would heal. That she would learn to love someone else. That she was young, with so much future ahead of her. But when he opened his mouth, all he could say was, "It will get easier."

Her lips twisted to the side, revealing her doubt. "I need to get back to work."

He let his hand fall to his side. He nodded at Michael, and a knowing glance passed between them. The burly cook would watch over his protege.

An hour later, Chuza joined Antipas and they strode across the sunny field to meet Vitellius. One of the governor's guards led them through an orderly camp where men sat before their tents and the scent of campfire bread hung in the air.

The flap to the governor's tent was tied open, and Antipas left his guards outside as he strode in. The space was divided by a hanging cloth. The main area was given over to a large table, where a handful of men in simple garb gathered around a detailed map.

"My lord," the guard said, "Herod Antipas is here."

The men turned, and one stepped forward. He was a large man, perhaps forty, with cropped hair and a beardless face. His eyes were deep-set beneath unruly eyebrows, giving him a calculating air. He strode purposefully to greet Antipas, and clasped his wrist with brisk formality.

"Welcome, Tetrarch," Vitellius said. "Come and join us."

A servant gave Antipas and Chuza cups, and they sipped their wine as the other men discussed borders and cities and acceptable hostages. Chuza feared his master would be humiliated by his inability to offer advice, but when they returned to their tent that evening, the tetrarch was beaming.

"I'm so pleased Tiberius requested my presence at these nego-tiations." Antipas clapped his hands and rubbed them together. "I can hardly wait to meet Artabanus. I may only be the mediator, but I will turn this to our benefit, mark my words."

Leah squinted against the bright sunlight as Chuza hurried toward them.

Days had dragged by while the king and governor met on the strange bridge that floated on the sluggish river. Antipas seemed delighted with the whole event, but Leah had spent the past few days with her belly in an anxious knot. She and Michael were supposed to prepare a feast fit for kings—with little notice and fewer amenities. If they failed and embarrassed Antipas… she didn't even want to contemplate the fate of her career.

Chuza's determined face told Leah everything she needed to know. "It's time," he said. "Prepare the feast."

Michael and Leah shared a glance. Butterflies fluttered in Leah's stomach as she pushed up her sleeves.

Michael slaughtered the sheep and the quail. As he prepared the lamb, Leah plucked the four birds. The kitchen slaves kindled a fire and hung the lamb on a green cedar branch.

Leah rubbed the poultry with oil and spices and set them to roast. Before long, the hiss of dripping fat and the fragrance of seasoned meat floated tantalizingly on the breeze.

She took a bowl of leavened dough and shaped it into braids. A slave slid the loaves into a makeshift clay oven and crouched to keep watch.

Leah and Michael tossed wheat kernels in oil and seasoning before roasting them in a large pan. They stewed dried apricots in wine and syrup until they were soft and plump. In a large pestle, chickpeas were ground into a paste, mixed with sesame butter and roasted garlic, and drizzled with golden oil. The slaves measured almonds and raisins into pretty dishes, and mixed the wine with water in the krater. The sealed jar of brined olives was opened, releasing its delightfully tangy fragrance.

380

As the sun sank, Michael carved the lamb and arranged slices of meat on a platter with bowls of sauce.

Before Leah knew it, the servants were whisking dishes to the center of the pontoon bridge, where Antipas had erected a stunning pavilion. The bleached wool panels glowed in the twilight, and its red fringe waved in the breeze. Hanging lamps swung gently, and elegant furniture filled this picturesque, if rather unusual, dining room. Antipas, Vitellius, and Artabanus reclined together, and polite conversation drifted toward shore as the first stars emerged in a purple sky.

Leah shared a look with Michael. They had done everything they could.

Leah watched anxiously as the platters returned, relieved to see them so depleted. The servants grinned at the anxious cooks.

"Everything found favor," one said. "Antipas seems pleased."

Michael wiped his brow. "The next time Antipas plans something like this, I'm staying home."

Leah couldn't share his sentiment. She was exhausted, but the challenge had been invigorating.

Late that night, as the powerful men retired to their separate camps, the servants and guards feasted on the leftovers.

Chuza came to join them, grinning from ear to ear. "Spectacular." He clapped one hand on Michael's shoulder, the other on hers. "You two should be proud."

Leah tried to smile. She was proud. But perhaps the best part about the whole feast was that she had forgotten about Jovian, if even for one day.

Satisfaction coursed through Antipas' veins as he strode out of Artabanus' camp. His final conversation with the Parthian king had gone even better than he hoped.

He squinted across the river. Chuza was waiting for him. Antipas crossed the floating bridge and pretended not to notice his steward's nervous frown. "Did you need something?"

"Do you?" Chuza's gaze darted over Antipas' shoulder.

Antipas chuckled. Always the worrier. "Come, walk with me." He made his way through his chaotic camp where the servants were dismantling tents and canopies.

Chuza fell in beside his master, and Antipas spoke in tones aimed for his ears alone. "I told Artabanus about our situation with Nabatea. Out of gratefulness for my assistance here, he wishes to give me a gift."

"A gift?"

Antipas' pulse fluttered with excitement as he leaned closer to his steward. "He's giving me armor and weapons, more than enough to replace what I lost to Nabatea. Enough for seventy thousand men."

Chuza stumbled to a halt, and his mouth hung open.

Antipas laughed and slapped his shoulder. "You should see your face!"

"My lord, you cannot accept such a gift!"

Antipas waved his worries aside. He had known Chuza would have reservations. The steward was a careful man, as he should be. But a ruler needed to take risks when necessary. "Artabanus insisted. Consider it a loan, if it makes you feel better."

Chuza glanced toward Vitellius' tent as if afraid the Syrian governor would overhear. "But you don't *have* seventy thousand men. An army a quarter that size would be seen as sedition."

"Don't worry. We'll put it in storerooms, somewhere out of the way. No one needs to know about it, except you and me."

Chuza dragged both hands through his hair. "This is a mistake."

His reaction rattled Antipas more than he cared to admit. But he refused to be humiliated by Nabatea again. He needed this armor, and once Chuza got over his shock, he would agree.

Antipas strode for his tent. It was nearly empty. He stopped a slave carrying his writing materials and retrieved a sealed scroll. He held it out to Chuza. "I want this sent to Tiberius immediately."

Chuza hesitantly accepted the scroll. "To the emperor?"

Annoyance flickered through Antipas' chest. "Of course. I stayed up late preparing a detailed report."

"My lord, it would be wise to give Vitellius a chance to send his report first."

Antipas' frustration grew. Soon the steward would be telling him when to eat and sleep. "The governor can send his own report whenever he wishes."

"My lord, please reconsider. You risk offending Vitellius by—"

Antipas cut him off with a glare. "Tiberius asked me to be here. He obviously wanted me to report back to him."

Chuza spoke tightly. "As you wish, my lord."

Antipas stomped out of the empty tent. Chuza followed and both men watched as the stakes were loosened and the tent collapsed in a heap.

Antipas strode away to his horse, eager to put Chuza and his needless anxiety behind him. Armor for seventy thousand men. He whistled lowly. Herodias would be so impressed.

Leah walked beside the wagon. The massive wheel creaked and rumbled as it rolled over the rough track. The noise was deafening, but not enough to drown out her thoughts. They were heading back to Sepphoris, and Jovian wouldn't be there.

The wind whipped her hair as she peered over the field, watching the tall grass swaying like waves on the sea. She needed to get her emotions back under control before they returned home.

She blinked rapidly, and let the wind carry away her tears.

# FORTY-EIGHT

36 AD
WINTER

Clouds scuttled past the sun as a cold wind crept down Jovian's neck. He hitched his cloak higher and scanned the Samaritan countryside. A local shepherd drove his sheep to water, their bells clanking as they ambled through the coarse grass.

The caravan was back in Pilate's territory, slogging its way north toward Galilee before they would continue on to Syria. Then the loop would begin again, a monotonous circle of trade.

Their route followed the mountain ridge that included the Samaritans' most sacred site. According to Amichai, there used to be a temple atop Mount Gerizim—until a Jewish king destroyed it. Jovian pressed his lips together. No wonder Jews and Samaritans didn't get along.

Their fearless leader Zahur had decided to press on to the Samaritan city of Sychar. Depending on sales, they would stay for a few days or even weeks before moving on to Galilee.

While there were exciting moments, guarding a caravan meant days of tedium—with far too much time to think. Which meant thoughts of Leah consumed most of his hours.

The longer he was away from Sepphoris, the more Jovian feared he and Leah could never go back to being just friends. The look in her eyes when she saw he was alive warmed him from within. But it was chased by guilt.

He should be doing everything in his power to break the tie that bound him and Leah together, but instead he had concocted a plan that could draw them even closer.

He sighed. It would be easier to harness himself to a chariot and win a race than to forget the woman who captured his heart.

Jovian turned to walk backward, inspecting the line of camels with their loads swaying side to side. Amichai lifted his hand in a wave. His past as a highwayman had become Amichai's greatest strength. He was adept at spotting risks along the road. Thanks to Amichai, the caravan had avoided trouble and wiggled out of a few tight spots with only minor injuries on either side.

Jovian turned to face forward. They were approaching a small village, and raised voices traveled on the breeze. Trepidation rippled down his spine, and he glanced back to make sure the other guards were on alert.

The caravan line contracted as they approached the noise. As Zahur led them past the village, Jovian saw a man standing atop a wagon and speaking to the crowd.

"I'll show you all," the man said. "We'll go at first light, and I promise you, we will restore the glory of Samaria!"

Men roared in approval.

Jovian called to a man standing with his arms crossed. "Shalom, my friend! What's going on?"

The man scanned Jovian and the caravan. "This man claims he found some ancient relics Moses buried. He plans to lead the men to Mount Gerizim in the morning." His lips twisted doubtfully.

"You don't believe him?"

"Why should I?" The man scoffed. "And I have to wonder, what does he benefit by whipping the people into a frenzy?"

Jovian scanned the fevered crowd again, but the caravan was

386

plodding onward, and he hurried to resume his position. Whatever was going on, his responsibility was to Zahur and the caravan.

They arrived at Sychar an hour later. Men trickled out of the city gates and strode toward the outlying village, some looking curious, others determined.

The caravan paraded into the city and aimed for the open market. Jovian helped unload the camels as usual, but he couldn't get the zealous crowd out of his mind. He had seen men stirred up with religious fanaticism before. It had not ended well.

Jovian and Amichai were assigned to water and picket the camels outside the city. As Jovian gathered up the lead ropes, Zahur approached.

"Be on your guard," Zahur said in his thick accent, and he fingered the knife in his belt. "I sense trouble."

Jovian and Amichai led the camels to the well outside the city, and studied the horizon.

All was quiet now, but Jovian would sleep with one eye open tonight.

The thunder of pounding hooves woke Jovian. He jerked to his feet, and his blanket slid to the ground. He shivered in the moonless night, sucking in a deep breath of the fresh air.

It was Amichai's watch. He stood with his back to the low fire, watching shadows pass in the darkness. It sounded like at least a hundred horses.

Jovian stepped beside Amichai. "What's happening?"

"Nothing good."

The sun rose on a bleak morning, the sky overcast with dark clouds.

The city gates opened on their creaking hinges, but few travelers went in or out.

Jovian and Amichai broke their fast with bread and dates. Other groups of travelers stirred in their makeshift camps, but they kept their voices down as if they sensed a storm on the horizon.

Two men stumbled into view, weaving their way down the road as if they were drunk—or injured. Jovian stepped toward them instinctively, but Amichai held out his arm and shook his head.

The city guards drew together, gripping their spears. Just outside the gates, the men fell to their knees and poured dust over their heads.

"What happened?" a city guard demanded.

"Pilate attacked us. We barely escaped with our lives."

Jovian and Amichai shared a dark glance.

"Pilate does it again." Amichai's lip curled. "He has to be stopped."

Jovian couldn't agree more. The banners, the golden shields, slaughtering Galileans at the temple altar, crucifying an innocent man, and now this attack against the Samaritans—Pilate's violent ways had killed hundreds, if not thousands.

As the day wore on, more reports trickled in, until a full picture of Pilate's cruelty emerged in grisly detail. His soldiers had mowed through the Samaritan farmers and tradesmen. Those who surrendered were executed without mercy. The wails of lamenting women filled the air until there was no escaping the sound.

Finally, Zahur decided the caravan should move on. There was no profit to be found in Sychar, only mourning. To Jovian's relief, Zahur aimed for Sepphoris. Hopefully Chuza would be there. The steward needed to know what Pilate had done.

Chuza's joy at seeing Titus faded as he scanned his friend's face. "What happened?"

Titus' fist clenched by his side. "Pilate."

As Titus described what had happened near Sychar, Chuza's anger battled with dismay. When Titus finished, Chuza sat heavily at his desk and rubbed his face with both hands. How could God let a man like Pilate rule Judea?

"Can you do something?"

Chuza winced. "Antipas can write to Caesar, but other than that…" He lifted his hands and let them fall.

"I know there's not much you can do, but I had to try… something."

Chuza understood the feeling all too well. "I will do what I can." Despite his efforts, his influence over Antipas was weakening further.

Chuza realized he hadn't even offered Titus a drink. He rose and poured each of them a cup of wine.

Titus took a sip.

"I have a son now," Chuza said.

Titus choked on his drink and Chuza chuckled.

Titus wiped his mouth, his eyes wide. "Joanna had the baby! Is she well?"

"They are both well." Chuza's chest warmed with pride. "We named him Ira, after Joanna's father. He's three months old already, and so determined." He twisted his lips ruefully. "If we can survive his stubbornness now, he will make a strong leader someday." A man who could protect his mother and sisters when Chuza was gone.

Titus fiddled with his cup. "And how is Leah?"

Titus' casualness did not fool Chuza. "Between her work at the palace and among the believers, she keeps herself busy. She'll be happy to see you again."

Titus scoffed doubtfully. "I know she thinks I'm a fool. I could go home, but instead I work for bad pay in Israel while refusing to convert to Judaism."

Chuza hesitated, not wanting to push. "You still feel the same about converting?"

"My mother would never forgive me if I was circumcised. Not that I'm eager for it myself." He chuckled, but it shifted to a heavy sigh. "Taking on Judaism would put an impenetrable wall between myself and my family. I'm not ready to cut ties. Not yet, anyway."

Chuza had hoped that experiencing the power of the Holy Spirit would finally convict Titus. But while the Greek man was fully convinced that Jesus was the Messiah, he still refused to become a Jew. It was a shame, in more ways than one. Titus had a gift for leadership, but as long as he remained merely a God-fearer, none of the believers would let him use his gift for the Lord.

Failure pressed on Chuza's throat. There had to be something he hadn't said, a way to persuade Titus that he hadn't found. Titus looked up, and Chuza smoothed his face.

"Ignore my rambling." Titus smiled sheepishly. "I'm just glad to be home."

"How long are you here for?"

"A week at least. Maybe more, if things are selling."

"And how is Amichai?"

Titus beamed. "Amichai is great. I don't know if I could do this job without him."

Jealousy twinged Chuza's chest. He still didn't understand why Titus had chosen to go with Amichai instead of staying in Sepphoris.

"I owe him." Titus seemed to read Chuza's mind. He leaned closer. "I know he's caused your family no end of trouble. But he not only saved my life, he stayed by my side even when he believed I was his enemy. I promised myself I would help him find a new path."

Chuza spun his cup on the desk. Without Amichai, Titus would not be sitting here. Chuza smiled. "He's lucky to count you as a friend."

Titus drained his cup and rose. "I should go see Leah. When I left, things were still—" he twisted his lips to the side "—tense between us. I can't leave again until I know she understands."

That was no small task, but Chuza nodded. "She's in the kitchen."

Titus strode from the room.

Sensing a presence, Leah turned and her stomach swooped. Jovian was back. He needed a haircut, but his eyes twinkled as they met hers, and his lips curved invitingly. She hastily reined in her thoughts.

"Welcome home," she said, and was frustrated as heat bloomed in her cheeks. "You must be starving. Sit."

Jovian slid onto one of the benches around the long table. Her hand trembled as she poured him a cup of wine. She kept her back to him as she prepared a tray.

Finally, as her pulse slowed, she turned and set the dizzying array of food in front of her guest. Jovian eyed it with appreciation, then grinned at her.

"I obviously can't eat all of this alone. Sit with me."

Leah opened her mouth to protest, but the earnestness in his gaze stilled her tongue. She swiped her hands down her apron and sat on the opposite bench. He shifted the tray so it was between them, and waited for her.

She plucked a piece of bread from the tray and tore off a corner to dip in the seasoned olive oil. He dug in, eating with enthusiasm. She smiled. It was almost like old times. She wanted to ask about his journey, but the words were trapped somewhere below the butterflies in her stomach.

Jovian cleared his throat. "I've been thinking, and I know what I'll do after I'm done working for the caravan."

She raised her brows. "You mean you don't plan to be a caravan guard forever?" It came out more sarcastic than she intended, and she blushed. If she could ever tame her foolish tongue, she would be a happy woman.

"Well, it'll be a year at least," he said. Excitement spread over his face. "But I've decided I want a business of my own. It does depend on one thing." He glanced around the empty kitchen. "I'll need you."

Leah nearly dropped her bread, and her voice came out squeaky. "You need me?"

Now it was Jovian's turn to blush. "I mean, I need your skills. As a cook. I need the best cook for my restaurant."

She pushed any dangerous thoughts back where they belonged. Jovian and she were just friends, and they both knew it.

"You want to open a restaurant? In Sepphoris?"

"I've given it a lot of thought. I want to offer daily meals, but also have a banquet room for meetings, dinner clubs, or even wedding feasts."

Leah pursed her lips. "It sounds… Roman."

"I know, but I've been thinking about what you said before. How good food brings people together."

She blinked, surprised that he remembered.

"Maybe we can bridge a little of the gap between Gentile and Jew, right here in Sepphoris. And you'd have your own kitchen."

She glanced around the room. Michael had all but implied he would hand her his apron when he retired, but that would mean she'd have to move from palace to palace, never having a settled, permanent home.

He leaned closer. "So, what do you think?"

Leah toyed with her bread. The idea was intriguing, but besides her doubt about a Greek man opening a restaurant in Sepphoris, she and Jovian would work side by side every day. It would test any friendship, never mind one where the cook loved her employer. "I'll need to think about it."

"There's no rush. Like I said, I don't have the money yet."

They both reached for a date and Jovian gave her a grin that made her pulse flutter. His restaurant would keep him here, in Sepphoris. It was what she longed for, but perhaps it was more than she could handle.

# ONE YEAR LATER

# FORTY-NINE

37 AD
SPRING

A ntipas stood with his arms crossed and rubbed his lower lip with his ring. The cold jewel soothed his anxious nerves amid the uncertainty that surrounded him. His furniture was draped with robes, coats, and belts as his frazzled body slave wrung his fool hands. But Antipas' worries surpassed mere clothing.

Pilate's reign was over. It had been more than a year since he attacked the Samaritans, accusing them of revolting, when in reality, they had been searching for holy relics.

Vitellius had heard about the bloodbath and sent Pilate back to Rome to face charges of cruelty. Vitellius had also dislodged Pilate's chosen High Priest, Caiaphas, and set another man up in his place. Two men who had wielded power in Judea for a decade were both gone. It was… unsettling.

Herodias' perfume teased Antipas' nose, and he turned as she entered the room, dressed in flowing robes of bright pink. She laughed brightly as she saw the disarray.

"Can't decide what to bring?" she asked, plucking at an embroidered coat draped over a chair.

Antipas frowned. "I've decided to meet Vitellius' army on his way south. I need to make the right impression. Authoritative, but not arrogant." Now that Tiberius had finally agreed to send Vitellius to pound Nabatea into proper submission, Antipas needed to look like a ruler who deserved the emperor's favor—and his help.

Herodias came to him, wrapping her arms around his middle and tipping back to peer into his face. "Relax, my love. Things are finally going your way."

Antipas was not so certain. "Are you sure I don't look weak, depending on Syria to defend my borders?"

Herodias scoffed. "You are the longest reigning ruler in all of Israel. Your brother Archelaus lives in exile. Philip is dead. Pilate and Caiaphas are both disgraced and discarded." She squeezed him tighter. "But you remain the tetrarch of Galilee and Perea."

A smile teased at the corner of his mouth. She was right. He had outlasted them all.

"You know," he said thoughtfully, "I should invite Vitellius to stop at Jerusalem on his way. Show him the temple and the palace."

Herodias nodded eagerly. "Yes, remind him of your powerful heritage. You are a valued ally."

With Vitellius' help, Antipas would recover both his stolen land and his honor. Maybe Herodias was right. Things were finally going his way.

"I nearly forgot the food." Joanna shook her head at herself as she came out of the house with a basket. The sun glinted off her dark hair and kissed her cheekbones. Chuza blinked at her. She was just as beautiful as the day they met.

She furrowed her brow at his expression. "What?"

He grinned, taking the basket. "Nothing. Just that I love you."

Joanna grinned and raised an eyebrow. "Just that? Well, I love you too."

As Chuza set the basket among the overflowing two-wheeled cart, little Ira toddled out of the house. Short curls framed his chubby face and bright, brown eyes.

"Oh, better pack this, too." Joanna scooped up the eighteen-month-old boy and pretended to toss him at Chuza like a sack of grain.

"Ah, yes." Chuza played along and gently tossed his son into the luggage. "Can't forget this."

The boy squealed with delight as he landed amid the bundles and baskets.

"Toss me too!" Nadia said, running out of the house.

"More luggage!" Joanna grunted as she swung the giggling girl at Chuza. "This one is heavier."

Chuza plunked her in beside her brother, and both children giggled.

"Are we ready?" Chuza swiped his brow in an exaggerated manner.

Joanna's playfulness faded, and she glanced back at the house. This journey came with baggage that could not be contained in baskets or bundles. Caiaphas' downfall had brought change into their life—not unexpected, perhaps, but difficult all the same.

Dalia and Alexander were moving back to Jerusalem. With Saul still missing and Caiaphas deposed, they had decided it was time.

Chuza squeezed Joanna's arm. "Are you sure you don't want to move with them?"

"I feel called to shepherd the believers in Sepphoris." She drew a deep breath. "We'll celebrate Passover in Jerusalem, but then we need to come home."

Chuza glanced down the street. Sepphoris had become their home, and they had friends and neighbors. But it would still feel empty without the rest of the family.

"I'll see if Leah's ready," Joanna said.

Chuza nodded. "I'll get Balaam."

Chuza wound his way around boxes, baskets, and bundles as he made his way to the stable.

He found Alexander in the dim, dusty space, harnessing his own donkey.

"Nearly ready?" Chuza asked.

Alexander grinned. "We'd better be. If we take any longer, we might as well stay the night."

Chuza chuckled and let himself into Balaam's stall.

Alexander tightened a buckle and lowered his voice. "Do you think Peter is back yet?"

Chuza pressed his lips together as he lifted Balaam's leather harness from its hook on the wall. "I'm not sure."

Peter had been preaching the good news along the coast, but strange rumors were spreading. They said Peter was going into the homes of the uncircumcised and eating with them. The news had sent a schism through the community of believers. While some, like Joanna and Chuza, permitted God-fearers to eat with them in Jewish spaces, Peter had done the opposite and eaten in a Gentile house.

"Do you think the rumors are even true?" Alexander asked.

"I guess there's only one way to find out."

Chuza's feet ached as they joined the slow queue at the massive city gates. Passover was only a few weeks away, and for the first time in a decade, Pontius Pilate would not oversee the massive influx of pilgrims. Satisfaction spread through Chuza's limbs like warm sunshine.

He tugged on Balaam's lead and they joined the clogged streets of Jerusalem where men and women jostled each other and small children rode on shoulders, donkeys, or in carts. The scent of warm bodies mingled with spices as smoke rose from the temple mount.

"It's good to be back," Joanna said, and glanced over at her eldest daughter.

Leah walked with her arms folded across her chest, her back hunched as if remembering the strikes across her skin. Chuza's chest tightened protectively, but it had been four years. He and Joanna shared a glance. The persecution was over.

The crowds thinned as they moved further up the city. Alexander lengthened his pace and led them down familiar streets and up to the two story house. A few neighbors called out surprised greetings, welcoming them home. Chuza drew his cart to the side, and he, Joanna, and Leah waited as the house was unlocked and the others went inside. They could hear Samuel shouting to his sister as he saw the familiar rooms.

Chuza helped Nadia jump out of the cart.

"Why do they need to move?" Nadia asked. The little girl had never lived without her extended family. It would be a huge change.

He crouched so he was peering up into her damp eyes. "We will see them again. Every festival."

"It won't be the same," she muttered. She tipped her head to the side, her innocent eyes probing his. "What about your family, Papa? Why don't we see them?"

Joanna's gaze flew to his, but Chuza rose and smiled at his daughter, setting his hand on her narrow shoulder. This wasn't the time to tell her about his painful past. "You are my family," he said softly. "You, Ira, Leah, and Mama." He gestured to the house, where happy voices spilled into the street. "My family is here, and I will see them every time you do."

Joanna picked up Ira, setting him on her hip as she spoke to her daughter. "I know you're sad, but try to be happy for Mary. Her family can finally go home." Homesickness shone in Joanna's eyes. No matter how many years passed, he knew she would always miss her vineyard.

Joanna reached for Chuza's hand and said, "We can't always be together, but we're a family, no matter what."

399

Joanna twisted her fingers in her belt as she and Chuza wove through the twilight streets. They were about to reunite with the other believers, but anxiety pervaded her eagerness. Peter had arrived in Jerusalem, but no one knew what he would say. If one of Jesus' closest friends had fallen away from the truth, what would that mean for The Way?

They arrived at a large house. Light seeped through the closed shutters and the hum of conversation filtered into the dusky air.

They knocked and were let into a house crowded with people and high emotions. Joanna's gaze was drawn straight to Peter. The former fisherman looked the same as ever with his tanned face and unruly hair, though there were more lines around his eyes.

Peter stood with his wife and his brother, Andrew. Despite the tension filling the room, Peter seemed at ease.

"Joanna!" Maryam called. Joanna rushed forward to embrace her friend. Chuza and Manaen clasped hands, their greeting subdued in the unsettled atmosphere.

One of the older men grew tired of waiting. "Peter," he said, and the room fell silent. "Is it true that you've been eating with uncircumcised men?"

"It'll take a few minutes to explain," Peter said mildly. "Do you mind if I sit?"

No one protested as Peter took a chair near the front of the room. He rubbed his palms down his knees as if preparing himself for his story. Everyone shifted a little closer.

"When I was in Joppa, I received a vision," Peter said. "I saw something like a great sheet, and in it were all kinds of four-footed animals and crawling creatures of the earth and birds of the sky. A voice said, 'Get up Peter, kill and eat!' But I said, 'By no means, Lord, for I have never eaten anything unholy and unclean.' The voice chastised me. 'What God has cleansed, do not consider unholy.'"

Joanna blinked in surprise, and she saw the others furrowing their brows, trying to understand.

Peter said, "This happened three times, and immediately the object was taken up into the sky. Before I could understand what the vision meant, three men came to the house, looking for me. They were sent from Caesarea by a God-fearer named Cornelius. I went to his house and preached the good news of Jesus to his whole household. As they were listening, the Holy Spirit fell on them, and they spoke in tongues."

Gasps filled the room, and Joanna stared in stunned silence as exclamations tumbled like leaves in the wind.

"They received the Holy Spirit, just like us?"

"Gentiles?"

"What does this mean?"

Peter gestured to a group of men and spoke over the tumult. "These brothers were with me. They saw it all. The Holy Spirit fell on the Gentiles, and I could see no reason why they should not be baptized."

"Greeks," Maryam said in shock. "You baptized Greeks?"

Peter spread his hands. "I now understand that God does not show partiality. In every nation, the one who fears God and does what is right is acceptable to him."

Silence filled the room at this daring proclamation.

Joanna's lips parted as her mind spun with the implications. Gentiles could join the kingdom of God without first becoming Jews? That would change everything. It seemed so… strange. Foreign. A nervous shiver ran down her spine. The walls of ritual cleanliness had protected her people for so long. Without them, who would they be?

But her nervousness was quickly replaced with wonder. The prophets had spoke of a time when all the nations would come to God, and this was that time! Warmth poured into her chest and came out as an astonished laugh.

She turned to Chuza, but his gaze was full of dismay. Her joy immediately dissipated. "What's wrong?"

"Titus," he whispered. "We've insisted he must become one of us to receive the Holy Spirit." His eyes grew anguished. "What if we had baptized him long ago? Is this what the Lord wanted all along, but we prevented it?"

"How could we have known?" She glanced at Peter. "The twelve didn't know."

Chuza made an amused noise in his throat. "We think of Peter as our leader, but he's not really doing the leading, is he? The Holy Spirit has been pulling us along, and we're all just running to keep up."

She wrapped both her hands around Chuza's. "Now that we understand, we can make this right. The next time we see Titus, we'll tell him everything. We'll tell him we were wrong. Jesus has called him, just as he is." A wide grin stretched her cheeks, but Chuza dragged a hand over his face and down the back of his neck.

"I just hope he'll forgive me."

# FIFTY

Chuza stood in the palace gateway with his hands gripped behind his back and his shoulders tight as bowstrings. God had opened The Way to the Gentiles, but he wished one particular Gentile was not coming to Jerusalem. The Syrian governor had sent his army around Judea to avoid unease, but Chuza could almost feel the pounding of their feet as they marched for Nabatea.

Antipas had intercepted the Syrian governor, and he was bringing him to Jerusalem to make special sacrifices. Vitellius was forbidden from entering the central temple courtyard, so they would stand in the outer courts and watch the smoke rise to the heavens. Then Antipas would throw a three-day feast in Vitellius' honor. He'd already invited all the leading men of the area.

But it wasn't the sacrifices or feasts that niggled at the back of Chuza's mind. It was the changes he saw in his master. A few years ago, Antipas would never have chosen battle over diplomacy.

Cheers rose from the city. Antipas had ordered servants to lead the procession, tossing bread and coins. To Antipas, it didn't matter if the cries of welcome for Vitellius were genuine, as long as they rang loud through the streets.

When the procession came into view, Chuza strode for his office. It would take a miracle to stop Vitellius' army.

Chuza smoothed his robe before he knocked. A servant pulled the door open, but Chuza hesitated as Herodias' angry voice flooded the hall.

She bit off her words as Chuza entered Antipas' chambers. With a glare, she crossed the room to peer out the window, her shoulders taut.

Chuza raised his eyebrows at his master. A marital spat couldn't be the reason he'd been summoned.

Antipas beckoned Chuza closer. "Agrippa was arrested for treason."

Chuza stiffened. "But, I thought—" He cut himself off. Agrippa had finally made it back to Rome. When the family refused to loan Agrippa more money for the journey, Cypros had raised the funds herself. According to his last letter to Herodias, Agrippa had bought his way back into Tiberius' good graces.

But apparently not for long.

Chuza glanced between Antipas and Herodias. "What about his friend, Tiberius' nephew? Couldn't Gaius help him?"

Herodias made a disbelieving noise as she flounced away from the window and flopped onto a soft couch.

Antipas toyed with his large ring, spinning it round and round. "That friendship was his downfall. Agrippa was overheard saying the emperor's death would be a good thing for Gaius."

Chuza pressed his lips together as he smothered a sigh. Cypros must be reeling. "Will you write to Tiberius? Ask for mercy?"

Antipas drummed his fingers on his desk. "I don't want to do anything to upset the emperor, not while I need his help. I can't give him any reason to recall Vitellius."

Herodias stifled an angry sob.

So this was why she was so upset. Not only was her brother in prison, but her husband refused to help.

"Keep an eye on the staff," Antipas said, and he rose to his feet. "No whisper of this scandal can reach Vitellius, understand?"

Chuza inclined his head.

Antipas looked at Herodias and frowned. "It's nearly time for the feast. Can you control your emotions long enough to join us at supper, or shall I make your excuses?"

Herodias' eyes flashed with anger, but she stood gracefully and bowed to her husband before striding from the room.

Antipas pursed his lips. "I understand she's upset, but maybe in prison, Agrippa will finally learn he's no longer a pampered prince." He chuckled mirthlessly and summoned his body slave.

Chuza stood quietly out of the way in the Great Hall. It was the third day since Vitellius' arrival, and Antipas was taking his guests on a tour of the finer rooms in Herod's Palace. The men held cups of wine, and Antipas was doing a good job of mixing history and wit.

Vitellius laughed loudly at something Antipas said. He seemed at ease, but Chuza suspected his focus was not on tapestries and mosaic floors, but on the campaign ahead. Chuza shuddered. How many innocent citizens would suffer because two powerful men cared more about their pride than their people?

One of Vitellius' servants crossed the hall, his pace clipped, and Antipas' voice trailed off as the servant bowed to his master.

The servant held out a scroll. "From Rome, my lord."

Antipas' expression flickered with panic, and his gaze swept the room until he locked eyes with Chuza.

Chuza silently hurried forward. He couldn't rip the scroll out of Vitellius' hands, but he could possibly temper Antipas' reaction if the emperor had decided to withdraw help from Antipas on Agrippa's account.

Vitellius stepped away from Antipas, broke the seal, and began to read. His face paled.

Tension rolled off Antipas in waves as Vitellius stared at the parchment. A flicker of hope danced in Chuza's chest. If Vitellius was recalled, Antipas would have no option but to renegotiate peace with Nabatea.

Finally, Vitellius turned and regarded Antipas soberly before scanning the room. The other guests stood silently, clutching their cups as they waited to hear what had disturbed the Syrian governor.

Vitellius cleared his throat. "The emperor is dead."

Chuza's pulse skipped a beat as he stared at the governor, his mind strangely blank.

Astonished mutters filled the room, but Vitellius cut them off. "Gaius has succeeded his uncle's throne. You will all kneel and proclaim allegiance to Gaius Caesar Augustus Germanicus."

Chuza and Antipas shared a stunned glance. Tiberius was dead? The implications spun in Chuza's mind like a skein of wool in the wind.

But Vitellius was waiting. Chuza went down on one knee, and a moment later, the rest of the room knelt as well, Antipas kneeling last of all.

Vitellius went down the line, hearing each man pledge his allegiance, one by one, until he reached Antipas.

Antipas' voice rasped as he spoke his vow before the Syrian governor. Chuza suspected his master was squirming inwardly as Vitellius flexed his authority, but there was nothing Antipas could do.

When Antipas had finished, Vitellius held out his hand. Antipas hesitated, but then accepted the offer and stood. The rest of the men rose silently as well.

Something flickered in Vitellius' eyes as he smiled at Antipas. "I'm afraid that this change in leadership means I must withdraw my army."

Antipas blinked, his lips parting with dismay.

"I will return to Syria until I receive word from Emperor Gaius. You understand, of course. And I'll be sure to send a *detailed report* about my time here."

As Vitellius emphasized the phrase, Chuza blinked. It had been more than a year since Antipas usurped Vitellius' right to report to the emperor, but clearly the governor had not forgotten.

Antipas' mouth opened and closed, but Vitellius was already turning away. Chuza caught the satisfied grin on the governor's face as he left the tetrarch gaping behind him. If the governor had been waiting for his chance to snub Antipas, he had found the perfect opportunity.

Chuza stepped into the dining hall and winced. Antipas sat alone. Lamplight glistened off the golden dishes as the table sagged under a staggering selection of culinary delicacies imported from all over the world.

Chuza pressed his lips together. He'd been so busy overseeing Vitellius' departure, he had completely forgotten to cancel tonight's feast.

Antipas sat in the seat of honor with his elbows propped on his knees, staring moodily into a cup. He lifted his head and their eyes met. Accusation filled Antipas' eyes, followed swiftly by resignation.

"I suppose you're happy," Antipas muttered. "No war. At least not yet."

"I will always prefer peace, my lord."

Antipas shook his head. "But what am I supposed to do now? Perhaps Nabatea will withdraw, at least until Aretas takes his measure of this new emperor." He scowled and leaned forward to tear a leg off a perfectly roasted pheasant. "Who is this Gaius, anyway? I can't even put a face to him. If he's friends with Agrippa, his judgment is certainly questionable."

Chuza glanced around to make sure none of the servants had

overheard. "My lord, Gaius is the emperor now. You need to be careful how—"

"Yes, yes." Antipas' lip curled. "I was just trying to reason out what sort of man our new emperor is." He leaned back, sighing bitterly. "I suppose Agrippa will be freed."

Chuza blinked. He hadn't thought that far yet. He cleared his throat as he studied Antipas' face. "Cypros will be so relieved."

"Herodias too." Antipas heaved himself to his feet and tossed the half-eaten pheasant leg onto the table. "For once, the fool made friends with the right man."

# FIFTY-ONE

Chuza's sandals whispered on the stairs as he left the palace. Word of Tiberius' death would spread quickly throughout Israel. While the people would rejoice at the news, Chuza just hoped the transition of power would be peaceful. The last thing they needed was some revolutionary hot-head deciding this was their opportunity to liberate Israel from Roman rule.

Vitellius was marching his troops back to Syria. Chuza was grateful for the unexpected miracle, but now his focus turned to a more personal situation. He still needed to make things right with Titus.

Guilt flickered in his chest. He never meant to shut a door that Jesus had opened. He'd been so sure Titus was resisting God's plan, but maybe Titus had sensed something Chuza was too blind to see.

He lifted his hand to rub his forehead, but he was distracted by a smudge of ink on his finger. He turned his hand, examining it. It was the hand of a steward. But, somehow, the Spirit had worked through this ordinary hand to do the extraordinary.

Chuza's hand closed. Titus had no idea he could experience the indwelling of the Spirit for himself, and it could be months before he returned with the caravan. Chuza's fist squeezed with frustration.

Leah glanced up from her pot as Chuza entered the courtyard. Nadia raced to her father as usual, Ira toddling just behind.

"Papa's home!" Nadia shouted, and Leah tensed. This wasn't their home. If it was up to her, she would throw their things back in the cart and return to Sepphoris immediately—and take the rest of the family with her.

Chuza picked up Nadia and gave her a loud kiss before doing the same to Ira. The children giggled, oblivious to the risk they lived under, just by being in the city.

Chuza wandered over to her. "Where's Joanna?"

"At the market with Dalia," Leah said.

Chuza nodded, and Leah finally noticed his eyes were lined with stress. "What's wrong?"

"We have a new emperor," Chuza said.

Leah blinked in surprise. The emperor had nothing to do with them, but Chuza seemed concerned.

He squeezed her shoulder. "Vitellius is on his way back to Syria."

"Before the feast?" Poor Michael. All that work for nothing.

"Most of the leading men swore allegiance to our new emperor," Chuza said. "I'm hoping that heads off any revolutionary ideas."

Jerusalem was filled with those discontented with Rome. She darted a glance at the table before whispering, "Can't you convince Alexander that moving back here is a mistake?" It had seemed risky before, now it seemed insane.

"Try not to worry. They gave this decision a lot of thought and prayer." He patted her shoulder. "I know it's hard to say goodbye, but God will watch over them."

Leah forced a smile, but as Chuza walked away, the smile slid from her face faster than oil on a hot pan. Families were supposed to stick together. But Alexander wanted to reclaim his ancestral home and Joanna felt called to shepherd the believers in Sepphoris.

Leah turned back to the oven and checked the lentils, clattering the pot lid in her frustration. Why did everyone else seem so certain about where they belonged, when she couldn't even decide something as simple as her career?

Leah tasted the lentils and added a pinch of salt. She still needed to decide if she would take Jovian up on his offer. The challenge of starting a restaurant and running her own kitchen was tantalizing. But could she really work beside him every day without breaking her own heart?

She turned as Joanna traipsed into the courtyard with a cheerful greeting, her eyes sparkling with joy. She strode toward the kitchen with her overflowing basket, huffing an exaggerated sigh of relief as she set it on the work table. She pulled out a handful of spring herbs and offered them to Leah with a flourish.

"As you ordered, my lady."

Leah fetched a shallow bowl to prepare a salad. "You're in a good mood."

Joanna raised her eyebrows. "And why aren't you? I thought you'd be rejoicing after Peter's proclamation."

Leah blinked in confusion. "I'm happy for Jovian. This will change everything for him."

"Just him?"

What was Joanna implying? Heat flooded her face. "I don't think it will change anything for… us, if that's what you're getting at."

Joanna's brows tipped in disbelief as she pressed her lips together.

Leah's temper flickered. "You act like everything is going to change. But if we start preaching that the Gentiles are clean in God's eyes, the persecution will start again, worse than before." Her back trembled with painful memories.

Joanna's smile softened. "I have faith that our people will come to accept it, in time. Don't let fear of the future steal your joy from this moment. Titus will be our brother." She wrapped an arm around Leah's shoulder, squeezing as she whispered, "And perhaps, someday, he'll be something more."

Heat poured into Leah's cheeks, and she smacked her adopted mother's arm. "I thought you didn't approve of him."

"I didn't." Joanna grew serious. "But these past years have shown the depth of his character and faith. I have admired him as a God-fearer for some time, even if I didn't think he would make a good husband for a Jewish woman."

Leah pressed her lips together. "It would cause a scandal. A Jew and a Gentile."

"It might. But we're already considered scandalous, preaching our crucified Messiah." Her grin returned. "And I haven't seen you sneaking glances with any of the Jewish believers." She waggled her brows and strode away.

Leah twisted her lips as Joanna joined the others at the table. She was in high spirits, and Leah didn't want to quash her joy. But Joanna wasn't being practical.

If Leah actually allowed herself to imagine a future with Jovian, how would that work? If they were blessed with a son, would Jovian refuse to have him circumcised? Would the child be ostracized in the Jewish community as Jovian had been?

Leah tucked a strand of hair behind her ear, her frustration rising. Joanna had warned her to distance herself from Jovian all those years ago, but how could a fourteen-year-old girl ignore a man that was not only kind and brave, but funny, contemplative, and loyal? Now that she was twenty-one, she still hadn't met a man who rivaled Jovian in her heart and mind.

She shook her head, trying to shake off these pointless worries. Jovian planned to go back to Antioch someday. And it didn't sound as if his family would welcome a Jewish bride into their home.

She drew a deep breath through her nose. She needed to stop thinking about herself. When Jovian found out about the Gentile inclusion, he would be overjoyed, and she would rejoice with him, as his friend. He could finally worship with them without any sense of division.

That joy would have to be enough.

Immediately after Passover week, Antipas took his household to Sepphoris for the summer months. He and Herodias lamented Galilee's distance from Rome as they waited hungrily for news about Gaius and his plans for the empire. The reports that trickled in from Rome were favorable. It seemed the people welcomed their new Caesar with open arms.

Herodias also awaited news about her favorite brother, confident that Gaius would not overlook the man who had paid a steep price for his loyalty.

Chuza and Joanna returned to their quiet house in Sepphoris. Chuza tried to ascertain where Jovian's caravan was now, with the hopes of riding out after him to give him the good news. But, for once, his sources failed him, and there was nothing to do but wait.

# FIFTY-TWO

Antipas jumped in his chair as Herodias burst into the room, a sheet of papyrus clutched in her hand. Chuza cut off his report, his stylus poised above his tablet. Herodias strode forward and flung the papyrus on the polished desk.

Antipas stared at the crumpled letter with a sense of foreboding.

"It's Agrippa," she snapped.

Antipas looked up at his wife, gauging her pale face and burning eyes. Resentment rolled off her in waves, and a perverse hope flickered in his heart.

"Dead?"

"Worse! He's a king!"

Antipas glanced at Chuza, and the steward blinked uncertainly. They had expected Agrippa to be freed—but crowned?

He eyed his wife. "What are you talking about?"

"Gaius gave him your brother Philip's land. But he's not a tetrarch, oh no, not Agrippa." Sarcasm dripped off her full lips. "After living off our charity for years, my spendthrift brother is now a king!"

Antipas' stomach soured. Agrippa's gamble had paid off.

He sniffed and tried to appear careless. "If the emperor wishes to honor a fool, so be it."

"But it doesn't make any sense! Agrippa spent the last few years fleeing from city to city, and now he's a king? But you, who loyally ruled Galilee and Perea throughout Tiberius' reign are only a tetrarch?"

"Why, thank you dear wife, for that succinct summary," he muttered.

Chuza's brow furrowed the way it did when he was trying to work out a complex problem. Herodias paced the room, her robes swishing and her earrings catching the light.

But a deep exhaustion crept up Antipas' legs and pulled him deeper into his chair. They were looking for solutions, but what was the point? A man could strive his whole life, and still end up with nothing.

Herodias whirled back to face him. "How many times did he come to me, begging for money?" She jabbed a finger at her chest. "I helped him escape Rome. I got him that position in Tiberias, which he ungratefully abandoned. And now, the next time we meet, I must bow to *him*?" Her eyes shone with angry disbelief. "How could you let this happen?"

She was blaming him for this mess? Resentment curdled his stomach. "Perhaps if I could flit about the world like your brother, spending my time in social games instead of ruling, I could have befriended the emperor's heir. As it is, I'd be hard-pressed to pick Gaius out of a crowd."

Herodias' voice turned shrill. "You haven't even met Gaius?"

Antipas rolled his eyes. "Gaius is, what, twenty-five?" He looked at Chuza for confirmation, who nodded. "I'm sure I met him, but he would have been a young man, still studying under his tutor, and I paid him little heed."

Herodias digested this, and then lifted her chin. "Well, I think we ought to meet him."

"The emperor?" Antipas lifted his brows.

"No, the emperor's tutor," Herodias snapped. "Yes, the emperor! You can pay him your respects and ask to be honored for your years of service."

He had never thought her a fool before. "*Ask* for honors?" he said incredulously.

Chuza shifted his feet as if unsure whether to leave the room or pretend he was part of the furniture.

Herodias flapped her hand. "You know what I mean. The request doesn't have to be… blatant… but Gaius needs to be reminded of all you've done for Rome."

Antipas stood and pulled every ounce of authority he claimed into his voice. "No."

Herodias blinked in shock.

Chuza surreptitiously took a step back and intently studied his wax tablet of notes.

Herodias came around the desk, and her sweet perfume filled his nose. She spoke softly, but it was edged with accusation. "After years of shame and debt, Agrippa is a king. And you don't care?"

Antipas gritted his teeth. "I am almost sixty. I have power, money, and friends. What is a title to me?" His eyes bored into hers. "I have no child to bequeath it to, no heirs to grow my fortune for. This life is all I have." His voice rose with his temper. "Why won't you let me enjoy it?"

Herodias let out a strangled cry, halfway between a groan and a screech. She whirled around and stormed away.

Silence filled the room, and Antipas sighed. Herodias would never let this go. Shaking his head, he picked up the letter on his desk.

Chuza cleared his throat. "Should I draft a letter to Agrippa?"

Antipas didn't look up, but his jaw clenched. "Whatever for?"

"To pave the way for friendship. He will rule the neighboring territory, so it would be wise to make peace."

Antipas would rather tie himself to a cart and pull children through the street like a donkey. He sniffed loudly and pretended to read the letter. "If Agrippa wants friendship, he can write to me."

"Do you really think he'll write first? You said some cutting things back in Tyre."

"I said nothing that wasn't true."

"Sometimes," Chuza said slowly, "when I quarrel with my wife, the best thing is to apologize first, even if she is also wrong."

Antipas sat back in his chair and scowled at his steward. "Am I married to Agrippa?"

"No."

"Then keep your relationship advice to yourself." He tossed Agrippa's letter aside, and it fluttered to the floor. He shook his head and muttered, "Whose side are you on, anyway?"

Jovian's fingers drummed on his sword hilt as the caravan plodded through the busy streets of Sepphoris. They were back, and ahead of schedule. It wasn't the first time the caravan leader changed course based on how a handful of bones landed on a mat. But for once, they had fallen in Jovian's favor.

Amichai came up beside him. "So? Am I about to lose my travel companion?"

Jovian was ready to feel settled again, to wake up each morning in his own bed. He had enough money to open his restaurant, but his plan hinged on a woman he could not have. Not in the way he wanted.

"I'm not sure," he admitted. "It depends on a few things."

"Or on one in particular." Amichai winked. Jovian rolled his eyes and looked away.

Once the caravan was settled in the market, Jovian and Amichai received permission to take a few days off. It was nearly supper, and Jovian's belly growled as they strode for Joanna and Chuza's house.

They stopped at the front door and knocked. A minute later, the door opened.

"Jovian!" Chuza stared at him in shock, and something passed over his face. Something akin to guilt.

Jovian tensed. "You've never called me that before." It had always been Titus. Something was going on. "Is everything alright?"

Chuza gave his head a shake. "Yes, of course. Come in, both of you."

Jovian and Amichai stepped into the portico, and as Jovian caught the scent of cumin and fresh bread, his stomach rumbled audibly in the small space. Amichai laughed and smacked him on the back.

As they entered the inner courtyard, Jovian furrowed his brow. The house felt strangely quiet. Joanna and Nadia were setting the table while Ira sat nearby, playing with a toy horse.

Joanna set one hand on her hip. "How do you always arrive at mealtime?"

"Everyone has some sort of talent," Jovian said sheepishly, and Joanna laughed.

"Where is everyone?" Amichai asked, looking around.

"They've moved back to Jerusalem," Chuza said.

"Really?" Jovian said in surprise.

Joanna looked at her brother with sympathy. "Mama went with them."

Amichai's face fell with disappointment, and Jovian patted him on the back.

Amichai looked at his older sister. "Why didn't you move with them?"

"We must tend our community here," Joanna said, spreading her hands. "And the new emperor makes things complicated for Antipas. Chuza wanted to be on hand to help."

Jovian gripped the hilt of his sword. Chuza was always sacrificing for his master, but rarely did Antipas seem to appreciate his steward.

As the men sat on cushions, Joanna brought a pot of red stew to the table, along with a stack of flatbread, a dish of dried fruit, and greens tossed in oil and vinegar.

They chatted about simple things, but as Chuza began pouring the wine, he glanced at Jovian. "I'm not sure if you heard, but there were rumors that Peter was going into unclean houses and eating with uncircumcised men."

Jovian stared at his food. *Unclean. Uncircumcised.* He took a sip of his wine to cover his discomfort.

Joanna leaned forward. "But Peter had a vision that led him to the house of a man named Cornelius. A good man, but a Greek."

*But a Greek.* Jovian tried to not let the words sting. After all, Joanna and Chuza had welcomed him into their circle, and defended his right to be here.

Chuza spoke carefully. "Peter was told in his vision that he should not call unclean what God had made clean. When he was preaching to Cornelius' household, the Holy Spirit came upon them mightily."

The hair at the back of Jovian's neck tingled. Long ago, he had accepted that the Holy Spirit was not for the Gentiles. He leaned forward. "What does that mean?"

"It means that through Christ, we are equal in God's eyes."

Amichai leaned an elbow on the table and stared at Jovian, covering his mouth with one hand.

Jovian licked his lips. "I still don't understand." A Jew and a Gentile were like two separate islands, even if they were joined by the sea.

Joanna spoke earnestly, her eyes alight with wonder. "You don't need to become a proselyte. You can be a Greek and still be one of God's people. Peter said that every nation that believes in God and that does what is right is acceptable to him."

Jovian fidgeted in his seat. "But... does what is right... isn't that the same as following the Law?"

"It seems some laws are changing," Chuza said.

Jovian's neck reared. "Changing? How can laws that stood for thousands of years change?"

Joanna spoke carefully. "Jesus said he came to draw all nations to God. We thought that meant that the nations needed to become like us—to become Jews—but Jesus opened the way for the nations to come to God as they are."

Jovian closed his eyes for a long moment, trying to understand. "So there is no difference between a Jew and a Greek in terms of ritual cleanliness?"

Joanna said, "Jesus told us this would happen, but we didn't understand. First, the Holy Spirit was in Jerusalem. Then, when Peter and John laid their hands on the Samaritans, they were filled with the Holy Spirit too. And now, the Holy Spirit has shown itself within the Gentiles. Jesus told us to take the good news to the nations, and this is it!"

Amichai shook his head in shock.

"Don't you see, Jovian?" Chuza's voice was thick with emotion. "God accepts you, just as you are."

This made no sense. He had spent years wishing he could be accepted and not merely tolerated. There had to be a catch. He was on his feet before he even realized he was moving.

The others stared up at him in concern, and pain filled Chuza's eyes. "I'm so sorry, Jovian," he said. "I wish I had understood sooner."

"I'm tired," Jovian said flatly. "I'll see you tomorrow."

He turned and strode out of the house, ignoring their calls.

He was halfway down the street before he heard footsteps running behind him. Instinctively, he braced himself, but it was only Amichai. Jovian sighed, and strode down the street.

"What's wrong?" Amichai fell in beside him. "I thought you'd be happy."

Jovian scoffed. "Do you believe Gentiles and Jews can be one big, happy family?"

Amichai chuckled. "My experience says families are not always happy. Especially when bringing in outsiders. But look at Chuza. My family hated the steward, and now he's one of us."

"It can't be that simple."

"Kind of like how you insisted a man like me can be forgiven, just because I repented?" Amichai jabbed a finger into Jovian's shoulder.

"Doesn't that sound too easy?"

"But you were already one of God's chosen people. Just a little… turned around."

Amichai laughed. "That's one way to put it."

They walked in silence for a few steps, and Amichai spoke slowly, as if thinking aloud. "You know, Abraham was called by God before he was circumcised."

"So?" Jovian said. "God told him to be circumcised, and then later God gave all kinds of laws for the Jews, what to eat, what to wear, how to live—"

"That came after generations of my ancestors being steeped in Egyptian ways. We needed that separation so we could learn God's ways."

"And now you don't need that separation?"

"I guess not." Amichai shrugged. "I mean, before I knew you, I thought all Greeks were terrible people. But you're not. You're loyal, honest, generous, and you believe in God."

Jovian's neck heated, and he shoved Amichai with his shoulder. "You're going to give me a big head."

Amichai chuckled. "I'll shrink it for you later. But my point is, how does my circumcision make me a better man than you? I think God is reaffirming what he's been trying to tell us through the prophets."

"And that is?"

"It's not an outward mark on the body that saves a man, but his faith."

Tears burned in Jovian's eyes. He blinked fast, trying to stop them before they fell. Was it possible? Was God throwing open the gates and calling him home as a son?

Jovian stumbled to a stop as his mind reeled. Jesus didn't just come to save the Jews. He came to save all the nations—including a Greek from Antioch who was struggling to find his place in the world. Jovian's knees trembled, and Amichai's arms came around him.

Jovian leaned into Amichai, gripping him fiercely. They had come full circle. He had preached Jesus to Amichai, but he had needed Amichai to preach Jesus right back.

Jovian drew a shaky breath. "Come on." He wiped his face on his sleeve. "I need to talk to Chuza."

"Oh, thank goodness." Amichai sighed as they turned back. Jovian looked at him. "I did not want to sleep in the market again."

As they approached the house, a cart rumbled up to the door and Leah hopped down. Jovian's heart back-flipped as their eyes met.

Everything might be changing, but what did this mean for the two of them?

# FIFTY-THREE

Leah's knees quivered. Jovian was back early, and he seemed agitated.

"Chuza told me about Peter," Jovian blurted.

Leah's heart fluttered. "It's incredible, isn't it?"

Jovian peered into her eyes as if searching for more, and her cheeks warmed.

She fumbled for the door handle. "Coming inside?"

Their footsteps followed her as she hurried into the courtyard. The children were happily eating, but Joanna and Chuza sat at the table, holding hands and praying. They stood as they saw Jovian, clearly relieved.

Jovian walked around the table and pulled Chuza into a hug. Chuza gripped him, and a long moment of silence passed as Leah blinked back tears. This was what Jovian had longed for, but believed he could never have.

His gaze turned to her. Everything had changed— everything except her feelings for him. But she was afraid to know if he felt the same.

Jovian looked at Chuza. "Can I be baptized?"

Chuza blinked. "Of course! We used the public mikveh before."

Jovian hesitated. "Will I be allowed? I mean, considering…"

Chuza and Joanna shared a glance, and Leah bit her lip as Jovian's shoulders tensed. He was well aware that acceptance by God did not mean acceptance by Jews.

"I'll talk with the rabbi," Chuza said.

Jovian stepped down into the cool water, soaking the hem of his plain tunic. Another step, and he was up to his waist. Chuza was already waiting for him, a wide grin on his face.

"It's a little cramped," Chuza admitted. The pool of fresh water was only meant for one.

Jovian glanced to the side. A dozen men and women had squeezed into the dim little room that smelled of damp stone. He met Nathan's eye. The elderly man had questioned a Gentile's right to partake of the Lord's Table, but now he inclined his head in approval.

Jovian's gaze was pulled to Leah's shining eyes. For years, they had been companions in faith, not always side-by-side, but on parallel paths. She, more than anyone, knew what this moment meant to him. Gratitude warmed his chest, but goosebumps were spreading fast over his arms and legs.

"Jovian Titus," Chuza said solemnly. "I've watched you grow from earnestly seeking God to accepting Jesus as your Lord and Savior. I am proud to baptize you in Jesus' name."

He gripped Jovian's shoulders, and Jovian's pulse raced.

"I baptize you in the name of the Father, the Son, and the Holy Spirit."

He pressed Jovian back, and Jovian allowed himself to sink into the water. It closed over him, muffling all sound. Time seemed to slow as he died with Christ. But then Chuza hauled him back to his feet, and both men stumbled to regain their footing.

Jovian gasped a breath and blinked the water out of his eyes. It felt as if the sun glowed in his chest. Chuza pulled him into a tight hug, slapping his back.

After Jovian had time to dry off and change, the group returned to Chuza's house for a celebration. Leah complained they hadn't given her enough notice to prepare a proper feast, but Jovian's mouth watered with anticipation as he saw the dishes spread on the table. It looked like a king's banquet to him.

The afternoon passed with laughter and good food. Jovian prayed among The Way—not as an outsider, but as an adopted brother.

As the guests left for their own homes, Amichai approached. "The caravan leaves in a week. Have you made up your mind?"

Jovian looked at Leah. She laughed at something Nadia said and leaned forward until her long brown hair swept over her shoulder. His heart galloped like a runaway horse. After years of denying his feelings, he was afraid to give them free rein.

Amichai patted his shoulder. "Well, I can see you're not sure. Whatever you decide, I'm here for you."

Jovian nodded absentmindedly. Drawing his courage, he crossed the courtyard to join Leah. She looked up at him, and her eyes widened.

"Will you walk with me?" he asked.

Leah answered breathlessly. "Just let me tell Joanna."

Jovian's palms dampened as he waited, and his ears nearly burst into flame as Joanna looked his way. Leah hurried back, her cheeks a pretty pink.

They left the house and meandered down the street. Curious eyes followed their progress, and Jovian yearned to pull Leah into some quiet place where they could be alone. He grappled for the right words, but his mind was muddled.

He drew a breath for bravery. "Have you given any thought to working with me in the restaurant?"

She hesitated. "Your idea sounds amazing, except..."

"Except what?" Whatever it was, he would fix it.

"I don't think it would be right. Me, working for you."

He stared at her as dismay poured into him. He had never imagined she would be like the rest of them, unable to look past his heritage.

Her eyes widened. "No, not like that!" She gripped his arm. "It's something... else."

Relief swamped him, chased by confusion. "Then what?"

A deep blush spread over her cheeks, and understanding dawned. Relief flooded his veins, making him ridiculously giddy.

But he schooled his features. "You know, it might be less awkward if you weren't my employee. We could be business partners."

Her chin tightened. "Partners."

He worked to keep his face neutral as he shrugged. "I mean, you'd need to buy in."

Anger flitted across her features, and he couldn't keep the ruse going. He took her hand, and her breath caught.

"Or," he said, "you could marry me."

She stared at him, her mouth open, and for a terrible moment, he feared he had misunderstood her feelings.

"I love you," she blurted. "I've loved you for so long." Tears welled up in the hazel depths of her eyes, and his heart leaped into his throat.

"I love you too," he said, and he dared to brush his thumb over her soft cheek. "Could you spend your life with me?"

She leaned against his hand, and her lips parted. But then she stepped away. "Things would be difficult for us." She gazed down the street, where curious eyes peered their way. "To most of the world, we are still a Greek and a Jew, two people who don't belong together."

"But now, the world is wrong." He took both her hands. "If God approves, what does anyone else matter?"

Leah's fingers tightened on his. "Do you mean it?"

"I mean it with everything I am. We can find a way forward together, you and me."

Leah trembled, her lips parting. "Then yes," she said, and a burst of laughter loosened a tear. "I will marry you."

Jovian couldn't help himself. He whooped in delight and picked her up, holding her against his chest as he spun around. She threw her arms around his neck, and laughter floated around him like music.

Chuza reached for Joanna's hand, needing her support. Jovian had only been baptized yesterday. The young man certainly hadn't wasted any time.

Jovian and Leah sat opposite at the courtyard table, their faces nervous as they waited for his answer.

As much as Chuza had expected this moment, he felt unprepared. He looked at Joanna, and she nodded with a warm smile.

"Yes, of course we give our blessing," Chuza said. "To be honest, we're not surprised." He winked at Leah.

Jovian's expression eased, and Leah blushed.

"But," Chuza held up his hand and fixed Jovian with a stern look, "we need to sort out a few things. How do you plan to support my daughter?" There was no way Jovian could continue as a caravan guard once he was married.

"I've been saving up to start my own business. I plan to open a restaurant." He glanced at Leah as Chuza's brows rose. "I know it seems odd, a Greek opening a restaurant in a Jewish city. But, I think, if Leah and I work together, we can help bridge the gap between the Jews and the Gentiles here. Perhaps we could even pave the way for the good news."

Joanna's eyes widened. "A bold idea. I like it!"

Leah looked proudly at Jovian and squeezed his arm.

Chuza hesitated. It was bold. But it was also true that Jovian's leadership skills would serve him well as he managed a business. And patrons would come from far and wide to taste Leah's excellent cooking. But it was still a risk.

"I've always wanted my own kitchen." Leah grinned at Jovian.

"Luckily for me, I have some savings to buy into the partnership."

Jovian flushed and shot Chuza a nervous glance. "I was only teasing."

Joanna tilted her head to the side. "A family business would be better than working for Antipas. And you could continue working, even after having children."

Leah blushed and Jovian sat taller.

Chuza folded his hands. "Well," he said slowly, "I think it could be a good plan. But I hope you'll start off small. Test out the idea, so to speak."

Jovian nodded, clearly relieved.

Chuza drew a breath. "Well, if that's settled, all we need to do now is set the date. How about next summer?" He hid his grin as Leah bit her lip.

Jovian leaned closer. "Seeing as we've waited for years, do you think we can set the wedding date a little closer?"

Joanna chuckled and bumped Chuza's shoulder with her own. "What about this autumn? We need enough time to invite the family."

Chuza opened his mouth to reply, but he stiffened as the front door crashed open.

Amichai rushed into the courtyard, and Chuza and Jovian jerked to their feet. A thousand fears spun through Chuza's mind in a heartbeat.

"There's been an earthquake." Amichai gasped out. His gaze was pained as he looked at Jovian. "It hit Antioch hard."

Stunned silence gripped the courtyard. Chuza blinked. He had never experienced an earthquake, but he had heard of the destruction they could cause.

Jovian turned ashen. "Are you sure?"

"I heard it from another caravan. Everyone's talking about it in the market." He walked toward Jovian but stopped a few feet away, as if unsure whether or not to console him.

Leah stared up at Jovian, stricken.

Chuza came around the table. "It's a large city. I'm sure your family is safe."

Jovian didn't answer. His eyes were distant as he dragged both hands through his hair. "I have to go home," he muttered. His gaze locked with Chuza's. "I need to know if they're alright."

Chuza wouldn't have expected anything else.

"I'll go with you," Amichai said at once, and Jovian grasped his shoulder in silent thanks.

Leah pressed her hands over her lips, her eyes welling with tears. She rose to her feet.

"I'm coming too."

Chuza stiffened, but Leah's chin came up.

Jovian set his hands on Leah's shoulders. "You can't. I need to leave as soon as I can. Tomorrow. There wouldn't be time for a proper wedding."

"I don't need a proper wedding." Leah said, and then blushed furiously. "I mean, we can say our vows tonight."

Jovian shook his head. "I wish that was possible. But—" He looked at Chuza, and his eyes spoke with greater eloquence than a poet.

"Tonight?" Joanna gasped. Panic wrote itself across her face.

Chuza opened his mouth to protest. There was no way. It was impossible.

But then he saw the way Leah stood, ready to support Jovian as he faced the unknown. Leah was twenty-one. She was strong, capable, and full of faith. If this was where the Spirit was leading her, Chuza couldn't get in her way.

"Alright," Chuza said, but he had to swallow twice.

Leah met his gaze and pressed her lips together. He held out his arms. Leah launched herself at him and wrapped her arms around his waist.

"Thank you, Papa," she whispered.

Chuza squeezed his eyes shut as he kissed the top of her head, a tear slipping into his beard. "May God make you like Sarah, Rebekah, Rachel, and Leah."

Her smile lifted her shoulders, and she stepped back. "If I can be like Maryam, Susanna, Naomi, and Joanna, I will be blessed."

Joanna shook her head. "It's too soon." A tear tracked down her face.

Leah reached for her, and the three of them formed a circle.

Chuza pushed down his fear and smiled at his daughter. "Let's plan a wedding."

# FIFTY-FOUR

Joanna's hands trembled as she spread Leah's best robe on the bed. There was no time to weave Leah something new. Opening a small leather pouch, Joanna laid out the jewelry she had worn at her own wedding—thin gold bracelets and a necklace of gold coins. She shook her head and blinked rapidly. She refused to cry again.

Instead of preparing a wedding feast, Jovian was packing a cart to haul supplies to Antioch. And instead of a bridal week, Leah and Jovian would walk for days, not knowing what they would find when they reached their destination.

"I'm sorry, Mama," Leah's voice came softly.

Joanna hastily wiped her cheeks. "You have nothing to be sorry about."

Leah stepped closer. "You cried on your wedding day too. I wish I could make you smile and laugh."

Joanna drew Leah into her arms and rested her chin on the smaller woman's hair. "I'm sure every mother cries when her daughter is married. But I am happy for you."

"Really?" Leah pulled back to peer at Joanna's face. "You're not disappointed I'm marrying a Greek?"

Joanna rubbed her palms down Leah's arms. "I've considered him part of the family for some time now. And there is no separation between Jew and Gentile in God's eyes. We are all his children."

Leah smiled with relief and turned to smooth a wrinkle out of her best robe. "It's hard to believe it's actually my wedding day."

Joanna squeezed her shoulder and went to fill a basin with water. Leah and Jovian had a hard road ahead of them—both literally and figuratively. She prayed God would keep them both safe on their journey to Antioch, and every day after that.

While Nadia watched with wide eyes, Joanna helped Leah to wash and dress, scenting her with fragrant oils and braiding Leah's waist-length hair. Joanna lavished all the love on Leah that she wished she had received on her own wedding day. Somehow, it worked healing oil into a wound Joanna hadn't realized she still carried.

Joanna stepped back to admire her eldest daughter. Leah was radiant. "You're ready."

Fear flitted across Leah's features. "Are you sure?"

Joanna gave her one last hug. "Yes."

Chuza stuck his head into the room. His gaze softened as he saw Leah. "They're ready downstairs."

Joanna and Chuza shared a glance. Were they ready for this moment?

Jovian fought the urge to smooth his freshly washed hair as anxiety coursed through his veins. He wanted this more than anything, but it was happening so fast.

He gazed around at the courtyard, finally noticing the colorful ribbons tied around boughs of greenery. Chuza had gathered up their neighbors and friends, and they were all smiling and cheerful despite the unusual situation. Children ran laps around a table spread with food and wine, giggling and teasing each other.

Chuza and Amichai had accomplished so much in only a few hours, but would it be enough for Leah? Surely no woman pictured her wedding day looking like this.

Maybe he should have delayed the wedding until his return. He had no idea what he'd find in Antioch. If his family was trapped in the rubble of their home—

"Are you alright?" Amichai murmured near his ear. Jovian flinched. How was he supposed to answer that?

"I'm about to be married," Jovian muttered, "but all I can think about is my family. What if they're hurt? What if they're waiting for me to rescue them?"

To his surprise, Amichai frowned.

"Don't let fear steal this moment from you." Amichai gripped his arm. "The woman you have loved for years is about to be yours."

Jovian's throat burned. "I know, it's just—"

"Give your family to God. Worrying won't ease your burden or do your family any good. We'll be there as soon as we can."

"But—"

Amichai squeezed his arm tighter. "Be here, in this moment, right now. Or you'll regret it forever."

Everyone turned as Chuza stepped into the courtyard with Leah on his arm.

Her skin glowed in the afternoon light, and her eyes shone as she scanned the dozens of faces. Jovian forgot to breathe as he fell into her hazel gaze. He could face anything with her by his side.

As Chuza led Leah forward, a hushed whisper of admiration circled the waiting guests.

Jovian's heart pounded with awe as the most beautiful and wonderful woman in the world walked toward him. Her hand was placed in his. The guests drew closer, encircling them.

Joanna stood beside her daughter. "Leah, do you wish to take this man as your husband?"

Leah nodded. "Yes, with all my heart."

"Jovian," Amichai said, "do you wish to take Leah as your wife?"

"Yes." Jovian stared into Leah's eyes, those green and gold pools that gazed back at him like untapped wells of love. He leaned toward her. "Leah, I never imagined this moment would come, but I pledge myself to you, to provide for you, shelter you, and love you, for always."

Her fingers tightened on his.

They signed the contract Chuza prepared. Leah proudly marked her own name.

Chuza began the blessings, and the guests joined in. Their voices faded into the back of Jovian's mind as he stared at Leah, but the words wrapped them in God's promises.

Jovian flinched as Amichai let out a celebratory whoop, and the guests clapped and cheered. The women surrounded Leah, laughing and hugging her, as the men slapped Jovian on the back.

The rest of the evening was a blur. Jovian only had eyes for Leah, and as they sat side by side eating a simple feast, he was overcome by the glances she gave him, full of love and admiration.

"I wish I could have given you a grand wedding," Jovian whispered in her ear. "You deserve so much more than this. Dalia and Alexander aren't even here, neither is Miriam."

Leah set her fingers on his lips and his pulse leaped like a bucking stallion. "There's no way I could let you go back to Antioch on your own."

He grinned. "Worried I wouldn't return?"

Her brow arched. "I would have gone to fetch you back."

He chuckled, and then immediately felt guilty for enjoying himself when his family could be suffering. Leah's eyes softened with understanding. "We'll leave at dawn and walk as fast as we can." Her lips quirked. "And then you will introduce me to your mother."

Nervousness fluttered in the depths of her eyes, but he ached with longing. Thea had to be safe. She had to meet her new daughter-in-law.

Knowing the new couple had to be on the road as the sun rose, the guests left early.

Amichai stepped up to Jovian, grinning. "I've prepared a room for you."

Jovian blinked. When did Amichai have the time? Leah blushed and the reality of the moment hit him. His stomach flipped.

Amichai beckoned, and Jovian held out his hand for Leah. They followed him into a lamp-lit room. A large bed was piled with bolsters. Colorful cloth draped from the ceiling, turning the simple room into a romantic bower. Flowers filled a vase, their sweet scent mixing with burning incense, and refreshments were arranged on a low table.

"You did this?" Jovian raised an eyebrow at Amichai.

"You're welcome," Amichai retorted. Grinning, he left, shutting the door behind them.

Jovian and Leah were alone. The enormity of the moment pressed on him, and his mouth was suddenly dry.

Leah exhaled and stepped into his embrace. Her scent filled his lungs, and his eyes closed involuntarily.

"I remember the first time I went into your arms," she said. "I remember I felt completely safe."

His arms tightened around her. "I remember that you fit perfectly, as you do now."

He lowered his head until his lips met hers, and then he forgot everything else.

Chuza swallowed repeatedly as he squinted into the rising sun, watching the trio grow smaller on the road leading away from Sepphoris. Joanna leaned on him, Ira on her hip. Nadia slipped her fingers into his, and Chuza squeezed his daughter's hand.

"They're coming back, right?" Nadia asked.

That was the plan. But once Jovian returned to Antioch with the woman he loved, he might not want to leave again.

"Of course," he said. He just hoped he was right.

## FIFTY-FIVE

"I think we should go back to Jerusalem," Joanna said.

Chuza realized he had been staring mindlessly into his supper. "What? Why?"

Joanna leaned both elbows on the table. "I miss my family more than I expected," she admitted. "We could go for Pentecost. Stay for a little while."

Chuza scanned his wife's face. She had been quiet ever since Leah left, and this big empty house didn't help.

"I'll talk to Antipas, but I'm sure it'll be fine."

"They're going to be so surprised!" Nadia giggled as they neared Alexander's house. The sun beat upon Jerusalem, baking the paved streets and radiating heat over the weary inhabitants. Chuza swiped his brow as sweat trickled down his spine. But the little girl seemed oblivious to the oppressive heat.

He ruffled her hair. "Do you want to tell them about Leah and

Jovian?"

"Yeah!" she said, and added a skip to her step.

Grinning, Chuza glanced back at Joanna. She walked by Balaam's side, carrying Ira on her back.

They stopped at the red door, and Joanna tucked a hair behind her ear. "It feels weird to be here without Leah. Do you think they're alright?"

Chuza squeezed her arm. "Jovian has a good head on his shoulders. He'll take care of her."

"And they've got Amichai." She chuckled. "Who'd have thought I'd trust my brother with my daughter's safety?"

"What are we waiting for?" Nadia interrupted, putting her hands on her hips.

"Nadia," Joanna chided.

But Chuza grinned and knocked on the door.

The door swung open and Alexander blinked at them in shock.

"Surprise!" Nadia cried out, throwing her arms in the air.

Alexander shot the girl a hasty smile, but then he gripped Chuza's arm. "Get inside, quickly."

Chuza stiffened. "Why?"

"Saul's back."

The hair on Chuza's arms stood on end as his pulse skipped a beat.

As Joanna rushed the children inside, Chuza trotted Balaam around the house to the stable entrance.

He couldn't draw a full breath until the stable door was shut behind him. He stroked Balaam's neck, trying to slow his racing pulse. It had been years since Saul terrorized The Way. Where had he been? And, more importantly, why was he back?

Chuza joined the others in the courtyard. Miriam knelt with her grandchildren in her lap as Joanna stood with her arms wrapped around her middle, speaking with Dalia and Alexander.

Alexander looked sheepishly at Chuza. "Sorry to alarm you, but you caught me off guard. We were discussing what we should do when you showed up."

Chuza cast Joanna a worried glance. "What's Saul done so far?"

"Not much," Alexander admitted. "He's been trying to infiltrate The Way, insisting he's one of us now."

Doubt twisted up Chuza's throat and came out as anger. "One of us? After what he did?"

Joanna's lips pressed together. "What are the twelve doing about it?"

Alexander spread his hands. "I'm not sure. But we could visit Manaen and ask if he has news."

Joanna brushed her palms briskly down her robe. "Alright. Let's go."

Chuza blinked. "Now?"

Joanna nodded with determination. Chuza glanced at Alexander. They all needed to know if their family was safe.

They left the children with Miriam and Dalia and wove down busy streets to a simple home in the Lower City. Alexander rapped on the door. A young serving girl opened it a few inches.

"Is Manaen at home?" Alexander asked.

The girl hesitated. "Who's asking?"

"It's all right, Hannah," Manaen's voice said. The girl stepped back, and Manaen pulled the door open. He saw Chuza and hauled him in for a hug so tight he couldn't breathe.

"This is the Lord's timing if I ever saw it," Manaen said. "Come in!"

Confused, Chuza followed him into the house, but he drew up short as a trio of men rose to their feet. Chuza's eyes skipped over Barnabas and Joses and landed on the small man with thick brows over pale eyes.

"You!" Chuza stepped protectively in front of Joanna.

"Peace, Chuza." Manaen held out his hands. "Barnabas took Saul to meet the apostles. They believe him. He's one of us now."

Chuza's mind reeled, and he pointed at Saul. "That man? The

one who persecuted Jesus' followers?"

"Yes."

Chuza's pulse raced as he glared over Manaen's shoulder at the man who whipped Joanna and Leah. Who oversaw Stephen's stoning. Who went into houses, dragging men and women to prison and voting for their death.

"Impossible," Chuza hissed, anger flooding his veins.

Manaen gripped Chuza's shoulder. "Nothing is impossible with God."

Chuza wrestled inwardly, and he turned to check on Joanna. Her lips were pressed together, and her eyes flickered as she considered. She stepped forward and stared into Saul's eyes. "What changed?"

Chuza saw the moment Saul recognized her. Anguish passed over the man's face.

"I am the worst of sinners," he admitted. "Yet Jesus, in his infinite mercy, appeared to me on the road to Damascus. A great light surrounded me, and I was struck blind. Jesus spoke to me out of heaven and sent me into the city." He took a tentative step forward. "I fasted and prayed, and I received a vision that a man named Ananias would lay hands on me and restore my sight."

Chuza twitched, recognizing the name. He glanced at Manaen.

Saul stepped closer. "Ananias came to me, and even in my blindness, I could feel his hesitation." He smiled wryly. "Could you blame him? I carried letters that granted me the authority to drag him back to Jerusalem. But Ananias laid his hands on me, and I was healed. I was baptized, and after proclaiming Jesus Christ in Damascus, I left."

The story was incredible. Perhaps too incredible. Chuza crossed his arms. "Let's say you're telling the truth. You've been gone for years. Where have you been?"

"Arabia." Saul said. "But, eventually, God sent me back to Damascus. I preached openly and the Damascus Jews turned against me. My escape involved a basket and a lot of rope." He chuckled.

Chuza tensed. "You laugh, but you caused a great many of my

friends to flee Jerusalem. Including my family."

Saul's smile faded. "I will live with that for the rest of my life. I am deeply sorry for the pain I caused."

Joanna's head tilted. "Jesus truly spoke to you?"

"He did." Awe tinged his voice. "I may never know why he chose me, but I will spend my life telling the world what Jesus has done."

Joanna set her hand on Chuza's arm and whispered, "I believe him."

Chuza flinched at the ease of her belief. But years ago, they had prayed for a miracle to stop Saul. Perhaps Jesus had answered in an unexpected, incredible way.

Saul inclined his head to Joanna. "You're one of the women who followed Jesus in Galilee, weren't you?"

"I am."

"I would love to hear your eyewitness account, if you don't mind." He gestured to a couch.

As she sat, the tension in the room eased. Chuza looked back at Alexander, and they shared a look of stunned disbelief.

"I'll go back and tell my family," Alexander whispered. "But I'm not sure if they'll believe me."

"Hannah," Manaen called. "Will you bring us some refreshments, please?"

Chuza took a seat near his wife. The conversation was stilted at first, but as they talked about Jesus, the atmosphere eased.

Chuza absorbed it all, his mind spinning. Four years ago, this would have been impossible. But his old mentor was right. Nothing was impossible for the Lord.

Chuza and Joanna walked slowly back through Jerusalem, holding hands.

"I wonder what Leah will think when she hears about Saul," he said.

Joanna peered into the distance. "We did the right thing, didn't we? Letting her go with Jovian?"

Chuza ran his thumb over her knuckles. At the time, it seemed the only logical conclusion. But if Jovian returned home and found the worst, Leah would bear the weight of his grief. That was a lot to put on the shoulders of a young bride.

"They travel with the Holy Spirit," he said. "I have to trust in that."

# FIFTY-SIX

Their ship slid down the Orontes River, and all the passengers grew silent as they approached Antioch. The port bustled as usual, but several of the nearby warehouses resembled nothing more than scorched skeletons. The smell of smoke stung his nostrils as Jovian's chest constricted. The damage was extensive, but he had half-expected the whole city to be rubble and black smoke.

The sailors directed the ship into its berth and the gangplank slid out.

"Ready?" Jovian glanced at Leah and Amichai.

Leah searched his face and nodded. She had not complained once on the journey, despite their grueling pace to the coast and their grim journey by sea. Guilt twinged his throat at this bleak honeymoon. He would make it up to her, somehow. But first, he had to find his family.

They carefully disembarked with the donkey and cart, an extra expense that had eaten into Jovian's savings. But he didn't know what his family would need, or what the city would be able to supply.

Jovian's anxiety spiked as they passed a group waiting to board, wearing slings and bandages. A man pulled a two-wheeled cart while

445

his family walked alongside, their faces bleak.

Jovian stopped a man walking by. "What's been happening in the city?"

The man scanned him from head to toe. "Well, the fires are mostly out."

Jovian tensed. "How bad were they?"

"The west and north side were nearly engulfed, and the Grove of Daphne is gone. The fire brigade has been working day and night."

Jovian's journey to the grove felt like another life. His throat tightened. "Are many dead?"

The man gawked as if Jovian was insane. "It was an earthquake! What do you think?" Muttering to himself, he walked on.

With every step of this journey, Jovian had swung between confidence that his family was safe, and fear that he was coming back to dig their bodies out of the rubble. Now he was afraid to find out.

Amichai patted his shoulder. "Come on."

Jovian tugged on the donkey's lead, focusing on the familiar creak of the cart behind him and nothing else.

The extent of the damage struck them the moment they left the port and entered the city. Men cleared stones from a collapsed building, their skin and clothes white with limestone dust. A house was missing a wall, revealing the furniture within, but the next was intact. It was frighteningly random.

They passed two men carrying a bloated corpse out of a ruined house, rags tied over their faces. They tossed the body onto a cart and Leah made a pained noise.

Guilt stabbed him. He shouldn't have brought her here. He turned, reaching for her hand. She gripped his fingers.

Government booths lined the street, doling out bread to a long line of weary-bodied men and women.

"This isn't how I wanted you to see my home city," Jovian said to Leah.

"I know."

He prayed his neighborhood had been spared from this level of destruction.

He led them down streets, picking their way when rubble blocked the narrow roads. At one intersection, beggar children swarmed them, trying to see what was in the cart. It hurt Jovian's heart to chase them away. Leah stared after the skinny boys and girls with tears in her eyes.

They finally reached Jovian's street. His pulse leaped into his throat. The house on the corner was flattened, a mass of stone and wooden beams. Jovian dropped the donkey's lead and broke into a run as tears burned his eyes.

His home was still standing. Relief flooded him. He yanked open the front gate. The front courtyard was empty. He charged into the house.

"Mother!" he called. "Father!"

No one answered. Jovian tore through the house. He stumbled to a stop as he turned a corner and light poured in from above. He blinked up at the sun, then down at the broken beams and tiles that blocked the hallway, obscuring the alcove where his mother prayed to her idol. His pulse quickened, and he stepped tentatively closer.

A dark stain covered the floor.

"No," he gasped, fear clawing up his throat.

A footstep crushed a broken tile behind him, and he whirled around. Leah looked past him, her gaze landing on the pool of dried blood.

"There's no one here," she said.

His mind would not work properly, and he just stared at her.

"Where would they have gone?" Amichai's voice broke into his muddled thoughts. "A neighbor or friend?"

"I don't know," Jovian said stupidly.

Leah turned to Amichai. "Let's ask the neighbors."

They turned away, leaving Jovian to stare numbly at the wreckage. If he closed his eyes, he could see his mother kneeling at the altar.

Had she fled here for safety when the earthquake struck, expecting her idol to protect her? He blinked back tears and realized the goddess was gone. He shifted through the wreckage, searching for it.

"Jovian!" Leah's voice called, and he turned. Her face was flushed from running. "They're at Flavius Horace's house. Do you know where that is?"

He didn't even answer as he strode past her in his hurry.

The walk to Horace's house passed in a blur, and he didn't pause as he entered the lower-level shop, barely registering how bare the shelves were as he strode toward the man who almost became his father-in-law.

Horace's jaw dropped as he saw Jovian.

"Where are they?" Jovian demanded.

"Upstairs," Horace said, but as Jovian moved to pass him, Horace gripped his arm. "Jovian," he said softly. "Your mother isn't well."

Jovian stared into his eyes, hating the sympathy that flickered there. "What happened?"

"A beam struck her on the head. She's been drifting in and out of consciousness. She hasn't opened her eyes for two days."

Pain stabbed Jovian like a knife, and he pushed past Horace and took the stairs two at a time to the upper level. He burst into a living space, and Horace's wife and daughters leaped to their feet in alarm.

"Jovian!" Persephone gasped.

"Where is she?" Jovian demanded.

Persephone gestured to a doorway, closed off by a hanging cloth. Jovian jerked the cloth aside and stepped into a family bedchamber. His breath caught. His mother lay on a low bed, her face pale. Bandages were wrapped around her head, and her hands were gently placed on her middle. If it wasn't for the soft rise and fall of her chest, he would have believed she was already gone.

His father, brother, and sister-in-law sat by the light of a single lamp, keeping vigil.

Belen turned his head toward the doorway and flinched. "Jovian?

How?"

Jovian waved aside his words. He stepped around Sergio and crouched to take his mother's hand. Her slender fingers were cold. Jovian snatched a blanket off a nearby bed and flung it over his mother's thin form. As he tucked it around her, he saw the missing idol standing near her head. Grief contracted his throat.

Tears poured down his face as he bowed until his forehead rested on her chest. "I'm so sorry, Mother," he whispered. If he had convinced her there was only one God with power, she would not be lying here.

He lost all sense of time and place until a gentle hand rubbed his back. He tensed, expecting Persephone, but the voice he heard was Leah's.

"Let's pray for her."

Jovian grasped the words like a lifeline. "Yes," he said, jerking upright. "We can pray for her to be healed."

His father gestured weakly. "We've given offerings at the temple of—"

"No," Jovian snapped. "She needs the help of a real God." He seized the cold idol. "Take this thing out of here. Throw it in the rubbish heap."

Belen's eyes widened. "It's your mother's. She would want her goddess watching over her."

"This is no goddess!" Jovian shook the idol in his fist. He was tempted to hurl it across the room. Sergio snatched the idol from Jovian's hand and ducked under the doorway.

Jovian reached for Leah's fingers and pulled her beside him. "Where's Amichai?"

Leah glanced nervously at Belen. "He's waiting in the other room."

"He needs to pray with us," Jovian said, and swiped a hand over his damp face. God had granted them the Holy Spirit for this moment. He knew it.

# FIFTY-SEVEN

Leah studied his face, then turned and called for Amichai. Cassandra rose and let Amichai take her place. Belen stared at the Jewish man, and then at Leah's hand encased in Jovian's.

Jovian gripped Thea's fingers. "Jesus, we acknowledge you as Lord, and we ask you to heal my mother. Let her awaken so I can teach her about you, and about your ways. Heal her body, Lord…"

He prayed for minutes, and then an hour. When Jovian's throat became hoarse, Leah took over, and then Amichai prayed.

As time slipped by, fear climbed up Jovian's throat. Chuza's prayer had healed him at once, but Thea lay unchanged after hours of prayer. What if his faith wasn't good enough? What if God would not heal Thea because she worshiped a false god?

Jovian blinked and realized Leah and Amichai had stopped praying and were quietly singing a hymn. He glanced over his shoulder. Sergio and Cassandra had fallen asleep on one of the beds.

His chest heaved with pain. "She's not better."

Leah's eyebrows contracted, and she let the song drift to silence.

Jovian blinked rapidly. "Is God punishing her? Or me for not

451

teaching her the truth? The roof only collapsed on her. Her and her idol. The rest of the house was fine. What if God—"

"No," Leah said, and gripped his hand. "God isn't like that."

Jovian shook his head. "I've heard the stories about what God did in his wrath."

"Jesus said that when we see him, we see the Father." She leaned toward him. "Would Jesus pull that roof down on your mother? Of course not." She cupped his cheek. "Sin pulls pain in on itself. It's just the way of it. Whatever happens now, it's not God's will that your mother suffers."

"Then why not heal her?" Jovian gasped, his chest rending like shattered pottery. "If God is all-powerful, it would take just a moment. Less time than a breath and my mother would be healed."

Leah was quiet for a long moment, and he realized, belatedly, that she had sat at her mother's side and watched her die. He wrapped his arm around her shoulders. Leah looked up at him, tears flooding her eyes. Somehow, she had lost everything yet kept her faith in God. He ached for such faith right now.

Leah took his hand and traced the tendons and knuckles with her fingertip. "Life is all we know," she whispered. "So we are afraid to go on the next journey, afraid to let our loved ones go on without us, afraid they will be alone, or scared, or lost." Tears coursed down her face. "But someone is waiting on the other side, someone with unimaginable love for the hurting and the lost, the one who was willing to die for us. He conquered death."

Jovian ached to accept her words, but his fear would not allow it. "But my mother doesn't know Jesus. If she's not one of God's people, then how can she be part of the kingdom and the resurrection?"

Leah leaned her head on his shoulder. "I don't know. But I know God loves your mother, too."

Jovian leaned back on his heels and tipped his face to the heavens. "God, please be with my mother, no matter what happens next. I place her in your hands and plead for mercy."

He swiped his eyes and realized Belen was watching him. Lost in his grief, Jovian had forgotten his father was even here. His neck heated. Belen had heard his prayers, his words with Leah, all of it.

"Who is the man?" Belen asked. "The one who conquered death?"

"Jesus of Nazareth," Jovian said, though he had tried explaining it to his father before. "He went up to heaven, but he sent the Holy Spirit, and Jesus' followers have been performing miracles as they teach the world about the kingdom of God."

"I don't see a kingdom of God here." Belen gestured helplessly at his wife.

Jovian looked at Leah, who gave him a sympathetic smile.

Humanity had grappled with death since the dawn of time. Jovian knew victory was coming for the world, but he bowed his head and prayed for death to be vanquished in this room right now.

The lamp began to flicker. Leah rose and refilled it. She stepped around Amichai, who was slumped in a doze. Jovian slept sitting up, his head leaning on his hands, his elbows on his knees. She fetched a blanket from an empty bed and draped it over his shoulders.

She realized Belen was watching her.

He spoke quietly. "Are you his wife?"

Leah nodded and sat beside Jovian again. This wasn't the introduction she had hoped for.

Belen scratched his stubbly cheek. "You seem to be a woman of wisdom."

Her cheeks warmed. "Thank you."

"Are you the reason he went back to Judea?"

Leah hesitated. This wasn't her story to tell, but her father-in-law was waiting.

"No," she said at last, and then smiled wryly. "He actually did his best not to marry me." Belen blinked in confusion, so she added,

"Because I'm a Jew."

His face flushed in the dim light. "I figured, but I thought he must have—"

"Become a Jew too?" she finished for him. "No. We didn't marry until we understood Jesus came for the Greeks too. We are equals before God."

Belen licked his lips. "I don't understand. The Jews welcome the Greeks among them now?"

"Let me start over. I'll tell you what happened when Peter was in Joppa."

When she finished recounting Peter's experience at Cornelius' house, Belen lifted his brows. "If half of what you and my son say is true, something strange is happening in the world. I'm not sure what to believe."

She smiled ruefully. "I've seen wonders beyond anything I could explain. But it's easier to accept once you've seen a dead man come back to life."

Belen shifted, seeming uncomfortable. He gestured to the side, where Amichai snored. "And this one? Who is he, your brother?"

"My uncle."

"And your parents are back in Judea?"

"Yes," Leah said, leaving the full explanation for another day.

"And you and Jovian plan to go back after..." He drifted off and gazed at his wife as if afraid to consider the future.

Leah hesitated. "I'm not sure." Before she saw Antioch, she never would have considered leaving the promised land. But the sight of the poor and suffering pulled on her. What if this was where the Holy Spirit wanted them? She glanced at Amichai. Living in Antioch would keep him safe from Antipas. And, she admitted to herself, she and Jovian would be more accepted as a couple here than in Sepphoris.

Belen gave her a small smile. "Well, I'm glad I had the chance to meet my son's wife."

"I'm happy to meet my husband's father." And now he was her

father, she realized. This room was filled with her family, too. She glanced at Sergio and Cassandra, slumbering in each other's arms. She studied Thea's face. She ached to meet this woman who had shaped a son like Jovian.

She took Thea's hand. "When she recovers, I'll make my new family a feast."

Thea's fingers twitched, and Leah gasped. The sound woke Jovian, and he jerked upright.

Belen leaned forward. "Thea?"

Leah's heart pounded in her chest. She had felt Thea move. She was certain of it.

"Mother?" Jovian said. "Can you hear me? I came back."

At the sound of Jovian's voice, Thea's eyelids fluttered, then stilled. Her mouth moved soundlessly, and then she whispered hoarsely, "Jovian?"

Belen cried out, and Jovian bent over his mother, gripping her hand. "Yes, Mother, it's me. It's Jovian. I'm home."

Sergio bolted awake.

Thea's mouth moved again, and Leah scrambled to her feet, searching for a drink.

She swept the curtain back and saw Horace's family sleeping on makeshift beds. Leah picked her way through the prone forms to a pitcher and sniffed the jug. Water. She poured out a cup and began making her way back.

"What's happening?" a man's voice spoke into the darkness. Horace.

"She's awake," Leah said.

He gave a huge sigh of relief.

Leah ducked around the curtain and passed Jovian the water. Amichai was on his feet, making room for Sergio.

Belen gently lifted Thea's head, and they helped her drink several mouthfuls. When she shook her head, they laid her back down.

"Where am I?" she asked, squinting her eyes as if the lamplight hurt her head.

"We're at Horace's house, remember?" Belen said.

"Oh, right," she said. "But how is Jovian here?"

"I came home," Jovian said. "And I brought my wife."

Thea's mouth pulled together in confusion. "Your wife?"

Jovian beckoned, and Leah tentatively came forward, hoping this wasn't too much for the injured woman.

A smile softened the high planes of Thea's cheekbones. "How lovely," she whispered.

Leah flushed.

Belen stroked his wife's cheek. "But you must rest now," he said. "We're all here. I will watch over you."

Thea's eyes closed sleepily. "I was having a lovely dream. I was sitting by a stream with a man. I felt as if I knew him, though I'd never seen him before." Her breath deepened as if she was enjoying a restful sleep.

Jovian stood and wrapped his arm around Leah's shoulders, trembling with relief.

"Come on," she said, and tugged him toward an empty bed. "You need to sleep as well."

He sat, pulling her down beside him. She glanced to where Belen lay beside his wife, wiping a tear from his face. Sergio and Cassandra whispered on one bed, and Amichai slipped out of the room. Embarrassment crept up Leah's neck. She and Jovian had slept side-by-side throughout the journey, but it felt strange to share a bed here, among his family.

But it had been a long journey, and exhaustion overwhelmed her embarrassment. She lay down beside Jovian, and he wrapped an arm around her, tucking her against his warm body. She yawned. In the morning they would plan for the future.

# Two Years Later

# FIFTY-EIGHT

39 AD
LATE SPRING

Chuza's ribs felt too tight as he faced his family. Joanna stood in the doorway with one hand on Nadia's shoulder. He blinked at his daughter. When had she gotten so tall? Ira jumped up and down, gripping Joanna's skirt with one sticky hand. He grinned up at his papa, not fully understanding.

Chuza crouched and held out his arms. His children threw themselves forward, and he held them tightly, inhaling the sweet scent of their hair.

Nadia squeezed his neck. "Don't go, Papa."

Chuza lifted his eyes to Joanna's. Her gaze filled with sympathy, but she spoke brightly.

"If he doesn't go, he can't bring you something from Rome."

Chuza cleared the thickness from his throat. "That's right. What would you like best? A new necklace? A toy?"

"A toy!" Ira said, jumping again. Chuza chuckled as he rocked back on his heels. The boy never quit moving.

Chuza gently disentangled Nadia's arms from around his neck and chucked her chin. "Help your mama with Ira, alright?"

"Yes, Papa," Nadia said. Her large brown eyes shimmered with tears. "Just make sure you come back."

Chuza ruffled her curls as he stood. Nadia had never forgiven her older sister for not coming back from Antioch.

Chuza picked up his satchel and slung the strap over his shoulder. Joanna stepped into his arms, and he buried his face in her hair, craving her strength, her confidence.

"I'll pray it goes well," she whispered.

"Have the whole community pray," Chuza said.

Antipas was going to need it.

The wind whipped through his hair and threw sea spray in his face. Chuza clutched the thick, wooden railing. Behind him, the sailors sang a rhythmic song as they worked in tandem, heaving on ropes to adjust the sail. Their ship whipped past little boats where fishermen labored beneath a cloud of gulls, and sped past small villages crowded near the shore. After three weeks of travel, they were about to arrive in Rome.

Chuza sighed and turned away from the view to gather his belongings. Herodias' voice drifted from Antipas' large, leather tent.

"It is no less than you deserve," she insisted. "Caesar must understand everything you've done for Rome. Trust me, on the voyage back, you'll be thanking me."

Chuza shook his head and ducked into his own tiny tent. He angrily rolled up his bedding and lashed it with a strip of leather. If this plan was truly as good as Herodias insisted, she shouldn't need to keep convincing Antipas of it, over and over again.

Chuza smoothed his face as he followed Antipas and Herodias

through the entrance and into the emperor's palace. Massive columns of white, blue, and gold supported a soaring roof. Bronze statues stood in alcoves, and the sharp scent of incense soaked the air. Antipas and Herodias wore their best robes and trailed a parade of servants bearing expensive gifts. Antipas' hand trembled as he smoothed his gray hair, but Herodias walked proudly. After two years of cajoling her husband, she was right where she wanted to be.

One of his scrolls slipped, and Chuza hastily corrected his grip. With this stack of records, he could show how Antipas had increased revenues, paid taxes promptly, and bettered the lives of his citizens. Antipas and Herodias intended to prove their worth, but what they needed—more than balanced ledgers—was sheer luck.

Chuza followed his master into a throne room arranged with art, statuary, and flowers. Men in togas talked in small knots, and musicians plucked calming notes in a corner.

Gaius sat on a raised platform. Exotic animal furs softened his throne, and a pair of hounds chewed on bones near his feet. Chuza studied the newest Caesar with misgiving. The emperor was young, with short hair and a beardless face. His features were startlingly normal for a ruler growing in fame for his cruelty and perversion.

Gaius saw their approach and inclined his head. As the servants spread the gifts at the emperor's feet and left the room, Gaius' gaze roved over the tetrarch.

Herodias shot Chuza a look, and he cleared his throat and bowed low. "My lord, may I present Herod Antipas and his wife, Herodias."

Gaius leaned his elbow on the arm of his throne. "Herodias," he said thoughtfully, narrowing his eyes. "Your brother is Agrippa, son of Aristobulus?"

She smiled sweetly. "He is. My favorite brother too, I might add."

"Hmm." Gaius didn't seem convinced.

Antipas cleared his throat. "My steward has prepared accounts to show that I have ruled Galilee and Perea justly, and to the benefit of Rome."

Gaius flicked a hand toward his servant, who came to relieve Chuza of his scrolls. Chuza reluctantly handed them over, suddenly sure that his hours of work would be shoved in some dusty corner and forgotten.

"So, why have you come?" Gaius leaned back in his throne and drummed his fingers on the armrests.

Antipas began his meticulously crafted speech, but hurried footsteps echoed in the room. Antipas trailed off, confused by the interruption.

A well-dressed man strode toward the emperor. "My lord, I bring important information regarding Herod Antipas."

Antipas and Herodias shared a startled glance, and Chuza stiffened. This couldn't be good.

Gaius crooked his fingers to the newcomer, who climbed the steps and set a scroll in the emperor's hand.

"What's going on?" Antipas whispered.

Gaius broke the seal and read the letter, his expression darkening. His gaze snapped to Herodias. "Your brother has written to me." Antipas flinched as if slapped. "He learned you were on your way here and wanted to ensure I fully understood the... situation."

Chuza's mouth dried. What had Agrippa done?

"Situation?" Antipas repeated.

Gaius' frown deepened. "He claims you have a secret alliance with the king of Parthia."

Chuza's jaw dropped, and Antipas sputtered. "No, my lord!"

Gaius' voice rang accusingly through the throne room. "Did you not feast Vitellius and King Artabanus after they reached a peace agreement?"

The room fell silent, and the music ended discordantly.

Antipas paled. "Yes, I did."

"And did Artabanus gift you a generous sum of armor and weapons? Enough to outfit an entire army?"

Chuza's stomach plummeted as Antipas hesitated.

Gaius rolled the scroll closed, his mouth pinched with cold sarcasm.

"Will I find that inventory in your careful records?" He flicked his hand to where the servant held Chuza's accounts.

Chuza forced his face to remain calm, but his mind was spinning.

"My lord," Antipas stammered, "I accepted the gift when there was trouble with Nabatea. This was back when your uncle was emperor. I would, of course, never use the armor without your permission. I would have mentioned it, but its mere existence completely slipped my memory," he finished lamely.

Gaius' frown deepened. "Why did you come here? Did you hope I'd make you a king like Agrippa?" He rose to his feet and thrust his finger toward Antipas. "Agrippa proved his loyalty to me, but you come here with lies! Your own family accuses you of treason and the best you can say is that you forgot?"

Antipas looked at Herodias, panic coloring his face. She opened and closed her mouth soundlessly.

Gaius sneered. "You came to me for honor, but you will leave with shame. I strip you of your tetrarchy and give it to Agrippa."

Chuza's knees wobbled in shock, but Gaius was not finished. The emperor's words echoed with terrible finality. "I banish you to Gaul for the rest of your life."

Antipas swayed, and Chuza rushed to support his master, panic lancing his heart.

Gaius turned to Herodias, who stared at her stricken husband, unable to move. His voice softened. "Herodias, you may keep the money you brought to your marriage. Your brother wishes for no harm to come to you, and invites you to live with him, in his house."

Herodias jerked to attention and drew herself up to her full height. "You must act as you see best, my emperor, but just as I have shared in my husband's prosperity, so I will share in his misfortune."

Gaius' face darkened with anger. "Then I strip you of your estate and give it to your brother. You will go with your husband into exile." He flicked his fingers in dismissal.

Chuza tugged on Antipas as they were surrounded by guards. He needed to get his master out of the room before Antipas collapsed and faced further humiliation. They turned away from the emperor, the expensive gifts, and Herodias' grand ambition.

# FIFTY-NINE

The guards marched them deeper into the palace. Chuza had no idea where they were going, but Antipas had just gone from a tetrarch to a banished ruler. The implications were horrifying. If Antipas was sent to Gaul, what would happen to his slaves? Sweat broke out on Chuza's brow.

"I wish we'd never come," Antipas wheezed, pale and sweaty.

Herodias overheard and had the decency to look away.

The guard stopped outside a heavy door. "You will remain here until passage can be arranged for Gaul."

Antipas blinked. "I can't return home to pack my things?" he said weakly.

"You may send someone to collect them. But I must examine everything, to ensure you're not taking more than you are entitled to."

Antipas sputtered, and Herodias' glared, but the guard was unfazed.

Without waiting for further insults, Chuza opened the door and led his master inside. To his relief, it was not a stark room, but amply furnished guest quarters, with polished tables, soft couches, and a window overlooking the gardens.

Chuza turned back to the guard. "My master and mistress have left their body slaves at the inn. If Gaius insists my master remain here, I will need them brought, along with their luggage."

The guard inclined his head and strode away, but he left two guards behind. Chuza closed the door, shutting the guards out.

Herodias sank onto a couch, the picture of defeat. She leaned forward and covered her face with her hands.

Antipas sprawled on the other couch, still deathly pale. Chuza glanced at the sideboard for wine, but it was empty. He swallowed around his dry throat and sat on a stool near his master. His limbs felt heavy, his mind sluggish.

Antipas' brother had been sent to Gaul thirty years ago. What did Archelaus' steward do? Looked for a new position, most likely. Chuza's hand trembled as he smoothed his hair. His situation was different, but he couldn't allow Antipas to drag him into exile.

Master and bondslave locked eyes, neither of them saying anything for a long moment.

At last, Antipas sighed. "This is not how I envisioned my end." His voice was rough. "Forty years of rule overturned in five minutes."

Chuza licked his lips. "We need to send someone to settle your estate and collect what you and Herodias need for your new life." Herodias groaned with dismay, but Chuza pressed on. "I could return to Galilee to arrange your affairs and gather your clothes, your gold and jewels, and anything of sentimental value."

Herodias barked a cold laugh. "The rats are already deserting the ship."

Antipas glared at her. "It was your brother who did this to us."

"Only because you were so cruel to him," she snapped.

Antipas' brows lowered. "All you ever do is complain about your brother becoming a king. Do you truly think your words did not reach Agrippa's ears?"

Herodias huffed angrily and jerked to her feet. She strode to peer out the window with her arms crossed over her chest.

Chuza folded his trembling hands and turned to Antipas. He had to hold his ground. "I will gather your things and send them to you."

Herodias' sniffed knowingly and shook her head.

"Send?" Antipas' gaze narrowed. "You will bring them to me. We will travel to Gaul together."

Chuza's mouth was bone dry. He shifted to the edge of his seat and leaned toward his master. "My lord, I have a wife. Two children."

"Then bring them," Antipas said with a dangerous glint in his eye.

Chuza's insides were unraveling, but he forced himself to remain calm. "My lord, I have served you faithfully for most of your life. I have been your body slave and your steward, and I would like to think, your friend. I am asking you, as your friend, to release me from my vow."

Antipas stared at him.

Chuza's heart pounded against his chest. He had believed he would serve Antipas until one of them died, but today everything was thrown into chaos. He prayed God would soften Antipas' heart.

Antipas drew a breath. "No." Chuza's stomach twisted and turned upside down. "I need you, more than ever. You will come with me to Gaul." As Chuza opened his mouth, Antipas cut him off with a slice of his hand. "I have decided."

Anger climbed up Chuza's throat, and he jerked to his feet. The stool clattered behind him. "My lord," he cried out. "You can't do this!"

Antipas heaved himself upright with startling speed. "I am your master!" Antipas roared, spittle flying. "If I command nothing else in this world, I command you!" His hand snaked like a viper toward Chuza's ear, and Chuza gasped with pain as he was jerked forward.

Antipas clutched Chuza's gold earring between his fingers as his eyes blazed with rage.

Chuza's hand flew to his burning ear as he stared at his master in shock. In all his years of service, Antipas had never drawn his blood.

Antipas shook the earring in front of Chuza's nose. "You will never be free. Until my dying breath, you will serve me."

Chuza's pulse pounded with horror. He should have waited a day or two. He shouldn't have reacted with anger. He should have—

It was too late. He must go to Gaul.

Chuza bowed to his master and a drop of blood landed by his feet. He spoke with all the calmness he could muster. "I will collect your things and be back as soon as possible." He could not look Antipas in the eye.

For once, Herodias was silent.

Spinning on his heel, Chuza strode across the room, pulled open the door, and marched past the guards. He ignored the stares as blood dripped from his ear and stained the shoulder of his best robe. Without a word to anyone, he left the palace.

He wove through the packed streets, hardly watching where he was going, and made his way to the inn. The palace guard was already there, gathering the confused slaves and Antipas' luggage. Chuza hooked his bag over his shoulder and aimed for the port.

He found passage on the first available ship heading in the right direction and boarded.

As the ship pushed away from the harbor, Chuza began to tremble and his pulse filled his ears. With a roar, he slammed his fist on the railing again and again, unleashing the bitter rage that boiled in his chest.

An arm grabbed his wrist.

"Do we need to take you back to port?" The gruff sailor demanded.

Chuza shook his head.

The sailor studied his face for a moment before dropping Chuza's wrist. "All right then."

As he strode away, Chuza turned and saw the other passengers watching him warily. He didn't even care. He turned back to face the shore, tears burning in his eyes. How would he explain this to Joanna?

Joanna drifted through the quiet house. She missed the days when these rooms overflowed with family. But she missed Leah most of all.

Joanna had expected Leah to go to Antioch for a few weeks, or perhaps a month or two. They had eagerly awaited for the newly-wed's return, but instead, they received a letter. When Leah and Jovian saw the devastation left by the earthquake, they felt compelled to help the poor and suffering in Antioch.

Joanna praised their compassion, but she had wept in private. She still missed Leah, not only as her adopted daughter, but as one of her closest friends.

Joanna crossed the courtyard and entered the dark stable. Balaam dozed in his stall. Joanna leaned on the railing and stroked his neck, drawing comfort from his warmth.

She heard footsteps behind her and turned, expecting to see Nadia. But it was Chuza's shadow that filled the doorway.

Joanna gasped and threw herself into his arms. He clung to her, and she gripped him tightly, breathing in his scent and dust from the road.

"How are you back?" she asked, pulling away. "I didn't hear Antipas had returned."

He took her hand and led her to the table. They sat, and fore-boding grew in her belly. Something was wrong.

"Gaius sentenced Antipas to exile," Chuza said without preamble.

Joanna blinked at him. "What? How?"

Chuza explained, and Joanna shook her head, trying to understand. "Just like that, Antipas must leave Galilee? Forever?"

As she saw Chuza's face, she realized what this meant. She could barely form the words. "He's making you go with him?"

Chuza's eyes were hollow. "I hope that you'll go with me."

"No!" she cried out, jerking to stand. As his face crumpled, she cupped his cheeks. "No, I mean you can't go. Enough is enough. You made that vow when you were hardly older than Nadia! He can't make you."

"I swore to serve him for life. I swore it before God," Chuza said heavily.

"And he helped kill God's son!" Joanna dropped her hands and balled them by her side.

Chuza lifted a hand toward his ear, but let it drop. "I, more than anyone, know who Antipas is. His fears, his hopes, his failings. Antipas won't let me go because he's afraid of being alone."

"He has Herodias."

Chuza pulled her to sit beside him. He rubbed his thumb over the back of her hand as the noise of the city filtered into the courtyard. The bark of a dog. A baby's cry. The rumble of wheels and the murmur of voices in the street. They were the sounds of Sepphoris. The sounds of home.

Tears burned in Joanna's eyes. "I don't want to go to Gaul. Our lives are here."

Chuza stared at their joined fingers. "I know. And I won't make you come with me."

Two hot tears slipped down her face, and Joanna wiped them roughly away. She wished he would order her to go, so she could pout and mope and wail. Instead, she tipped back her chin, stared at the blurry stars, and prayed.

# SIXTY

Chuza stepped into his Sepphoris office and years of memories stole his breath. He blinked, staring at the familiar room as if for the first time.

Someone cleared their throat behind him, and Chuza turned.

The staff leaders stood in the hall. Michael bobbed his head. "You summoned us?"

Chuza fixed a smile in place. "Come in. I have news." He moved behind his desk but did not sit.

The staff filed into his office, Michael's broad shoulders taking the space of two men. As Chuza met the eyes of the men and women who had served Antipas alongside him, nostalgia tightened his throat. He had never counted his coworkers as close friends, but he had known some of them for decades. Their shared purpose had forged a community he was about to leave forever.

He folded his hands. "Antipas and Herodias are not coming back."

The others murmured in shock, and Chuza explained. Stunned silence answered his account.

"What about us?" the cupbearer asked, and glanced around at

the others.

"That is up to Agrippa. I suspect he will keep most of the staff, but he is your master now."

The lead laundress covered her mouth with her hands, and Chuza hastily added, "Agrippa has ruled his lands with a fair and just hand. I think you will find him a reasonable master."

Michael crossed his arms with a frown. "But what about you, Steward?"

It was a moment before he could form the words. "I will go with Antipas to Gaul." The staff gasped, and their concern was a small comfort. "I will take a few servants with me, but only if they are willing." He would not force anyone to leave the promised land. If Antipas needed to hire foreign servants in Gaul, so be it.

The staff leaders drifted out of the room to inform their subordinates, and Chuza sank into his chair. How had it come to this?

Chuza was engrossed in his work when Michael strode into the room, a tray in his thick hands. Chuza rose in surprise, but Michael waved him back down.

"I thought you could use some supper." Michael set the tray on the desk.

Chuza glanced out the window, surprised to see it was growing dark. He pressed his lips together, knowing he'd have to face Joanna sooner or later. He turned back to the head cook. "Thank you."

Michael rubbed his palms on his apron. "Any word from Leah?"

"Nothing recently," Chuza said around the tightness in his throat. "But she sounded happy in her last letter."

Michael nodded, then shook his head. "It's hard to think of our girl far away in Antioch."

Chuza fiddled with his stylus. "She's grown into a capable and kind woman. You were a big part of that."

Michael waved his hand dismissively, but he looked pleased.

"What about you? Are you going to stay and work for Agrippa?"

"I'm thinking it's time I retire. I've saved a tidy sum, and my nephew has a place for me."

It was strange to think of the household without Michael.

"Well, in that case," Chuza rose and opened his money box, "Antipas is happy to reward you for your years of faithful service." He counted out a generous amount and set the coins in Michael's palm.

Michael raised his eyebrows. "I wasn't expecting anything but my wages. Thank you, Chuza." He tipped the coins into his apron pocket and extended his arm. "I hope you and Joanna do well in Gaul."

Chuza gripped Michael's strong hand and blinked rapidly, knowing this was only one of many goodbyes.

Chuza's stomach churned as he let himself into the house. Shame at his late arrival crept up his spine. The courtyard was quiet, lit by a few lamps. The children must already be in bed.

Joanna knelt in front of the oven. She turned at his footsteps and pulled a tray from the coals. "Come and eat."

She stood, and her long braid swung over her shoulder as she set the tray on the table. A cake of fine flour bubbled with brown, gooey dates. His eyes filled with tears. He didn't deserve a treat. He didn't deserve any kindness at all.

Joanna slid his bag from his shoulder and gently pushed him onto a cushion. She poured them some wine, and the sound was loud in the quiet courtyard. He accepted his cup but didn't drink. With effort, he met her eyes, fearing the bitterness, the resignation, or even worse, a hint she had decided to remain in the promised land to wait for Jesus' return.

But her eyes were only filled with warmth as she sat down across from him. "How did the staff take it?"

He cleared the emotion from his throat and told her about his day.

She pressed her lips together. "It feels like the end of an era, doesn't it?"

He sighed. "I wonder how Antipas will be remembered. Will future generations speak of the cities he built, of his many years of peaceful rule, or will they only remember his role in Jesus' death?"

Joanna made a disgusted noise in her throat. "I know what I'll remember." She reached across the table and grasped his hand.

Chuza winced. "Is it pathetic that I pity him?" Lamplight flickered in her eyes. "He has no faith to cling to, only the memories of his mistakes and a wife who brought him as much harm as joy."

Her brow furrowed and he dropped his gaze, ashamed that he still loved his master, in some strange way.

He gripped her hand. "I should hate him. Part of me is so angry I could burn all his belongings. But then I think of Jesus, forgiving those who killed him. How many have come to faith because of Jesus' love for his enemies? Perhaps, if I love Antipas, even though he doesn't deserve it, he too will see the power of faith, and come to know Jesus as his savior."

He peeked at her face, afraid he would see disgust as he spoke of loving the man who was tearing their lives to pieces.

Joanna stared at the table top, her lips pressed together. "I've been praying about what to do, and I'll confess, God has been silent." She raised her eyes to his. "But the scriptures say two are better than one." She tipped her head, and a smile played on her lips. "You will need me in Gaul, I think."

"More than anything," he said hoarsely.

She came around the table and sat next to him, leaning her head on his shoulder. "We have faced challenges before, and God has always seen us through. Perhaps we can take the good news to Gaul. Start a new community."

He wrapped an arm around her shoulder and felt the tension in her posture. Leaving their fellow believers would tear a gaping hole in their lives.

Chuza shifted so they faced one another. "If we do this, we may not return for years, if we can return at all." Gaul was a world away from Galilee. "You have family here. What if Leah comes home and—"

"I will miss them all. Terribly," Joanna said thickly. "But my heart is with you. My place is with you."

Her words both soothed and seared his heart. He pulled her into his arms. "I'm so sorry I swore that vow. I wish, more than anything, I could turn back time and snatch the words from my lips."

She squeezed him. "We can only move forward, not back. God will go with us."

His heart threatened to burst in his chest. Whatever difficulties he would face in exile with Antipas, he would not face them alone.

# SIXTY-ONE

Chuza drew Celer to a halt. The bay horse shook his mane, and Chuza patted his neck. "How many times have we taken this ride, old man?"

He peered over the Sea of Galilee. The deep blue water shimmered, and hills hedged the inland sea. The walls of Tiberias blocked the valley ahead, stretching down to the water's edge.

This was Chuza's last stop. After he finished here, Antipas' affairs would be closed and it would be time to leave Galilee.

Chuza nudged Celer's side with his heels. The horse walked on, and Chuza absorbed the surrounding sights, knowing he might never gaze on them again. He had heard strange things about Gaul. Forests so dense sunlight could not enter. Snow that fell until the grass was covered. People with skin as white as milk. Chuza shivered despite the heat.

He and Celer rode through the city and up to the palace. He slid from the saddle and a groom came forward, his face pinched.

"Is it true, my lord?" the groom asked, taking Celer's reins. "Antipas isn't coming back?"

Chuza untied his bag from behind the saddle. "Agrippa is on his way here with his family. You have a new master now."

The groom shook his head and led Celer to the stables.

Chuza steeled himself and entered the palace, aiming for his office. He was stopped repeatedly by staff desperate for news. Chuza answered them calmly, though his inner tension tightened to the point of snapping.

Finally, he made it to his office. He shut the door and leaned against it with a sigh. He scanned the room. Joanna's touches were every-where he looked. This had been their first home. He peered into the bedchamber beyond, where he first saw Joanna after she was miraculously healed. Their lives had never been the same after that.

He turned to the desk and set down his bag. He had much to do before Agrippa arrived.

Chuza stood in the courtyard amid the jingling of tack, the rumble of cartwheels, and the cheerful conversation of carefree men. He could almost believe time had rolled backward and Antipas was making his yearly circuit.

But Galilee's new king strode into the courtyard, his step lively and ready to command the day.

Chuza bowed.

"Ah, good!" Agrippa strode closer. "I was hoping you'd arrive before me."

Chuza folded his hands behind his back. "I've gone over the accounts, my lord, and everything is ready to hand off to your steward."

"I expected nothing less from you." Agrippa grinned as he slapped Chuza's arm. He turned as Cypros came into the courtyard, trailed by her four children and their nurse. Cypros' eyes softened as she saw Chuza, and she swept toward him.

"This must be so hard for you," she said. Chuza glanced at Agrippa, but the king nodded in agreement. Cypros tilted her head to the side.

"Come and dine with us tonight."

Chuza hesitated, but Agrippa squeezed his shoulder. "I'm eager to hear about your plans for the future."

This attention was unexpected, but Cypros' smile seemed genuine. Chuza inclined his head. He could not refuse the king and queen.

Chuza stood to the side as the children followed their parents through the courtyard, delighted at their new palace. The oldest boy and his sister walked arm in arm, but then broke into a run, racing to see who could get inside first. Chuza smiled despite himself.

He arrived at the triclinium promptly, but the large room was empty. The golden ceiling reflected lamplight onto the vivid murals painted on the walls. Antipas had held many feasts in this room, including one where he attempted to get Phasaelis drunk with the hope she would be unfaithful and justify a divorce. But Joanna had thwarted that plot. Chuza grinned.

He turned and approached the servant. "Who is dining with Agrippa tonight?"

"Only you and the queen," the servant said. Chuza blinked with surprise, but the servant held up his pitcher. "Wine?"

The cup was barely in Chuza's hand before Agrippa arrived with Cypros on his arm. He led his wife to a couch and ensured she was comfortable before he took his place. Chuza was pleased to see it. Cypros had borne her fair share of difficulty as Agrippa's wife, but now she shared in his success.

Chuza sat, and a young servant brought in a basin of water. His brows rose, but he said nothing as Agrippa ceremoniously washed his hands and blessed the bread in the Jewish way. The ritual felt strange in this space.

Agrippa inclined his head to Chuza as the servants began passing around food. "I know my family has been faithful in name, but I am determined to live out that faith."

"It will win the favor of the people, I'm sure."

Agrippa smiled. "I'm not doing it for politics."

Chuza hoped, for Galilee's sake, that Agrippa spoke the truth.

Agrippa popped a grape in his mouth. "What are your plans now that Antipas' tetrarchy is finished?"

"I'm going to Gaul."

Agrippa's brows rose. "Really? You wish to go into exile with him?"

Chuza hesitated. "I am his bond slave. He wishes me to go, so I go."

Cypros frowned. "That doesn't seem fair. After everything you did for him?"

Chuza couldn't help wondering why she cared.

She seemed to read his face, and she smiled. "We haven't forgotten how you helped Agrippa leave Tyre. And you were always trying to help me."

Chuza shifted. "I was just trying to do what was right."

"You cared," Cypros insisted. "Believe me, I have seen enough carelessness to know the difference."

Chuza wiped his fingers on a napkin and inclined his head to Agrippa. "I may have helped you leave Tyre, but the rest you did on your own."

"With Cypros' help." Agrippa lifted his cup to salute his wife. "You were right, she is my greatest ally. Someday I'll tell you how she wheedled me a loan worth thousands of sesterces, all while keeping her virtue."

Cypros laughed.

Agrippa leaned closer. "But Chuza, if you don't want to go to Gaul, I can send another man in your place."

Chuza's heart leaped at the possibility, but he shook his head. "I made a vow. I belong to Antipas."

Agrippa regarded him as Cypros frowned.

"You know, Gaius gave me permission to stop you from taking anything I feel belongs in Galilee," Agrippa said. "It is by my kindness that Antipas and my sister can travel into exile with money and clothing."

Chuza blinked. Antipas would need his clothes and jewels to live upon.

"I assure you," he stammered. "I will take nothing beyond what I feel is fair to Antipas."

"Oh, but you are," Agrippa said. "You're letting him take you."

Chuza's mouth dried. "What are you saying?"

"I will not allow you to go with Antipas into exile. I claim you as my slave, for the good of Galilee. "

Chuza stiffened. "Antipas will not agree."

Agrippa laughed. "Antipas has no choice! Seize this chance, Chuza. You don't have to follow Antipas anymore."

Chuza's mind stumbled over the idea. What would life be like without Antipas?

If he took Agrippa's offer, he had no guarantee his new master would be any better. But at least he and Joanna could remain in Galilee. He could probably convince Agrippa to let him work in Sepphoris. Or perhaps Joanna would rather live in a different city. Possibilities spread before Chuza like a feast, and a smile bloomed on his face.

"I think he is amenable," Cypros said, laughing.

Agrippa turned to a servant. "Send in a scribe."

Chuza cleared his throat. "I can scribe for you—"

Agrippa cut off his offer with a friendly wave of his hand. Chuza tried to eat as they waited, but his stomach was filled with butterflies. The whole situation felt unreal.

The scribe arrived and Agrippa leaned back on his couch, studying the golden ceiling as he searched for the right words. "I, King Herod Agrippa, grant Chuza his freedom. I grant him a release payment equal to ten years' wages, for services rendered." He looked at the scribe. "I want three copies, understand?"

Chuza was numb. Agrippa had owned him for mere minutes and was now offering him his freedom?

"Why?" he blurted. "Why are you doing this?"

Cypros smiled. "We want to repay you."

Under his breath, Agrippa added, "Getting one over on Antipas doesn't hurt either." He laughed as Cypros made a face and flicked a grape at him.

The scribe warmed a bit of wax and poured it on the bottom corner of the papyrus. He held the portable desk out to Agrippa, who pressed his ring into the wax. Agrippa held the precious document for a moment, then handed it to Chuza.

"There," he said. "You are a free man."

Chuza took the papyrus in a daze.

Agrippa again turned to the scribe. "The second copy goes in our records, in case there is any doubt. Send the third copy to Antipas, along with his tunics and cloaks."

Chuza stared at the sheet of papyrus as his mind spun. He had gone from Antipas' slave, to Agrippa's, to a freeman within a few breaths.

Agrippa reached for his cup, grinning with self-satisfaction. "So, Chuza, what will you do now?"

Chuza stared at him blankly. "I will need to ask my wife."

Agrippa roared with laughter and raised his cup. "That's the right answer!"

Chuza smiled wanly, but then he remembered. There was one thing Joanna would want.

"My lord," Chuza said, speaking carefully, "Antipas took my wife's vineyard. It has been in her family for generations. Torah would support returning it as ancestral land."

"It is hers." Agrippa waved his hand airily. "I will arrange the documents before you leave."

It was all too much. Chuza's hand twitched toward his maimed ear, feeling the split in his lobe. It could never hold an earring again.

"My lord?" a servant said, stepping into the dark room with a lamp.

Antipas held up a hand to shield his face, wincing at the light. He sat up, and his foot struck an empty amphora. It wobbled noisily across the floor. Herodias was passed out on the other couch.

Antipas licked his lips, trying to clear his head. "What do you want?"

The servant picked his way through the room. Robes and leftover food were strewn among cushions on the floor. His servants had run away weeks ago, and high and mighty Gaius had not sent anyone to replace them.

"Your things have arrived."

Thank God. Chuza was back, and he could make some sense of this mess.

Antipas reached for his cup, but it was empty. "Where is he? Where's my steward?"

The man hesitated. "I have a letter for you. From King Agrippa."

Antipas' nostrils flared. "You will not speak that name in my presence!"

The servant shrank, but he would not be deterred. "Gaius has already read it. It says your steward is not coming."

No. It couldn't be true. Chuza would not abandon his vow. Antipas shook his head slowly, trying to make his mind work properly.

The servant continued, "Agrippa claimed Chuza as his own property, and then he freed him. It's all in the letter." He held out the scroll again.

Antipas trembled. All his suspicions about Chuza conspiring with Agrippa returned with painful clarity. Betrayal poured into him like molten steel and hardened into despair. How could Chuza do this to him?

"Get out," Antipas muttered.

The servant didn't move.

Antipas picked up the amphora and hurled it at him. It shattered against the wall. "Get out!"

The servant dropped the letter and fled like a whipped dog.

Antipas' chest heaved as Herodias sat upright, blinking blearily.

"Well, my dear," Antipas snapped. "It looks like it's just you and me."

"Hmm," she grunted, and reached for a new amphora of wine.

# SIXTY-TWO

Joanna couldn't wait any longer. She picked up the front of her skirt, grabbed Nadia's hand, and raced down the lane. Her heart skipped as her daughter laughed with delight.

Home. She was coming home.

The rows of vines were thick and verdant on the gentle slope under a late summer sky. The two-story villa stood proudly in the tidy yard. Behind the house was the sturdy storeroom, the vegetable plot, and the pens for the sheep and goats.

She drew up to a stop before the house, panting as Nadia leaned against the door frame.

"Shalom!" the young girl called. "Is anyone here?"

"Shalom!" Tirzah's voice came from inside the house. Joanna's pulse increased as the woman who maintained the property came to the door, wiping her hands on a towel.

"Joanna!" Tirzah said, delighted. The women embraced. Tirzah looked down at Nadia. "You've grown, little one." Nadia stood as tall as she could, and Tirzah gestured to the house. "My boys are having their midday meal. Why don't you go in and join them?"

"Ira too?" Nadia asked, and turned to peer back down the road. Chuza strode up, Ira riding on his back.

"Of course," Tirzah said. Chuza set his sturdy son down, and Nadia grabbed the little boy's hand and led him into the shady house.

Chuza grinned at Tirzah. "Is David here? We need to speak with both of you."

Tirzah's smile wavered as she looked between Chuza and Joanna. "Yes, of course. He's working in the field."

"I'll get him," Joanna said.

She practically skipped around the house, taking the well-worn path she had trod a thousand times before. A flock of birds was startled out of the fig tree as she walked with her arms swinging. She opened the gate and walked down the rows of leafy vines trained to follow the trellises. Thick clusters of grapes basked in the heat, almost ready for plucking. She rubbed a leaf between her fingers and rejoiced in the familiar feeling.

David's surprise shifted into a wide smile as he strode toward her. "Now this is a sight for sore eyes."

"As are you," Joanna said. David was as much a part of the vineyard as the vines themselves.

"We're almost ready to harvest. Will you be able to join us?"

"We'd love nothing more, but first, I need you to come back to the house. Chuza is waiting for us."

David scanned her face, just as Tirzah had. "Something has changed, hasn't it?"

Joanna couldn't help grinning. "Just come back so we can tell you together, alright?"

David accompanied her to the front of the house where Tirzah had brought out a tray with a pitcher and cups. Chuza was already sipping, his eyes alight with contentment. Joanna and David accepted cups of their own.

"So?" David asked. "What's the big secret? You two are grinning like a pair of fools."

Joanna glanced at Chuza, and he nodded.

"Chuza is a free man," she said, and threw her arms wide, sloshing her wine.

Tirzah and David exclaimed in delight.

"And," Joanna reached for her husband's hand, "he convinced Agrippa to return the vineyard to my family."

David gaped in astonishment as Tirzah gasped.

"It took very little convincing," Chuza said humbly. "Agrippa is feeling very benevolent as Galilee's new king. I'm almost sorry I didn't ask for more." He chuckled, and Joanna shook her head at him affectionately. Their fates would have been entirely different if Chuza hadn't helped Agrippa or been kind to Cypros.

Tirzah glanced at David, then turned to Joanna. "So, you're moving back?" The uncertainty in her voice was unmistakable. This had been David and Tirzah's home for years. If Joanna moved back to the vineyard with her family, everything would change.

Joanna drew a deep breath. "Actually, no." She stepped closer to Chuza. "We've decided not to move onto the vineyard. We're moving to Antioch."

Tirzah and David stared at her in shock.

"Antioch?" Tirzah echoed.

"Are you sure?" David asked. "You don't have to worry about upsetting us."

"We can move back into town," Tirzah said. "Or build a small house somewhere on the property."

Joanna said, "That's not it. Believe me, when Chuza first showed me the deed, I had every intention of moving back here." She scanned the vineyard, a place filled with a thousand memories, most of them good. "When I was young, I hoped to live on the vineyard forever. I wanted to watch my parents grow old and to raise my children here." Her gaze landed on Chuza, and he gave her an encouraging smile.

"But my dreams have shifted," Joanna said, looking back to Tirzah. "I am glad the vineyard has returned to my family. My father's legacy will continue. We can support ourselves with the revenue. Perhaps one of my children, or one of Dalia's children, will want to raise their family here. But I feel called to live out in the world, to share what I witnessed and what I learned at Jesus' feet. I can't return to a quiet life. At least not yet."

Tirzah tilted her head. "But why Antioch?"

"Leah and Jovian have been working to help the poor there," Chuza said. "We will help, and share the good news of Jesus."

A thrill ran down Joanna's spine, an unexpected eagerness for this new adventure. "Our friends Manaen and Maryam are going to join us, as well as a few others. It's time to spread the good news outside of the promised land."

David wrapped an arm around his wife's waist. "We will continue as the vineyard's caretakers, if you'll have us."

Joanna blinked in shock. "Oh, of course! We wouldn't have it any other way."

"Mama?" Nadia called, running out of the house. "Can you show me where you slept when you were a little girl?"

Joanna looked at Tirzah, who nodded.

Joanna grinned. "I can show you everything."

Autumn sunlight filtered through a fine layer of construction dust. It had been two years since the devastating earthquake, and Antioch was bustling. The scent of crushed olives drifted into the city from the surrounding groves.

Tall insulae lined the streets with shops on the ground floor. They passed booths selling everything from simple pottery to exotic silks. The Greek language filled the air, mingled with smatterings of Latin, Aramaic, and a host of other tongues.

A bridge took them over the river, and they paused to admire the beautiful architecture of the circus and the palace.

Joanna swallowed hard. Antioch was very different from Sepphoris or Jerusalem. She had been to Tyre, Petra, and Alexandria, but she had never considered making a home anywhere other than the promised land.

Until now.

"Are we almost there?" Nadia asked with an exaggerated sigh.

Joanna glanced back at the cart where Nadia sat cross-legged beside her sleeping brother. Behind them walked Manaen, Maryam, and Joses. Gratefulness surged in Joanna's throat. Moving to a new country was intimidating, but it was easier with friends.

Balaam pulled their cart, and Celer was tied behind, bearing some of the lighter items on his back. He was no pack horse, but Chuza would never dream of leaving him behind.

"Not long now," Chuza answered Nadia.

Joanna shared a glance with her husband. She couldn't fault her daughter's impatience. After two weeks on the road, her feet hurt and she was ready to eat a proper meal. But above all, she was eager to see Leah.

Chuza consulted Leah's letter. "We turn here, I think."

They rounded the corner and rumbled past a construction site. The air was punctuated with chisels, saws, and the grunts of men at work. At the end of the street, they eyed a ruin, abandoned and eerily silent.

They turned again, down a quieter street lined with small, private homes.

"It should be down here somewhere," Chuza said. "Look for a blue front gate."

"I see a blue gate!" Nadia called out, standing in the cart and rocking precariously.

"Sit down," Joanna chided, but Nadia was right. The blue gate gleamed in the sunlight like a beacon. Her pulse quickened.

A servant answered Chuza's knock, a young man who scanned them from head to toe. He smiled. "You must be Leah's family."

Joanna fought the urge to peek over his shoulder into the courtyard.

"Is Leah here?"

"They just got back." He held the gate open so they could enter. Chuza held out his arms to Nadia, and she jumped into them enthusiastically. Joanna scooped up Ira, the little boy warm and heavy. He curled his head into her neck and slept on.

"Follow me," the servant said. "Vera will watch your carts."

A young woman smiled shyly as she joined them in the street. She stroked Balaam's neck with delight.

The travelers walked silently through an atrium and into an inner courtyard. Joanna's heart leaped as she saw Leah and Jovian sitting among two other couples.

"You're here!" Leah cried out as she saw them. She leaped to her feet and ran into Chuza's arms.

Chuza held her close, kissing the top of her head as he blinked rapidly. Leah leaned back, and her cheeks were wet with tears.

"I don't know why I'm crying." She laughed as she wiped her face. "Perhaps it's the baby." She ran her hand down her middle, revealing a round bump.

"You're pregnant?" Joanna cried out. She shifted Ira's weight and gave Leah a one-armed hug. Happy tears filled her eyes. Just hearing Leah's voice was a reminder of how long they'd been apart.

Jovian and Chuza clasped hands before the men laughed and hugged instead.

Leah rubbed Ira's back, her expression wistful. "He's grown so much. I'm afraid he'll have forgotten me."

Joanna squeezed Leah's arm. "There will be plenty of time to get to know one another again."

Leah led the way to a couch where a woman with thin eyebrows and prominent cheekbones smiled brightly. Leah introduced them.

"You must be exhausted," Thea said. "Why don't you lay your little boy down here?"

Joanna gratefully laid Ira down, and Thea rose to hug her with unexpected warmth. "Leah has missed you all."

Thea's motherly embrace was a bittersweet reminder of the mother Joanna had left behind in Jerusalem. But now was not the time to be homesick.

Jovian grinned at Chuza. "So, you're not a steward anymore?"

"I'm just plain, ordinary Chuza."

Jovian tilted his head, pursing his lips as he scanned Chuza critically. "Well, I wouldn't say 'plain'." Chuza made a face and Jovian slapped him on the shoulder with a laugh.

The rest of the group was introduced and Tomas handed around cups of watered wine.

"Rishon is eager to meet you," Jovian said to Manaen. "He has a thousand questions I don't know how to answer. He's hoping you'll speak in the synagogue."

"I'm eager to set my hand to the plow." Manaen rubbed his palms together.

Maryam patted his arm with a grin. "Maybe we should get settled first."

"Speaking of being settled," Joanna turned to Leah, "your letter said you've found a place for your restaurant?"

Leah's eyes danced. "We hope to open next week."

"Well, you have your first patrons," Chuza said, and spread his arms. "I, for one, have missed your cooking." He glanced at Joanna hastily. "As compared to camp food, I mean."

As Joanna shot Chuza a mock glare, Amichai's voice cut through the laughter. "When did you get here?"

His crooked smile pulled Joanna back in time, back before he met his revolutionary friends, back when they had been children on the vineyard with a whole future ahead of them.

She blinked and crossed the space between them, throwing her arms around him.

He stiffened in surprise, but then held her close.

"I'm so glad you're here," Joanna said, and she meant it.

Amichai squeezed tighter. "Me too."

Joanna stepped back, and Amichai covered his embarrassment by picking up his niece and swinging her in circles until she giggled wildly.

Joanna scanned the courtyard, her heart overflowing.

Leah leaned on Jovian's arm, beaming around the courtyard. Belen talked with Chuza and Manaen, and Maryam sat beside Thea. Joses, Sergio, and Cassandra were discussing the layout of the city.

Leaving her homeland was one of the hardest things Joanna had ever done, but God had been preparing a new family, and a new home.

Chuza turned and they locked eyes. Every difficulty over the past decade, every tear, every uncertainty, had led to this moment. Chuza inclined his head to her in understanding as the courtyard hummed with conversation, laughter, and possibility.

# AUTHOR'S NOTE

This series has been both a joy and a challenge to write, and I hope you've enjoyed your time with Joanna, Chuza, and all their friends and family.

Whenever I finish a historical fiction novel, I always wonder which parts were true and which were imaginative. If you're like me, these notes are for you.

*Joanna and Chuza*

All we know for certain about Joanna and Chuza comes from two verses:

> "…and Joanna the wife of Chuza, Herod's steward, and Susanna, and many others who were contributing to their support out of their private means." -Luke 8:3

> "Now *these women* were Mary Magdalene, Joanna, and Mary the *mother* of James; also the other women with them were telling these things to the apostles." -Luke 24:10

Joanna's family and her service to Phasaelis, as well as Chuza's vow to become a bondslave, are from my imagination. I look forward to the resurrection and being able to sit down with Joanna and Chuza to hear their real story.

Leah and Jovian Titus are completely fictitious characters, even though they feel very real to me.

But, never fear! There is a lot of history within this novel.

*The Way*

I call the believers "The Way", taking my signal from Acts 9:1-2. They were not called "Christians" until sometime later in Antioch, according to Acts 11:26. Some say this is also when the word "church" began to be used to describe the believers, though the word is far older.

I had a difficult time trying to discover what Jewish traditions The Way kept in those early years, and which they didn't. It seems they were still attending synagogues. They were going up to the temple at the hour of prayer. They were still circumcising their baby boys. But were they making sacrifices? Were they performing the rituals needed for cleanliness, particularly the ones that required a priest?

Questions like these are difficult to answer. I hope I showed some of the struggles of Jews adjusting their lives to line up with Jesus' sacrifice on the cross. For me, it resonated with the 'deconstruction' movement we see today, where believers are breaking down traditions that grew over centuries, and are rebuilding their faith with Jesus as their cornerstone.

*Timeline*

In this novel, I followed the biblical account up to Acts 11:19. I'll admit, I had a hard time recreating a timeline for these astounding events. When reading Acts, it seems as if the action is coming so quickly, with one thing tumbling right after the other. How much time transpired between events is widely debated by scholars. I added years and seasons to the chapter headings to try to help the reader, but if they are not helpful to you, please disregard them.

The greatest surprise for me was how many years may have passed between Pentecost and the pouring out of the Holy Spirit on the Gentiles. This was really interesting to explore through Titus' eyes, a man who believed in Jesus' resurrection but who wasn't willing to become a Jewish proselyte. His grafting into the chosen people was life-changing for him, as it should be for all of us.

### Saul

Saul's history is taken from a few places. We see he is a Roman citizen in Acts 22:25. He describes himself as a Pharisee in Philippians 3:5, and that he was born in Tarsus but raised in Jerusalem and trained under Gamaliel in Acts 22:3.

Saul arrested both men and women according to Acts 8:3, but these believers are not named. We don't know how many were sentenced to death by the Sanhedrin, but it does seem as if some died when we read Acts 26:10-11:

> "And this is just what I did in Jerusalem; not only did I lock up many of the saints in prisons, after receiving authority from the chief priests, but I also cast my vote against them when they were being put to death. And as I punished them often in all the synagogues, I tried to force them to blaspheme; and since I was extremely enraged at them, I kept pursuing them even to foreign cities."

### What I didn't include

Due to the nature and limits of fiction, I was not able to give details on everything that happened in the first twelve chapters of Acts. My intention was to follow my specific characters on their journeys of faith, and their struggles living in and near Herod Antipas' court. I invite you to return to the Bible and reread these stories for yourself, and imagine what it would have been like to experience them firsthand.

*Real Biblical Men and Women*

I include several biblical figures as fictional characters. Besides the well-known figures of Peter, Andrew, Matthew, Stephen, and Saul, Manaen is mentioned in Acts 13:1. Mary, who I give the alternative spelling of Maryam, is one of the women at the tomb, and the mother of James (one of the twelve, the son of Alpheus) and Joses. She is mentioned in Luke 24:10 along with Joanna, and again in Matthew 27:56. I give the mother of the sons of Zebedee, James and John, the name Naomi. Some believe her name was Salome.

*The Extra-Biblical History*

I used the writings of the ancient historian Josephus to recreate the historical context surrounding Pilate, Antipas, Agrippa, Herodias, and Cypros.

Josephus gives a fairly detailed picture of Agrippa's debts. There really was a feast at Tyre where Agrippa was insulted by Antipas and moved to Syria, and Cypros did raise the funds while they were in Alexandria to send Agrippa back to Italy. Josephus has Agrippa being sent to prison before he's made a king by Gaius. (You may know Gaius better by his famous nickname, Caligula.)

The battle with Nabatea is challenging to place in a timeline, but it is recorded by Josephus, along with Antipas' crushing defeat and his need to get help from Vitellius. Josephus places Vitellius in Jerusalem when word of Tiberius' death reaches him, and tells how he took his armies back to Syria.

Pilate's attack on the Samaritans and his subsequent dismissal is also recorded, along with Caiaphas being deposed at the same time.

Josephus also records how Agrippa heard Antipas was going to the emperor to ask for honors, and that Agrippa sent a letter to put a stop to it. For the sake of simplicity, I didn't include Agrippa's second accusation of Antipas conspiring with another ruler against Tiberius, and scholars aren't sure whether it was true or a wild accusation. Scholars also debate whether Antipas really did have seventy thousand sets of armor, or whether that was a scribal error on Josephus' part.

Most scholars place the end of Antipas' career in 39 AD. Josephus states that Herodias went with her husband into exile. Salome, her daughter, was remarried by that time, to her cousin.

In this novel, we do not get as far as James, the son of Zebedee, being beheaded by Herod in Acts 12:1-2, but scholars generally agree that refers to Herod Agrippa I, not Herod Antipas.

## A *few more thoughts*

I am well aware I may have made some choices that readers might not agree with, such as my timeline or not capitalizing the pronouns for Jesus or God.

But I suspect the more contentious issue will be Joanna sitting on a teacher's seat, leading communion, and baptizing Phasaelis.

According to the scriptures, women were the only witnesses of certain vital historic moments. I propose that the crowds, trying to ascertain the veracity of the resurrection, would have wanted to hear it from eyewitnesses whenever possible.

I also postulate that if Saul was arresting women and throwing them in prison, then these women had done something blasphemous in his eyes. Had they been speaking openly about Jesus' resurrection, just like the men?

I also invite you to consider the many women mentioned within the New Testament who served as prophetesses, disciples, deaconesses, teachers, letter carriers, and who hosted churches in their homes. The Old Testament also includes wise women and prophetesses who instructed and led men.

When I have Joanna hosting a gathering of believers in her home, I give her a prominent leadership role because she traveled with Jesus, heard him speak firsthand, witnessed many of his miracles, and was there at his resurrection. Perhaps you imagine that she would step back and let her husband lead. But if Chuza spent most of Jesus' ministry with Antipas, why would he insist on leading?

I also propose that because these early churches were happening in private homes, women, even in a patriarchal society, would have had more opportunities to speak and teach than if they had been in a public setting or synagogue.

But I also wanted to include another viewpoint in this novel. All women are called to live out their faith, but not all are called to take leadership roles. Early in this novel, Leah compares herself to Joanna and feels inferior. She worries that a leadership role is the only way to be a good follower of Jesus. I hope I showed through Leah's story that there are many ways to live out our faith and love those around us.

My dear friend, thank you for journeying with me through this trilogy. I pray it inspires you to find your place within the great story that God is still telling.

*"The Lord bless you, and keep you; The Lord cause His face to shine on you, and be gracious to you; The Lord lift up His face to you, and give you peace."* -Numbers 6:24-26

# DISCUSSION QUESTIONS

1. Are you a fan of biblical fiction? Why or why not?

2. At the beginning of the novel, Chuza's personal life has recently changed, but his surrounding circumstances have not. Has that ever happened to you?

3. The author has Joanna speaking publicly about Jesus in Solomon's Portico in the temple. Do you think that is plausible? Why or why not?

4. Do you think Leah found confidence through serving in quieter ways? Who do you identify more with, Joanna's outgoing faith, or Leah's quiet service?

5. Chuza hopes to steer his master onto a better path. Is he just being naive, or should Christians try to influence the people of power around us? Considering how Antipas ended up, was it worth it for Chuza to keep trying?

6. How did you feel when Chuza refused to denounce Jesus, even if it would have saved Joanna and Leah? How did you feel when Keturah was forgiven for denying Christ?

7. At the beginning of this novel, Jovian is struggling because he believes in God but fears God is cruel or indifferent. Have you ever faced those kinds of thoughts? How did you work through them?

8. Joanna struggles emotionally after they must leave Jerusalem. Did you sympathize with her grief over losing her community? Have you ever had to start over with a new faith community?

9. We see the start of Phasaelis' journey in the first book of the trilogy, but she doesn't come to faith in this book. Have you known someone who took years to come to Christ? How can we keep from becoming discouraged when our loved ones refuse to believe?

10. What do you think about Joanna baptizing Phasaelis? Do you feel the same about Chuza baptizing Jovian?

11. Jovian believes in God, yet he refused to become a Jewish proselyte because he didn't want to cut himself off from his family. Do you think he made the right choice in that moment, before he knew God was bringing the Gentiles into the people of God?

12. Do you think the early believers struggled with knowing which traditions and laws were reinterpreted in light of Jesus' sacrifice? How do you handle questions that challenge your understanding of faith and church practices?

13. Do you practice "open" or "closed" communion? Do you think Nathan was right to exclude Jovian from the Lord's Supper?

14. What did you think about Balaam? If you lived in ancient Israel, do you think you'd have wanted a pet? What kind of animal would you have picked?

15. Were you happy with where Amichai's story ended up? How can our past still haunt us, even after our sins are forgiven?

16. How do you think the Gentile inclusion was received in the Early Church? Do you think Jovian and Leah would have been accepted as a couple?

17. How did you feel about Antipas, Herodias, Cypros, and Agrippa throughout the story? Were you satisfied with how their stories ended? Did you suspect that Agrippa would help Chuza?

18. If it had been up to you, would you have wanted Joanna and Chuza to stay on the vineyard or go to Antioch?

19. How has reading a fictional story helped you understand the events surrounding the book of Acts?

# ACKNOWLEDGMENTS

First, I want to thank God for giving me a love for stories. It is God who gives me the strength to keep writing even when I am discouraged or weary. I couldn't do this without him!

I need to say thank you to my husband and children, who are both supportive and understanding as mom types away on her computer at all hours.

A huge thank you to my early readers: Lee Patmore, Alison Bonsan, and David Snethen. I truly appreciate you reading the rough draft and giving me valuable feedback and encouragement!

Big thanks to Cay Danielson for creating the amazing map of Joanna's world.

Thank you, dear reader, for allowing me to share this story with you. Your support means more than I can say.

The grace of our Lord Jesus Christ be with you all.

Katrina

# About the Author

Katrina lives in Alberta, Canada, with her husband and four children. She began her indie-author career in 2019 with her debut novel *Dividing Sword*, and she is grateful for the book-loving friends she has made and the opportunity to do lots of research. She welcomes comments and questions on her website:

katrinadhamel.com

## BIBLICAL FICTION FROM KATRINA D. HAMEL

Dividing Sword
As the Stars

## Court of the Tetrarch Series
Joanna
Wife of Chuza
Herod's Steward

Printed in Great Britain
by Amazon

36468120R00292